HERITAGE

GENE RODDENBERRY'S EARTH: FINAL CONFLICT
Novels from Tor Books

The Arrival
by Fred Saberhagen

The First Protector
by James White

Requiem for Boone
by Debra Doyle and James D. Macdonald

Augur's Teacher
by Sherwood Smith

Heritage
by Doranna Durgin

Visit the *Earth: Final Conflict* Web site at
www.efc.com

GENE RODDENBERRY'S

EARTH
FINAL CONFLICT™

HERITAGE

DORANNA DURGIN

TOR®

A TOM DOHERTY ASSOCIATES BOOK

NEW YORK

GENE RODDENBERRY'S EARTH:
FINAL CONFLICT—HERITAGE

Edited by James Frenkel

A Tor Book
Published by Tom Doherty Associates, LLC
175 Fifth Avenue
New York, NY 10010

www.tor.com

Tor® is a registered trademark of Tom Doherty Associates, LLC.

ISBN 0-312-87822-2 (hardcover)
ISBN 0-765-30208-X (trade paperback)

First Edition: November 2001

Printed in the United States of America

0 9 8 7 6 5 4 3 2 1

For the denizens of Dancing Horse Farm, where July in the desert is too hot to do anything but write, and for the canine companions of North Fork, who know the greatest weapon of all is actually shafartava

ACKNOWLEDGMENTS

Endless thanks to Jennifer's ruthless reading—I only got what I deserved after making her sit through all those videotapes. And thanks, too, to those in the EFC community who were so helpful with resource material.

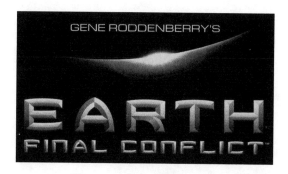

GENE RODDENBERRY'S

EARTH
FINAL CONFLICT™

HERITAGE

Earth shone brightly below the Taelon Mothership. The colors of planetary clouds, land masses, and oceans were unimpeded within the ship's bridge by anything as mundane as ship bulkheads. Taelon virtual glass might provide the Mothership walls, but the Earth and stars against a backdrop of black space made its wallpaper. And the bridge, though it was lined with cubbies of Taelon flight engineers and contained by the occasional swooping, graceful structural member, offered a view that was anything a Taelon could want.

From the single command chair on that bridge, Zo'or stared out at Earth with an expression of calm detachment. Thoughtful, his blue mottled features serene . . . none of his true feelings were revealed by anything but the glitter of intent in his eyes.

Unless that glitter was actually cool malignance.

Upon their arrival at Earth, the Taelons had presented a united front of benevolence, sweeping in to cure human ailments of all sorts, to offer alluring gifts of technology and culture. They took pains that their own appearance—all their features in approximately the right place despite universal baldness, blue-tinted skin, and graceful androgynous bodies—was encased in flesh, and thus didn't routinely send humans screaming away in fear. At first, the Taelon focus on their collective goal of acceptance by humanity kept them harmonized within and without the shared awareness of their Commonality.

Zo'or stared at the Earth, his body resting in quiet repose within the multipart chair in which the humans found it all but impossible to sit. With no one else here but the natural, energy-defined forms of the distracted flight engineers within their cubicles, he let himself relax, letting down his guard. Letting some of that cool malignance seep through to his expression.

It hadn't taken long for the Taelons' individual philosophies to surface—for Da'an to grow soft and to identify far too easily with his human subjects and subordinates. Now Da'an even sometimes lost sight of Taelon goals—of the desperate needs of the Taelon race, their fight for their very survival—in his concern for how Taelon activities affected the human race.

Zo'or had a clearer vision. The Taelons were an advanced species, much more advanced than the humans—who were in turn much *less* advanced than Da'an somehow imagined. And the Taelons had long established a precedent of using less advanced species to gain their own ends. Zo'or had no qualms about doing the same with humans, and didn't care if that meant lying to, manipulating, or intimidating them. These things were far easier than conducting experiments in a truthful atmosphere, because humans didn't understand the concept of acceptable loss among experimental subjects. Nor, lately, did Da'an . . .

Although he used to.

So it became easier, as well, for Zo'or to conceal his most radical projects from Da'an. Not that Zo'or, as Synod leader, owed Da'an any explanation in the first place—but the less conflict he had with Da'an, the less time he spent on unnecessary and annoying discourse, and the more time he could devote to his projects. Which meant if he did bother to conceal a project, he'd best conceal it very well—for when Da'an uncovered clandestine activity—the unfortunate Earth Defense project came readily to mind—he was very . . . uncooperative.

Zo'or had become quite adept at covering his tracks.

It wasn't important that sometimes he spent more effort covering those tracks than he did in seeing that the projects were competently carried out; it didn't concern him that sometimes this resulted in more of what Da'an and the humans would consider unacceptable losses. It was worth the effort as long as he got results; as long as he brought the Taelon race closer to salvation.

Because Zo'or had a goal, and he didn't really care what happened to Earth and its humans along the way.

Liam Kincaid sat in a folding porch chair on the roof of the Flat Planet café, unintentionally camouflaged in a snug black ribbed turtleneck, black leather jacket, and black jeans. If not for the pale reflection of the moon on his face and the glint of color in his short brown hair, he might as well have not been there at all. But there he was, sitting and silent, and troubled by an uneasy prescience he couldn't define.

The prescience came thanks to that third strand of alien DNA winding around the human DNA of his parents, and thanks to the gifts of Siobhan Beckett, his Irish Companion Protector mother, who'd had the gift of seeing things. *Ansuz.* She'd chosen Sowelo as her personal rune, but it might as well have been Ansuz. *Communication from within.*

Thanks also to the Taelons, who thousands of years earlier had tampered with humankind to provide them with such sight.

Tonight it gave Liam neither rest nor answers. Tonight it kept him out on the roof, one of his rare evenings home alone and undisturbed by his duties as Protector to Da'an, the North American Companion. He nursed a champagne punch from Suzanne's hand down in the Flat Planet, feeling the cold slats of the chair against his back and thighs, and trying to chase down the elusive feelings of disquiet, of impending trouble, and to separate them from the normal vexations of the day.

As if he could know what was normal. As if anyone— born of man, woman, and Kimera, grown in one agonizing, confusing day—could truly understand *normal*. Deprived of the memories of his own childhood, he had instead Ha'gel's Kimera racial memories, and those of his human parents as well—sometimes clear and striking, impossible to ignore; sometimes an obscure morass of awareness that didn't quite seem connected to who he was.

And sometimes the world still seemed fresh and new— but a moment later he'd see something he'd seen a thousand times in a thousand lifetimes, and it made him feel so old he didn't know if he'd ever move again; he floundered at the thought of trying to express such moments, such knowledge, to those around him.

Still, he wondered what it was like to have a first day at school. Or that first bike ride without training wheels, and the scraped knees that went with it. He remembered Ronald Sandoval's first crush; his first kiss . . . he knew how Siobhan had lost her virginity. But he'd done none of those things himself.

This body had come ready-made, grown almost to the end of its third decade within its first day. It knew how to do things that he hadn't learned firsthand. He honed it and its skills; he gathered experiences and information almost faster than he could process them, plunged as he'd been into this tense thrust-and-parry undercurrent between the Taelons and the human Resistance, and with the Taelon enemy, the Jaridians, on the verge of breaking the situation wide open.

Liam knew how to fight. He knew how to run tactical operations, was learning how to use the astonishing shaqar-ava that blossomed at will in the palms of his hands. He knew to hide his heritage from all Taelons save Da'an—and knew what would happen if he didn't. He was cool under fire, dedicated to his cause, skilled in his profession.

But he wasn't sure he knew how to live.

He rubbed a thumb thoughtfully over his palm as foreboding tightened the muscles between his shoulders, crowding out the tension from more personal thoughts. It seemed he'd have to figure out *how to live* on another day.

This next one seemed to be booked by trouble.

TWO

Augur had to hand it to the Taelons. They were good. Very good. He'd never have predicted they could accomplish *this*. Still, as he gazed pensively at the stick-borne morsel in his hand, he had to admit there was something . . . *unfulfilling* . . . about biting into a corn dog now that it was a healthfully nutritious snack instead of the calorie-, fat-, and sodium-laden guilty pleasure of old.

Along with the guilt went the pleasure, it seemed.

He took another bite, chewed thoughtfully, and dropped the remaining two-thirds of the corn dog into a convenient trash bin. He'd derive *more* pleasure, he decided, by slipping into the files of the company who'd hired the Taelon-trained food engineers and stealing the process to create the enhanced corn dog. Not that he'd do anything with the information. Knowledge for its own sake, that was good enough. The thrill of the chase.

Unless, of course, it afforded him the chance to turn an unexpected profit down the road.

He wiped his fingers on the paper napkin that had come with the impaled corn dog and dropped that in the trash too, looking out over the colorful, people-packed lawn of the morning Constitution Gardens, keeping the Vietnam

Veterans Memorial at his back so he could take in the bulk
of the crowd.

People and *Taelon*-packed lawn, he corrected himself.
Not many Taelons, but they'd definitely made a showing at
this nearly spontaneous fair, especially considering they
were spread out between several major cities around the
globe. A *Celebration of Accomplishments*, they'd aptly named
the event, although quite typically humankind immediately
shortened it to *the Fair*—a joint Taelon-human celebration
of everything the two species had achieved together in the
few years of their acquaintance. Along with the creation of
unprecedented conveniences, they'd conquered hunger and
disease—aside from the ever-mutating flu strains, one of
which was sweeping the nation right now. The Fair even
came complete with slick outdoor displays and booths to
commemorate and explain events, inventions, and new
technology. In between the healthful corn dog stands and
the portable Ferris wheel, of course. And there were probably pony rides around here somewhere . . .

Augur was betting there was no mention of Second
Chances. In fact, he was betting that the recent spectacular
failure of Second Chances—the revelation that Taelons had
used their rejuvenation process to plant false, pro-Taelon
memories in their subjects and the resultant murmurs
of distrust about the Taelon Companions—was the very
reason this worldwide Fair had so swiftly progressed from
inception to actuality. Especially given that March in Washington, D.C., was hardly the time to plan *any* major outdoor
event. Nor was Tiananmen Square, for that matter, or
Hyde Park in London, though Torrey Pines State Beach
outside San Diego probably had it pretty well.

Not that D.C. didn't.

Augur squinted at the sky with a skeptical eye, looking

up at where the Mothership would be, could he see it. Intense blue sky, pleasing fluffy clouds, the barest hint of a morning breeze . . . it made him wonder . . .

Nah. Not even the Taelons were *that* good.

"Augur."

Augur removed his gaze from the sky and aimed it at Captain Lili Marquette instead. Ah, yes, just as fine as usual, her dark blazer looking no-nonsense and as tailored and shapely as Lili herself. There was an enhanced pistol at her side under that blazer, and her slacks and shoes were both made for action.

Augur often thought he might like to offer Lili some action, but then again he usually thought better of it. As in, better safe than sorry. Because while she seemed mildly beguiled by his occasional lascivious grin, he'd hate to lose the edgy chemistry that had bloomed between them upon first meeting. Old enough to know what she wanted, young enough to belie her experience and accomplishments, Captain Lili Denner Marquette—marine, space shuttle pilot, and Companion Agent—didn't suffer fools *or* annoyances lightly. Or bad guys, for that matter.

"Keeping a low profile?" she asked him, raising one winged dark eyebrow and meaning, of course, that he was doing hardly that.

"The people who want me won't look for me here," he said with assurance, shrugging off her concern with a quick smirk he liked to consider charming. Besides, the people who currently wanted him were all under surveillance by his excessively powerful and multitalented computer, which would signal his global if it were time to disappear for any reason.

"If anyone's looking for you, they'll see you from orbit," Lili suggested, eyeing his patterned Day-Glo lime shirt, a nice body-hugging lycra knit that his red-hooded black leather jacket did nothing to downplay.

"It matches my shoes," Augur said, which should have been obvious to a woman of Lili's observational powers. And the shirt set strikingly against his hot-chocolate skin, outlining a body that was buff enough to impress the women without scaring them off.

"It matches your attitude," she said, looking away from him to scan the crowds. Always on duty, that was Lili.

"That's the point," he told her, which she also should have known. Come to think of it, she probably *did* know. She hadn't really come over here to talk about his clothes.

He followed her gaze as it hesitated, aimed at the small stand of bare-branched cherry trees beside the pond. He spotted the Taelon first—not surprising, considering those spangly dark blue-patterned jumpsuits they all wore, molded so tightly to their neither-he-nor-she bodies that even Augur didn't have an outfit to rival the look. This particular Taelon had Da'an's height and body language, but from the look that had settled on Lili's face, she wasn't looking at the Taelon. She was looking at the Companion Protector who shadowed Da'an—and after a moment, Augur spotted him, too: Liam Kincaid, Boy Wonder, hanging in the background. Dressed dark, as usual, and in a characteristic mix of casual and expensively formal—gray turtleneck, those black jeans—and a lean black leather duster. A favorite, but too dark for Augur's taste.

An odd one, that was their Liam. Who knew where he got *his* tastes, especially with all that Kimera blood in there. Even now, apparently relaxed, standing hipshot and watching quietly while Da'an chatted up some ecstatically impressed young woman, Liam had that look. Along with the grace his mother had given him, sinuous in repose—and only waiting for an excuse to explode into the same efficient action of Ronald Sandoval, an unwitting and so far oblivious father. That *look*, as though he was watching the same thing everyone else watched and yet saw something entirely different.

"Something's up with him," Lili muttered. A bright foil balloon floated free behind her, causing a small roil of pandemonium as people tried and failed to catch it, then tried and failed to hush the child who broke into loud tears at its loss.

"Moody," Augur said, as if that were answer enough. "The kid's not even a year old yet, Lili. Gotta have some growing pains. You really oughta let me take him out on the town one of these nights—"

She cut him short with a look. "With you? The same man who gave him champagne within his first twenty-four hours?"

"What did you expect, mother's milk? Lighten up. Liam's only problem is the responsibility you Resistance people keep putting on him." As if Liam wasn't just as much Resistance as anyone else.

"He's the best choice to lead us and you know it," she said, but it was an absent defense; she didn't even bother to point out that along with his many other profitable pursuits, Augur put in plenty of hours on Resistance needs. "No, that's not it. If he weren't ready, there's no way I'd back him. It's something else." She gave Augur a sharp look, her attention riveted back to him, and not in the way that he'd like it to be. "Augur, what *did* happen when you were with him in the sleeper farm near-death state? You and Maiya . . . what did you see there?"

"Whoa, whoa," Augur said. "What's *that* got to do with anything?" As if he wanted to think about *that*, and *now*. Behind them, a gaggle of teens giggled in giddy unison as a

Taelon passed nearby. Augur didn't know him, which was just as well. Very few of his interactions with Taelons had left a positive impression on either party.

"All right," Lili said impatiently, breaking her resumed scan of the crowd to narrow those lusciously tilted eyes at him. "What did *Liam* see there?"

His father Ha'gel . . . the doorway to another plane of existence . . . the answers to all of his questions within reach—but not grasped. Liam had left them behind, untapped, when he chose to return to this world of humans and Taelons.

Hedge. Time to hedge. If Liam wanted to tell Lili about that intensely personal experience, he would. "What did he *tell* you he saw?"

Her eyes narrowed a touch farther; then she released him. He relaxed tension he hadn't known he'd held, which annoyed him. The Taelons had had their hands on him a number of times, and never for any good purpose—but they had no hold on him as long as he could walk away untouched inside. Or as long as he could convince himself he had.

Not long before the hullabaloo of Second Chances, the Taelons had harvested humans to mine mental energy and help patch a hole in the Taelon Commonality. Never mind that the humans involved, stuck in an artificially induced near-death state, eventually wavered and crossed the line to death. Augur and Maiya—and Liam, who'd come to haul them home—had almost taken that step. Liam had had more choice about it than the rest of them, had been so close to joining the weird, memory-based construct of his father that for a few moments Dr. Park and that tough old son-of-a-bitch Jonathan Doors had thought him dead in truth.

Augur had walked away from his father, too. But at least

Augur had known what he was walking away *from*. Liam's questions were left unanswered.

He shrugged, although Lili wasn't looking at him anymore. She'd see it anyway. "Look, Lili—you'll have to talk to him about that. It's his thing, not mine. I'm *over* my thing."

"I doubt that," she muttered, but she wasn't talking about that particular nasty experience, and Augur smiled, more to himself than anything else.

"Relax," he said. "Enjoy the pretty day and the pretty Taelon fair and all the happy people. It's rare enough when something goes right with Taelons involved."

"Say *that* a little louder, why don't you," Lili grumbled, glancing to make sure the teenagers had moved on.

Augur just smiled. Maybe he'd try another corn dog.

Brian Cowley sat on a bench by the pond and angled his body so he could glare at the Taelon from behind his sunglasses. Today he wore what was left of his presentable casual clothes, remnants of a life he no longer lived.

With a wife who no longer lived.

Thanks to the Taelons. To *this* Taelon.

Da'an.

He hadn't wanted her to go. She'd had all the radiation, she'd had all the chemo . . . and she'd had enough. It had been time to come home and spend her remaining days with him in the house he would lose shortly after she died, unable to pay the medical expenses and the mortgage both.

But she hadn't known that. At least, he'd been so sure she hadn't known.

He'd never understand why she changed her mind and accepted the Taelon offer to participate in initial joint efforts to cure this human illness. He'd never trusted them, not from the day of their arrival. But they'd fed her lies—they had to have done so, behind his back, to have convinced her—and false hopes and hyperbole of cure, and off she'd gone.

Never to come back.

So here he was, a young widower with no home and no job—he'd lost that shortly after her death, when he'd failed to show up for work one time too often—sitting in a park during a Taelon fair and glaring at the presentations. Glaring at the Taelons.

Glaring at *this* Taelon, whom he well recognized, and against whom he cultivated a well-fed hatred.

Why he'd come, he wasn't quite sure. It hadn't been to attend the presentations and applaud. He'd found himself in front of one of the displays, a modest stage with a protective railing and sinuous Taelon-grown backdrop that flowed upward into a partial roof, as though the speaker had been real and not a fancy datastream display. Briefly trapped in the crowd, he'd been horrified to realize that the presentation revolved around the very project in which his wife had participated.

Apparently, there had been some successes.

Too bad his wife hadn't been one of them.

He looked around for something to throw, but the park itself was groomed far too thoroughly to provide him with stones, and the litter from the Fair was gathered almost as soon as it fell. So he'd shoved his way free of the crowd, eliciting irritation and comments that he barely noticed, and found himself this park bench, mentally flagellating himself across not-so-old wounds. Ripping them open. It was a wonder no one else saw the blood.

Or maybe they did. No one came to sit by him, although bench space was at a premium.

He watched the Taelon, and poured his hatred out of

his sunglass-shuttered eyes, feeding his emotions with revenge fantasies . . . what he would do if Da'an weren't so
closely shadowed by his pet Companion Protector, a capable-
looking man of his own age whose apparently casual facade
didn't fool Cowley for a moment. This one was on *their*
side, and would choose Taelon life over human life anytime. He had an unusual look on his clean-cut features, distracted and alert all at the same time, and one that puzzled
Cowley until he decided it was the look of a man who
knows he's seeing the world differently than most anybody
else. Better-than-thou, attached to his Taelon master. No
doubt he had a weapon of some sort under his long leather
duster. Particle beam guns, that's what they gave the best
of the Companion Agents . . . those who didn't already
have skrill.

Skrills. Another Taelon abomination, those bio-engineered
creatures who attached themselves to Companion Protectors and gave themselves up for use as energy weapons.
Cowley knew all about them. Know thy enemy—he'd made
a mantra of that. And he knew he was outgunned, even if
he'd had the means with which to buy a gun in the first
place. Outmanned, too, with this one . . . for the Companion Protector had looked his way several times, and now
settled his gaze on Cowley long enough so there was no
mistaking his recognition—however unlikely—of Cowley's
carefully hidden malice.

Cowley looked away, though at that moment he hated
himself for backing down as much as he hated the Taelon
for existing. When he glanced back, the Companion Protector was murmuring to his Taelon master, and though the
Taelon had been speaking to a young girl, the pair immediately drifted away from the pond, heading for the memorial
at the other end of the park.

Cowley watched them go. Even when the Companion

Protector glanced back at him, Cowley watched. If Taelon Volunteers swooped down in their wake to accost him, his life would be no better or worse than it already was. But he doubted it would happen. They didn't know him. Didn't know what drove him, or how deeply, or how little he had to lose.

But they would.

Someday, they would.

Not a true threat. Liam took another glance at the seated man, gave an internal shake of his head. Not today, anyway. At first glance, the man looked about forty; a second glance had changed that estimate to thirty—haggard and hard-used, dressed in clothes that had seen better days even if they *were* clean. He was unhappy, and had definitely come here more to glare than celebrate—but not to do anything about it.

All the same, Liam bent his head to Da'an and murmured, "We've been here awhile. I'd feel better if we moved on." Because he knew better than to ignore the little nudge of warning he felt, no matter what he saw.

Da'an's acknowledgment came in the form of action; only once they were angling away from the pond did he say, "That man seemed sad to me. What about him concerned you?"

It wasn't a challenge of Liam's reaction . . . just Da'an, ever trying to discern the unfathomable about humanity. In this case, Liam couldn't be of much help. He shook his head. "Just a feeling," he said, struggling to define it; Da'an watched him, clearly waiting. Finally, picturing the man again in his mind, Liam said, "He was too quiet within himself. He was holding something back."

"Ah," Da'an said. "And you speculate that since this

venue, especially, is meant for people to express themselves, then he holds back something unacceptable to your society."

"Something like that." The supple leather duster swished against his legs as they walked, a constant and not unpleasant reminder of its presence. He barely needed it today, with what he understood—and recalled, if he chose to hunt out Sandoval's memories—to be an unseasonably warm day. A gorgeous day, and something about it made him want to stretch and grin foolishly and bask on a hill in the sunshine. Barring that, being here at the Fair by Da'an's side—one level of him always scanning for trouble but the rest free to enjoy—was fine enough. He held out a hand to act as a bumper for the two youngsters charging their way, their gaze riveted skyward to watch a hot-air balloon; one of them bounced off him without even noticing and continued on his pell-mell way. He did grin, then, watching them dash away and glancing at Da'an to share the moment.

Da'an didn't quite seem to understand what had inspired his reaction.

No matter. It was still a gorgeous day, Liam was out doing what he did best—and the foreshadowing of the previous days, while it still lurked, lurked quietly enough to let him grin while watching cavorting children and imagining what it would have been like had he, too, had those carefree days.

Ta'en looked up as Zo'or entered the Mothership lab facility, built so deeply within the bowels of the ship that Ta'en never took in so much as a glimpse of the stars—or of the planet they worked so hard to mold to their needs. The captive Jaridian had once been kept here; now it fell to the recently reassigned Ta'en and his human assistant, Dr. Peter

Bellamy, to work with what remained of the escaped prisoner. A few crucial samples, a more refined process . . .

Zo'or had informed him in no uncertain terms that there was not to be a repeat of the dangerous incident with Joyce Belman.

Ignoring the fact that it had been Zo'or's interference that had caused all those problems in the first place, Ta'en had indicated his understanding to Zo'or. And had resolved to maintain secure conditions in the lab at all times. Phe'la, the new head of medical security, assisted him in this matter, providing a coded virtual barrier at the lab entrance and physically isolating the computer systems.

Ta'en had admired Da'an's original project with the Taelon/Human Genetic Research Facility, and regretted its loss—but the Taelon Synod wasn't about to risk another human with the combined human, Taelon, and Jaridian powers Joyce Belman had obtained; they considered themselves fortunate that Belman continued her journey on another plane of existence, and had not remained to interfere with the Taelon agenda on Earth.

Not to mention their existence as a whole.

Now, instead of being allowed to reestablish that enlightened program with stricter protocols, Ta'en had been forced to scale back the original idea, isolating only the elements of the Jaridian genetic material responsible for the shaqarava organ—the powerful energy doorway in the Jaridians' palms. He was, however, happy with the challenge of creating a virus in which to insert the material. He'd make it transmissible only by injection at first, and then when it proved successful, he'd alter it to an airborne version, much as the Kimera had done to the Taelons' parent species, the Atavus, so many millennia ago.

The Atavus, a dying species, had turned to Atavus-with-shaqarava, newly energized and profoundly alive. And not long after that came the philosophical split between those who would retain the shaqarava and those who sought to subsume it within themselves, creating the energy web of the Commonality.

Ta'en supposed that someone knew how much longer it had taken for the Taelons and Jaridians to split into two distinct races, one with shaqarava and one with Commonality; he did not. He knew that to have any hope of prevailing over the seemingly infinite numbers of the quickly breeding Jaridians, the Taelons needed the shaqarava as a tool—but were unable and unwilling to introduce it into their own race.

That left the humans.

Bellamy lifted a recently analyzed vial to eye level—the Beta-S virus—and regarded it with much pleasure. "Flying colors," he said, somewhat cryptically, though there was no mistaking the smile on his face.

Ta'en did not ask him to elucidate upon the strange phrase; he'd learned he wasn't truly interested in the answers he elicited with such questions, and Bellamy's expression made his meaning plain enough. "Excellent," Ta'en said. "Has Phe'la seen to the acquisition of volunteers?"

Bellamy hesitated, his smile fading. He was a tall man with a refined but long-boned face; when he grew somber, the natural lines of his face enhanced the expression to the point that even Ta'en could easily discern it. "He has supplied a roster of potentials," he said, replacing the vial in its stand. The clear contents looked faintly violet in the reflected light of the Mothership's veined interior walls. "But . . . I don't like the looks of them. They've all been convicted of violent crimes. Are they really the right subjects to provide with shaqarava?"

"That," said Zo'or from the archway leading into this initial laboratory chamber, "is not your concern." He waited, pointedly, for Ta'en to disable the virtual glass barrier at the entrance; Ta'en hastened to do so. Zo'or came through with a stride that was at once casual and purposeful. Ta'en had seen it enough to recognize it. Though it held all of the usual Taelon grace, it held too the potential for more . . . for the unusual ruthlessness Zo'or was known to possess. It was not something for one of the scientist caste to understand.

Merely to avoid.

Bellamy said nothing at first; he, too, knew better. And then, though he was less skilled at sycophancy than many of the non-implanted humans who worked with the Taelons, he touched one hand to his chest and held the other out in a respectful Taelon greeting and told Zo'or, "I only meant to serve you better."

But Bellamy meant it. Bellamy, though often rough with his phrasing, was more reliable than many humans with smooth acquiescence and cultured smiles. He worked hard; he truly appreciated the rewards. Indeed, once Taelon doctors had quietly cured his little girl's blindness—a simple matter, really, but one still out of reach of human medical science—he had worked with unflagging devotion.

Perhaps someone had mentioned to him that the procedure used on his little girl was reversible, but Ta'en didn't think so. The human's slight hesitation upon reassignment to this project had surely been only surprise, and not reluctance.

"Yes, of course," Zo'or said, inclining his head to Bellamy. "But do not trouble yourself. These initial volunteers will be suitably placed in a situation where their enhanced abilities can only help your human race, never harm it."

Fighting the Jaridians, of course. An efficient way to dispose of these first experiments.

But Ta'en knew this already. He also knew that Zo'or

didn't make appearances without reason. "My current report will be available shortly," he said, a guess at the purpose of this visit. "As you can see, we are precisely on schedule."

" 'Precisely on schedule' is no longer good enough," Zo'or said, circling the central lab stand as he eyed the contents. "Something has come up. An . . . opportunity. I require the virus now."

Ta'en was too surprised for diplomacy; such was not a scientist's strength, anyway. "*Now*, Zo'or? It is not ready!"

"Did I not just hear Mr. Bellamy say that it was?"

How long had Zo'or observed them before making his presence known? "You heard Mr. Bellamy state that the initial phase of testing was successful, nothing else. We have yet to run human trials, as you know." Human trials, to confirm the expected course of the virus—several days of immediate flu symptoms, followed by the unfortunately painful development of shaqarava. A week, perhaps eleven days, from beginning to end. A week to reshape an entire species.

"That will have to be good enough," Zo'or said, and implicit in his tone was his willingness to move forward regardless of any of Ta'en's protests.

And regardless, Ta'en could not help but protest. Borne of a caste who long valued the experimental procedure above all else—and not being of the subset who pursued their science in unstructured exploration of new places and things—the very energy of his being seized to a momentary, offended halt. "It is not good enough," he said stiffly. "We had too many failures in human testing of the Alpha-S virus—including deaths—and may I remind you that it, too, passed initial evaluation with Mr. Bellamy's *flying colors*."

"The failures are of no consequence," Zo'or said. "You

also had successes, did you not?" He looked from Ta'en to Bellamy, who glanced at Ta'en, then squared his shoulders as if taking on a load. Ta'en could not blame his assistant for then responding with what was only the truth.

"Several," Bellamy said. "Volunteers with actively functional shaqarava. Although," he added, in an offhand tone Ta'en associated with a human about to say something potentially offensive without wanting to give offense, "they're all medical volunteers." People who were promised cures for this ailment or that, in return for accepting the virus into their systems.

Not already dangerous prisoners, was what he was really saying. Briefly, Ta'en admired that. Briefly. But his true attention lay on more significant things. Zo'or sought to interfere with the experiment, to sully the procedures. The outcome would be tainted, its success possibly ruined. "Zo'or," he said with a scientist's blunt assertiveness, "I am in charge of this project. It is running on schedule. I cannot help it that the schedule you initially requested no longer suits you; I will not have the project subverted. It is just such meddling that created the Joyce Belman disaster."

"That project was flawed from the start, as its outcome proved." Zo'or circled the lab stand again, stopping to gesture fluidly at the vial, running long fingers down the length of it without ever actually touching it. "If you have concerns, Ta'en, you may take them up with the Synod. Until such time as they override my decision, I expect you to abide by it."

By which time it would be too late. Bellamy knew it, Ta'en knew it . . . and most importantly, a glance at Zo'or's serenely confident expression showed that *he* knew it, too.

Ta'en inclined his head slightly, unable to help the slight bluish energy blush that passed over his fleshly features and briefly revealed his energy patterns. "What is it," he asked, "that you require us to do?"

"In truth, very little." Zo'or's face held a brief glimmer of his victory, but nothing more. "I have already coordinated with Phe'la to take advantage of this opportunity. He will see to the distribution of the virus among our test subjects—young, healthy humans of both sexes, conveniently already gathered."

"The Fairs," Bellamy said suddenly, with an unusual flash of insight and initiative—at least, none he had ever shown Ta'en. "The worldwide Fairs."

Zo'or inclined his head. "Yes." When he looked at Bellamy again, it was with a moment of increased attentiveness. "We are fortunate, are we not, to have such a perfect venue? The attendees will gather, selected subjects will acquire the virus, and then they will all disperse. The virus distribution awaits only a supply of the virus—which I expect you can synthesize in short order. We have little time to waste if we are to accomplish my—the Synod's—goals."

As rushed as the inception and execution of the Fairs had been, time had existed for Zo'or to express his needs to Ta'en before this. But as Ta'en opened his mouth to say so, he caught a strange look in Zo'or's eye . . . and realized anew that he could not hope to win this kind of argument with the diplomat-caste Synod leader. Realized, too, that if Zo'or had *not* expressed his needs before now, there was a reason. And that Zo'or himself had already provided that reason, in his own way.

Given more warning, Ta'en would indeed have taken this issue to the Synod, which—however unlikely—might even have overridden Zo'or's desire to act so precipitously with Ta'en's powerful virus. With Ta'en's detailed reports, Zo'or had known precisely the stage of Ta'en's work—and that it would suit his sudden needs.

Outmaneuvered. All that was left was to take it gracefully enough that Ta'en might continue on the project, might salvage something of it after all. He said, "I need only to know the amount you require."

"Excellent," said Zo'or. He looked at Bellamy and added, "There is something else."

Bellamy's squared shoulders seemed to hunch in on themselves a little. Or perhaps that was Ta'en's imagination; he had not made a close study of the humans, but merely absorbed what he had to in order to function with them on the ship. Bellamy said, "How can I be of assistance?"

"A small matter," Zo'or said. He picked up one of the quick-shot injectors from the lab table, a finger-held device just large enough to hold a dose of virus and the painless, instant mechanism of injection, and handed it to Bellamy. Bellamy took it, though not with any understanding; his brow pulled together in a way that made his forehead uneven. Nor did Ta'en understand. Surely Zo'or didn't expect this valuable assistant, a doctor, to risk himself by taking the virus—

But no. Zo'or did not.

"Liam Kincaid," he said, and Bellamy's brow went from bunched to raised.

"Da'an's Protector?" Bellamy asked, as if there could be any other. On the other hand, it suddenly seemed to Ta'en to be a reasonable question, because surely Zo'or didn't mean to tamper with *that* human.

"Da'an's Protector," Zo'or confirmed, as if he'd made a perfectly ordinary request. "A non-implant who has been allowed to remain so for far too long, without even a skrill to safeguard our valued North American Companion."

"The virus cannot give him a skrill," Ta'en said, with as much protest as he dared. It was common knowledge among Taelons that Kincaid lacked the Cyber-Viral Im-

plant that allowed the use of a skrill and that Da'an preferred it that way—*preferred* to depend on this human without the CVI-supplied security of the motivational imperative
that put Taelon interests above all else. Should Bellamy be
caught, Ta'en would lose his assistant's skills on this project,
and then he *would* be behind schedule.

"Of course not," Zo'or said. He gestured at the quick-
shot. "But it *may* give him shaqarava."

"And if it kills him?" For some of the Alpha testers had
died, horrible deaths that Ta'en would wish on no human.
And this was a human that Da'an counted on, had quickly
cultivated to a crucial position. This, too, was one of the
rare humans who occasionally spent free time on the Mothership, inquiring of Taelon ways in a respectful way that had
gained him a reputation for being pleasant yet still capable
of challenging discourse.

"If it kills him," Zo'or said, apparently unaffected by the
thought, "then Da'an will be required to choose a new Protector, and I will make sure *this* one becomes an implant. Either way, Da'an is benefited. And what benefits Da'an
benefits us all." Again, he indicated the quick-injector. "He
knows of you. You can easily contrive of some reason to
place yourself closely enough to use this, where he will not
let a stranger close enough while protecting Da'an. But Major Kincaid *will* be injected with this virus. After all"—and
he turned his full gaze on Bellamy, repeating his words in a
meaningful fashion—"what benefits *us* also benefits *you*."

Bellamy only nodded. It was, Ta'en knew, the only thing
he *could* do. For with Zo'or, that kind of statement always
had an opposing corollary. *What harms us also harms you.*

Early afternoon at the celebration, and Da'an remained the
ultimate diplomat, smiling at children—the Taelons' fasci-

nation with children was one of their few dependable reactions—making the right comments at the right time to the adults, showing deep concern when someone worked up the nerve to approach him with complaints. Halfway through the day, Da'an was still tireless.

Just as well, Liam thought, since he was the one Taelon whose presence was a must here at the D.C. location. Unobtrusively placing himself between Da'an and a man who'd had a little too much to drink—not that alcohol was available on the grounds—Liam touched his earpiece and murmured directions to Companion Agent Lassiter. Lassiter was smooth; he'd have the man escorted out of Constitution Gardens and thanking him for it.

Above all, there were to be no scenes at this celebration.

Perhaps that's why the population of Volunteers—all CVI-enhanced to some extent, with implants to improve their strength and speed—seemed to have doubled within the past hour. Wouldn't they just be delighted to know that the Resistance was also out in force, prowling each of the celebration locations and on the alert for some little chink in the Taelons' united front, some tidbit of information that might come in handy in the future—tomorrow, or the next day, or ten years from now.

The Resistance was in it for the long haul.

Eyeing the Volunteers, he thought of the foreboding he'd felt the evening before. "Is Zo'or worried?" he asked Da'an, not turning to look at the Taelon as they drifted from the pond toward the Vietnam Veterans Memorial. Da'an had somehow managed to dispose of the gift of helium balloons he'd accepted from his most recent child encounter, which was a blessing. They bore an unfortunate resemblance to the shape of his head.

Da'an responded as obliquely as ever. "I see you, too, have noted them."

"And so will everyone else. Not exactly conducive to the cheerful and benevolent atmosphere you're trying to promote, are they?"

"They have done nothing. I am confident that whatever their purpose here, they will not interfere with our goals for this celebration."

"Meaning you don't know what's going on, either," Liam said, with as dry a tone as any human ever used with a Taelon.

But then, Liam did a lot of things that *not any human* would do. Especially when it came to the Taelons.

He felt Da'an's gaze upon him, but as often happened, Da'an did not respond. A handful of children ran by, shrieking as loudly as children could and followed by the bellow of a desperate older child being ignored. "Tad! Mary! Get back here! I'll *tell*—" and by the time quiet conversation was possible again, the wall loomed before them, black and stark and unyielding.

"I have always felt," Da'an said, looking like an astonishing physical non sequitur against the backdrop of the memorial, "that this structure speaks most loudly about the barbarity of humanity."

"I have always felt," Liam said, unhesitating, "that it speaks of the struggle to *be* human."

"And is it, do you think, a successful struggle?"

Liam grinned. "Interesting question. I think time will tell." He did not add, *it depends on the success of the Resistance.* Nor did he add, *I think humanity deserves the chance to figure that out for itself.* They'd had *that* conversation before. That, and other similar conversations about which Zo'or would never learn. Not for Da'an's sake; for Liam's.

A frisson chased down his spine, one not born of the unusually pleasant spring breeze; his palms itched, and he clamped down on the impulse to allow his shaqarava to bloom. It was the one instinctive reaction he could never allow himself to express.

Especially not with so many Volunteers around.

Though right now, none of them were in sight. He saw no one in the Gardens but Fair-goers, heard nothing on the breeze but conversation and happy shouts and a stray balloon or two. There was nothing around them but the wall and its never-ending pile of tributes and gifts and flowers.

All the same, he rested an unobtrusive hand on the grip of his weapon and left it there, drifting back toward the end of the wall while Da'an perused the chiseled names. *Timothy Dahl, Randall Ellis, Arlan Gabel.* As he put a finger to his earpiece, about to request a team com check, he caught a blur of foresight—*the immediate future imprinted over the present, a flash of danger and impending conflict, the screams of a crowd, Da'an, the defensive bloom of shaqarava light*—

—and jerked around at the end of the wall just in time to catch a full body blow. He rolled with it, off his feet and right back up again, beam gun drawn and aimed steadily at the astonished face of . . .

. . . Peter Bellamy? Bellamy, who'd stayed so quietly in the background while Joyce Belman made her own fateful decisions in an attempt to save the tainted project they'd been working on?

Liam narrowed his eyes, and though he lowered the weapon slightly, he kept his aim true.

"Major Kincaid!" Bellamy said, his face bright red against his fair coloring, his hands out in what—until the Taelons' arrival—had been considered a universal gesture for *no harm meant.* Liam knew this from both Beckett and Sandoval—and from Ha'gel he knew it as a sign of danger, of shaqarava exposed. His knuckles whitened on the grip of the weapon while his instincts clashed.

"Liam?" Da'an said, a gentle inquiry behind him.

Right. Here and now. No harm meant. Bellamy had come barreling around the end of the wall and broadsided him, that was all. It was no surprise that he was at the gathering, not with his livelihood tied up in Taelon ventures and his little girl a walking advertisement for what the Taelons had accomplished for humankind. Liam lowered the weapon and secured it.

"I'm so sorry," Bellamy said, and smiled weakly. "Kids . . . so damned independent when it's the least convenient." He held out a hand. "Please . . . I meant no harm."

Liam took it, allowing the man a brief two-handed clasp as he said, "No. Of course not. I overreacted." Shaking hands. He hated that. The gesture held great intimacy for him; for those with shaqarava, it was generally a prelude to intensely private sharing.

Bellamy nodded away from the wall, where several clusters of people watched them, whispering and pointing and trying not to be too obvious, which of course they were. "We've provided some excitement, anyway."

"Not the sort we were hoping for," Liam said, but lifted a hand to acknowledge and reassure the ones closest to them before putting his back to them in a not-so-subtle cue that the excitement, for what it had been worth, was over.

Bellamy chattered on a few moments, moments in which Liam's attention, despite his appropriate responses, was anywhere but on the conversation. Why had he seen such a trivial thing in foresight—not all of which had come to pass? Why did he feel the unease that had settled upon him? Da'an, in full diplomat mode with Bellamy, showed no signs that anything was amiss—but while at times Da'an's smooth features and pearl-gray eyes spoke volumes, he could also be as inscrutable as they came.

At the moment, he was at his most inscrutable. He inquired after Bellamy's child, he allowed Bellamy to uneasily evade answers about his current assignment—evasions that probably meant it was one of Zo'or's projects—and he spoke in glowing terms of his pleasure regarding the day's events. He then provided an opening for Bellamy to say he had to find his child, which Bellamy seized, shaking Liam's hand again unbidden and offering Da'an an automatic Taelon gesture of respect.

Liam watched him go, and almost didn't hear when Da'an spoke from behind him.

"Liam, are you well? You seem not to be at ease this day."

Glancing at him, Liam didn't answer immediately—or when he did respond, directly. "Let's just say I'll be glad when it's over, and you're not in the middle of a crowd."

But they had the rest of the afternoon before them.

Peter Bellamy made it to the nearest bench before he started shaking. He wasn't meant for this kind of work. He didn't even think it was *right*. From here he could watch Kincaid; the man hadn't had a chance. *Didn't* have a chance. Even so, he'd been so quick . . . almost as if he were expecting trouble. And the look on his face . . .

Bellamy thought of the beam gun, inches from his own face, and knew he'd had a closer call than either of them had let on.

He glanced at the discreet quick-shot still nestled in his palm and closed his hand around it; in another moment he thrust that hand into his jacket pocket and shook the quick-shot free, closing his eyes so for the moment, he didn't have to see Kincaid.

Once he wouldn't have thought much about it. He'd been proud of his associations with the Taelons, proud of the advanced level of work he was doing, and prouder still to be tapped by Zo'or for a special assignment. He hadn't hesitated to introduce Jaridian DNA into Joyce Belman's experiment.

But Joyce had paid the price, a price more profound than he had ever imagined.

It had been a loss of innocence; a loss of hubris. And it made him suddenly aware of the price he, too, could pay for his work with the Taelons.

"Daddy!"

Approaching from the Ferris wheel, his Eileen tore loose from the hand of her nanny—where she'd been all along, Bellamy's comments to Kincaid notwithstanding. She ran straight to him, her eyes clear and bright, and flung herself at his lap. He hoisted her up and turned her to sit sideways across his thighs, hoping she wouldn't notice his residual trembling. "You look like you've had a grand time," he said, his voice a little too hearty. The nanny noticed; her eyes narrowed briefly. Over the top of his daughter's silken black hair, he gave the smallest shake of his head; the nanny subsided.

"I had a balloon," Eileen said. "It was silver! But I lost it."

"That's easy to do. But this is a fair day . . . you *should* have a balloon. Would you like another?"

She wiggled enthusiastically. "Blue this time! Blue for Taelons!"

The nanny reached out her hand, and his daughter readily slid off his lap, slipping her small hand into the neatly manicured grip of her caretaker. "Blue for Taelons," the woman agreed.

"Wait here, Daddy," Eileen commanded, supremely confident in her ability to boss him so.

With reason enough. He'd stopped shaking. By the time she returned, the quick-shot would be gone from his pocket, and he'd have only a few more moments of stolen time before reporting to the Mothership. *Yes*, he'd tell Ta'en and Zo'or. *Liam Kincaid got a nice strong dose of the virus, and he suspects nothing.*

The first was certainly true.

Somehow, he wasn't so certain about the second.

THREE

Ronald Sandoval stood at the open entrance to the lab in which the Jaridian had once been kept. This place was nothing more than a reminder of failure.

Sandoval was in a position where he could not afford failures.

Within the lab, Zo'or, Phe'la, and Ta'en gathered around a monitor in a back niche of the organically asymmetric room. Structural ribs defined several such niches, one of which Sandoval recognized as a human workstation; the up-tilted, embedded monitor held a small print image photo at the corner.

The main work station, a flat combination of touchpad, inset monitor, and workspace braced by two swooping floor-to-ceiling ribs and abutted by open, head-high storage of neatly placed lab equipment, ran the length of the room, set just off center. At first glance, the area still looked abandoned, as it had been once the Jaridian escaped—but that photo on the display screen told a different story, as did the coffee rings on the flat area beside it. Someone was at work here, a human under supervision by Ta'en, most likely, since Phe'la had his own station elsewhere.

From Ta'en's expression, things were not going as he liked. None of them were inclined to look up and notice him; Sandoval glanced to make sure the virtual glass door was disengaged and moved into the room, standing quietly to listen to the sibilant and incomprehensible Taelon language. Its incomprehensibility didn't matter; body language would tell him what he needed to know for now.

Zo'or's frequent and fluid gestures—not to mention the infinitesimally raised and tilted angle of his head—meant he was pleased and felt in control of this situation. Phe'la, too, was pleased—and deferential, never lifting his head above the angle of Zo'or's, his gestures more subdued.

Ta'en seldom looked entirely pleased, and now was no exception. If Sandoval had dared, he would have described the scientist as prissy. The corners of Ta'en's mouth resided in a place of permanent tension, and his gestures, while more graceful than any human's, were jerky in comparison to Zo'or's. Nor did he ever seem to stand entirely straight, scuttling from place to place within the lab—though Sandoval hadn't figured out if this was mere impression or actuality.

Nor did he intend to spend enough time with Ta'en to find out. His place was with Zo'or—where the power was. Where things happened, and where enough authority bled to Sandoval that the FBI agent and Companion Protector could learn what he needed to know, influence what he needed to influence.

Where he could push around those whom he needed to push around.

"Ah," Zo'or said, noticing him. "You have finally arrived."

"Yes, Zo'or," Sandoval said, stepping forward without attempting to point out he'd been here for quite some time, or that he'd arrived only moments after being summoned.

Sandoval had a home—but he didn't see it very often.

"Attend this display," Zo'or said. "You may have occasion to utilize it in the near future, and you should be familiar with it."

Sandoval joined the three Taelons before the complex monitor as Zo'or gestured a command and brought the display up to its transparent holographic format. Standing quietly attentive, his hands clasped behind the back of his impeccably tailored suit, he assessed the display.

Clearly Earth, spread out in a flattened Mercator projection. Tiny pinpricks of light clustered in a handful of areas—eastern and western United States, Bolivia, England, Russia . . .

All areas in which the first annual Taelon/human celebration was being held.

And the lights? He looked more closely at the clusters, picking out the individuals, noting that some of them had spread from each thick nucleus, strung along uniform travel lines. Roads.

"You've marked some of those who attended the day's fairs," he concluded. "For what purpose?"

"We are tracking certain individuals who are participating in a project of mine," Zo'or said.

Ta'en said, as primly as a Taelon was able, "These tags would have had much more significance had you allowed us the time to create a unique marker for each subject. In that way we would have been able to follow the individual progress of each, and note how the virus affects different humans. All *these* markers do is give us a general awareness of where the subjects are going."

"Nonetheless, it suits my purpose," Zo'or said. "It is enough that we will be able to locate our subjects among those who are unaffected. If there is an occasion of unexpected development, the circumstances will make the subject easy enough to track."

A virus. The Taelons were fooling with a virus. Didn't

they know how strong a buzz word that was among humans? Hadn't they learned from the infection that had nearly killed Da'an and Zo'or, along with countless humans?

Of course, that virus hadn't been of their doing. In Zo'or's eyes, that would make it another matter entirely. Nonetheless, Sandoval couldn't *not* say something. "Just what sort of . . . *virus* is this, Zo'or?"

Zo'or glanced at Ta'en with something of triumph in his expression. "It is not transmissible. There is nothing to occasion the concern I hear in your voice."

"My concern is reserved solely for your benefit, Zo'or. You've had a taste of how humans react to the thought of plague, especially one they haven't encountered before. Should those on Earth discern what you have done, it could seriously harm public opinion of the Taelons."

"You are being overly dramatic. This is certainly no plague. This is a small experiment and it will remain a small experiment, with its details known to no one outside this room aside from Ta'en's human assistant."

Sandoval again considered the dots—how small they were, yet how there were enough of them to make the fairgrounds glow within the hologram. "If this virus is not transmissible, how was it dispersed to so many?"

"Volunteers," said Phe'la.

Sandoval gave Zo'or a pointed look.

Zo'or had been with humans—with *Sandoval*—long enough to interpret that look easily. "They know nothing," he said. "They are advanced units, assigned to this ship. They pose no security risk."

"Respectfully," Sandoval said, "one of my duties as your Companion Protector is to advise you on matters pertaining to human behavior and security. I cannot perform those duties when I know nothing of your decisions regarding those matters until irrevocable action has already been taken."

"In this case," Zo'or said, lifting his head to the angle Sandoval knew so well, "I did not find it necessary to ask your advice. Nor do I, now. I am informing you of the existence of this project and its tracking system, so that you may use it to our advantage in any way that becomes necessary."

Sandoval knew when to back off. He knew when to acquiesce on the surface despite the frustration of being plunged into yet another untenable position.

Once, he never would have felt that frustration at all. Once his eagerness to please would have been entirely unfeigned, thanks to the motivational imperative included with his Cyber-Viral Implant. The implant had let him partner with his skrill—Raven, its creator had named it, but Sandoval was so closely entwined with it in symbiotic relationship that he rarely thought of it in separate terms at all. The implant had also prompted him to commit his wife, DeeDee, to a governmental facility that housed other "special cases"—people who simply stood in the way of the Taelons' goals. Later, the CVI motivation imperative had failed, allowing him independent thought and freeing him to rush to DeeDee's side, to rescue her from that horrible place and the deeply drugged existence she led. And he had freed her . . .

Long enough to run straight into death.

Then Sandoval had gotten a second CVI, one with the same motivational imperative—to serve the Taelons, to do nothing that acted against their interests. Not even to love a wife.

But having found free will again, he had not let go of it so easily. The second imperative had not held, not deeply. And now, while he let it guide his responses and his actions, he also reserved a part of his mind for himself.

That part now quietly groaned, knowing how badly things would go if this project—this *virus*—got out of hand. And he didn't even know what the virus was *for*.

But he had the feeling he'd find out.

Zo'or said, "One other thing. Be alert for any odd behavior on the part of your fellow Companion Protector, Major Kincaid."

Sandoval's head came up sharply; he couldn't stop himself. "You've introduced this virus into the major?"

"It served me to do so," Zo'or said, an immediate and meaningful comeback. "I think you'll be pleased with the results. I look forward to them myself."

Oh, yes. Sandoval had the feeling he'd definitely find out. Sooner rather than later—

But not soon enough.

"It's better than meeting in the warehouse, don't you think?" Hayley Simmons, Northwest Pacific Resistance cell leader, gestured at the brittle, winter-burned grass, the sluggish canal water on one side, the cold Potomac River barely visible on the other, and the few bare-branched trees scattered around them. Her voice held only a hint of sarcasm.

Liam strolled along the Chesapeake & Ohio Canal Path beside her, his gloved hands jammed into the pockets of his lined leather jacket, glad for both the turtleneck and the scarf he wore. Normal early spring Washington weather today, unlike the astonishing weather at the Fair the day before. "It's Washington," he said. "It's made for clandestine meetings and assignations, warehouse or not."

Hayley smiled to herself, one of those woman's smiles Liam felt he should be able to interpret but somehow never quite could. With all the lifetimes of memories lurking in his mind, clouded or hiding or right there on the surface to

grab him, he was still a man like any other, unable to decipher the Mona Lisa. She asked, "And which is this?"

"Oh," Liam said, and looked away, smiling into his
scarf, "I don't believe in limiting things with premature
definitions."

"*That* was nicely done," she said, but the mockery in her
voice was affectionate. In a moment, she sobered. "I can see
why, though. I guess that's just what I did to you."

"Limited me?"

"Limited my belief in you."

"Because you'd heard about my parentage." He didn't
wait for her nod; she'd as much as said so once before. "Lili
shouldn't have told you."

Hayley shrugged, scrunching her scarf up around her
short honey-dark hair. "I put her in a tough position. She
gambled. It worked out—and I haven't told anyone. I
won't."

Liam looked out over the canal, a small ribbon of seren-
ity on the edge of Georgetown. "Good," he said. "Don't."

She took an extra step to get ahead of him, stopping in
front of him, an assertive hand on his arm. Assertive, that
was a good way to describe Hayley Simmons. Or maybe
downright aggressive. A fit, capable young woman who deserved her own self-confidence—physically, probably just
Liam's age. Chronologically, she had quite a head start.
"You think I don't know the stakes?"

"I think," Liam said, a deliberately mild counterpunch,
"that the stakes are higher for me than they are for you."

After a moment, she dropped her hand. "I suppose
that's true." She sighed, twisting her mouth to make a face
at him. "But I'm in deep enough. Anything that hurts the
Resistance hurts me."

"That makes me feel so much better," he said dryly, but
not with any true concern. He resumed walking—a stroll,

really, for they weren't going anywhere but this conversation, and she kept pace. "You or your people spot anything unusual yesterday?"

"You mean besides that big influx of Volunteers wandering aimlessly about? I wanted to put a KICK ME sign on someone's back."

"Not without warning me, I hope." He raised an eyebrow at her with that less-than-subtle reference to her recent precipitous actions during the Second Chances crisis—when she'd snatched the Taelons' star spokesperson for the project during a very public gathering.

It had turned out all right; it had even given them needed information. But for the short term, it had also made things very, very hot for Resistance members—and set Liam and Hayley against one another from their first introduction.

Now she scowled at him. "Let it go, Liam."

"Let it go, yes," he said. "Forget it, no. You call the shots in the Northwest, Hayley. I call them here."

"If things keep up as they've started, you'll call them everywhere. Lili's backing you to replace Jonathan Doors. The others will, too."

Liam gave a short shake of his head. "Doors kept things too centralized. He wanted too much control. It's not the best way for us . . . not the safest way. If anyone takes me down—takes down anyone from a central headquarters—the whole organization goes, too. We've got to spread out a little . . . trust our cell leaders."

"Even me?" she said, looking straight at him to make it the kind of challenge she couldn't seem to keep herself from throwing down before him.

You don't want to go up against me, he'd told her once. On the large scale, she'd accepted that. On a personal basis, though, he didn't think she'd ever stop testing it.

And that's what made her such an asset to the Resistance.

"Even you," he said, but before she could react, added, "Usually."

She glared. "Dammit—"

He cut her off with a shrug. "Prove me wrong," he invited her. And since he meant it, she just looked back at him, cut off from her anger.

"I will," she said, just as simply. And rubbed a gloved thumb over her forehead, frowning a frown that seemed to have little to do with either him or the conversation.

"You okay?" he asked, stopping again to watch her more carefully. She looked tired . . . but then, Resistance work and double lives tended to do that to them all. He himself rarely spent two consecutive nights in his own bed; more often than not, if he made it home at all, he'd only get as far as the sleek black recliner in front of his desk, where a few moments to down whatever it was he'd grabbed to eat and drink would turn into solid sleep.

If he'd grown up sleeping in a bed, it might bother him. But he'd grown up in the course of a single day, and it didn't.

Hayley wrapped her arms around her oversize light winter jacket, outlining the much shapelier form beneath. "Yesterday fooled me . . . I didn't dress for temps in the forties. That's all."

"Let's go back, then," he said, turning around to face the Key Bridge again. "We're through here, unless you've got something you haven't told me."

She shook her head, tucking her hair behind her ear in what proved to be a futile gesture; it was too short to stay there. "Nope. Looks like the Taelons didn't do anything but run a bunch of happy-happy fairs yesterday . . . nothing more nefarious than that."

"Ne*fair*ious, you mean."

She stared at him in disbelief. "Oh, God, Liam. You should die for that."

"Not today," he said, and after a moment grinned at her. Lighthearted moments were not to be taken for granted; there weren't enough of them.

Hayley looked at him a moment, until her habitually intense, live-every-moment-with-assertion faded to something lighter, and she rolled her eyes and offered him her hand.

Just as habitually, he hesitated, and she said, "It's not a defining action, Liam. We're not limiting things like that, remember? Just call it a truce."

"It's—" *not that*, he started to say, and stopped. She didn't understand; she couldn't. So he just smiled and took her hand, glad for the gloves between them, feeling the tingle in his palm despite them and wondering suddenly how the Atavus had dealt with such things when that precursor race for both Taelons and Jaridians had suddenly found themselves developing shaqarava. And wondering too, why—

—He stood before an enclave of huts, primitive huts with baked clay slathered on the woven-branch roofs, giving them the appearance of houses with hats. Clustered at the entrance to the huts were the enclave's occupants.

The dying occupants.

Covered with the same hut-mud in a primitive attempt to draw healing from the sun that beat so pleasantly on his borrowed, hard-scaled exterior, they tended one another, their craggy features showing little of the sorrow reflected in the rough keening that rose from several of the huts. That sun, too, beat down upon his borrowed Kaluuet exterior, spun from Kimera powers and placed over his own form so he could walk freely among these natives.

As it turned out, an exterior borrowed from a being who

sickened from the same illness as the other beings here, beings who had proved extraordinarily sensitive to the minor changes in their sun.

Beings whose mud would do them no good, and who would soon die out altogether.

The last he'd been here, the Kimera had considered this race to be one with great promise. Fierce, emotional, and yet . . .

And yet despite their primitive state, their hunting and bloodshed-based society, they'd been discriminating in the application of their violence. He himself had witnessed—

But his borrowed body, his ailing, borrowed body, betrayed him. It spasmed with pain, buckling at the knees, slipping into the last stages before its coma and death. It was time to—

"Liam!" Hayley said sharply, her voice making no sense to him; something jerked at his arm. *"Liam!"*

Memories. It had been a memory.

Someone else's memory . . . Kimera. Of what the Kimera had known as Kaluuet and the Taelons had only ever called by the human term *Atavus.*

"Liam!"

Finally he focused back on the here and now, and found Hayley trying to extricate herself from his bone-crunching grip on her hand. Instantly he released her.

"What was *that* all about?" she demanded, massaging her hand.

He blinked, ran a hand over his face, then couldn't help looking at the hand to see that it was still his.

Memories. Kimera memories.

Never before had he had more than a glimpse.

Never before had they carried him away from himself, stealing his very consciousness to insert him in another being's experience. Ancestral experience.

The hand was his. The glove was still creased with the

strength of the grip he'd applied to Hayley. "I'm sorry," he said, and for the moment it seemed the only thing he *could* say.

"Sorry, hell," she said. "You didn't answer my question. What *was* that?"

He didn't have the wherewithal to shrug her off, to offer some vague but satisfying answer, as he would have had to give Sandoval had this happened in front of that unyielding Companion Protector. He could only tell her, "I don't know."

"Liam—"

"I don't *know!*" he said, voice rising in uncharacteristic frustration.

She stared at him a moment longer, her blue eyes narrowed into shadow. Finally she said, "Okay. We're both tired. Let's go in."

She'd let it go . . . but she wouldn't forget.

And he didn't blame her.

Liam strode out in front of her and Hayley, feeling unaccountably tired and irritable, watched him go, juggling a plethora of reactions. Part of her simply watched the view, admiring it and glad he'd worn a short coat and tight jeans—but part of her felt the ache of her hand and knew this was someone she could never take for granted on surface appearance, no matter how attractive that surface was.

Not that she'd ever been tempted, not once she'd learned of his unusual . . . *ethnicity*, she supposed one might call it. And especially not where the Resistance was concerned. Despite her decision to support him, she intended to keep a close eye on how Liam dealt with the business of leading the Resistance.

Although Hayley Simmons was not one of those people who was afraid to mix business and pleasure.

Jonathan Doors. Former Resistance leader, ruthless boy billionaire—about to make a play for the presidency of the United States. Sometimes Augur admired his bold, decisive strokes of action; sometimes he even leaped to support them. And sometimes he ignored the man and went his own way.

Now he said, "What do you want, Jonathan?" in a flat, bored tone, far too interested in the current financial venture his computer tracked for him, displaying complex graphs and rows of figures over the three monitors evenly spaced on his circular standing workstation. "This isn't your home anymore. It's mine. Remember that, the next time you reach the point where knocking would be appropriate."

Doors stood just beyond the high-security elevator and said, "Then you'd better lock out my personal code," in deep, gravelly tones devoid of contrition. He did, after all, maintain the right to sequester here in the event of emergency.

"Damn," said Augur. "I knew I forgot to put something on my *to do* list." He frowned at the screen—those stocks should be performing better than that, he'd seen to it personally—and hot-keyed a request to gain access to proprietary information he wasn't even supposed to know about. "What is it you want?"

Doors didn't respond immediately, which was fine with Augur. No doubt he was looking the place over. Not long ago it had been the Resistance headquarters—a place of crowded high-tech equipment and medical resources where a team of dedicated people tried to second-guess the Taelons . . . and to heal those who had been affected by

them. Sahjit Jinnah had died on his way back to these facilities, shot during a mission to keep crucial information out
of Taelon hands; his fiancée, Rayna, had been killed by a
Jaridian probe. And Liam had been born here.

Now it was Augur's, thanks to Doors' decision to go
high-profile—and running for president was about as high-
profile as it got—instead of continuing his deeply clandestine life here in the hideout. And now, instead of the sterile,
occasionally military presence of the Resistance, the carved-
rock cavern had personality and style. With frameworks of
piping to act as token walls and hold Augur's beloved art
collection, his hand-built, ever-evolving computer system
lining one side of the huge cavern, and more private space
in the back rooms beyond, the spacious lair was—in Augur's opinion—much improved. Little remained of the Resistance aura, aside from the sleek conference table not far
from his computer nexus. And half the reason he'd kept that
was because it was a perfect way to showcase Picasso's
Guernica, a painting that deserved a minimalist environment so its own splendor could be more completely appreciated.

Augur glanced back to the elevator where Doors stood.
Still. "You're not getting it back," he said bluntly.

"I don't want it back," Doors said, just as bluntly.

Augur almost asked, for the second time, what Doors
did want—especially now, with the evening barely about to
start and so many more entertaining possibilities for spending one's time springing to mind—when he realized. The
man was stuck between. Not yet active as a presidential candidate despite his announcement of intent, and not quite
out of his role as Resistance leader. And while Augur was
not normally of a mind for distractions that didn't somehow
prove profitable or pleasurable, he decided to let Jonathan
Doors hang out for a while.

Not that he could resist a little dig. "Quit worrying. The Resistance is doing fine. It *will* do fine, under Liam's guidance. He's got an insider's point of view like none of us could ever have."

"I know," Doors said darkly, finally moving into the room to drape his overcoat over a conference table chair, as conventional as always in a dark patterned sweater over dress slacks. The man definitely needed someone to do his shopping for him—and those off-the-rack suits would be the first thing to go. "That doesn't mean it's the right choice for the Resistance to make. Or that it's not premature. There's so much we still don't know about him—"

"Then I'd say we'll find out sooner with him on center stage," Augur said cheerfully, unaffected by Doors' doom-and-gloom persona.

Holo-Lili, Augur's lifelike computer interface, pixeled to miniature life in her display tube unbidden, which meant she'd come across something in one of his many active background alerts. He'd chosen a current persona that he'd thought would please the real Lili . . . *if* the introduction was done just right.

Warrior Princess Holo-Lili glared meaningfully at Doors, not about to impart her news with a security risk around. Dressed in a short leather skirt, a striking metal bustier, and slouchy boots with totally impossible heels that lengthened her already long legs, she put a hand on the pommel of her stout sword and took up a posture that indicated she was waiting for an explanation of the intrusion. Augur waved away her concern. "Never mind him. What's up?"

"You asked me to keep an eye on enemy activity in the sky," Holo-Lili told him, keeping one narrowed eye on Doors. "Something's up."

Augur translated for Doors. "The Mothership air traffic

control," he said. "Pretty boring stuff, usually, but you never know." To Holo-Lili he said, "Details, sweetheart."

She shifted her narrowed gaze to him and tightened the hand on her sword. "Watch your tongue if you want to keep it."

Augur winced. Maybe he'd been a little too enthusiastic when he'd programmed this version of Holo-Lili. "Okay, okay. Forgive me. I got carried away. Now, what have you found?"

"I was out scouting, and I noticed an unusual amount of activity in the docking bay. Both Major Kincaid's and Captain Marquette's shuttles have been rushed through a maintenance cycle. Four other shuttles have been activated for imminent use."

"Something *is* up," Doors said, coming closer to the monitor array and ignoring Holo-Lili's reignited glare. "Do we have anything vulnerable going on right now?"

We? "The *Resistance*," said Augur, "is having a communal day off. Recovering from all that intense fair-watching yesterday. One too many merry-go-rounds, you know. Tiring work. Besides, nothing's happening."

"*Someone's* in trouble," Doors mused.

"Someone is," Augur said. "But it's not us. Display it," he told Holo-Lili, adding a hasty "Please," when she took up a wide-legged stance, fists on hips. Yes, this persona definitely needed a little fine-tuning.

If he could get close enough.

The Mothership air traffic control data flickered to life on the monitor array, replacing columns of figures he was just as glad to have away from Doors' ever-perceptive gaze anyway. Liam's shuttle, Lili's shuttle . . . vague destination figures put the planned action somewhere in the middle of Texas. "Saddle up, Liam," he murmured to himself, and looked at Doors, assessing the man's avid attention.

Nope. You could take the man out of the Resistance, but you couldn't take the Resistance out of the man.

Northern Texas already knew it was spring, even if Washington, D.C., didn't. Liam stood outside the darkened shuttle and debated whether to shuck his jacket, trading it for the warm evening breeze—and then decided that he, like Hayley, had never quite managed to shed the chill of their early morning walk.

Behind him, Volunteers disembarked from his shuttle, passengers who'd had little to say either to him or among themselves. They joined the silence of the larger gathering of Volunteers, all shuttled in from the Mothership, all armed with heavy weapons and sidearms. The final shuttle—Lili's shuttle—burst through a sudden bloom of interdimensional space, swooping gracefully to a precise landing next to Liam's. In a moment she was powered down, and Sandoval emerged—as suited and dapper as ever, despite the apparently rushed nature of this operation.

Liam, at least, knew nothing about it; he let the question show in his expression.

"The Resistance, Major," Sandoval said briskly, coming to his side. "We're acting on an unexpected tip. There was no time for a briefing."

There were always the globals. But give Sandoval his illusion of control; Liam knew there were no active Resistance cells in this area and tonight he simply didn't care about the details of what was really happening, even if he should.

Lili had no such compunctions, coming up to join them as she settled her sidearm more securely in its holster. "Resistance? I haven't heard of any activity in this area." She'd left her tailored jacket in the shuttle and blended into the night in a close-fitting vest and dark, cuffed-sleeve T-shirt. Her global blinked on quiet standby and as she noticed its light, she thumbed it off. Dangling from one hand were a couple of night-sight goggles; she handed one to Liam as he inserted but didn't activate his ear com. "We aren't going to do the Taelons' public approval rating any good if we barge in on a sleeping family."

"Our orders are clear," Sandoval said, as if she hadn't spoken. "This farm houses a major Resistance gathering. They're armed and considered dangerous. We'll go in peacefully, but if they don't immediately surrender, our Volunteers *will* open fire."

Lili slapped her arm. "This farm houses mosquitos the size of . . . *Texas.*"

Sandoval chose not to hear that, either—while Liam didn't have to worry about it. Mosquitos, even hungry early mosquitos, left him entirely alone. One of the little perqs of being partly alien.

Sandoval addressed the Volunteers, assigning them back and front egress and informing them there would be no premature movement on the house; they were to wait, poised for assault, until clear voice orders to move in. He glanced at Liam and said, "I'll handle initial contact."

"And I'll just come along for the ride," Lili muttered, standing close enough to Liam so only he could hear. "I think he's forgotten I'm more than an automated shuttle system."

"I'm sure he just wants to protect a valuable pilot," Liam said, but he was expecting the light blow that landed on his shoulder. "Come on. Let's get this over with. These people aren't Resistance . . . I can only hope we're not going to wake up some peacefully sleeping All-American family."

"No such thing," Lili muttered. "Not these days. Besides, even if they *were* sleeping, they're awake by now. We didn't come in *that* far from the house."

"It was far enough," Sandoval said, moving just close enough so they could hear him. "Maintain silence until I say otherwise."

Liam nodded at him; Lili followed with her own nod a heartbeat later. Sandoval didn't know his tip was bad; couldn't know there was no Resistance here. And neither should they, which meant acting the part. Goggles in place, they moved through a squishy-damp fallow field, heading for the house in silence. No barking dogs, aside from those in the distance; no shouts of alarm from the house. Nothing more than the occasional muted clink of metal against metal and the rising odor of disturbed wet soil.

—The sun beating down so harshly on his back, the comforting images of his own ferocity during his last hunt attending his own dying moments—

Liam stopped short, closed his eyes hard, his face tight with strain. *Not now.* No repeats of this morning. As much as he wanted access to those ancestral memories . . . he didn't want to be at their mercy.

"Liam?" Lili came up close, carrying the single word on the ghost of a whisper.

He shook his head, moving forward again. Almost there. Let Sandoval wake up whoever lived here, and they could leave.

They passed the backyard outbuildings, passed what looked like an old outhouse. Without direction, Volunteer pairs rushed in to plant heavy-duty halogen stand lights, jamming them into the ground to surround the house.

"Goggles off. Turn on the lights." Sandoval's tone was conversational, his expression just as quiet as he raised a wireless, palm-sized voice-amp to his mouth and nodded.

Liam jammed the goggles into his pocket as light flooded the yard, reflecting brilliantly off the white farmhouse and splintering shards of light back from the windows. But for all the visual explosiveness of the moment, there was no sound. No response from within the farmhouse. A huge farmhouse, three stories and two dormers, windows framed by recently painted blue shutters and lace curtains visible within.

A huge, silent farmhouse.

"This is Agent Ronald Sandoval of the Taelon Companion Protectors," Sandoval said, sending his voice echoing into the night. "We know this is a Resistance location; you are surrounded. Exit the house one at a time with your hands on your heads and you will not be harmed."

Silence.

A moth found the light reflecting from an upper-story window and beat itself against the glass.

"I don't like this," Lili said.

Neither did he. It wasn't Resistance . . . but your basic Texas farm family should have thrown on the lights and stumbled out of the house.

"Maybe Augur . . ." Lili said, without completing the thought; she faded back to one of the sheds and slid behind a corner.

Liam looked away from her just in time to see Sandoval's hand rise into the air, an impending signal to the Volunteers. "No!" he said, a harsh whisper that startled Sandoval into jerking around.

"This is *my* operation, Major," he said.

Territorial in all issues of power, that was Sandoval. Liam gave a short shake of his head. "I just meant," he said, "that without a better idea of what's in there, wouldn't it be wiser to send in a lone man? If you storm an empty house and the press gets wind of it, the Companions will look foolish. If you storm an innocent family, the Companions will look *worse* than foolish." If they *killed* a family . . .

"The press," Sandoval said, and snorted derisively. "The press is not here." But he hesitated, unable to shake the possibility . . . and perhaps aware of Zo'or's ongoing willingness to rid himself of the annoyance named Liam Kincaid. "Go, then. I expect a constant stream of feedback." And he touched his earpiece meaningfully.

Liam walked quietly up to the house, beam gun in hand and up at his shoulder to point at the sky—ready, but not poised. He tried the doorknob; it turned easily under his touch. "Door's open," he said. "I'm going in."

Augur's incoming calls forwarded automatically to his main monitor when the lair's system was active; now Lili's name blinked in high-res lettering as Doors, responding to the locator map on a secondary monitor, said, "Texas? We're not doing anything there right now."

"Tell me something I don't know," Augur said. To Holo-Lili, he said, "Go away. I don't want my two warrior Lilis clashing right now." Not until he refined this programming, anyway.

Holo-Lili said, "But I'm in the mood for a good battle—"

"What are you, Warrior Princess on PMS? Go, or I'll flatline you." Augur reached for the keyboard, and although Holo-Lili scowled mightily at him, she also pixeled out of her tube. "Incoming global, go ahead," he commanded, and Lili appeared before him. More or less; all he could see were the pale angles of her face, sheathed by darkness. And some kind of . . . building in the background. "Is that an *outhouse*?" he asked in disbelief.

"Shh! Keep it down. I've already got my global as low as it goes. Listen, Augur, I need—"

"My help. Like I said, tell me something I don't know."

She evidently didn't care that he'd started her in the middle of a conversation, and that got his attention as much as her words. "Liam and I are in Trinia, Texas—Sandoval's got us raiding a farmhouse he says is Resistance."

"It's not."

"I *know* that," she hissed, working to keep her voice down. "What I want to know is what it *is*. If it's not Resistance, what are we doing here?"

"Hold on," Augur said. He slid his wheeled chair down the length of his workstation, frowned, buffed the local monitor with a red and black patterned silk sleeve that did nothing but smear it, and invoked his personal search macro. The Internet, his private database, other private databases . . . "We'll start with Trinia."

"Be quick about it, would you? Liam's just gone in there."

"Alone?" Doors said sharply, moving into range of the digicam perched on the main monitor.

"Jonathan," she said, half in surprise and half in question. "Yes, alone. Hell, it's probably just some poor family that doesn't even lock its doors at night, but—"

"Or not," Augur said, his brow raising as he watched information scroll by on the smeared monitor.

"First floor's clear," Liam told Lili and Sandoval, speaking into the ear mike as he took a last, careful look around the old-fashioned sitting room beside the stairs. "No sign of anyone. I'm going up." Top to bottom; if anyone was flushed out, they'd go straight to Sandoval. Cautious despite the lack of movement within the house, he hugged the wall on the way up the stairs to the second floor, moving out into a long hallway with careful steps. Sandoval's FBI training had been bred into this body; warrior instincts from a thousand races, absorbed and remembered by Kimera, kept him moving lightly without second thought.

"Major." Startling, and in his ear.

Liam tapped the earpiece twice, an acknowledgment, and a signal that he wasn't going to respond verbally. Not until he'd swept this floor. Intuition, no matter where it came from, was not to be ignored.

As quiet as it was, he wasn't alone up here.

"Or not *what*?" Lili demanded of Augur, her face white in reflected halogen light, the night blacker than ever behind her. She shifted so she could glance over her shoulder at the house, giving Augur the glimpse of one side of it through her global.

"Quit thinking innocent farm family," Augur told her. "Start thinking *militia* instead."

"Mil—" she said, cutting herself off as she jerked her head back to look at her global. "I haven't heard a thing about militia here—"

"Yeah, well, you wouldn't, would you? That's why you came to me, right? The Texas governor is trying to keep it quiet. Looks like he figured out a way to get it taken care of before things got out of hand, with a little help from his Taelon friends and their Volunteers."

"If *we're* here, things are already out of hand," Lili snapped. "And Liam's in there—Sandoval—" She quit spitting out half-finished thoughts and put a hand to her ear. "Liam! Liam, come in, dammit!"

•   •   •

"Come in, dammit!" Liam's earpiece squawked at him and before he could reach up and tap acknowledgment, Lili forged ahead, blurting, *"Militia, Liam!"* even as Sandoval overrode her on the frequency and snapped, "Captain! Stay off this link!" With the jumble in Liam's ear came the simultaneous slam of a door against his shoulder, flinging open to jam him up against the wall with the beam gun caught at an awkward angle and ripped from his hand. A man—heavyset, heavy-moving—bolted past, intent only on escape. *Militia.*

"That's it, I'm coming down," the man whispered harshly into an old model walkie-talkie, already halfway down the stairs and either not noticing or not caring that he'd encountered the enemy on the way.

Not caring, Liam thought, and in that moment something in him rose up in rage and his talons ripped into the haunch of the huge foodbeast he and his tribemates had captured, another memory of a dying Kaluuet complete with the blood singing in his ears and urging him to chase that which now ran—

Liam pressed the heel of his hand to his forehead and said between gritted teeth, "Not. *Now.*"

The earpiece clamored at him, Lili's and Sandoval's voices overlapping into nonsense until he ripped the thing free and threw it across the floor, barely catching Sandoval's final shout—*"We're coming in!"*

The man had been running. Had been running *from* as much as running *to.* Militia, always prepared for a raid . . . never going down without a fight . . .

Liam scooped up his beam gun and stepped around the open door.

Explosives.

Wires leading from this room through a connecting door, more leading out the window and presumably back into the window of the opposite neighboring room. A series of explosives placed around this second floor, ready to rain destruction down on the house below—and here was the timer, glowing fast-changing little red numbers at him.

The entire second floor, rigged to collapse on the heads of anyone who stormed the place—and those who were about to do it.

Liam didn't think about the beam gun, didn't think about the consequences . . . didn't think about much of anything at all. He dropped the gun and flung up his hand, and the energy gathered from somewhere within him and somewhere without, channeling through his shaqarava with an unprecedented agonizing, ripping sensation that startled a cry out of him—startling him into fear and second thoughts.

Too late for that.

On Augur's monitor, Lili stopped her increasingly frustrated attempts to contact Liam, punctuating her defeat with a sharp "Damn!" while Augur, watching through her global connection, spotted what she couldn't see—Volunteers running toward the house behind her.

She must have heard them, though—she heard *something*—for she whirled around, making the global view tilt and dance; she shouted something—a warning, he thought—and then it was too late.

The side of the house bloomed with explosive fire, licking out to fry the edges of the old camper-truck parked in the side drive, instantly melting the cheap aluminum house siding, breaking the glass of halogen lights with its heat and shock wave.

Fire, driving the Volunteers back and to the ground.

Fire, limning the horrified lines of Lili's face as she shouted, "*Liam!*"

And then she dropped the global, leaving Augur staring at a disconnect screen.

"Whoa," he said.

"I knew it," Doors said. "I knew it. Premature."

"Go away," said Augur, displaying intense annoyance in every line of his face just in case Doors didn't get the message. "Begone. Leave this place."

For Lili's global wasn't his only eye to the world, and Augur wasn't about to be left wondering.

He had work to do.

FOUR

L ili Marquette was having none of
it. Not after the moments of hor-
ror she'd endured . . . not after Liam had come staggering
out of that half-dismembered house, allowing her fear to
turn to fury in response to his foolishness at having walked
into such a situation in the first place—and at Sandoval for
letting it happen. A good leader *didn't*. So she let Liam play
the game out with Sandoval; she even joined in. But she
was having none of it.

Then again, Sandoval didn't necessarily *lead*. He con-
ducted. And he did what was necessary to protect the
Taelons, without the loyalty to his fellow humans that Lili
had come to take for granted when she was in the marines.
Semper Fi. Not a phrase in Sandoval's lexicon.

"You were lucky, Major Kincaid," Sandoval was saying,
having joined Lili and Liam at the edge of the outbuilding.
They stood in the aftermath of the blast; half the house had
collapsed in on itself with surprisingly little in the way of
fire beyond the initial conflagration. "If the blast of the
bomb hadn't been directed outward—"

"I took a chance," Liam said, arms crossed. Or—and
Lili narrowed her eyes—not crossed at all. The left over the
right, obscuring his right hand. Hiding it. "It wasn't much

of a choice—shoot out the initial device in the relay or let the whole house come down around me."

"Nonetheless," Sandoval said; he pulled out his pocket watch, glanced at it. "Very lucky, Major. Now if you'll excuse me—"

"You knew it was militia," Lili said, not excusing him but also refraining from adding the obvious. *You knew and you sent Liam in there without telling him—because you knew he wouldn't play along.* Never mind that Liam, theoretically expecting Resistance tactics, could well have been killed.

"I told you what I knew, Captain." Sandoval returned her anger with unaffected composure. "And I don't see your point. Resistance or militia; of the two, which do you suppose is more dangerous?"

"I don't recall the Resistance being prone to this kind of senseless violence," Lili said darkly.

"True," Sandoval admitted. He thought about it another moment and gave a short nod. "The Resistance prefers to work covertly. But I have no doubt its members would fight if cornered."

"Neither do I," Liam said dryly. "But it's always nice to be prepared. And it strikes me that we've saved President Thompson a lot of grief here tonight."

"Not to mention all sorts of congressional hearings," Lili added, watching Sandoval, her eyes again narrowed.

"Oh?" said Sandoval, his Asian features bland. He couldn't make it any clearer; he didn't particularly care about the question *or* the answer. "And how is that?"

Oh, he'd known all right. A favor from Zo'or to President Thompson, that's what this had been. A militia nest cleaned out in one fell swoop, and without the risks posed by using conventional forces—standoffs weren't likely with the superior Taelon firepower in play. Zo'or wouldn't have allowed the charade unless he had good reason.

Unless he wanted something to hold over Thompson's head later on.

"Think about it," Liam said, surprising Lili with his shortness, surprising even Sandoval, whose evenly hand-some features grew a little harder in response. His dark eyes could be expressive if he let them . . . Lili had seen him smile, once—had found it stunning in its charm, the way it changed his entire demeanor.

But never did he smile while under the influence of his CVI. The good old Taelon imperative.

He was definitely not smiling now. "I don't have time for this," he said. "Major, I'll expect a full report on my desk in the morning. If you're injured beyond the obvious, have yourself seen to." And he turned away to attend his senior Volunteer, his appearance entirely unruffled by either the walk across the field, the explosion, or the conversation.

Lili eyed Liam openly. Now the game was over—she was through playing. He stood on the edge of the halogen glare—lights that had been quickly replaced with the arrival of another shuttle, this one right in the driveway. The look he returned her was unusual in its defiance. Not that she hadn't seen defiance from him; plenty and often. But rarely did he aim it her way. And it was unique to find him defiant as now, when he was scorched at the edges, a bruise darken-ing by the minute along his jawline, stray splots of blood brought up by flying debris, and . . . *something*. Something else. She considered and discarded the idea of modulating the anger in her voice. She felt it; let him hear it. "Don't try to tell me you caused that mess with a *beam gun*. What *really* happened up there, Liam?"

He just as clearly considered and discarded the idea of prevaricating before he glanced over at Sandoval striding toward the captured militia and then back at her to say in a low voice, "I'm not sure."

"You're not sure? What do you mean *you're not sure?* There's more to it than what you told Sandoval, I know that much." Her global beeped; she ignored it.

He shrugged, shifting his weight to one leg in what she normally considered a relaxed and confident posture on his part but what right now simply looked wary. "The bombs were there. Are *still* there, except for the one I destroyed."

Lili looked at the half-melted house, thinking again of the blast she'd seen, of how little actual fire there'd been. "You destroyed it. You didn't *detonate* it. You just—" Her global beeped again; she snatched it off her belt, knowing who it was even before she glimpsed the caller ID. "Not *now*, Augur! We're fine, okay? Everything's fine." She slammed the device closed, ignoring Augur's startled expression. He'd pout—but he'd get over it, and she had the feeling that if she gave Liam an inch he'd be out of there. So she looked at him and said, "You did it. Not the beam gun, not the bomb. *You* did it."

"I'm still sorting it out," he said.

"No you're not," she shot back at him. Pushing him, and trying to push hard enough to make him push back.

Which he did. "It's all *right*," he said, bringing himself fully upright and yet belying his words with the tight, strained look on his face.

"Listen," she said, "you can pull that stuff on Sandoval, but don't you dare try to pull it on me. We're *on the same side*."

And that's when he did it, when he looked away. Just for an instant, but it was long enough. She *knew* that look. She'd seen it before, when he'd once thought himself responsible for the future scene of carnage in the Resistance hideout—when he'd struggled through getting a handle on the Kimera within himself, the abilities that no one else had and no one else could guide him through the use of.

Yeah. *Something* was going on, all right. She'd pushed him far enough to learn that much. And now she'd hesitated long enough so he'd gotten his balance again. At some point he'd shoved his hands into the pockets of his light jacket, and now he said, "We're on the same side, all right. But just because I was born within the Resistance doesn't mean the movement owns my every thought. Or were you ready to tell me the details of your brother's death?"

Lili winced. Low blow, and that wasn't like Liam either. "No," she said. "We don't own your every thought. But if what's going on with you affects the Resistance, you can bet I'll keep asking. And if I don't, someone else will. We're at a crossroads, Liam. You know that. We can't afford to take the wrong step right now. We've got to be able to depend on each other."

"You *can* depend on me," he told her. "But that doesn't always mean you're going to agree with me. Or that I have to agree with you." And there was no evasion in his gaze now, not as the brightly artificial light surrounding the house hit his blue-gray eyes at just the right angle to light one and put the other entirely into shadow.

How appropriate, said a wry little voice in her head. One part of him telling her the absolute truth, and the other part of him telling her nothing at all. Out loud she offered a formal—if temporary—retreat. "You're right. You don't. I just hope you know when you cross the line between your personal issues and Resistance business."

"I know," he said. "As much as anyone can."

She didn't find that particularly reassuring. But it was as much as she was going to get, and Sandoval was eyeing her in that way that meant he wondered what they were talking about when she ought to be assisting in the cleanup for this messy little operation. So with one last meaningful look at Liam, she left him there by the shed.

Liam watched her go. Captain Marquette she'd been for that conversation, and not Lili. Not the woman who, along with Augur, had helped him through his first difficult days, but a ranking member of the Resistance, putting the welfare of the Resistance before all. As would Doors, if he heard about this. No, Doors would go further; Doors would turn him over to the Taelons if he felt it was best for the Resistance. Doors would have Liam killed . . . or do the job himself.

So Liam stood and he waited, waited until Lili was fully involved in conversation with Sandoval and both of them were moving out of sight. Then he let himself sag back against the shed, let his head fall back against it, lifting his hand to look at the glowing shaqarava there, pulsing with the same agony that had gripped him within the house and never let go. Not both shaqarava, just this one, the one he'd instinctively brought to life at the threat of the bombs. "Go away," he muttered at it, words clenched with the pain of it. He closed the hand into a fist, covering the unearthly light, trying to squeeze it out of existence. "Go. *Away.*" And glared, reaching for that place within himself, the feeling of closing himself away from the energy rush of activated shaqarava. It hammered at him, unrelenting, ripping right up his arm and trying to burst out his hidden palm.

"Please," he breathed, on the verge of giving in, of letting it happen. "Leave me alone."

The light leaking from between his fingers faded; the

unaccustomed pain of it faded as well. Slowly, he opened his cramping fingers, disbelieving the relief of it, not under-standing either why it had happened or why it had gone away.

And not knowing when it would happen again.

omething's up," Lili said firmly, not to be put off by Augur's mutterings about growing pains and *Liam's just a kid* and give him some time. Because it didn't matter if it was true, it didn't matter what the unusual circumstances were and how reasonable it was for Liam to hit growing pains. Not with the fate of the Resistance riding on his actions. "Something's up, and I need you to find out what it is."

She could see from Augur's face that he was about to dig his heels in. Not a good time for that. Walking briskly through the Mothership's organically curving corridors while she spoke casually into her global as though this particular call was within the Taelons' best interests would only get her so far; she ducked down the corridor to the empty lab that had once held a Jaridian and tucked herself behind a wall rib as Augur said, "You know, Lili, he outgrew that Big Brother stuff somewhere around his thirty-eighth hour."

"He still comes to you and you know it. Besides, he's not talking to *me*. That doesn't leave us a lot of choice, does it?"

"I'm telling you, it's probably nothin—"

Lili cut him off, keeping her voice low in its intensity. "Then find out for sure and you can say *I told you so*. Think of this as a rare opportunity." She'd barely glanced at the global, watching the quiet stream of traffic in the main corridor instead—but now she looked at him, finding with much relief that he had that look on his face, the one that no amount of camouflage behind high-tech cam-glasses and splash-of-color clothing could hide. The one that said she'd finally intrigued him.

"You'll owe me dinner," he said, a counteroffer.

"Yes, yes, I'll owe you dinner. Just do it, okay?"

He held up both hands. "Doing it, doing it. Next time I see him. Good enough?"

"It'll have to be," she muttered. But to Augur Lili nodded shortly. "I'll check back with you."

He waved her off dismissively and the screen went to dial-tone blue; Lili slid the global closed against her hip and hooked it over her belt. She stood there with a thumb and forefinger lightly touching each brow, taking the moment to sort out the complicated pieces of her life.

Sandoval had known about the militia presence last night; therefore so had Zo'or, and Zo'or never did anything without a reason. Meanwhile, whatever happened to Liam had been no simple close call with a cranky detonator—not even a close call with the cranky bomb attached to that detonator. But she had no further data bits to add to either event, so it was time to file them away—not for good, but just until something else happened to make them make sense—and get back to working on the post-Fair reports from the various Companion security teams, assessment and reassessment of their strategies. Sandoval hadn't asked for them yet, but when he did, he'd expect them to be ready.

She realized, rubbing her fingers against the outer edges of her eyes, that Liam's report had not yet been filed.

Voices permeated her thoughts, human voices, and low enough so she thought they might have been there all along. Wonderful. Now *she* was getting careless.

Except that she wouldn't anticipate voices in an empty lab.

Not so empty?

And if not, what new project had the Taelons initiated?

Lili moved toward the lab, not concerned about being caught—checking out human presence in a closed area was a perfectly good excuse for her own arrival.

All the same, when she got close enough to recognize Sandoval's voice, she slowed. And she thanked the Taelons for their pleasantly asymmetric, entirely alien architecture as she pressed herself behind a slight projection just before reaching the lab's faintly scintillating new virtual glass barrier. She made no attempt to see the interior herself; she didn't have to. She put her global on high-res record and let it do the peering for her.

She made her escape shortly after Sandoval's voice and tone shifted, into getting-ready-to-issue-final-commands-and-leave tones, and then—just to see how he'd react—she reversed course once she reached the turnoff from the main corridor, playing her investigative role.

"Captain Marquette," said Sandoval in displeased surprise. "What is your reason for being in this area?"

"Just wondering the same of you," she said. "I heard voices. I came to see who was using an empty lab."

"Security of this lab is not your concern." He shot his cuffs more properly into place, especially the one over his skrill. As sleek as his suits were, he hadn't found a tailor who could make a sleeve fall properly over the bio-engineered weapon.

"Not directly," Lili said. "Although I consider anything that affects the Taelons to be my concern. I don't have to have a CVI for that."

He looked at her a moment, the look she could never

read, not until he opened his mouth and sometimes not even then. Half the time she thought it meant *who do you think you're kidding* and the other half she thought she had him completely buffaloed.

And oddly enough, sometimes she thought he simply chose not to act on what he saw.

This time, he said, "You no longer need concern yourself with this area."

"So I see," she said. "If you'll excuse me, then—"

She'd made it a few long-legged strides away from him when he called out after her. Damn, how *did* he always time it so perfectly?

"Captain," he said. "About those security reports from the Fairs—"

Double damn. "They're almost all in," she said, stopping, turning her head to respond but not quite enough to actually look at him. "I'll get them to you as soon as I've compiled them."

"*Almost* all? Which areas have failed to report?"

"Tiananmen," Lili said. "And D.C."

She didn't have to see Sandoval's eyebrow go up. She could feel it in his silence.

"I see," he said. "Thank you, Captain. That is all."

Dismissed, she thought, and just as glad for it; the global at her side clamored silently for attention with its clandestinely gathered data.

A few minutes later she sat in her docked shuttle—as private as it got, this shuttle, especially with the personal modifications she'd given it. Aside from the increased performance in atmosphere and during the interdimensional transitions—modifications Liam had adapted to his own assigned shuttle—it would also subtly warn her anytime any being came within a certain range, depending on the current default setting.

In dock, she couldn't give herself much of a buffer; there was always an Advanced Drone—a well-trained *human* drone—servicing this or that shuttle, always someone going to and fro. But it was enough so she could sit in the back of the shuttle with her legs crossed and attend to her global—an activity she did often enough—whether she was working, making a call, or contemplating her navel while Sandoval kept her waiting—that it drew no attention.

Besides, it would be uncharacteristic of Lili Marquette, marine pilot and SI war veteran, *not* to have a proprietary attitude about her shuttle.

"Marquette," she told the blank, open global. "Voice authorization. Play back last recording. Magnify centrally, times two."

Sandoval. Sandoval's back, to be precise. Talking to a lab tech in the requisite white coat—the Taelons went for a subdued teal, but allowed the humans their habits—both of them attending a holographic midair datastream display, their voices no more distinct than she'd heard from the corridor.

The tech looked familiar; she'd figure his identity out later. "Increase volume," she said quietly, automatically glancing out over the docking bay floor in spite of her shuttle's warning system. "Increase magnification centrally."

Well, it was a little crooked, but that's how she'd been holding the global. She thumbed the pause button, putting the conversation on hold while she frowned at the datastream display. Those things could be hard enough to sort out in person. But suddenly the visual clicked into place, and she realized she was looking at a very faint flattened world map. Within the map were smears of light, and she bumped the magnification up again, enough to discern that the smears were discrete clusters of individual lights. Stray, faint lights showed up on their own here and there, not attached to or near any clusters, but not many of them.

Okay. Clusters of light. The locations had to be significant, whatever the lights indicated. There seemed to be two different sizes of clusters—large, diffuse ones across the globe along with much smaller, more concentrated areas within North America—and occasionally there was even a small concentrated area within a diffuse area. The map had nothing but sketchy land features, so it wasn't going to be of much help. She'd have to take it to Augur, see if he could superimpose it on another world map.

Yet even as she was about to release the pause and listen to the conversation, the pattern of lights caught at her, tugged at something familiar in her thoughts. She drummed her fingers against her knee, frowning, and finally gave up, decreasing the magnification and releasing the pause with the memory tug unresolved.

"There," the lab tech said, pointing to a hazy grouping. "You can't tell from the map, of course, but we've got the computer keeping track. We lost one, here."

"Can you pinpoint the area?"

"Not any more precisely than what you see. That's why Ta'en was displeased with the arrangements."

"Never mind," Sandoval said. He slid his global open and said, "Section Seven, acknowledge."

The reply was unintelligible. Lili suspected it didn't matter.

"We have an alert," Sandoval said. "Have you been monitoring communications as instructed?" A pause. "Good. Contain the situation. Sandoval out." He tucked the global away, returning to his conversation with the lab tech as if there hadn't been any interruption. "And can we expect more of these problems?"

"No. I mean, it shouldn't have happened—not if Phe'la's

Volunteers targeted as Ta'en instructed. Of course, it's not always possible to tell the health of an individual, especially not with the flu season—"

"I'm not interested in excuses," Sandoval said. "I simply need to know to what extent my teams should be prepared."

The lab tech said quietly, "If it's containment you want, I suggest you prepare them well."

"Thank you," Sandoval said, and seemed to mean it; Lili could understand that. It was hard enough to do an efficient job on a need-to-know basis when what the Taelons *felt* their agents needed to know was so different from what their agents *did* need to know. But Sandoval didn't dwell on it; he indicated a grouping of lights. "Dr. Bellamy," he said, "what is the significance of these smaller groupings?"

How convenient. Just what *she* wanted to learn.

Bellamy shifted uneasily. Bellamy—she *knew* he'd looked familiar; Dr. Peter Bellamy, a med lab employee she'd seen in the Jaridian's holding area right after the being escaped. He hadn't said much, then, hadn't struck her one way or the other. Now he struck her as worried. Then again, he was dealing with Sandoval. Worry might be entirely appropriate. He said, "We haven't figured that out yet. Obviously, the large groupings represent the original sites. But due to the inaccurate nature of the tracking tags, it's difficult for us to gather data on actual location—"

"I'm not interested in what you *can't* tell me," Sandoval said. "Only in the answer to my question."

Bellamy cleared his throat. "Perhaps you'd prefer to speak to Ta'en?"

"Ta'en isn't here. You are." Sandoval again pointed to several small clusters. "You targeted youthful subjects, did you not? These could be secondary learning institutions."

"They could be," Bellamy agreed, grabbing at the notion.

Sandoval turned away from the datastream to look at Bellamy, that passive-aggressive *I'm going to nail you but I'm going to make you wait for it* look that Lili had learned to ignore. Then he said, "Or they might not be. Find out, Mr. Bellamy. Immediately."

"But that's not what I—"

"Are you questioning my orders?"

And then Bellamy got some backbone, surprising Lili—even generating a little cheer for the doctor. "I question whether your orders take precedence over my responsibilities to Ta'en."

"Let me resolve your dilemma," Sandoval said. "I speak for Zo'or."

And Lili smiled, for Bellamy stuck to his guns—and in this case, it meant a delay for Sandoval, and more time for her to download the information to Augur and set his genius on the challenge. Which, for Augur, wouldn't be much of a challenge at all. Her hand curved over the end of the global, preparing to punch in Augur's code, as Bellamy said, "I would be happy to serve Zo'or. But it isn't my place to make that decision. Ta'en will return shortly . . . discuss this with him so he can release me from my current duties and I'll immediately start work on your request."

Sandoval gave him The Look. And then he said, "I'll be back, Dr. Bellamy."

Lili stopped the replay, staring thoughtfully at the paused global. If Sandoval was smart—and he was—he'd forget about Bellamy and go straight to Phe'la, whose work in medical security made him the best one for the job, anyway. That's probably where he'd been headed when she'd bumped into him.

Damn. That gave them less time than she thought to stay a step ahead of him.

But as her glance fell on the global again, on the datastream map between Sandoval and Bellamy, she froze; the concentrated tags—whatever they were for—fell into place in her mind, perfectly fitting a crucial pattern.

Resistance hangouts.

The Flat Planet in D.C., Cleveland, Denver, and New York City—Augur's franchise, if you were clever enough to track him down on paper, which no one ever was. The Orbital Spin in L.A., Palo Alto, Seattle, and Phoenix—Doors had owned those at one time, but someone else fronted them now.

Lili's fingers tightened around the global. The Taelons were up to something—tracking people for study?—and somehow, they'd caught and tagged a significant number of Resistance members in the process. Even if Sandoval hadn't figured that out yet, he soon would.

Too soon, no doubt.

Lili wiped the display, keeping the file in upper RAM for ready download, and hit the code that would dial Augur's number. None of her Resistance contact numbers resided in easy storage and recall . . . all she'd have to do was drop this global and have the wrong person pick it up and she'd expose not only herself but everyone else. Resistance numbers were stored piecemeal, coded . . . a jumble of meaningless numbers.

She gathered her jumble of numbers and called Augur; let him finish identifying the cities involved. And she called Liam, who looked tired and took the news with so little re-action that she thought he was probably hiding much more of one. And then, signing off with him, she stared at her blue dial-tone screen and hesitated.

Liam would see it as a betrayal. Augur would think it stirring up trouble. Outspoken Hayley Simmons might be annoyed enough to delay her imminent return to the Pacific Northwest.

In the end, she made up her own mind. She called Jonathan Doors.

The Flat Planet had never seemed so empty. Liam was expecting it, but when he eased into the bar, the lack of familiar faces took him aback anyway. There were customers aplenty—it was prime dining time, after all, and the Planet offered more than exotic drinks in the evening; savvy D.C. diners knew they could depend on the small kitchen to deliver personalized if pricey meals along with the house specialties. From the charmingly named curdled milk sticks—fried cheese of all varieties—to complex vegetarian dishes . . . the eclectic menu served to draw in enough business to camouflage the Resistance clientele.

But he'd gotten Lili's call; he'd gotten the generalized message from Doors afterward, passed from person to person within the Resistance thanks to a viruslike program Augur designed to automatically forward the message even while deleting it from the originating global. He'd been met by Kwai Ling at the door, handling hostess duties even as she silently cued Resistance members that it wasn't safe. She'd only frowned at him and shrugged him by, though. Given that he lived in the attached apartment, it would be odd if he *didn't* end up there, tagged or not.

Tagged. They had to find out what the tags were for. Had to figure out a way to get rid of them.

Augur met him from behind the bar, took one look at Liam, and shoved the drink he'd been about to sip across the curving red surface to Liam. "Here," he said. "You look like you need this more than I do."

"Thanks," Liam said, not stinting the sarcasm.

Augur was dressed in casual spiff mode this evening, the perfect café au lait tone of his shaved head gleaming, the single lock of hair at the back of it braided tightly and looking as though it might be oiled. The body-hugging orange and red shirt he wore probably broke a zoning code somewhere along the line. He leaned on the counter and said, "Tough day at the office, huh?"

"What do *you* think?" Liam responded, and tried the drink—a sparkling wine cooler of some sort, it made a nice sweet zing in his mouth. He nodded his thanks, saluting Augur with the glass, and took another sip. Tough day. Sandoval's report was done, at least—a hack draft, but Lili had insisted on taking it anyway, and he hadn't fought her on it. He hadn't asked her about her call to Doors, though she'd been trying to find a way to bring it up herself, had almost done so a couple of times, each time opening her mouth slightly but only giving her lip a quick bite instead of coming out with words.

He didn't ask her about it. He didn't need to. He'd shaken her up at the raid, and she'd done what she'd thought best for the Resistance as a result.

He just wished she hadn't.

For Doors didn't hesitate. He didn't consult, discuss, or commune. Resistance leader status notwithstanding, he *ordered*. He sent the warn-off about the Flat Planet and Orbital Spin, and as near as Liam could tell, he'd spent the afternoon hovering over Augur's shoulder while Augur played with the download Lili had sent him.

Didn't the man have a political interview somewhere? Doors' son and campaign manager, Joshua, was surely sharp enough to hang on to the momentum Doors had achieved with his outspoken interviews during the Second Chances debacle. In fact, as little as he felt like it at the moment, a call to Doors was probably overdue. He pulled his global off his belt and put it on the bar, working up to it.

A sudden shiver ran down his back, startling him; he

looked at the drink and then at Augur, then didn't ask. Augur knew better than to give him unexpected recreational drugs. He set the drink down anyway. "Not the best idea for you to be here."

"Pshaw," Augur said with much dismissiveness, actually saying the word. *P-shaw.* "I own the place, don't I? Not that anyone's going to be able to prove that on paper, of course, but still . . . with all those little dots mapped in this city, it'd be surprising if one or two of them weren't here."

All those little dots. "Could you make any sense of Lili's data?"

And Augur gave him that look. "You wound me," he said.

"Yeah, yeah." Liam drew his jacket closed. "Let me put it this way. What does Lili's data mean?"

"That's more like it." Easily and cheerfully appeased, Augur provided himself with another drink like the one he'd given Liam. "Interesting thing, that map. I can tell you some things for sure . . . the rest we'll consider an educated guess."

"I'll take what I can get."

"You're a grouch, you know that?" Augur eyed him conspicuously.

A grouch? Maybe so. He had reason enough, waiting for the next ancestral memory not only to hit him, but to carry him away. Waiting for his shaqarava to reveal themselves at some excruciatingly inopportune moment. He was tired, and unrelentingly cold—as if his body had acclimated to spring in the single warm day of the Fair. "I guess I am," he said. "I'm sorry." Together, they waited for Angie to serve the two customers who came to lounge against the bar. On another day, one of the other Resistance members might move in to serve as buffer, or even distraction, but today they were on their own.

When they had decent privacy again, Augur skipped ahead in the conversation. "Here's the thing," he said. "All of the tags—those little dots of light—are localized around an area that hosted a *Celebration of Accomplishments*—" His tone left no room for doubt about his feelings there, though he paused and said, "You know, those Taelons need a better PR firm. 'Celebration of Accomplishments'? What kind of holiday is that? It hardly rolls pleasurably off the tongue—"

"From what you've said, I'd have thought you already had plenty roll pleasurably off your tongue," Liam told him.

Augur flashed him a brilliant smile. "So I do. But enough about my personal life. Take what Lili heard—for whatever reason, the Taelons have attached tracking tags to a large number of people, and they apparently chose them at the Fairs. Young, healthy people. Now, as a group, how would you describe the Resistance members we had patrolling the U.S.-located Fairs?"

"Young and healthy," Liam said, knowing that the conclusion should therefore be obvious to him and finding himself too tired to think it through. The Resistance had members of all ages and abilities, hidden away in unlikely and crucial positions within government, industry, and services. But of those who did fieldwork, few were past their prime, and few dealt with obvious health problems. The nature of the game didn't allow it.

Augur waited a moment, giving Liam the chance to fill in the conclusion, and then grew impatient. "However and whyever they've established these tags, the Resistance was the perfect target. Lili was right—the small areas of intense concentrations, overlaid on precision mapping provided by *moi*, turn out to be either Flat Planet or Orbital Spin locations."

"Then Doors did the right thing to warn us off," Liam mused. "I just wish he'd talked to me about it first."

"Yeah, well, you know how he is," Augur said. "He's having a hard time letting go. The siren call of power and all that."

"He's not going to do the Resistance any good if he creates confusion about its leadership," Liam said darkly.

Augur said abruptly, "Lili's worried about you."

It threw Liam off stride. He closed surreptitious fingers around his right palm, then relaxed them. In response to Augur, he just absently shook his head—which was no response at all, but then, Augur hadn't exactly asked a question, either. Out loud he said, "We've got to find out if they have records of that tag scan Lili saw—and if so, we've got to destroy them somehow. Sandoval's way too smart not to go back to that scan when he sees his interesting little areas of concentration have dispersed. And we've got to figure out . . ." he trailed off, losing his train of thought.

Augur, used to thinking faster than other people could talk, filled in for him without missing a beat. ". . . why they're tracking people. If it was a ploy to expose Resistance members, they came way too close to success. If Lili hadn't found that lab—"

"We've got to find a way to scan for those tags ourselves," Liam said, briefly turning his back to the bar and surveying the room, wondering how many people here had been at the Fair, and of them, how many had been tagged. "That's the first step."

"Already on it," Augur said, *of course* unspoken in his voice. "And then we'll come up with a way to negate them."

"Good," Liam murmured. Lili could be working to learn what she could aboard the ship, while Liam . . .

Liam thought he might just ask Da'an.

Augur nudged his arm in a silent bid for attention, then directed his gaze at the giant flat-screen monitor in the corner of the bar. Other patrons had noticed as well; someone was interested enough to turn it up. Catherine Shaw, the anchorwoman with all the scoops, had a most serious expression on her face as she said, "The bizarre incidents defy explanation; medical experts are unable to explain the witnessed, spontaneous destruction of Kenneth Roy's body, a young man who was otherwise described as being in excellent condition until this incident claimed his life."

The view cut to a grieving woman of the right age to be a sister or girlfriend, coming into the interview in midstream to start her in the middle of a babbling sentence. "—hadn't been himself lately, but we never thought—I mean, we would have gone to someone for help if . . . he just turned inside out! It was so horrible—"

And back to Catherine Shaw, who said, "The incident happened in the middle of a heated argument, but officials have dismissed the idea of foul play. Meanwhile, across the country in San Diego, another strange incident occurred in which a young woman disappeared right in front of her family. Witnesses say she screamed and then vaporized in a shimmering blue light. Authorities have turned to the Taelons; Da'an, our North American Companion, has promised to apply Taelon technology toward solving these two tragic riddles."

"Yeah, I'll bet," Augur said, low enough for Liam's ears only.

Liam shook his head, turning back around to let Catherine Shaw talk about the stock market without his attention; he reclaimed the wine cooler. "Don't sell Da'an short," he said. "If this is related to some project the Taelons have going, my bet is that he doesn't know about it."

"*If,*" Augur said skeptically.

"If," Liam repeated. "Those energy-eating bugs from ID space weren't their doing. Not everything is." Another shiver struck him, foreboding—*screaming, his own shaqarava light*—and . . . *not*—strong enough so he lost his grip on the cooler glass, recovering just in time to avoid creating a wine cooler lake.

Augur frowned at him, skewing his precisely trimmed mustache and goatee. "That's not right," he said, and removed the glass from Liam's hand. "Look at you, Liam, all bundled up when I've got the heat settings to *tropical* in honor of the night's specialty swordfish. If it were anyone else I'd say you had the flu that's going around—" He stopped short, narrowed his eyes, and asked in honest curiosity, "Can you *get* sick?"

With as much of a cutting edge as he could dredge up, Liam said, "I was hoping *not.*"

But two-thirds of him was human, and humans caught the flu with alarming regularity. What, he wondered, would a low-grade fever do to the other third of him, that part with which he'd had so much trouble lately? Or—he shivered again, trying and failing to dredge his Beckett and Sandoval memories for references—a high-grade fever?

He was, he thought, about to find out.

"Here," Augur said, fishing into his pocket. "Virex. Take it; it'll help you fight the flu off. It's even engineered to get this season's top bugs. Over-the-counter and everything."

Liam winced. "No thanks. After what happened when I tried *over-the-counter* headache caplets, I think I'll just stay away from that sort of thing altogether."

"Oh, ri-ight," Augur said. "You weren't much good for a while. Though it's been a while since I heard you giggle."

Liam sighed. As a sympathetic ear, Augur had some work to do. "Let's just consider it making up for lost time. I don't think I had the opportunity while I was a kid."

"There's that," Augur agreed, removing the wine cooler from the bar top. "But hey, at least your first time wasn't a stomach virus. Ugh, nasty." And as Liam raised an eyebrow at Augur's proprietary possession of the drink, Augur added, "You need something warm, not *this*."

Bemused, Liam said, "What, are you my mother?"

"There's an excellent book by that name. I recommend it to you. Written by a man named Seuss. Here, drink this tea." And Augur replaced the cooler with a traditional teacup, proving that the Flat Planet was always a place of surprises. "And turn off this global," he said, commandeering Liam's global to suit action to words. "Go upstairs, and get some rest. No playing out on the roof, now."

"You *are* my mother," Liam said, but took the tea, holding it in both hands. Not a bad idea, at that. Beckett would approve. Beckett would pull out a rune—Hagalz, for the destructive forces of nature—add a drop of whiskey and honey to the tea, and suggest that there was no point in ignoring what his body was telling him.

But he sighed, and reached for the global—which somehow still wasn't there, although Augur glowered at his intent. Liam nodded at where it had been. "You know I can't do that." No telling who was trying to reach him, or how vital their message.

"Yeah, well, you should," Augur said, Keeper of the Global. "There's more to life than the Resistance, my friend. You need to figure that out."

"There's not more to *my* life," Liam said. "Not right now."

"Be blind, then. Ignore my words of wisdom."

"The global?" Liam was not up for this little game. Not up for it at all.

"Drink the tea," Augur said implacably.

Liam said a word he rarely used, which only made Augur laugh. And he drank the tea.

·   ·   ·

Nothing truly wrong, then, Augur decided, although Liam was clearly closing in on miserable, heading for the door to his apartment with nothing of the usual spring in his stride and another mug of tea pressed into his hands. Lili had been right—something was up, all right, but it was nothing more than half the people in Washington put up with each winter.

Except, of course, that it was Liam's first time, and he hadn't been able to define the problem on his own. Augur gave an exaggerated little shudder. When he thought of *first time*, this wasn't exactly what he usually had in mind.

Suzanne came up behind him, returning to the bar with a tray of empties. "Is he okay?"

"Yeah," Augur said absently. Lili needed to know—she'd practically assigned him to find out, after all—but from the look of the group that just crowded in, things would be hopping here for a while. "Just the flu."

"*Just* the flu?" she said. "And he's going home to that apartment? It doesn't even have a decent kitchen. Someone ought to take him soup or tea or something—"

"Did that." Augur grinned, though he turned away as he did it, pulling out clean glasses from beneath the bar. Suzanne had acquired an endearingly awkward crush on Liam the first time she'd seen him—but never the nerve to do anything about it. "You know, you should just go ahead and ask him out."

"Do you think?" she said, glancing somewhat longingly at the discreet entrance to Liam's apartment.

"I think," Augur assured her. "I definitely think."

"Chocolate," she said, tapping her lower lip. "If he doesn't need feed-a-fever food, then feed-the-soul food might help."

Augur gave her a briefly skeptical look and then let it go. "Whatever," he said, and nodded to where the new group had pulled two tables together. "Just take care of those customers first, okay?"

"Chocolate," she murmured thoughtfully to herself, nodded, and headed back out to the floor.

Augur dumped the remains of Liam's drink and washed his hands in the small sink set beneath the bar. No use in taking chances.

Ta'en was not particularly pleased; he knew this fact reflected in the pinched corners of his mouth, but could not smooth the expression away. However, Zo'or seemed reasonably satisfied, and there was something to be said for that.

"All location teams are alert and ready for containment," Sandoval said. He looked tired, a distinction Ta'en was acquiring the skill to discern; Ta'en recalled that the hour was late for Sandoval's Earth locale, although that never seemed to prevent the Companion Protector from being available. Sandoval, like Ta'en, now stood on the elegant first level of the Mothership bridge, where sometimes the silence was soothing, and sometimes it was intimidating.

Of late, Ta'en had found it intimidating.

"Good," Zo'or said in response to Sandoval's assertion, sitting regally in the bridge command chair. "Then we can expect no further news reports from Catherine Shaw on Ta'en's failures."

"There would be no need for containment if you had allowed me to proceed with my planned methodology," Ta'en said instantly, straightening to an unusually upright posture. "I will take no responsibility for them; they are a result of your own decision."

Zo'or did not respond—in itself, an admission of sorts.

Sandoval filled in the gap. "The errors in judgment that

resulted in public knowledge of the failures have been corrected. I expect no recurrences."

"Excellent." Zo'or turned the chair away from them both, affording himself a view of the stars. "And you, Ta'en—what do you expect?"

Ta'en took this as a genuine request for information. "I speculate that the majority of the failures are a result of the human influenza virus interfering with our own retrovirus—you note that the concentrations of failures are in the cities hardest hit with the influenza virus. Those in which *our* virus has gone awry for whatever reason will likely evince the results before the successful adaptions. Starting a week after the virus introduction, your teams should be also alert for those with the power of the shaqarava. I assume from your previous comments that you will want to acquire them for your own use?"

"I will want to interview them, certainly. I believe," Zo'or said, looking out to the stars and smiling faintly to himself, "I believe that once they understand the options before them, they will choose to volunteer in the battle against the Jaridians."

"Options?" said Ta'en. "What options do they have? The retrovirus will have changed their very nature. Their sole option is to live with that fact."

"True," Sandoval said. "But we certainly cannot allow those with such dangerous power at their disposal to wander unchecked among others in Earth's population. For the good of all, we would be forced to detain them in a Taelon facility. No human facility has the resources to deal with those so empowered."

Ta'en thought the practice of taking subjects from those already imprisoned held greater merit, but did not say so. Such a suggestion was pointless at this stage of the project.

Sandoval frowned, which Ta'en thought little improvement to his habitually serious face. Humans were more interesting, he felt, when allowed their full range of emotions. Of course, they were also less predictable, which made the CVI and its imperative a useful thing in humans who operated with as much authority as Sandoval. "Zo'or," Sandoval said, "those who acquire the shaqarava are more likely to be able to hide it than those in which it has gone awry. It won't be possible to contain them all before word gets out. Meanwhile, President Thompson is already asking for our assistance in determining the cause of the . . . *incidents* that Catherine Shaw reported. As you predicted, his gratitude for the militia cleanup should prevent him from becoming too troublesome, but I have no doubt that Jonathan Doors will try to connect the incidents to the Taelons in some way—especially once those with developing shaqarava become evident. What explanation do you wish to use?"

Zo'or's pale eyes were serene in his satisfaction, his gestures liquid and composed. "The one that will align humanity with the Taelons against a common foe, of course. We will release our report on the recent arrival of another Jaridian probe."

Sandoval hesitated, the question evident on his face—the same question in Ta'en's mind. Another probe? When had it arrived?—but his expression quickly resolved. "I understand. Should I also mention the unfortunate injuries of the Taelons who acquired and dealt with the probe?"

"A very nice touch. Yes, I like that. It is unfortunate that the probe's destruction did not come quickly enough to prevent infection of humankind with this Jaridian virus. I will trust you, Agent Sandoval, to handle the timing of this revelation to the human United Nations."

Sandoval nodded, the slightest of motions in his still body, his hands clasped behind his back in a way no Taelon would ever choose to stand. Even Ta'en, as muted as his gestures were in Zo'or's presence, could not imagine choosing to limit his bodily vocabulary so.

Zo'or turned to Ta'en, inclining his head in a manner that made it appear as though he was about to bestow a favor on Ta'en. Ta'en suspected otherwise. "Ta'en, now that the weaknesses of your Beta-S virus have been made apparent, I expect you will take advantage of the opportunity to eliminate them. When we do choose to move to a full-scale inoculation of trained Volunteers, we will not want to waste any of them."

Ta'en quietly made the decision to proceed with his own methodology for testing Beta-S. He could combine his results with Zo'or's sloppier but more copious data for a better outcome. And then, abruptly, Ta'en wished he had managed to end his part in this conversation a few moments earlier, for Da'an entered the upper level of the bridge and moved down the gentle curving ramp to the bridge proper. No scientist would choose to insert himself between the edged barbs those in the diplomat caste used to give their positions potency.

Beyond that, the debates between Da'an and his offspring were legendary in their intensity. Ta'en chose to still himself, quieting the agitated gestures that clamored along his own arms and hands. Best to remain unnoticed.

Da'an proffered a respectful greeting gesture to Zo'or and said, "I would speak to you about what is happening on Earth."

"And what," said Zo'or, "is happening on Earth?"

"Do not play games with me, Zo'or. You know very well that the recent incidents in the human population are not natural to their biology. So do they. I have promised President Thompson I would obtain answers."

"A foolish promise," said Zo'or.

Da'an inclined his head. "Perhaps so. But as North

American Companion I could hardly do less without raising suspicion. And of late, we have given the humans enough reason for suspicion."

"And you, Da'an? What suspicions do you have?"

Da'an hesitated. "I regret to say that I believe we are indeed somehow to blame for what has happened. I wish it were not so."

"Save your wishes for those who deserve them, and save your efforts for the Taelon race," Zo'or snapped, turning on Da'an so suddenly that even Sandoval stiffened slightly.

"All the same," Da'an said softly, after just enough pause to acknowledge Zo'or's words, "I would like to offer the humans some explanation."

Zo'or's response was short. "No doubt." Then he seemed to reconsider, and said, "I will offer *you* the choice, Da'an. Which would you rather—to remain ignorant and thus respond truthfully so to all questions, or to know your answers and thus be forced to lie when you cannot reveal them?"

Ta'en felt his own mouth pinch with the cruelty of the choice. Like himself, Da'an was being forced into a position where he could not serve his caste to his own exacting standards—his well-known weakness for the humans notwithstanding.

It was a choice that Da'an apparently could not bring himself to make, for he remained silent, standing with the quiet dignity for which he was known. After a moment, Zo'or said, "I thought not. Go to the humans, then, and tell them you have no answers for them. When I am ready, an explanation will be provided."

Da'an blushed with a surge of personal energy, but he again inclined his head. When he left, Ta'en went with him, making his escape as he could and realizing with a sudden surprise that he much preferred working with the human Bellamy than interacting with his own Synod leader.

Bellamy, at least, tried his best to make life smoother for Ta'en. The same most certainly could not be said of Zo'or.

But the Synod had chosen, and it was not for Ta'en to question.

It was for Ta'en to give the humans shaqarava, and that was honor enough.

SIX

Lili grabbed her global from the brightly colored Formica tabletop with a sound of disgust, thinking that it might be nice to get through a decent dinner for once, even if in this case a "decent dinner" meant too many french fries, too late in the evening; King Street in Alexandria, and on the way home. *Captain Proton*, the caller ID told her.

She took it to mean Augur, rolled her eyes at no one in particular, and snapped the global open. "Augur," she said, by way of greeting.

"Ah, you recognized my alter ego," he said, and smirked in that way that no one else could have possibly made appealing, turning arrogance into an asset.

"Sure," she said. "When my global tells me someone with an absurd ID is calling, I know it must be you."

"Tsk," he said. "That's not very nice. Maybe I'll go away."

"Not without telling me what you found out from Liam, you're not," she said, tipping the global down so the fast-food restaurant logo wouldn't show in the background.

She should have known better than to try.

"Would you like fries with that?" Augur asked.

"You're not being endearing," she said. "Now what's up?"

"Couple of things," he said, leaning back in his chair before the main monitor; she could see the clustered monitor array behind him—a nexus of three monitors facing outward and encircled by a tubular steel track holding the keyboards and peripherals—and the hologram tube off to the side. And if she wasn't mistaken, it was occupied by the latest version of herself . . . in a . . .

Yes, in some kind of bronze bikini getup.

Augur must have seen some sign of it in her face; he shifted to block her view of the tube. Never mind. She'd deal with *that* later. "First of all," Augur said, a bit loudly at first until he was certain he had her full attention off of the holo-tube, "you can quit worrying about Liam. He's sick, that's all."

"He's *sick*?" she repeated, both surprised and doubtful. And since Augur had already scoped out her location, she chewed the end off a french fry, mulling his words even as he affirmed them.

"Yeah, even Superman gets the flu. Fever, chills, all that. I sent him to bed with some tea."

Bemused, Lili said, "I'll bet he took that well." She thought about obtaining the recently improved—thanks to the Taelons, of course—version of Virex for him, the immune system booster that most people routinely took for the flu, and decided against it. No telling how it would interact with the Kimera part of him . . . just like there'd been no predicting what something like the flu would do to him.

"He took it better than you'd think—that's how I know he's sick."

"But he's okay," she persisted.

"He's fine," Augur said, and it was his offhand delivery that assured her as much as the words. "But listen, Lili—we had a chance to talk about the maps. You know Dr. Park and I are already working on identifying the tags—probably some simplified nanobot kind of thing, isotope-carrying. No problem; I'm checking in with her first thing in the morning, and if we can figure out what to look for, I think I can tie into your shuttle systems and run our own little tracking scope. But in the meantime, we need to do something about those image files they've got on ice. The ones *before* Doors shoo'd the Resistance away from the Flat Planet, if you catch my drift."

She did. Sandoval wasn't so easily thwarted once something caught his attention, and they couldn't afford for him to have a map with giant pointers to Resistance hangouts. "You mean *I* need to do something about it."

He didn't bother responding to that. "The Mothership generally stays on an east coast schedule to align with the U.N., right? So you go in about dawn."

"Augur, there's some damn tight security on that area. I've got the codes to just about any area of the ship, and I still have no idea how to get in that lab." She'd already tried accessing the lab information from a random workstation within the ship; the workstation memory held no awareness that the lab computer even existed. It was behind a firewall, then, or completely independent from the rest of the ship. The only access must be within the lab itself.

The one behind virtual glass.

Augur smiled. "Leave that to me."

Leave that to me. Of course.

Which was how Lili found herself walking casually along the predawn main corridor of the Mothership, headed for the area from which Sandoval had specifically told her to stay away. Taelons didn't sleep, not exactly, but they required meditation and the opportunity to refresh themselves within the Commonality, and they had indeed fallen into the habit of keeping human schedules to do so. Those humans who walked the corridors at this time generally moved quietly, and with less intensity of purpose than during daylight hours. Though taut with the danger she was about to walk into, Lili was not unprepared. She'd carefully purged her global of the least incriminating fact, littered her small shipboard office with a data trail of the reports she'd been working on, and set the stage for her need to "clear her head" with a quiet walk. All a nice convincing alibi, should she need one.

She wasn't alone the first time she walked by the turnoff. She strolled on and doubled back, and this time took the opportunity to turn in, still not hurrying her steps, not looking like she was doing that which she ought not.

Until she reached the lab, whereupon she pulled from her close-fitting vest the one incriminating thing she carried—Augur's adapter cable to hook her global up to the Taelon keypad controlling the virtual glass door to the lab. It was small enough, she hoped, that she could unobtrusively rid herself of it if she had to.

The connection wasn't a smooth one; she had to curse at it several times and adjust the tiny prongs with gentle tooth pressure before it snicked into place—by then she was in full spy mode, fight or flight, and she took a deep breath to put herself back to the place where she could feign her way out of the situation if need be.

Not her strength. Lili preferred to go in with guns drawn, confronting the problem, taking on the fight if need be. Not slipping around its edges, sly with words and manipulations and shadows. To some extent, Doors was like that, too—and it had eventually driven him to leave the underground he'd created and challenge the Taelons publicly. Liam, she realized suddenly, was much better at this double life than she was. He lived with so many secrets inside him, with the necessity of keeping them just to survive, that dissembling to the Taelons came more easily.

Even so . . . the need to keep those secrets might simply be more of a liability than the Resistance could afford.

This wasn't helping. She took another breath and keyed in a call to Augur, who answered instantly; he'd been waiting. "Okay," she said quietly. "Do your thing."

"Stand back," he said, already going to work, "and watch magic in the making."

"Just make it *fast*," Lili muttered, watching her global respond, tripping through combinations of Taelon words and figures that Augur himself could barely comprehend. William Boone had been the only human to work his way through the Taelon language; Augur's further work in it was based on his interaction with Boone. Fortunately, one didn't have to understand the individual elements of a password to come up with the password itself—as Augur proved moments later when the code settled on a three-dimensional display of slowly whirling characters.

Relief flooded through her—dangerous relief, for she couldn't afford a letdown yet. "Augur, you *are* magic," she whispered into the global as she put her hand through the archway, unimpeded by the virtual glass barrier.

"I know," he said, utterly without humility. But he turned more serious and said, "Go get it, Lili. And *be careful*."

As if she had to be told. She slid the global closed with a quiet snick and eased into the lab, hunting the computer interface.

Ah. There. Against the back of the room, beyond the datastream display area. No need to call Augur in on this one. When it came to the Mothership, Lili knew the systems as well as any human aboard—and this one, tucked in this out-of-the-way lab with its newly secured perimeter—

had only the lightest of password protections on it. "Why bother?" she muttered. Token passwords behind a theoretically fail-safe barrier.

But she knew the answer. The Taelons were as prone as humans to follow patterns without thinking them through, a species quirk Lili had been quite pleased to discover they shared.

It made her job a whole lot easier.

It meant she knew the several systems they used for storing data . . . and recognized this one when she saw it, easily accessing the tag tracking log files. There she discovered the start date of the tracking—the day of the Fairs, not a big surprise—and watched, flipping through the file images, as the Fair attendees dispersed to the larger metropolitan areas around them, and as travelers went home. As the Flat Planet and Orbital Spin locations gradually acquired a steady-state concentration of tags.

Bent over the computer panel, working as quickly as possible, she identified the records up to the point of Doors' quickly disseminated command to disperse from the hangouts, erased them, and replaced them with copies of those records made since then. Someone would have to know exactly what they were looking for before they noticed the changes.

Done. She sighed relief. Almost free and clear; she'd have to loop in footage for the surveillance system, but that had to be done once she was gone, from a regular workstation.

And then, as she removed a specially treated tissue from her inner vest pocket and wiped the panel free of all traces of her touch, a quiet human voice spoke from the archway. "What are you doing here?"

Momentarily, she stiffened. But it had been a not-particularly-challenging voice in its quietness. Not one of the Taelons' human security drones. Bellamy. Had to be Bellamy. And she ranked Bellamy.

So she forced herself into casual mode, dispensing of the tissue in a mild sleight of hand as she turned to face him. "I'm reliving old times, I guess," she said. "I knew him, you know. The Jaridian who was here."

"Did you?" he asked in surprise, momentarily derailed. He took a closer look at her, and the puzzled look on his face resolved. "Captain Marquette. Yes. I guess you knew him better than any of us. He never spoke to us."

"He spoke to me plenty," Lili said, without enlarging on her comment. No point in telling Bellamy that the Jaridian had offered them crucial insight into the conflict between the Taelons and Jaridians . . . and that in many ways, they'd found him more reliable than the Taelons.

"It must have been a frightening experience," Bellamy said, moving into the lab. "It doesn't explain why you're here, though. Respectfully, this is a secured area. Agent Sandoval would have added you to my clearance list if you were supposed to be here."

Lili raised her eyebrows. "Secured? If that's true, then you've got problems. I walked right in."

Bellamy frowned. He was more sober than she remembered from her brief interactions with him earlier in the year; less cocky. Someone who, somewhere along the way, had realized how much he had to lose. He indicated the archway. "There's a virtual glass door here, Captain."

"Not when I walked through it," Lili said with some assertion.

Bellamy turned to the keypad, hitting the sequence that would reinstate the door; it shimmered into place, coruscating briefly when he pressed his hand against it. "Seems to be working fine," he murmured.

Lili joined him next to the door, eyeing it and the keypad, suppressing her unease at being locked in. "Occam's razor," she said. "The most obvious explanation—"

"Is the most likely," Bellamy finished unhappily. "I'm certain I keyed the door back into place when I left to eat." He had a right to be unhappy. He had, after all, apparently neglected to do that of which he was so certain—an error that would cause serious repercussions should Sandoval discover it.

"You're lucky it was only me," Lili said; Bellamy didn't look so sure about that—or else he simply wasn't buying the explanation she'd led him to consider. "Look," she said. "I was just walking out some kinks before tackling this report I'm working on. Not a big deal. Maybe a scare like this is a good thing . . . it'll keep you on your toes in the future."

"Agent Sandoval won't be so understanding," Bellamy said, absently keying in the code to open the door again.

Lili stepped through it, hiding her relief just as she'd hid her tension. "I don't see any particular need to tell him," she said. "He's got a CVI; sometimes he forgets what it's like to be you and me." And then winced inside, wondering if she'd overplayed that card.

Bellamy wasn't giving her any clues; distracted by his apparent lapse—or his silent disbelief of her scenario—his expression remained preoccupied as he put the door back in place. "Thank you, Captain," he said. "Please, for both our sakes, don't come back here."

She wasn't sure how to interpret that, except it certainly didn't sound like he'd go running to Sandoval, and that was as much as she could ask for. "Not unless Agent Sandoval requests it," she agreed. "Good day, Mr. Bellamy."

And then all she had to do was get down the corridor without being spotted, erase the surveillance records—for those were kept with all the other ship surveillance files, and she knew just where they lived within the main system—and get that report finished. Not only did it tie into her cover story, but Sandoval wanted it.

It was always best to give Sandoval what he wanted.

She found an empty workstation—for she'd long ago pegged which workstations were least populated by the Advanced Drones, and rotated her clandestine work among them—and quickly handled the surveillance data, looping in images of the empty lab. There. Finally. She could truly give that sigh of relief—even if she couldn't quite dismiss the niggle of worry that was Bellamy. Still . . . she'd handle it when it came up again, *if* it came up again.

For now, she turned to the worry that was Liam. She had more privacy here than in the small work area assigned to her in a much more active part of the ship. She'd much preferred when she'd worked alongside William Boone in his Earthside headquarters, a Taelon adjunct to an existing building. They'd had plenty of privacy, easy opportunities to pursue a Resistance agenda. But Sandoval would never be so separated from those he served, and that meant neither could she.

So she'd take advantage of these moments for a quick global call, although—she checked the global time display—it was probably still too early for Liam to answer, especially if Augur was right about the flu.

But Liam answered, though not right away. And Augur certainly appeared to have been right.

"Lili," he said. Drawn blinds kept his apartment shrouded in night despite the approaching dawn; she'd seen the rows of columnar candles lining his glass-and-metal shelves in the past, but had never seen them all lit as they were now. Beckett's influence, she thought, a complete dichotomy in mood from the rest of the sleekly modern space and no doubt something that centered him, as Beckett's runes and mystical edge had kept her firmly grounded in Ireland despite the turmoil of being a Companion Agent.

"Liam," she said, surprised by his appearance despite Augur's warning. "You should be in bed."

"Close enough." He shrugged, sitting cross-legged in the black recliner in front of the monitor on which he'd picked up the call. Shirtless—Suzanne would have a fit of envy—with a blanket slipping over his shoulders and fatigue smudged on his face, he'd clearly had a rough night. "I'm waiting to hear from Augur," he said. "What's your status?"

"I took care of the data we were worried about," she said, scrutinizing him, finding nothing more than a rumpled, bleary-looking human. "Wanted to check in with you."

"Nothing new," he told her, shifting in a way that made her think of all the achy flu bugs she'd ever had. "We need to find a way to scan people for those tags."

"I'm more concerned about finding a way to invalidate them," Lili said. "Until we do that, the Resistance is in serious trouble. I'll try to keep Sandoval distracted from following up on what he saw, but if he does, sooner or later he *will* figure out how neatly so many of us have been identified for him. Talk about a purge—Liam?" Something in his face had changed, his gaze gone distant, his shoulders stiffening so the blanket slid off . . . and he didn't reach for it—didn't seem to respond to her voice. "Liam?"

He responded, all right. His eyes rolled back; she could see the corded muscle in his neck.

"Oh, great," Lili muttered, restraining the urge to shake her global as if the gesture would transmit to him. She couldn't remember feeling more helpless. This was the *flu*?

Kimera-within-Kaluuet—clandestine, shape-changing anthropologist, absorbed in the community. Endowed with the memories and living the life of its host, Kimera-within wailed with anguish over the death of its child. A she-child it had been, healthy and strong in these days of wasting sickness. Dead not by that which each Kaluuet here had grown to expect, but because of the sheer carelessness of another warrior.

The Kimera-within faced the warrior over the body of the child, keening loud accusations that its community echoed—all had seen the carelessness, had seen the child run through only moments earlier, its blackish blood still dripping from the haft of the spear.

Limited by Kaluuet form and identity, the internal Kimera self howled for revenge—for the Kimera was at its core not-Kaluuet, and the stricture "harm not one of your own" that bound the Kaluuet did not hold for it. So the Kaluuet form snarled and tensed, rocking back and forth in its wide-legged stance, responding to the unusual Kimera-based urgings within.

The Kaluuet warrior just looked back, blinking, and then down to the blood on its careless hands.

Kimera-Kaluuet wanted revenge, ached for revenge, could think of nothing but that revenge. But within this host form, it found itself turning away. Turning its back. Just as did every other being in the community. No physical harm would come to this warrior who had slain a child of their own.

Within the Kimera-Kaluuet, anthropological wonder bloomed. If any creature were to kill one of its own kind, this moment would have been that to inspire it.

And it had not.

"Liam!" Lili said through gritted teeth, and this time she *did* shake the global, unable to stop herself. Then she froze, for on the small screen Liam had changed again, his strangely labored breathing—not physical strain, she would have said, but emotional—hitting a sharp gasp, and then smoothing to something more normal. And his eyes unrolled and his head tilted back, but he caught it and gave himself an infinitesimal shake. And though he looked a little confused, when his gaze met hers through the global, it quickly sharpened.

"And what," she said acerbically, flooded with anger on the heels of her worry, "was *that*?"

"Pay-per-view," he said, his voice as dark as she'd ever heard it.

"I'm not kidding around, Liam." And then he shifted slightly and she saw his hands, resting lightly on his knees, shone with a softly glowing blue light. "That's it," she said. A last straw of sorts, for as much as she worried about him, she also had to be able to *count* on him. The Resistance had to count on him. "That's really it."

He looked down at his hands, turning them palms up, and smiled faintly—though not with any amusement. "That's *what*? Giving up on me already?"

"That's not it and you know it—"

"No," he said, barely letting her get the words out, though he didn't much raise his voice. "No, I don't know it. I've got the infamous flu. I don't think much of how it makes me feel, and from what I've seen—from what Sandoval or Beckett experienced—it's not hitting me just like it would hit you or Augur or Doors. But if I *were* Doors, would you challenge my ability to lead the Resistance? If *Doors* got sick, would you challenge *him*?"

She shifted, a little uneasily. She'd trust Doors to look after himself, that's what she'd do—whether it meant going off to bed or pushing himself to the limit. But—"You're not like Doors. You're not like *any* of us. We don't have any idea how this will play out."

He met her head-on. "That's right, we don't. But do you really think it's best for the Resistance to create more turmoil within the organization right now?" He shrugged, rubbing his palms along his thighs, gingerly enough so she could tell they pained him—and that much, she knew, was unusual. But it didn't distract him, and he didn't let it distract her. "Don't be alarmist. Let me have the flu and get over it like anyone else."

Anger flared up all over again, for if there was one thing they couldn't afford to forget, it was this very fact. Her voice went sharp as she jumped on his words. "You're *not* like—"

He jumped right back at her, raising the energy from *some*where. "And I never will be, if you don't let me!"

They glared at each other a moment, and he scrubbed his hands over his face, coming out looking just as bleary as before; morning stubble against a pale face didn't help one bit, and she could see another shiver take hold and work its way from his shoulders down his back. She wanted to tell him to go to bed and forget all this. He said, "Look, this is me. This is part of what comes with the package. When you chose me, you chose to deal with my heritage. I never said it was going to be easy."

He was right. She was looking for guarantees in a world where there weren't any. And while most in the Resistance knew him only as the man who'd appeared so suddenly to prove himself within the organization, Lili had known exactly what she was doing when she chose to endorse him.

When she'd stepped away from the leadership role herself.

She took a deep breath. "Okay," she said. "Okay. But play it safe, will you? Stay right there, get some rest and get through this thing."

"Now you sound like Augur," he said, giving her a half-hearted grin.

"Yeah, well, there's a reason we give him all the tricky jobs," she replied, willing to let him take the conversation to a lighter tone. "Just do it, okay? I've got things handled up here, Dr. Park and Augur are working on the tags and will call as soon as they know anything, and there aren't any Taelon publicity stunts coming up—Da'an can do without you for a day or two. If you need anything, just let your fingers do the walking."

He gave her a slight frown of complete incomprehension.

Lili rolled her eyes. "Your global, Liam. Use your global."

He hesitated, getting that normal, faraway look that he sometimes got when sifting through all those memories. Not quite as startled a look as Boone had gotten when hit by his CVI-enhanced memory, but definitely elsewhere. And it was reassuringly familiar, with none of the intensity of whatever had happened moments earlier. *Pay-per-view.* Whatever the hell that was supposed to mean.

Now he came back to the conversation, and nodded slightly. "I'll take it as it comes," he told her, which was evasive but as much as she was going to get.

"Be good," she replied. "Or I'll set Kwai Ling on you."

She thought she saw him wince at the thought of the Flat Planet's domineering hostess, and she closed her global with satisfaction. *That* would keep him at home, in bed with the flu.

Just like anybody else.

Bellamy double-checked the virtual barrier function at the lab entrance, though he was sure he'd left it activated when he'd gone to grab breakfast . . . and just as sure that it hadn't failed on its own. Captain Marquette had not waltzed in here as easily as that.

The question was, why had she come at all? *Walking out the kinks* hardly inspired the effort it took to break into a secured area. Uneasily, he moved to the spot where he'd found her—next to his own workstation. Nothing looked unusual or out of place.

Nothing, that is, except for the lone paper tissue sitting at the bottom of his empty waste receptacle. He bent over the receptacle—an asymmetrical thing of clean and sweeping lines that, were it smaller, would be mistaken for a vase on Earth—considering whether to pluck the tissue up and examine it, as distasteful as the thought struck him. As it turned out, he didn't have to; he recognized the particular odor of the cleaning fluid imbued within it.

Not his tissue. Not his cleaning fluid. And no one else had been here since he'd gone on break. No one but Captain Marquette, of course.

Abruptly he sat, allowing his lab stool the moment to adjust automatically to the height of this particular workstation. Working quickly—he didn't want to have to make explanations to Ta'en or, worse, Sandoval—he drew up the surveillance tapes for the lab, skimming through the visuals to find the moments he wanted.

There she was. Working at this very station, invoking the datastream with a thoughtful but narrow-eyed gaze. Beautiful long almond eyes she had, blue in the light and dark in the shadows—but he'd seen them flash with displeasure and wouldn't want to be on the receiving end of that, no more than he'd like to be under the scrutiny of Sandoval's cold dark eyes. And if he wasn't mistaken, he was about to be caught between—

Hold on. What—?

His display flickered irritably; he closed the file and reopened it, long trained by human software to expect foolish anomalies that could be resolved with such a maneuver.

Only it wasn't the same file. No more Captain Marquette. No more visual record of her intrusion here. He'd stumbled into her very efforts to cover her tracks.

Successful enough, too. Because although Bellamy had no doubt he could spend his morning sorting through the system until he found what she'd accessed and determined for himself if she'd changed anything . . .

He chose not to.

He closed the file with a few unhesitating keystrokes, and went back to his own work.

Ah, Augur's favorite thing . . . skulking around capriciously changing Resistance-held warehouses, trying to look casual—to look as if he actually *belonged* here, which he did not, and so early in the day at that. He waved a cocky little wave at the unseen camera—there'd be one, no doubt about that—over the door as a spontaneous listing of his truly favorite things came to mind.

Oddly enough, skulking wasn't one of them. He much preferred to do such activities in the virtual world of data and phosphors. So he frowned, took a quick glance around to see if his much-wanted person was being watched, and invited himself inside.

Yes, he was much wanted . . . even if no one doing the wanting actually knew *who* they wanted. Augur was most careful about such things.

He sauntered into the warehouse, down the inevitable flight of metal stairs, and through an open space to the curtained-off area where Park had her equipment. She, too, moved where she was needed, although she also worked out of Columbia Hospital, where her good name was still her good name and her Resistance activities weren't even a figment of someone's imagination. Between her and Dr. Belman, they got the job done, and probably knew more about Taelon biotechnology than anyone else in the States.

Since Doors had abandoned the hideout that was now Augur's own personal underground palace, Park had developed an efficient and precise routine for breaking down her equipment and setting up at the next secure location— although it meant she was generally working with less than she needed. Didn't matter, not today; he'd tie it into his system if he had to—Holo-Lili was waiting, thews braced and loins girded.

He really needed to do something about that.

The warehouse was huge; there were plenty of other sections curtained off by plastic walls and pipe-metal infrastructures—bunking areas, tables with high-tech camping equipment to make up the kitchen, other sections for planning and training. Augur ignored them; Park and her medical toys were the reason he was here. She'd seen the recording Lili had made of the tag-mapping; she'd had the chance to draw plenty of Resistance blood and hunt through it for anything unusual. With any luck, she'd have an answer waiting for him, and then together they'd brainstorm some way to turn the things off.

But when he walked through the "door"—a surprisingly sturdy metal door set within a pipe frame, and already half open—he found her in a rolling office chair beside an exam table, her head cradled in her arms and her chic, light blonde hair in total disarray. Startled and alarmed, he took a few quiet steps and frowned . . . until he realized she was merely sleeping.

"Been in this Resistance thing too long, Augur," he chided himself quietly, setting down the small bag he carried—two cups of spiced coffee—and slipping out of both a streamlined knapsack and his leather coat, which he draped across the back of another chair. He put a gentle hand on her shoulder, his skin stark against the white lab coat she wore. "Doc, hey . . . Doc?"

She made a sleepy noise, turning her head to look at him through the fringes of her hair; her eyes widened slightly. "Augur," she said, and slowly straightened. "I'm sorry. Long night . . ."

"No problem," he told her, stepping back a little now that she was aware of his presence. She was like that . . . evoking respect even though she didn't demand it in so many words. Melissa Park was a mature woman—Augur made it a policy never to guess a woman's age, not even when goaded—but she was one of the lucky ones who was translating herself into a ripened version of what she'd once been. Different, but no less attractive—even now, with her hair going its own way and her face creased from her lab coat sleeve.

Ah, yes, Augur did like a sleepy woman.

He gave himself a little throat-clearing and said, "How's it going?"

She rose from the chair and tugged her lab coat back into place, resetting the stethoscope around her neck.

Stethoscope? For blood samples?

"I'm afraid I'm not where I was hoping to be in terms of tracking down the tags," she said, stretching her neck and kneading the stretch. "I got waylaid . . . but now that you're here, I hope we'll take care of that aspect quickly enough. Doing something about it is another thing again . . ."

"Let's just start at the beginning," Augur said, pulling out a coffee and handing it to her, nodding in response to her murmur of appreciation. "Do you have the blood samples?"

"More than you can imagine," she said grimly. She pulled open the shiny steel door of a small refrigerator alongside the portable but sturdy lab table and indicated the contents.

Samples. Racks and racks of them.

"Whoa," Augur said, eyebrows climbing. He resettled the small oval frames of his yellow-tinted glasses and looked again. "You have a convention in here?"

"Something like that." She removed a rack, smoothly and efficiently, and set it on the table. One hand pulled out slides, the other slide covers. "I don't think we'll have to go through all of these, however." She took one more sip of coffee and set it aside; if she wasn't already fully awake, she was doing a good imitation, setting up several slides in quick succession.

"You sound like you already have some ideas," Augur noted, arms crossed and fingers tapping against his forearm as they twitched with the impulse to do something. He wasn't used to doing the watching.

"Forming ones," Park allowed, inserting the slides into the multislot computerized microscope that would help her analyze them, scanning for unfamiliar structures and bringing them to her attention.

Within moments, a red light went on over each slide.

"Wow," Augur said. "Three cherries. Looks like the jackpot for you, Doc."

"I'm not sure I'd put it that way," she said, tapping in a few commands to bring up a three-way split screen on the monitor beside the scope machine. Cradling an elbow in her palm, resting a knuckle under her chin, she considered the screen.

There was nothing astonishing; nothing overwhelmingly profound. Within the center of each screen sat a small black dot. Augur reached beside her to type in a quick command, enlarging the screen significantly.

A structurally artificial black dot.

"Not very numerous," Park said. "Let's just see how many there are." She set the computer to counting them for each sample, and reacquired her coffee.

Augur said, "I'm more interested in *what* they are."

"Undeniably Taelon," she said.

"As if that was ever in question," Augur responded. "*Every*thing small and sneaky and hanging where it shouldn't be is Taelon." But he reconsidered and added, "Unless it's mine."

Park gave a small smile as if amused despite herself. "If we assume this device is part of the tracking system Lili discovered, then it doesn't really matter what you want to call it. What matters is how it works, and what we can do about it."

"All right," Augur agreed. "Let's call it a tagbot, then."

"Tagbot it is," Park agreed as the monitor screen flickered to a search results window. "Well, they're definitely here, but there aren't that many of them. Let's hope that makes our job easier."

"If I were a tagbot," Augur said, "I'd be sending a signal."

"Most medical imaging uses isotopes," Park mused. "But that seems too subtle a thing for off-planet detection."

Augur had to agree, although it had been his initial thought as well. But if not isotopes, how were the tagbots shouting their presence?

Maybe just by shouting. "Y'know," he said. "Could be the little guys are humming." On one frequency or another, a little chorus of tagbots combining to shout loud enough to turn into a blip on the Taelons scope. He turned to his knapsack, pulling out a notebook computer and his global, both of which he could link to his main system if he had to.

He didn't think he'd have to. Not with the global—*his* global, and thus not any ordinary global—hooked up to his laptop and slowly scanning wavelengths from one end of the spectrum to the other. The Taelons could do amazing things with technology, true enough—but he was betting that when restricted to tagbots so tiny, they weren't pushing their luck with an overly complex system.

Park had returned the tray of samples to the refrigerator; Augur retrieved them even as Park turned back to the samples within the scope, off on some mission of her own. A quick scan of the spectrum got him a myriad of radio stations; he programmed the global to ignore them and started again. "Ah," he said. "I've got you now, my pretties."

"And I might say the same," Park told him from her seat at the scope, whatever she was looking at. "Though I'd probably use different words."

"Everyone does," Augur said matter-of-factly. He gestured with the global, indicating the rack of samples. "I'm picking up a faint signal just into the ultrasonic part of the spectrum, but it's steady. And if my global can pick it up from here, you can bet the Taelons can read it from the Mothership. It's simple, but it's all they need to do the trick. And in Lili's global file, Bellamy *was* complaining about the lack of sophistication in the tags." Luckily, it'd be no big deal to rig up any number of global-detectors for use on Resistance members.

Eliminating the tags would be another thing altogether. Ah, well. One thing at a time. "What have you got?" he asked, replacing the rack in the refrigerator and going to look over Park's shoulder. The monitor showed a full-screen view of an organic lump, complete with 3-D protrusions. He answered his own question. "Something ugly."

She smiled, but it didn't hold much humor. "A virus."

"From the flu that's building up steam around here?" He had a dose of Virex on hand, yes he did, ready to take at the first sign of illness, and one in his system already even though the doctors said that was mostly a waste of time.

"I believe so. There's definitely an influenza structure

here." She tapped the scope with her finger, where all three LED indicators burned brightly. "Three cherries." And she glanced at him, a look full of significance.

"I don't suppose," he said, the ebullience of his tag discovery giving way to a familiar brand of dread—the Taelon-brand, fast becoming a household product—"that you think this is a coincidence." Virus and tagbot, hand in hand.

"That all three tagged samples show signs of the new flu? No. I very much doubt it."

Augur frowned. "Why would the Taelons want to give us the flu?"

Park shrugged. "There's no telling. Maybe so they can earn goodwill by helping us through it."

"*That's* something they'd do, all right." And it wouldn't matter to the Taelons that even in this day and age, the elderly still sometimes died from a bad case of flu.

Flu that Liam had. No doubt he was tagged as well. At least Augur now had a way to find out for sure. "But why," he said out loud, "would they bother to *monitor* humans with the flu?"

"That's a good question," she said. "One that bothers me." She stared at the virus a moment longer and mused, "It's pretty complex. It won't be easy to come up with a specific counteragent."

"What about Virex?"

Park shook her head. "It'll help. Enough so the CDC probably won't worry about coming up with an antivirus in time to help with this round of infections; they'll just let this one run its course, and add it to the cocktail in next season's flu shots. I doubt very much it's airborne—the tagbots certainly aren't, and it seems unlikely they would design the virus to spread in a manner they couldn't monitor, since they've gone to all the trouble to monitor it in the first

place. We should concentrate more on making the tags i
effective."

"It's a 'bot," Augur said, back on his turf. "It's got to
have an off switch."

Park swiveled the chair to face him. "Maybe it does,"
she said slowly. "But in this case it's more like a virus than a
mechanical thing. It's introduced into the system, and it
probably replicates until it reaches a certain population
level, at all times broadcasting its signal. *Off* is no doubt a
very unnatural thing to it."

"And why not work *with* its tendencies instead of against
them—make so many of the things that no single one of
them is significant." He gave her a gratified look. "I like the
way you think," he said. "You can come visit my place anytime."

"Why, Augur," she said, "you flatter me."

"At every opportunity." Crossing his arms, he leaned
back against the exam table, was taken by surprise when it
smoothly rolled away from him, and recovered to stand hip-
shot instead. "You know, Doc, Liam's got this thing. Looks
like hell. I tried to get him to take the Virex but—"

She was already shaking her head. "Not such a good
idea for him. But I wouldn't worry about it—with his system, he should fight this kind of infection better than you or
I. I'm surprised he got it in the first place."

"So was he." Augur looked at her, considering, two fingers rubbing his chin. She looked back at him without a
trace of doubt, so he shrugged and said, "Guess you're the
expert," and then reached over her shoulder to flick back to
the monitor view of the tagbot. "Okay, little 'bot," he said.
"Get ready to make whoopee. Because as soon as I learn
your secrets, you're going to be very, very busy."

Park reached for her coffee. "And then we can figure

out a way to distribute the tags widely enough to make the original ones meaningless. I think it's the best route to take. But let's not forget we need to provide the Resistance with tagbot detectors."

Augur waved a hand. "That's not a big deal; it doesn't take someone with my brilliance to whip one of those things up, especially not once they know what they need. Hayley's got some tech specs here, doesn't she? Why not put them to work? Keep them out of trouble."

Park shook her head. "It's not as easy as that, I'm afraid. Where do you think I got those samples?"

"Uh-oh." Augur didn't much like the sounds of that, or the tired tone her voice took on when she said it. He had the sneaking suspicion he knew why she'd been delayed in her work on the blood samples.

Park didn't wait for him to ask. Silently, she took him out of the plastic-walled work area, moving deeper into the sectioned warehouse where she opened a closed metal door and stood aside so he could see in.

Rows of bunks. Occupied bunks. Not only Hayley's people, temporarily shipped in from the northwest corner of the country, but faces he recognized from the local Resistance efforts. All faces he had seen at the Fair.

Miserable, sick, feverish Resistance members, tagged and bagged.

Augur closed the door and leaned up against it. *Uh-oh*, indeed.

SEVEN

Liam stuck his head under the high, arching faucet of the second floor's polished steel sink, scrubbing cold water through his hair and over his face and grabbing a few quick licks with a toothbrush. Ironically enough, it made him feel more human.

Though not much.

Nor had Augur's news done much to improve his disposition. He'd found the tagbots, yes, and even had a plan for invalidating the tags that made the Resistance so vulnerable. That the flu—the Taelon Flu, Augur called it—was somehow tied into the tags wasn't too startling, other than in the fact it was surprisingly benign for a Taelon project. They'd already decided the tags were tied to the Fair, so that meant those who had been at the Fair were the ones at risk. They'd been a nice bundle of vulnerable humanity.

But Hayley. Hayley and her willingness to barge in and barge ahead, this time with her clinic. *That*, he didn't want to deal with. Not even though he could understand and even respect her willingness to stick her neck out to do what she thought was right. If only her timing weren't so damned bad.

Or maybe it was *his* timing. He was the one who was

sick, after all, with all the dull, thick thinking that went with it, and the unexpected effect on his Kimera side.

His Kimera-within. He grinned at the irony of it, shaking his head and stretching out one sore arm. Persistent, overwhelming memories, always of the Kimera and their interference with the ancestors of the Taelons—the Kaluuet, a name he didn't ever expect to speak out loud. Of all the memories gifted to him by his heritage, he didn't understand why the flu-driven memory flashes seemed fixated on these events concerning Taelon heritage.

He'd learned to trust himself, even the unknown parts of himself, enough to believe there *was* a reason. He just didn't understand it yet. He might figure it out tomorrow, or next year, or he might never understand it at all.

There was certainly no point in trying to think it through *now*. Maybe some coffee . . .

He grabbed a ribbed silk knit turtleneck and didn't bother to replace the lightweight tai chi workout pants he already wore, fingering his hair into place. To judge by his glance in the mirror, it hadn't done much good, but he didn't bother to go back for a second pass, not with the turtleneck yet to pull on.

He took the narrow spiral stairs at a slower pace than normal, headed for the big monitor and what would probably turn into a confrontation with Hayley. The knock on his door took him by surprise, but the stairs spilled out right beside it and he answered it within seconds. From the other side, Suzanne gave him a startled look, obviously having expected to wait. He wasn't sure who was more surprised— she at his quickness or he at her very presence. The Flat Planet wouldn't be open for hours.

"Liam," she said, and seemed to get stuck there, staring at him. She held a large covered foam cup in one hand and a crumple-topped white bag in the other, and for a moment she just stood there. Then she thrust the cup at him. "Here," she said. "I heard you weren't feeling well . . . I thought some morning coffee might help."

He was never sure what to make of her. One moment she was relaxed and confident, serving drinks and flirting with customers, and the next she might as well be tied together at the knees and elbows like a putty woman. This seemed to be a putty moment, so he was somewhat wary as he took the coffee. "I was just thinking about coffee," he said, watching as she took in what was visible of the apartment from here—impressions of gleaming glass and metal furnishings, a combination of brick wall and the silvered, soundproofed walls contiguous with the Flat Planet interior. In doing so she forgot to release her hold on the coffee, so he waited patiently until she remembered, letting go so suddenly he almost dropped it himself.

"Sorry," she said, wincing. "It's still hot, so be careful." Then she seemed to remember the bag, and thrust it at him. "Chocolate," she said. "Not for breakfast, of course, but I thought later you might . . ."

When it became evident that she wasn't going to pick up the rest of the sentence, Liam took the bag and said, "Chocolate?" searching his memory for an understanding of how it fit in and not finding any clues whatsoever. He wasn't surprised; he felt like he needed to go stick his head under the faucet again.

"It always makes me feel better," she said hastily. "And from the way you look—" and then, as he reacted to that, "Not that you look bad, you always look good, I mean, *really* good—" and then she cut herself off and took a deep breath and said, "Anyway, I hope you feel better."

"Thanks," Liam said, and opened his mouth to say more . . . except she'd fled.

Maybe Augur could explain.

Then again, maybe not.

He headed for the recliner, standing in front of it to activate the monitor screen and place a call to Hayley.

She wasn't quick to respond . . . but as soon as he saw her, he knew why.

Of course she had it. She'd been at the Fair; she'd already had chills when they spoke the day after the Fair, chills both of them had chalked up to the weather. Now her short gold hair looked as finger-combed as his, and her pale face only accentuated the smudges beneath her eyes and the quirky little smile lines at the very corners of her mouth. Like him, she habitually wore dark colors; today they only made her look halfway to dead. "It's about time," she said, proving that her voice, at least, still had most of its normal vigor. Then she gave him a double take and a lift of her eyebrow and said, "Nice shirt. Looks good on you."

The shirt. Still in his hand. He pulled it on. "It's about *time?*" he repeated. "Funny, I was going to say the same to you. I just heard about your little clinic. Don't you think you should have discussed it with someone first?"

"What makes you think I didn't try?" she said, not taken aback for a moment. "I called you. Your global was unavailable. I made the decision I had to."

Unavailable?

Augur had turned it off. Not for long, but it had been off. Inwardly, he groaned. Outwardly, he didn't give her an inch. "I'm not the only one you could have called. Lili would have told you the same thing I'm about to—it's a bad idea. You need to disperse those people, and you need to do it now."

She laughed, short and sharp. "What makes you think I can?"

"Hayley, if those people are tagged, you're going to give

Sandoval exactly the signpost to the Resistance that we were trying to avoid when Doors gave the call to disperse."

"It was an *order*," she said. "Not that he had the right to give it. And of course they're tagged. I didn't know it when we gathered here, but Dr. Park has pretty much proved it. The Fair to the tags to the flu. Everyone here *was* at the Fair, by the way."

"I figured as much," Liam said. "And we'll figure out what the Taelons are up to, too. But you've got to get them out of there."

"Liam," she said wearily, "weren't you listening? I *can't*. They're *sick*. Some of them ought to be in a hospital."

That sick?

"Even if they could move, where do you expect my people to go, slinking around back alleys in this condition?"

"They shouldn't have been here this long in the first place," Liam said, one of those out-loud thoughts he would have known better than to voice if only his own head didn't feel so thick.

"That didn't stop you from using them at the Fair, and being glad of the extra coverage," she shot back at him.

He took a breath. "I know. I'm sorry." And another, as they watched each other somewhat warily. And then her eyes narrowed, and she looked at him even more closely, bringing her global closer and enlarging his view of her somewhat alarmingly.

"*You've* got it," she said accusingly. Of what, he wasn't sure.

"Yes," he told her.

She muttered, "Great, just great," and returned the global to its normal position, for which he was grateful.

He kneaded his forearms absently, one after the other, grown used to but not resigned to the sparking pains along the nerves there, and took his tone down a notch to ask with real concern, "How are they?"

She gave an automatic glance over her shoulder; he could only guess that she was within the same room as many of them. "It's a strange one," she said. "I'm not even sure it's the flu at all. No one's coughing and hacking or going through boxes of decongestant and tissue, except for the sickest ones at the start. It's just a fever that comes and goes, and these damned body pains. But the worst of them are pretty bad. Dr. Park is worried about organ breakdown."

Organ breakdown. What would that feel like? Would he know if it were happening to him? Did anyone? He hesitated, almost afraid to ask the next question. "And you?"

"Better than some. I'm carrying on a conversation with you." She gave him a wry smile.

Significant in itself, if some weren't able. And if they weren't, then she wasn't exaggerating when she said dispersing wasn't an option.

"How about it, Liam?" she asked suddenly. "Did Doors give that order because you weren't able to? Or are you stepping back from your commitment to us?"

"What do you think?" he said, and stopped himself from reaching for the blanket—chills again—to glare briefly at her—only to realize from her small if satisfied smile that she'd been hoping for just that reaction. If nothing else, Hayley Simmons brought out the emphatic side of him. Not necessarily a bad thing, but right now he was just too tired for it. "Doors gave that order because Lili went to him. That was her decision, and given what she knew about the tagging and my situation at the time, I can understand why she did it. It doesn't reflect my position with the Resistance. At least, not from my point of view. You may see it differently."

"Okay," she said, still with that quiet satisfaction. "Don't worry about me. I meant it when I said Doors was too exposed to lead us anymore. While you . . . you're good at quite a number of things we can use."

I ought to be. Beckett's and Sandoval's skill sets alone gave him that much.

"I don't know what Doors is up to," she said, "but he doesn't make decisions for us anymore."

"Apparently, neither do I," he said, indicating the sickroom behind her.

"I told you. I did what I had to do. Do you think you would have done any differently under the same circumstances?"

"I would have called Lili," he said bluntly, but then relented. "And . . . if I couldn't get her, I would have done exactly what you did." He sighed, picked up the blanket, and wrapped it around his shoulders. "Augur's working on a way to disable the tagging system. Meanwhile, I understand that the city's opening clinics tomorrow at Georgetown and Columbia; there's a shelter taking in people right now. With any luck, the Taelons—and Sandoval—will take your group to be something similar. *If* we can get past today."

"Maybe you should be here," she said, giving him a critical eye. "Safe with all the other sickies."

Where almost any of them would be witness to his own brand of Kimera-within. Not a great idea. He shook his head, but didn't get into his reasons. Anyway—"Augur wants to see if he can scan the city through my shuttle. It won't be a worldwide view, but we ought to be able to get an idea if the numbers are remaining steady, and how the dispersal looks."

"Yeah, you look like you're in great shape for flying," she said, as diplomatic as ever. But she sighed, and rubbed her neck with a wince, flexing her fingers afterward. "Just take care of yourself, okay? The Resistance is counting on you." She gave him an unfathomable look. "*I'm* counting on you." And the screen blanked out, leaving Liam to stare at it in silence as he drew the blanket more tightly around himself.

As if he needed the reminder.

Sandoval entered Ta'en's lab with a brisk stride and brusque demands. Earlier this day, he'd come to examine the tracking data and discovered the datastream had an entirely different appearance than previously; there were no intriguing gatherings of tagged individuals, other than a slow accumulation at medical facilities.

And when he'd gone back to find the records of what he'd seen, he'd discovered them corrupted.

Ta'en had been unmoved at Sandoval's irritation. He considered the tags little more than useless for his own purposes. "What does it matter how the people gather?" he'd said, and gone back to his own work.

But now Ta'en wasn't here.

And Bellamy was.

Bellamy, who showed appropriate understanding when Sandoval inquired after the health of his family, and attentively put aside his tasks to be of service to Sandoval.

"What happened to the earlier records of the tracking data?" Sandoval asked bluntly.

"Ta'en told me you'd encountered a problem. I tried to recall that data myself, when I heard about it. I'm afraid I couldn't." And truly, he didn't want to displease Sandoval. His expression made that clear enough.

Sandoval was, nonetheless, displeased. "That's not what I asked. I asked what happened to them."

And though Bellamy hesitated, after a moment he admitted it. "I don't know. I can't figure it out. I'm afraid you're asking me things outside my specialty—I'm a doctor, not a hacker. I can have a systems specialist in here to look things over if you'd like me to follow up."

"Do that," Sandoval said—and then had a sudden thought, that of Zo'or learning about this through other channels. Deliberately, he softened his manner. "On second thought . . . we'll leave it for now. Since Ta'en seems to feel it will have no impact on this project . . . tell no one of the anomaly." He pulled out his pocket watch, flipped up the cover, considered the time.

Not that it really mattered, or that it even often mattered. But the gesture often made people think he was calculating affairs that involved them, and that, in turn, made them more anxious and interested in responding as well as possible. Now he looked up at Bellamy as he tucked the watch away and prepared to leave. "However, I want to know instantly the moment you observe any like behavior on the tracking datastream. Instantly, Mr. Bellamy. Is that clear?"

"Yes," Bellamy said, straightening a little. "Absolutely clear, Agent Sandoval."

Sandoval turned his back and walked out as briskly as he'd come in. And without looking, he knew that Bellamy sagged a little behind him.

It served his purpose.

Even the glittery city of Washington had its homeless, its not-so-abandoned buildings, its low-rent areas. For all the amazing sweeping changes the Taelons had made in the world, ridding it of red tape, bureaucracy, and people who fell through the cracks of social programs had not been possible.

Cowley had fallen through the cracks more or less by

choice, without the heart or desire to take any of the helping
hands that might have hauled him back up again. And for
the first time he regretted that fact as he huddled in his
car—his home—and pulled a ratty blanket up over himself,
and a creased and battered piece of cardboard over that.
He'd been sick in the last few years, but never this sick.
Never so fevered that the metallic water in his dinged-up
thermos wouldn't slake his thirst, or that he couldn't pile on
enough of his belongings to keep warm.

It was no consolation that so many in the city were as
sick as he. Although . . . he'd heard they were setting up
clinics. If he could only find a few moments when he felt
better, well enough to crawl out of this car, he might for the
first time avail himself of one of those helping hands.

He didn't care about much anymore, but he cared about
living. Only in living could he seek that which truly mattered to him.

Liam ignored Lili's advice and ignored the clamorings of his
body, which wanted only to crawl into a cave somewhere
and sleep. He grabbed a tall orange juice from the Flat
Planet bar on his way out, downed it, muffled his hands in
thick gloves to hide the faint blue energy leakage from the
shaqarava that responded so unpredictably to this flu, and
grabbed a taxi to the Taelon embassy.

"Taelons, eh?" the driver said, a deeply black man with
a faint Caribbean accent. "Did you hear they've offered to
help us deal with the new flu? Don't know what they think
they can do . . . the flu's the flu. Always has been. Just got to
get through it." He met Liam's eyes in the rearview mirror
briefly, and frowned. "Man, what're you doing out with it?
Just spread it around to the rest of us that way."

Liam roused from the distracted state he'd settled into, watching K Street go by. "I wouldn't worry about it," he said. "It's not airborne. And I'm wearing gloves."

"Not airborne?" The man frowned. "What do you know, man-going-to-the-Taelon-embassy?"

Liam looked at his palms. They looked innocuous enough, their uniqueness hidden in gloves. Only days ago he'd been wondering about the secrets hidden within him, the memories that seemed so elusive, and the abilities this body doled out to him in dribs and drabs, things that came to him when he needed them. These hands had returned Da'an to the Commonality when he'd been lost; they'd protected Liam himself from a Jaridian replicant the very first time they'd spontaneously activated, a defensive instinct he hadn't known he could count on.

Now those secrets had forced themselves on him, no more explicable than when they'd been silent. From leaking shaqarava to explosively uncontrolled shaqarava, and visions that threw pieces of a puzzle at him without the framework within which to put them together . . . or to avoid them if he chose.

Nothing, that's what he knew. And a whole lot more of it than he'd known a few days earlier.

The taxi driver didn't believe him when he said so; that much was evident. They arrived at the embassy without further conversation. Liam offered him a cash card the man was obviously wary about taking, and tossed it into the front passenger seat instead. "Keep the change," he said, and left the man staring at it, double-parked.

The airlocked glass doors of the embassy opened for him automatically, depositing him in the warm lobby and its clean, efficient lines. Sheila, the guard at the desk—all freckles, with a tight braid coiled characteristically at the nape of her neck—stood up to greet him. "Major Kincaid," she said with some surprise. "I'd heard you wouldn't be in today."

"I'd heard the same," he told her. "Looks like I need to check something out in the shuttle."

"You'd think it could wait." She eyed him with a proprietary kind of disapproval, a look many of the guards had quickly assumed when he'd taken Boone's place at Da'an's side. *"They've already lost one,"* Lili had told him. *"And they liked Boone. Everyone liked Boone."*

Except for his enemies.

Liam shrugged at the guard. "Call me Liam," he said, as he always did. "And I only wish it *could* wait."

She tsked at him, but said merely, "I'll clear you through."

He nodded his thanks, heading for the elevator that went straight to the level of Da'an's offices—an organic Taelon addition that looked as alien as anything could in contrast to the otherwise straight lines of this building.

He could have gone straight to the shuttle; this elevator also went to the roof—an easy place for the dancing, lightweight shuttles to land; Lili's often sat next to his. But he went to Da'an's office instead, riding the elevator in a silence that only seemed to emphasize the memory flashes nibbling at the edges of his mind. Like falling stars at the extreme periphery of his vision, too fast to close his mind's eye against, not fast enough to go unnoticed.

As long as they stayed there, at the edges.

They didn't, of course—they crowded him hard, hard enough that he slammed a hand on the elevator stop button, fighting them off in ensured privacy.

Kaluuet, mud-roofed wattle huts, death and dying—

No. Not *now*.

Eyes closed, fists clenched, he fought against the unbound Kimera powers struggling for unbridled freedom within him.

Cautiously, he opened his eyes again, let out a slow and careful breath.

Relief. He could control it. He could keep his secrets as they were, his alone. Flu or no flu.

He released the elevator.

Liam found Da'an absorbed by a datastream display; Da'an's only acknowledgment of Liam's appearance in the curving entrance hall that spilled out into the spacious Taelon-grown veined and ribbed office was a raised hand, a request for silence. Liam complied, more intrigued by what had caught Da'an's attention so completely than by an immediate need to start the conversation that loomed between them.

Ronald Sandoval. He was impeccably groomed as always if a little more severe, his thick hair strictly under control even in the breeze that flapped the bottom edges of his fastened overcoat. Sandoval stood in front of the U.N., saying, "Out of courtesy, we provided this information to Earth's leaders before making it public, but there was nothing said that won't be general knowledge before this day is over." The microphones bristling before him shifted a little closer with reporter anticipation. "The Taelons have discovered and destroyed another alien probe. The scientists involved are still recovering, but the Synod regrets to inform Earth that it believes the probe is somehow responsible for the unusual incidents recently reported within the United States."

"Do the Taelons know anything more about the probe's purpose? Why did it cause the deaths of these people?" A faceless, nameless voice from behind the camera view, Middle East in accent, was the first to shout out the question on everyone's mind.

Everyone's mind but Liam's, perhaps. Liam—with all his thoughts tripping up inside him and the flame of fever racing down his arms to ignite in his palms—Liam's first and instant reaction added up to *how convenient.*

"That is still under investigation," Sandoval said.

And then some bright soul did what each of them probably wished they'd done, shouting out, "And do the Taelons think that the probe has anything to do with the sudden appearance of this devastating new flu?"

After the slightest of hesitations, Sandoval said, "I'm afraid I can't comment on that," with just the right amount of regret in his voice—a response of great impact, from this man who generally revealed so little. "However, I can tell you that the Taelons have extended an offer to assist Earth's medical communities in dealing with this new illness." He held up his hands, clad in fine black leather, shutting down the new questions in midvoice. "I'm afraid that's all I have to tell you. I'm sure your individual governments will make every effort to keep their citizens informed."

They shouted questions at him, of course, but he was already on his way to the shuttle awaiting him in the flag-rimmed courtyard; Liam instantly recognized Lili's silhouette in the pilot's seat.

With a gesture, Da'an blanked the datastream, only then turning to Liam.

Liam looked at where Sandoval had been, and shook his head. "He's good," he said. "I'll give him that much."

Da'an didn't respond, spending instead a moment in examination of his handpicked Companion Protector, the stained-glass effect of the walls muting his face to look more blue than it truly was. Behind him, carefully nurtured

Taelon flora—halfway between Terran tree and shrub—showed tiny blossoms at the end of the delicately frondlike branches. The setting as a whole was a distinct reminder of Da'an's alien nature, and of the careful balance he maintained when dealing with Liam. Liam perceived their relationship as a series of dances . . . sometimes intimately, painfully truthful, sometimes at a formal distance where revelations of conversation came more in what was not said than in what was.

It was certainly true that Da'an not only understood more of Liam's nature than any other Taelon even suspected, but that he held Liam's fate in his hands through his simple awareness of Liam's Resistance connections. That he chose not to reveal those connections, that he occasionally even chose to work through them, didn't for a moment fool Liam into thinking he could be fully trusted. If Da'an worked through the Resistance, it was for Taelon ends as much as human; that he chose not to reveal Liam's unique makeup meant only that he saw potential in it for the Taelon agenda.

And yet their relationship was more than that. The large-scale choices Da'an made—like those Liam made—ofttimes had nothing to do with his personal self. And on a personal level, Da'an was more mentor than employer, a guide along a crooked and puzzling journey.

And now, having carefully assessed his protégé—a stubborn, questioning, and often resistant protégé, but a protégé in many ways nonetheless—Da'an said, "I was told you were ill."

"Along with a hell of a lot of other people," Liam said dryly.

"So I understand. Although your president declines our offer of help, which I *fail* to understand."

So. Even President Thompson had a spine once in a while. "Chalk it up to human nature," Liam said. "We have a fine sense of when we're getting jerked around."

"I don't believe I comprehend the idiom."

"He suspects what I suspect," Liam said. "That the Taelons have something to do with 'the sudden appearance of this devastating new flu.' It makes us wary of accepting any help, especially when that help can only improve the public opinion of those we suspect of causing the problem in the first place."

Da'an inclined his head. "You have come to ask me what I know of the virus."

"Yes," Liam said, following Da'an farther into the office, where he stopped before his uniquely Taelon chair, gracefully disconnected parts that when viewed from afar could hardly actually be a chair, but when occupied by a Taelon, looked like it could be nothing else.

There Da'an hesitated, and apparently decided against introducing the distance of formality his presence in the chair inevitably produced; instead he turned to converse with Liam on a more intimate level. "You will perhaps find this difficult to believe, but I know nothing beyond what you have already been told."

"I don't find it difficult, actually," Liam said. "Others will, but I don't." Zo'or was quite willing to leave Da'an fumbling around in the dark—and if Da'an happened to stumble publicly while he was at it, so much the better. "I think I would have phrased my question differently, though. I'd like to know what you *believe* of the virus and the possibility of Taelon involvement."

"Ah." Da'an broke eye contact, a movement with no little significance. "You put me in a difficult position."

Liam was unyielding. "I know."

"And what would you do with this information, if you had it?"

Liam massaged the palm of his hand through his gloves, a familiar gesture with something of desperation about it. "Not much," he said finally, thinking it was only the truth. Without proof, the Resistance certainly couldn't spread the word, although Jonathan Doors might feel differently. Of course, he was a politician now, and had the tool of innuendo at his service. And the knowledge wouldn't make a significant difference in how the Resistance responded to either the tags or the virus. "It's important to me, I guess. To know that I can ask you."

"This, I understand." Da'an gave him a somber look, one of many in his subtle repertoire. "I appreciate your candor, Liam." His gaze shifted again, but this time it wasn't so much *away* as it was to his mind's eye. "I suspect that Zo'or is hiding something from me. More, I cannot say." With startling swiftness, he brought his full focus back to Liam. "And you, Liam? Do you hide something from me as well?"

At first, Liam didn't understand. Then Da'an held out a steady hand, graceful even in slightly cupped repose, and he realized. The gloves. Slowly, Liam removed them, tucked them under one arm, and held both hands out before Da'an, palms up. As hands went, they were not unusual. Big hands with long, sturdy fingers, human in the extreme.

Except for the glimmer of unsteady shaqarava, flickering in rhythm with the sharp pang running outward from the center of his being and down his arms to his hands.

Da'an caught his breath, taking one of the proffered hands to tilt it this way and that, then holding his own hand over top with several inches between, closing his eyes as if he could measure both the energy and the pain. When he removed his hand, it was with a long, quiet sigh. "I had not thought," he said, "that you would be vulnerable to purely human ailments. Or anticipated that they would have this affect."

"Join the club," Liam said, but without the edge the words might have had. He looked down at the shaqarava, overwhelmed for a moment by the clamoring voices of the past, layers of visions, of his Kimera ancestors living among the Atavus—the Kaluuet—intrigued by their unique mix of ferocity and strict moral code. "Your people were dying," he said, half in memory and half in the present, a hazy place that didn't consider the wisdom of his words and what they might reveal. "That's why the Kimera were so interested in them, isn't it? Because they could see something of beauty even in the violent creature you won't even give a name, other than what you borrow from the human language."

"The Atavus," Da'an said softly, no doubt beset by memories at the reminder of his own time bereft of the Commonality and reverted to that primitive state.

"Zo'or spoke of the Atavus as though it had no redeeming qualities whatsoever," Liam said. "But that's not true. They were intensely attached to their own, and their ferocity came of their environment, their need to survive ... even hurt and hungry, you—the Atavus—only offered violence in return for aggression. And no Atavus, no matter what the cost, would ever consider turning on another of its kind. Humans, for all their posturing, can't say the same."

Da'an, shaken from his initial reaction, spoke sharply enough. "No one knows these things. No one speaks of them. How is it you come by this information?"

"*It* seems to have come by *me*," Liam said, suddenly more firmly in the here and now and realizing how far he'd pushed Da'an. The Taelons' universal reaction to their ancestry was much like those in the Scopes trial who were horrified to learn they might somehow have primordial man in their chain of existence. Except Liam suspected that the Taelon horror and reticence had more to do with admitting their common roots with the hated Jaridians . . . as well as their need for alliance with the Jaridians themselves.

He shook his hands out in an abrupt motion that broke the mood, and replaced the gloves with a shiver.

"Liam," Da'an said, "take care with yourself. I am not easy with what I see here."

"You or me," Liam said. "But I think in order to do that—to *take care of myself*—I'll have to figure out just what Zo'or is up to."

And Da'an tilted his head in the quick gesture that always came with the blush that followed, like a visual Taelon punctuation mark of significance. "I am afraid," he said, "that you are correct."

"Maybe this wasn't such a good idea," Augur muttered to himself, standing in quiet Rock Creek Park and glancing once more at his watch. Liam was many things, but *late* wasn't generally one of them. And though the day was pleasant in a lightly overcast low-key way, standing out in it for an extended period of time hadn't been in his plans. Augur was a creature of underground warrens and mazelike warehouses who spent most of his time avoiding large empty spaces where his presence was so painfully obvious.

Well, there were the trees. Pleasant trees offering a certain amount of privacy, even without leaves. And he should be glad enough that the city in general was so taken up with its viral misery that it had obligingly abandoned Rock Creek Park to him and his unsanctioned little meetings. He bounced up and down a few times on his toes, thinking about warm activities. Steamy, warm activities. Mmm, yes. That was better.

The sky blossomed with quantum fire, just long enough for a shuttle to escape interdimensional space directly above him, and far closer to the ground than he'd been expecting. He backpedaled furiously as it hovered, insectlike and graceful, its ID generators folding into landing pods with the precision of a living thing; it settled to the ground in the spot he'd occupied during this cold wait and the virtual glass of its vast curving windshield blinked out.

"Cut that a little close, didn't you?" Augur demanded, even as he bounded up to the shuttle and inside, bringing his knapsack with him. "And where were you, anyway?"

"Delayed," Liam said, sliding the supportive arms of the pilot's chair open. "And trying to keep a low profile."

"Yeah, yeah," Augur responded, not paying much attention anyway as he pulled out his notebook computer and the modified global, setting them on the first passenger seat. "Put up the glass, why don't you. It'll be warmer." Not to mention that while they could see their surroundings perfectly, their own forms would be somewhat obscured by the scintillation of light off the virtual glass.

Liam obliged; by then Augur had the global fired up and aimed his way. "Oh, you glow, baby," he said. "You've got a healthy little population of tagbots chugging around inside there."

"Did you really have any doubt?" Liam said. "You're the one who saw Park and her samples."

"Always good to be sure," Augur told him. "Don't tell Lili I dragged you out of bed. She'll kill me."

Liam rubbed his palms along his thighs, looking thoroughly distracted. "I was up anyway."

Ah-ha. There wouldn't have been much that could drag him out . . . not unless it was finding out more about that which loomed large on all their minds. And that meant Da'an. "Learn anything?"

Liam shrugged, not looking particularly astonished that Augur had worked it out. "Not a lot. Confirmed what I thought, which was that Da'an doesn't know what's going on."

Augur shook his head, firing up the slim computer and flicking through several screens of password protection. "Those Taelons are worse than soap opera characters. Scheme, scheme, scheme. You'd think they'd find something better to do with their time. Something more constructive."

"From Zo'or's point of view, what he does probably *is* constructive."

"Yeah? Well, not from mine. And that's what's important. Gotta keep things in perspective here, Liam."

"Right," Liam said, oh-so-dryly. "I'd forgotten." He swiveled the pilot's seat around to get a better look at the computer. "Think this will work?"

Augur didn't say it. He just gave Liam a look of mighty disapproval, keyed in a few final commands, and said, "Open a link to the shuttle for me."

Liam turned back to the virtual glass, activating the shield interface with a precise gesture. "All yours," he said. "Try not to leave any fingerprints."

"Ha ha," Augur muttered, already working. "Good. This looks good. Take this baby up and we'll get a look at the city." And get you back home in bed, kid.

Up is where Liam took them, tapping a strange and most annoying pattern on the interface in the process. Straight up, to avoid the flight paths of the airplanes so quickly being replaced by ID portals. And there they hovered, while Augur, hooked into the shuttle sensor systems, took a quick scan of D.C. and gave Liam the word to drop back down again. No doubt they looked like a shuttle on a pogo stick, but the one trip would be enough for now.

Except they didn't drop back down; not all the way. A full story from the ground, the shuttle came to an abrupt halt. Augur didn't even look up; he was busy overlaying the scan on a grid map of D.C. "All the way down is fine," he said, but they didn't move—and when he glanced up, Liam's hands were still and quiet.

The wrongness of that quiet triggered his alarm. Shuttle pilots were in constant motion, their hands dancing across the shield interface to manage not only the nav clusters, but the life support, anti-grav, communications . . . with Lili at the helm, it looked like a graceful ballet. Liam's style was more straightforward, if equally assured, longer arms and larger hands making smaller and less extravagant movement. Augur had danced the dance once, fresh out of conscripted training—*brainwashing* was more like it—aboard the Mothership, and in dire need of escape.

He didn't particularly want to do it again.

Abandoning the computer even as it displayed the tagbot map, he grabbed the back of the pilot's seat and pulled himself forward. "Liam, what's—"

But he didn't complete the question—no point, not with his flu-ridden pilot sitting stiff as a board and probably lucky to be contained by the encircling arms of the seat itself. He quivered slightly, his eyes rolled back, and a faint smear of blood at the corner of his mouth. A fit? He'd looked sick, yeah, but not enough for *this*—

"Liam," Augur said most earnestly, giving Liam's face a gentle pat, then another, holding his hand there long enough to feel the heat of the flu burning there. "C'mon, kid, this is no time to let your mind wander." No response, and he thought about making the pat a slap, but thought harder about the fact that he was in a live shuttle with no one at the controls, and one story was still a very long way down, Taelon crash technology or not. So he turned to the shuttle instead, activating the static console with a barely remembered gesture—

Or not.

The shuttle ignored him. It ignored the command he remembered, it ignored the one he thought he remembered, and it ignored the one that had nothing to do with piloting whatsoever. And still they hovered, but by then Liam had taken a sharp breath and when Augur turned around again, Liam was gazing at fingers bloody from wiping his mouth and frowning in a dazed sort of way.

"Down," Augur said succinctly. "Put us *down.*"

Without comment, Liam resumed the annoying tap in the communications corner of the interface; the interface flickered to life and quite obediently, the shuttle sank quietly to the ground.

"And what was *that?*" Augur demanded as soon as they were down. Liam still seemed a little dazed, but there was no confusion on his face. He knew what had happened. And that meant he knew it *might* happen, even as he'd taken Augur up above the city. "What the *hell* was that?"

"Part of the way I'm reacting to this flu, I guess," Liam said, disengaging the seat's restraining arms. "Ha'gel's racial memories . . . *my* racial memories." He ran his tongue over his lip and said ruefully, "Guess that'll teach me to keep my mouth closed."

"What do you *mean*, part of the way you're reacting to the flu?"

"I thought Lili would have mentioned it."

"Yeah, well, you thought wrong." Though it explained just why she'd been so disturbed, if she'd seen one of these little spells. "You're doing this . . . this . . . *memory* thing and you're in the pilot's seat? What, are you *nuts?*"

Liam didn't rise to the bait. "Anything we did today, the shuttle can all but do by itself, and I programmed in a fail-safe." He tapped the annoying pattern on the console. "Without that input, it goes into auto-hover. A dead-man's switch."

"Let's not call it that, thank you very much," Augur snapped. "And you should have told me."

"I was hoping—" he said, and looked down at his hands. If Augur wasn't mistaken—and he never was—they were glowing faintly with the energy of Liam's shaqarava. That which he generally kept under excruciating control, given the consequences should the wrong person see them. Now Liam flexed his fingers and turned the palms into his lap, hiding what had barely made itself evident. "You're right. I should have. I thought . . ." He looked up from his hands to meet Augur's gaze with something reminiscent of his early days, the days when he was bewildered by the world as often as he forged his own path through it, and sometimes turned to Augur for answers. "I was sure . . . I thought I'd gotten control over it."

"Apparently not," Augur said, but he shifted his weight back, feeling for the seat opposite his computer and sinking into it. "Ha'gel's memories," he said, and nodded at Liam's hands. "And *that*. Anything else you're not telling me? You're not spontaneously transposing into ID space or anything like that, right?"

"Not as far as I know," Liam said, sounding more like himself. "They hurt like hell, which they've never done before, but nothing more dramatic than that."

"Good," Augur said in pronouncement. He thought of the Virex he still carried. "And you're *sure* you don't want—" But Parks had agreed; no Virex for Liam. Augur idly scratched his chin, smoothing the barely-there hair of his beard, and sent his thoughts in another direction. "Ha'gel's memories," he repeated. "You've got those all the time, though, don't you?"

"More or less," Liam said. "Things happen sometimes; I have an understanding of them I wasn't expecting. Or events will trigger memory. But there's so much . . . how do you remember something you don't even know you know?"

Augur blinked. "I hadn't thought of it that way."

"These are more than memories," Liam continued. "They're . . ." and he searched for words, finally shaking his head. "It's living the moment all over again. I don't get to choose. And I don't know why I'm remembering what I am."

Augur raised an eyebrow at him. "Learn anything? Anything useful?"

Liam shook his head, an immediate response that he cut short. After a moment of thought, he said, "The Atavus were into art."

Not entirely what Augur had been expecting. "Say that again?"

"They revered their artists. I just saw . . . I saw their reaction to the death of an artist, a male who worked in dyed cane-weave. They'd provided for him, so he wouldn't interrupt his work with hunting, and they kept vigil over him . . . and when he died, the whole community grieved."

"Of all the memories . . ." Augur said, and shook his head.

"That's what I'm seeing. The Kimera study of the early Atavus. It intrigued them. When the Atavus started to die off, the Kimera felt a great urgency about it."

Die off? They'd done anything *but* die off. They'd become the Taelons, and come to plague Earth. "For a dying race, they seem to have prospered fairly well," Augur said, all his usual sarcasm in place.

"Until now, at least," Liam agreed, too enigmatic for Augur's taste.

But not something he wanted to pursue right now.

They'd sat here in this shuttle long enough. The kid had
had a vision, the shuttle had responded as programmed, and
meanwhile they'd gotten the scan they needed. All was well
enough, and they might as well make use of their work.
"Okay," he said, shifting the notebook computer so Liam
could see the monitor more clearly; Liam rose from the pilot's seat to crouch by the computer anyway. "Here we are
with the tagbots, seventy-two hours into introduction—
assuming it was done at the Fair, which I don't think anyone
doubts."

"Had to have been, given what Lili's recording showed
us," Liam agreed. He gazed at the screen in silence a moment, taking in what Augur had already seen—that within
the randomly spaced tagbots of D.C., there were several
areas of tightly gathered and overlapping tagbots.

Augur pointed, swift stabs of motion. "Columbia.
Georgetown. Howard University Hospital. The YMCA.
And here . . . Hayley's little setup." The largest of them, of
course. The most conspicuous. Liam looked at it, worrying
a palm with his thumb; Augur felt like smacking it. He did
say, "Don't pick at scabs, Liam—they leave scars," which
got a startled and uncomprehending reaction, but was apparently distracting enough to do the trick anyway.

"We might be all right," Liam said finally, not sounding
entirely certain. "Once those other clinics increase in
size . . . there are a couple of shelters that will probably light
up, too."

"With luck, anyone who sees it will simply assume
they're all public gatherings of the Taelon Flu," Augur said,
though he felt as if he was trying to convince himself.

The answering look on Liam's face only increased his
misgivings. "Then again . . . this is Sandoval we're talking
about. Do we really want to rely on *luck*?"

Augur didn't hesitate. "On the other hand," he said, "I

think I'll just get to work on that tagbot replication." He flipped the computer shut, jammed it into the knapsack, and hopped out of the shuttle as Liam dropped the 'glass for him. "Go home," Augur said. "And fly *careful.*"

Liam raised a faintly glowing hand in response, restored the virtual glass, and lifted off as Augur backed away from the shuttle.

That, Augur supposed, was all the assurance he would get.

At least until they figured out what was happening with the Taelon Flu.

EIGHT

Sandoval was beginning to understand, and he didn't much like it. Zo'or had made no attempt to fully explain the project, but neither did he attempt to hide the facts of it as they discussed developments within the secure lab area that had once held a Jaridian. And the facts were beginning to add up.

Be alert for any odd behavior in Major Kincaid, Zo'or had told him. As far as Sandoval could tell, up until this point that consisted of contracting the same viral symptoms as everyone else the Volunteers had tagged. Except that now things were coming together . . . now hindsight was kicking in.

He saw in his mind's eye the Texas militia raid, and the astonishing explosion of cold fire lighting up the night sky. He wasn't sure exactly what had happened in that house, though he *was* now sure it hadn't entirely been the result of a militia bomb. But even if he took the results of this virus—this retrovirus and its deep-seated changes to the architecture of human DNA—into account, he couldn't explain it all. Such as why the major had been affected so quickly, and yet now seemed on the same course as everyone else, although he understood from Captain Marquette that Kincaid was very sick indeed. Or why he would fail to mention the truth of what had happened in the house. What did he have to hide?

For the moment, he shook these thoughts away, leaving himself free to concentrate on the conversation between Zo'or and Ta'en—and Peter Bellamy, although thus far the man was little more than a warm body off to the side, trying to avoid notice.

Sandoval didn't blame him. He, of anyone here, probably had the best understanding of the ramifications of the experiment—along with the personal ramifications should his performance in altering his fellow humans be seen as less than satisfactory. And while Sandoval understood perfectly the potentials of this project—of any of the Taelon projects—he had learned not to judge such things as innately good or bad, but by how they could be used.

Ta'en, as quirky a Taelon as Sandoval had ever seen— his movements less graceful and more jerky than most, with his tendency to bend slightly at the waist and a habitually prim set to his mouth—was in full-swing disapproval. "You have perverted this project, Zo'or. It was meant to be a precision measurement of a controlled reengineering of the humans. Now it is merely a circus."

Reengineering. For Taelon purposes, just as had been done to the skrill. Sandoval worked the fingers of the arm that bore the skrill, an entirely subjugated creature turned into a weapon. She made many demands of him—for food, for energy, for self-preservation—but he hadn't even known she had a name when he acquired her. Or that she deserved one . . . or that her species had been a peaceful and private one.

Raven.

He didn't say the name out loud, not even in solitude. But knowing it and thinking it reminded him of many things he could never afford to forget when dealing with the Taelons.

"I fail to see the problem," Zo'or responded, gazing

with satisfaction at the datastream tag map. "I am quite aware that you have continued the experiment on your own terms. This additional methodology merely expands the scope of the project." He gestured at the datastream. "Furthermore, look how easy the humans are making it to contain the successfully adapted subjects. We need merely to gain access to these clinics, and we can acquire the subjects."

Bellamy spoke up, if somewhat hesitantly. "If you send Volunteers to the hospital, there'll be a terrible outcry. It's like picking on little old ladies and kittens . . . it just isn't done."

For a thoughtful moment, Zo'or frowned—a look restricted to his eyes, but one for which Sandoval had learned to be alert. "I don't follow your crude analogy," he said finally, "but I believe I understand your concern. I am counting on Da'an to open the way for us, however unwittingly. Even now he continues his efforts to talk the Earth governments into accepting our help. If he succeeds, it will only be natural if we invite the most severely affected humans here, where we can best help them."

"That would probably work," Bellamy admitted.

Sandoval frowned at the datastream, and pointed at the area of the most concentrated tags, a spot along the coastal states. "Why is there such a gathering of people here? Is this the same as one of the earlier areas I asked you about?"

Bellamy shook his head. "No, I don't think it is. I think it's just a clinic that responded more quickly to the outbreak."

"You think," Sandoval said flatly.

Bellamy said nothing, but his glance at Ta'en recalled their earlier conversation.

Sandoval gave him a long, cold look . . . and dropped the question. He'd have to go to Phe'la for those answers; Ta'en had indeed refused to relinquish any of his assistant's time for Sandoval's whims, and Zo'or hadn't cared enough about those whims to press the point. So Sandoval shifted back to the thing that had concerned him when he so recently first realized the true purpose of this virus. "May I suggest," he said to Zo'or, "that we bring Major Kincaid to the Mothership."

Zo'or gave him a look Sandoval interpreted as baffled. "Whatever for?"

Sandoval was taken aback, enough so he even let it show. "He's a valued member of Da'an's staff. Now that he has this virus, he should be closely monitored. People are dying; Da'an will be distressed if Major Kincaid is one of them."

"Da'an's distress is of no matter to me," Zo'or said, lifting his chin as he turned his head aside, eyes closed, a completely dismissive gesture. "If Major Kincaid dies, it will relieve us of the problem he's been since Da'an acquired him. He has no CVI imperative, and is much too difficult to control. If he survives and acquires the shaqarava, he will at least be able to serve us better."

Sandoval forbore to mention it had been Zo'or himself who allowed Kincaid to become a Companion Protector without the CVI. Then again, neither of them had expected the man to live out his first day in the role . . . had, in fact, set him up to die along with Da'an. His survival had always been somewhat of a puzzle—and at this point, given the major's successes and Da'an's satisfaction with him, CVI or no CVI, Zo'or had little leverage with which to force an implant on Kincaid.

"I understand," Sandoval said to Zo'or. Understanding, however, was not the same as agreement. Sandoval would much rather have Kincaid where he could keep an eye on him, merely because of that facet of unpredictability. And . . . because although he'd gone along with Zo'or's initial plans to sacrifice the man, he now had no desire to break in another Companion Protector for Da'an. "But I'm concerned about how it will look to the public, should his condition be noted. We've offered to help others; it might seem like we're not taking care of our own."

"And if we bring him here, will it not seem like favoritism?"

And at that, Sandoval truly did understand. For each point of his own, Zo'or would have a ready counterargument. He didn't want Kincaid on the ship. Sandoval understood, too, when discretion meant survival. "True. It might also be easier to blame us, should something go wrong."

"Exactly," Zo'or said, satisfied as ever to . . .

Well. To get his own way.

"Tell me," Zo'or said to Ta'en, "what can we expect in terms of the virus progress?"

"You have my reports," Ta'en said, looking somewhat affronted that Zo'or hadn't memorized them. "You've seen its quick incubation. Soon there will be signs of developing shaqarava. Most people will remain fevered for several more days—at the end of which, their systems will either reject the changes and die, or they will acquire the shaqarava. It will take somewhat longer before they understand how to use them, of course—or before the underlying changes will be complete."

"Of course," said Zo'or. "All for the better. It will give us an opportunity to gather them up."

But as the meeting dispersed, as Zo'or gave Sandoval the look that could only translate to the human royal version of *attend us* and dismissed the scientists despite the fact that it was he who left and not they, Sandoval felt a sudden twinge of . . . something. Something he couldn't define, but which made him take out his global and hang back long enough to place a call.

Kincaid looked every bit as haggard as one would expect; Sandoval couldn't discern his location but he'd be surprised if it were anywhere other than the odd apartment the man called home. A place where he could, as he'd once told Sandoval, "keep an eye on things." For they both knew the Resistance had once made a foolish habit of hanging out at the bar located beneath that loft. Once. Before the sweeping roundups when the Taelons had needed subjects from whom to siphon away spiritual energy until their damaged Commonality was repaired.

Kincaid's presence there suited him; it would keep the Resistance from creeping back into the bar, and deny them their safe haven.

Unless, of course, Kincaid blew it up with his wild virus-spawned shaqarava—and himself along with it.

"What can I do for you?" he asked Sandoval, clearly making an effort.

"Major. I was wondering—" *if you knew you were developing shaqarava.* But Sandoval was not used to acting on impulse; he suddenly hesitated over the one that had led him to make this call—although it had not faded, and did not yet release him from the need to warn his fellow human being. Struggling to keep the conflict—discretion versus rare compassion—from showing, he started again, ignoring the puzzled look on Kincaid's face. "Captain Marquette informed me you would not be available to the Companions for an unspecified amount of time. I wondered if you knew when that time would end."

Kincaid's expression cleared. This, it now said, was the sort of thing he'd come to expect from Sandoval. "Not long, I hope. You'd do better to ask Zo'or."

Thank you, Major. It was just what Sandoval needed to regain his equilibrium. "And why would you say that, Major?"

Kincaid shook his head in a weary gesture. "Ask him. Or don't. But I can't tell you, except to say as soon as possible."

"Stay in touch," Sandoval said shortly, and slid his global closed with a decisive gesture—only to stare at it in his hand.

Zo'or perhaps had the right of it. Kincaid was too difficult to control . . . for either of their purposes.

Another restless night. If he'd been asleep, he would have called them intense dreams.

But he wasn't, and they weren't.

He was as awake as anyone stuck in lingering night fever chill, struck with intermittent bits of visions of the Atavus— its art among its ferocity, its moral code next to its efficiently merciless hunting habits. It occurred to Liam somewhere in the midst of it that the Taelons were just as fierce as they had ever been. They merely directed that energy in other ways, with less obvious bloodshed to mark their trail and less expression on their faces as they did it.

And by putting the stamp of civilization on what they did, they allowed themselves to roam across the universe committing terrible crimes in the name of their now-corrupted morality.

But it was too profound a thought to hold on to for long, especially with the wall monitor beeping in front of him, at first mixing bizarrely with the images he saw, and finally—persistently—breaking through to reality.

The caller ident was blocked, which meant Resistance. "Incoming call, go," he told the system, and even in the remaining haze wasn't entirely surprised to find Hayley looking at him.

"I need to talk to you," she said.

"You *are* talking to me," he told her, certain of that if nothing else. He was surprised at the desperation that crossed her face.

"I mean in person," she said. "Here. Now." As he checked his watch, she forestalled his comment about her wee-hours-of-the-morning timing. "Of course I know what time it is. Just get here, will you?"

He rubbed his hands over his face, working through the decision, and groaned expressively. But he said only, "Okay. I'll be there."

Easier said than done, catching a taxi this time of night, taking it just close enough to the northeast section of town so he'd only have a few blocks to walk, hoping to hold himself together on the way. But though he felt the memories pressing in, they didn't step in and take over; the cool night air cleared his head, for which he was manifestly grateful. With no one else around, he pulled off his gloves and let that cool air wash over his aching hands as well.

Hayley met him just inside the warehouse and wordlessly took him down the makeshift aisle of the divvied-up warehouse floor to a small, curtained area with a single bed. Her own space. When she turned to face him, swallowed up in a large jacket with her hands jammed in the pockets and the fever of the virus still sapping her color, the words he'd intended—short, to the point—died in his throat; he eyed her a moment instead of saying anything at all.

Uruz would be her rune, for her warrior's strength. When they'd raided the files at Second Chances together, he'd seen in her eyes then a hunger for action, a determination to dig out the truth about Second Chances. Maybe even the same bare-your-teeth exaltation in the challenge that sometimes grabbed him, especially when life was feeling particularly new.

All he saw now was fear.

It surprised him. Not so much that she expressed the fear, but that he reacted to it—something he'd never felt with Lili, whom he'd known . . . well, ever since he was born. But even though he knew Hayley was as capable as anyone—or more—of taking care of herself, he still felt the impulse to somehow lift that fear from her.

If nothing else, it softened his voice, though the words themselves remained the same. "What is it?" he asked. "What was so important that you needed me here? And *here*?" He looked around the private, empty room.

"I didn't want the sickest ones to see your reaction," she said, still pensive in the extreme, and strangely reluctant. Especially for Hayley; he didn't recall ever seeing her reluctant with words. "And I wanted to be able to speak freely about . . . well, about you. Things you might know that the rest of us don't."

Liam raised an eyebrow, taken aback . . . and waiting.

Slowly, she removed her hands from her jacket and held them out to him, palms up.

Within the centers pulsed a small and muted radiance.

He sucked in a surprised breath, reaching for her hands without thinking, intent on a better look, his shocked inner voice hissing *shaqarava* in a dissonant echo of thought—until he touched her. Instantly, he knew his error and—along with the sudden strong and intimate feel of Hayley's being, an awareness of her surprise at her equal perception of him—he felt the memories rush in on him. He had an instant's notice, a flash of auralike imminence, and then—

The Kaluuet, already dying as a race, sickened further. They lolled about within their tribes, unable to hunt, unable to tend their young . . . suffering. Even the Kimera-within-Kaluuet—who kept clandestine watch, transformed to this shape without his own shaqarava lest he catch the retrovirus with unpredictable and disastrous results—knew what to expect, and watched his palms accordingly. His entire being ached, but his arms . . .

His arms were on fire. They pulsed with it, spiraling to heights of pain he had not anticipated, could not explain. The flames within shot from the very center of his being, the very center of the power he knew would be his to command. It grew by the hour as he watched those around him, recording events for the Kimera racial memory and knowledge repositories. Growing yet more as those around him died—or emerged slowly from their mud-topped huts, dazed and bearing the shaqarava that would allow this species to manipulate and control the very sun energies that had been killing them.

Never mind their confusion, never mind the hut he'd seen literally explode into incandescent energy flames, never mind the first accidental murder, and the resulting suicide from the one who had never meant to do any such thing. He saw, too, the first time two Kaluuet touched, and realized the sharing they could enjoy. He saw the first—

He saw—

He cried aloud with the agony in his limbs; he tore at his own leathery, scaled skin with claws that rent terrible wounds. He thought dimly of abandoning this form, and then couldn't muster the concentration to do it. Another Kimera-within approached him, reaching for him.

And he watched his own hands erupt in a terrible violence of light, a meaty and literal explosion of self, black blood hissing as it sprayed through the flickering streams of energy.

And then he—

Liam's shout came incoherently to his own ears; he discovered himself bent over, clutching his hands with Hayley reaching for him but afraid to make the contact this time. He blinked, took a deep breath . . . straightened.

"And what kind of wild ride was that, Mr. Toad?" Hayley asked—though she, too, seemed affected by the instant of sharing they'd had before he'd broken away into memories—sharing he was sure would never have spontaneously occurred between two individuals with shaqarava under control.

He looked at his hands one more time, found them as they should be—more or less, if you didn't count the glow, a larger, more established presence than Hayley's—and dropped them to his sides. "A ride full of things we need to know," he said. At her puzzled look, he sat down on the edge of her spartan bunk and closed his eyes to let the images—free of the drowning pull of actual experience—wash over him. He let them mingle with what he'd seen before, all of it tinged by the sharing they'd had. Slowly, he said, "The Atavus were dying. Their own sun was killing them. And the Kimera saw something in them . . . something noble. Something they wanted to save, to study."

"The Kimera. Your people." It was all but an accusation.

"Yes. My people," he said, realizing suddenly that as far as humanity was concerned, *he* was the Kimera-within. "They gave the shaqarava to the Atavus . . . some kind of retrovirus. And the Atavus . . ." He looked straight at her, watching as his words sunk in. "The Atavus got sick. Some of them died in fever. Some of them . . . exploded in light. And some of them . . ." He held out his hands to her, much as she'd earlier revealed her own to him.

"Shaqarava," she said grimly, and then exploded into sudden vehemence. "*Dammit!* I knew it! I knew the Taelons were behind this!"

"Their motives don't seem to be the same," Liam said, his outward calmness a stark contrast to her outburst, "but I think they're doing to us just what my ancestors did to them. The difference is, we *know* what shaqarava do. And we know where they come from." The Atavus had been clueless. For how long? he wondered.

"Genetic material from the captive Jaridian who escaped," Hayley muttered, dropping to the bunk beside him, running her fingers through already untidy hair. It made him more aware of his own appearance—ruffled hair, face drawn; he hadn't changed out of the pants he'd slept in. And he hurt. Oh, he hurt. It lived in his eyes; he'd seen it. Hayley could see it, too; her expression said as much. She asked, "He told Lili some of this when he held her hostage, didn't he?"

Liam nodded. "Everything we know about Jaridian and Taelon history—which still isn't much. And it definitely isn't the same story the Taelons have told us about their war. Da'an once told me the Kimera had joined with the Taelons; that the shaqarava came from that joining. I think the Jaridian had the right of it—the Kimera couldn't make a single joining and affect the whole race. They had to provide all the Atavus with shaqarava as soon as possible. The Taelons are feeding us revisionist history."

"Big surprise," she said, still muttering. Then she tipped her head to look over at him with a sudden frown; the cot moved with the shift of her weight. "*You've* got it," she said. "They *gave* it to you."

"Probably Zo'or's doing," Liam said, feeling the inevitability of her thoughts fall into place, but not preempting them—just not particularly wanting to say them himself.

"They don't know you already *have* shaqarava," she said, her dismay growing stronger. "What will this virus do to you, Liam?"

He didn't respond right away, not until he'd gone over the answer in his mind, turning it this way and that as if he could find a more palatable way to say it. "I don't know," he said finally, heavily. "I don't think"—how to say it—"I don't think it'll be compatible."

She hissed a quiet curse, echoing his sentiments reasonably well. After a moment, she held up one hand, stopping short as though it were caught behind a mime's invisible box. After another moment, he put his own hand on the other side of the invisible box; nothing but a soft glow between them, and the sensation of brushing the surface of something deep and beyond description. Something purely *Hayley*, her warrior's determination and fatalism along with all the things she kept hidden from the world and sometimes even from herself. More personal than words, than mere skin against skin . . . and a type of communication this body ached for.

Until Hayley's fingers trembled slightly, and she dropped her hand. "Yeah, well," she said, as if they'd been in the middle of conversation instead of intense silence, "I guess we've got some calls to make. You want Lili, Doors, or your friend Augur?"

"Augur," Liam said, dropping his own hand to retrieve his global. "Doors might not like the fact, but he's not on my calling list anymore. I have no doubt he'll still hear about it as fast as anyone."

"If not faster," Hayley agreed. "But first, I want you to talk to Dr. Park."

He didn't respond right away. He sat looking at his hands, not really seeing them, and not at all sure he wanted to hear anything Park could say to him.

Liam was going to say *no*. He was going to try to slip away in the night, shaqarava forming over shaqarava, that utterly haggard look on his face and not much hope to go along with it.

Hayley wouldn't allow it. Surely now that the doctors truly understood what was happening, they'd be able to offer him help. She closed an aching hand around Liam's wrist, taking the chance it would be far enough from his shaqarava to prevent the unintended sharing they'd just experienced.

Not that that had been such a bad thing. Liam, warm

and solid and just as tangible to her mind as his wrist to her fingers . . . no, not a bad thing at all.

His pulse beat against her fingers. Bounding, not quite steady. "I mean it," she said. "They might be able to help."

"They can't help *you*." He left the rest unspoken, but she heard it anyway. *So there's no way they can help* me.

"Not unless you give them a chance," she said, her voice unrelenting enough to get his attention; he looked up at her, catching her gaze with blue eyes that were both angry and oddly at a loss. Quietly she said, "I can argue about this for quite a while. Don't you think it would be easier to just do it?"

For a moment she thought he was going to get up and walk out. And he did get up, making the cot creak with the movement, but then he stood there, waiting. Waiting and finally nodding toward the folding metal door. "Let's go, then," he said.

She tucked her jacket closed around her, overlapping the front flaps and realizing anew how astonishingly ill she felt. *They can't help* you, he'd said, and he'd been right. But she refused to believe they couldn't help *him*.

They walked down the hall with shoulders touching— or they would have been, had they been of the same height—and found the doctors in raised-voice discussion over the anatomy of the virus.

Dr. Belman was the first to break off and notice them. "Liam," she said. "I didn't even know you were here."

"Just arrived," he told her. "Hayley wanted to share the news."

Both doctors looked particularly grim. "The ramifications of this virus are horrifying," Park said. "We've known that the Taelons can alter us with their CVI technology, but that requires individual attention. This . . . this is mass production."

"We're lucky it's not readily contagious." Belman nodded at the image on the main monitor. "Only bodily fluid contact will spread it, and once it runs its course, we should be safe even from that."

Hayley moved farther into the room, leaning straight-armed against the lab table to make sure she had their attention. She knew all of this, even if Liam might not; it wasn't what she wanted to discuss right now. Her own Resistance-allied doctor would know that, but she'd gone back to the Northwest after the memory files exposing Second Chances had been released, and Hayley found herself without the patience to wait through a science lesson. "I'd like you to look at Liam," she said, startling both of them but too weary to modify her peremptory tone. "What I'd *really* like is for you to tell me you can do something for him."

From the doorway, Liam shot her a quick resentful look; a warning. *I can speak for myself,* it said.

"There's no point in dancing around it," she said. "You're too important to us."

"It'd be nice if people didn't keep reminding me that I'm important for *what* I am and not *who* I am," he shot back at her, but he moved in from the doorway so Belman, who was already reaching for some diagnostic device, could get her hands on him.

Taken aback and not used to the feeling, Hayley couldn't find the simple words to say *that's not how I meant it*. A flash of pain ran down both arms at once, fracturing her thoughts even further; she rubbed her fingers over her brow and tried to pull herself back together.

But all she could think of was that moment in her private sleeper, the one that had been all about *who* he was and *only* about who he was. She'd had some idea of what shaqarava did . . . only a small idea. She only knew of it as a weapon. She hadn't known . . . she hadn't expected . . .

And from the look on his face, neither had he.

Or maybe he'd just been taken by surprise, for if anyone among them knew the functions of the shaqarava, Liam was the one.

Finally, she shook off the lingering moment, reluctant to lose it but needing to bring herself back to this room, this here and now. She pulled herself together enough to say quietly—at last—"That's not what I meant."

Somehow in those moments of thought, he'd pulled off his leather jacket and draped it over the edge of the lab table; Belman was probing along the inside of one arm while Park watched. He winced at something Belman did and nodded at her murmur of apology, but his eyes were on Hayley. "Good," he said simply, and winced again, this time reflexively jerking his arm back.

Dr. Belman didn't attempt to recapture it. She patted his upper arm in an absent, motherly way and stepped back to give them both a serious look. "When I first learned you were sick, I wasn't worried—I knew your system could handle it. But with what we know now—"

"You think you were wrong," Liam said flatly.

She exchanged a look with Park, and Park was the one who nodded. She said, "Why don't you take a bed here, Liam? I'd like to have you on-site, where we can keep an eye on you."

Hayley knew it was coming; that short, sharp shake of his head, even as he looked as if he wanted nothing more than to sit down and not get back up again for a day or two. "It's hard enough to deal with what this virus is bringing on. I don't want to do it while I'm trying to keep everyone else from figuring out just how different it is."

"You can have my bed," Hayley said instantly. "The most private spot in the whole building, if you don't count the bathrooms."

He seemed to think about it. He closed his eyes, tipped his head back, and said from there, "Would it really make a difference? *Really?*"

And Belman said reluctantly, "Probably not."

He opened his eyes, this time to look right at Hayley, a final look to let her know this was a decision, and not something to argue about. "I'm going to make those global calls . . . and then I'm going home while I still can."

She didn't argue.

Lili closed her global and closed her eyes, the image of Hayley's exposed shaqarava burned permanently into her mind's eye.

She knew what it must mean for Liam—shaqarava on shaqarava, a battle that was burning him up from the inside out—and what that would mean for the Resistance. It was Liam who seemed to wander so freely among the Taelons, discussing their pet projects, understanding their individual philosophies. Who offered the Resistance insight it would otherwise not have, no matter how it annoyed Jonathan Doors to have to admit it—Boone had annoyed him in that way, also.

She knew what it meant for mankind, too—the changes and challenges they would face with two distinctly different communities—those with, and those without shaqarava. After all, the end of *that* story played out before them right now. Jaridians and Taelons . . . forever intertwined, forever enemies.

They'd do something about it. They *had* to do something about it. Starting with her . . . and with the lab where she wasn't allowed.

. . .

Augur cut the global connection and sat staring at the tag-bot map copied to his main system from his portable, not truly seeing it. The Taelon Flu. He'd been more right than he ever knew, calling it that. And all those dots on this map . . . each one a person being changed from their DNA out—and at least half of them on the verge of manifesting shaqarava. Their very beings, perverted by the Taelons—a feeling Augur knew well, though at the time their slick mind-bending techniques had fooled him into thinking he actually *wanted* their wretched tampering—*wanted* to become a lizard-brained fighting machine with enhanced strength and reflexes and none of the inherent charm of Augurness.

And here he was, still struggling to replicate tagbots while the crisis rushed ahead without him. While his good friend fought a battle alone, Augur sat here helpless to make a difference.

He'd already armed Kwai Ling with a modified global; no one with tags—assuming there was anyone left who was well enough to walk into a bar—would enter through its doors, or into any of the Flat Planet franchises he owned. But suddenly that wasn't enough. Suddenly he knew they'd have to find a way to counter this retrovirus, or the Taelons would achieve a victory over mankind that could never be won back, not as he'd won his own self back from their clutches.

This wasn't something he could do; this was for Park and Belman. What *he* could do, *had* to do, was replicate the damn tagbots, and make sure the affected cities were so in-undated with them that all the 'bots were entirely useless to the Taelons.

And that, he knew, grinning a sudden feral grin, would leave the Resistance free to act.

.   .   .

Jonathan Doors sat in his campaign headquarters, his suit jacket thrown over the back of his chair, his vest unbuttoned. Late-night hours, standard fare for both politician and Resistance founder. A cold half cup of coffee sat on his clear desk; empty Chinese take-out cartons filled the wastebasket, still redolent of kung pao chicken. And the words of his Resistance contact—currently hanging out in Hayley Simmons' clinic, healthy and playing nurse—filled his mind.

Shaqarava.

The man hadn't known what they were as he reported the news. Not many people did—but Jonathan Doors was certainly one of them. And to him, they meant one thing. One crucial thing.

He nodded slowly with his thoughts, a barely discernible smile altering the weathered lines of his face. *We can use this.*

Resistance members, fully armed with shaqarava. A populace containing members who could not be bullied by the Taelons and their pet Volunteers. They might lose Liam Kincaid, but with shaqarava on their side, they wouldn't need him.

Yes, we can use this.

NINE

owley made it to the YMCA. He wasn't sure just how, but he had, and that's all that mattered. There he'd at least—*finally*—gotten warm. And though they'd practically had to force the food down him, he'd had that, too.

And he'd survived.

Now he sat cross-legged on the cot he'd been assigned, wide awake in the darkness. Listening to the labored breathing of the man beside him—a man who'd been at the Fair, he said. He hadn't said he'd gone there to score the latest designer version of cocaine, but Cowley knew the signs. Young, apparently healthy . . . and going through withdrawal at the same time. Cowley listened to the man breathe . . . waiting for him to stop. He wouldn't be the first one here in the Y clinic, despite the IVs and good food and attentive nurses. In this particular population, Cowley found himself one of the hardier specimens.

And as far as he knew, the only one so far to come through the other side of the fever, sitting on his bed, his fingers curled around the slight glow of his palms. The only one to know what would happen to all the rest. And that made this his opportunity to act.

He had more contact with the Taelons than most. He'd avidly collected information, had read everything he could, watched every newscast. He understood the way they thought; he knew the different ways they used humanity.

He knew they'd done this to him.

But he didn't mind.

He didn't mind, because he'd wasted no time in understanding what *had* been done. To explore the changes and his control over them, and to realize the new energy conduits in his palms hadn't completed their development.

That the tiny bits of power he'd tossed around were only the beginning. Now he had what he'd always lacked; he was sure of it.

The right weapon.

But not if he stayed here. Not if anyone found out he'd what he had, and as soon as someone else showed the signs, they *would* know. Although the city—the *country*—had set up its own clinics to deal with this sudden plague of flu—of pseudo-flu—the Taelons were still trying to force their help upon Earth; he'd heard two nurses talking about it just this evening.

And if there was one thing Cowley knew, it was that if the Taelons ever got their hands on him, they'd never let him go.

So he waited until the overworked medical staff were deeply involved with one of the failing patients, and he quietly pulled out the IV he no longer needed. He took the pillow his neighbor no longer needed, too, and used it and his own to fashion a crude lump in the sheets. Just enough to fool a glance in the dark, but that's all he needed.

Then he gathered up the clothes that had been stored in a plastic bag under his bed, clutching them to his body as he slunk out of the room. The nearest bathroom was close enough; he emerged clean, dressed, and halfway to respectable.

He also emerged full of purpose. For the first time in a

long time, he felt not just aching determination, but the ebullient state of a man with his obsession finally in sight.

The Taelons, after all, wanted to be involved with the effort to nurse humanity through this flu. And when the Taelons wanted something in D.C., they sent Da'an to get it.

Soon, Da'an would come to him.

TEN

Liam walked a few blocks from Hayley's clinic, not nearly as alert as he should be at this time of night in this particular area. The streetlight glare threw halos of light around everything, presenting the street, buildings, and badly cracked sidewalk area in three flavors—black, glare, and haze. Instead of concentrating on the surrealistic effect, he found himself stunned by his new understanding of the Taelon Flu, the sudden obvious relevance of the memories that kept seizing him.

Shaqarava on top of shaqarava.

No. Not likely to be compatible.

As if understanding itself had destroyed his remaining defenses, the unmasked virus took gleeful hold within him, making the walk from the clandestine clinic to the first available taxi an exercise in muddled persistence. Hot, cold, dazed, his body too heavy to move, his head light enough to float away . . . one foot in front of the other, not thinking *I should have stayed* until he was far enough along to make going back as hard as going forward.

When he reached a main street and flagged down a taxi, the driver took one look at him and pulled abruptly away from the curb, leaving the smell of hot rubber behind.

Liam blinked at the cab's taillights for a stupid moment. Halfway down the next block was a streetlight and next to it a glass-fronted building; he took himself there and made a face at what he saw in the darkened window.

He wasn't sure when he'd last shaved, and it showed. He hadn't bothered to tuck his turtleneck in his belted jeans, and its neck was a crumple of cloth instead of a neat fold. And his hair . . . He dug around both back pockets of the jeans and eventually came up with a comb. Then he tucked in the shirt, straightened his jacket, and refolded the turtleneck. Nothing to be done about the stubble. He drew himself up into something approximating his normal assured posture and headed for the corner.

This time, the approaching driver let him get in the cab. He pulled the door shut with relief and told her, "The Flat Planet. It's just past Wisconsin on M Street."

"I know where it is," she grunted. The cheerful sort.

Good enough for him. He slumped into the seat, kneading one forearm, letting go of the facade.

"Hey," she said sharply, looking at him in the rearview mirror. "Have you got that flu? You do, don't you?" The cab rocked as she braked, already heading for the curb.

Ah, hell. Liam reached into his jacket, pulled out his ID, and snapped, "Companion Protector—you just get me where I want to go!"

He could see the decision warring in her eyes, the effort to decide which was the lesser of two evils. Eventually she cranked her window down and headed for Georgetown at a speed that would have made him wince under other circumstances but this time just offered him relief.

He let his head fall against the back of the seat with a sigh, and a wince of realization. He *must* be ill. He'd just pulled a Sandoval.

·   ·   ·

At the Flat Planet, the cabdriver hesitated just long enough to eject him and speed away. He didn't care. He'd made it home—though he didn't make it as far as the narrow bed in the apartment loft. Not up those tightly spiraled stairs, not a chance. He stumbled to the recliner—jacket, gloves, and all—rolling bonelessly into it and not moving once he had. And he gave up his fight against the clamoring memories.

The Kaluuet gloried in their new power. They let it feed them and their desires. They rampaged across their homelands, learning their new skills . . . how to transmute energy. How to enhance the physical with the unseen forces around them.

Kimera-within-Kaluuet—for there was always one, always someone in place to study this species that so fascinated them—rampaged with them, subsumed by her role.

They gathered in the early evening to hunt, under a setting sun whose rays no longer bothered them—a tried and true position above the waterhole in an earthcrack. The lumbering little foodbeasts would show soon; if not tonight, then the next. Succulent eating, the beasts were—surprisingly so, considering the diet of lichens and scrub they fed from on this craggy land. And surprisingly swift on their feet, too, if not so swift with their thoughts. For years untold, this very herd had helped sustain the local Kaluuet tribe. Tonight the hunt would be good; it had been long since the Kaluuet were free of sickness, and the herd would be less cautious than usual.

The rough ground bit pleasantly into her leathery skin; her eyes, newly enhanced by use of the shaqarava's energy manipulation, cared not at all that the light faded. The earthcrack dropped away directly before her, plunging into darkness; the breeze funneling up from it carried the scent of beast. She heard the scrabble of blunt, hard toes on rock—

The night lit up with the energy of shaqarava. The creatures screamed and bleated and blundered helplessly within the confined space, their terror a palpable thing as well as gamely odorous. The Kaluuet went wild with the hunt. Beside the Kimera, a female stiffened and cried out with pleasure as blue energies whirled around her, feeding the shaqarava, feeding *her.*

Kimera-within-Kaluuet had not known this use of the shaqarava, and without thinking allowed her Kaluuet form to try it. As did the male beside her, and another beside him, until the earthcrack was ablaze with light of a different kind. They drank unfettered, unthinking, uncontrollably, an orgy of feeding on the carefully hunted herd that had fed so many generations of them.

A herd they would hunt no more.

Afterward, there were few of the creatures left to bring back for meat; the rest were withered corpses. But the Kaluuet were bursting with internal glory, and foremost on their minds was locating another herd so they could do it all over again.

Seven days after the Fairs, the rest of the world was beginning to realize what Lili had known the night before. *Shaqarava.* Here at County Hospital in D.C., the tension and horror of it was written all over everyone's face—the doctors, the nurses, the visiting family . . . the patients. Patient population had doubled within the past few hours; word was reaching those who'd been waiting out their illness at home, too. The communicable diseases ward was full to overflowing, and the emergency department was crammed to a standstill. The Red Cross had mobilized to convert the D.C. Convention Center to a patient facility, although there weren't nearly enough medical personnel to staff it—it or any of the other spontaneous gatherings of those who had been waiting out their fevers and were now panicked at the knowledge of what lay ahead.

It didn't really matter. The ones who needed medical help were those with failing, fever-damaged organs, and those with signs of shaqarava rejection. The rest of them would survive with a little basic TLC . . . and none of them would ever be the same again. No, what they *needed* was the communal gathering, the comfort of being someplace official while this terrible retrovirus transformed them. They needed to feel they were in a position to receive help, should it somehow be forthcoming.

Publicly, President Thompson accepted the Taelon explanation of contamination from another probe—acceptance no doubt inspired by his continuing desire to keep the Texas militia incident quiet. Lili didn't know what Thompson thought privately, only that when the Taelons had offered advanced patient care and supplies, the president had drawn the line, suggesting they consider working on a cure instead.

This had not seemed to have occurred to Zo'or before, but officially, he was considering it.

Now Sandoval was here at the hospital, trying to suggest to the chief of staff that it was in his best interests to poll the patients—those who had already shown shaqarava—for volunteers to come to the Mothership where the Taelons could assist them in adjusting.

"I will not have you preying on these people in their vulnerable condition," the chief of staff said. Lili didn't know him well—didn't know him at all, in fact—but she had a feeling that the tall, lanky man had reached the end of his patience; his gesture factor had gone up, his voice had gotten harder. He seemed to find some of his missing patience in his beard, which he stroked in short, even passes. No hair on his head; gorgeous beard.

"I believe I was making an offer to help these people," Sandoval said, a study in contrast beside the doctor. Thick black hair, compact, his body language in quiet mode—Lili thought of it as camouflage—he had no apparent awareness of how far he had to tilt his head to confront the physician. "That's not how I define the term *prey*, Doctor."

"I suspect we define many things differently than the Taelons do," the man said, sounding calmer. The beard-stroking, then. Definitely helped.

"You're not talking to a Taelon," Sandoval said, which surprised Lili; Sandoval made no bones about the fact that he considered himself Zo'or's stand-in when Zo'or wasn't around.

"I might as well be," the doctor said. "Look, President Thompson has already told the Taelons how they can best help—by helping us find a cure to this thing. I support that request . . . and I will do nothing to undermine it."

"Not even if your failure to act harms the very patients you're trying to save?" Sandoval delivered the line like a knockout blow, and his tilted eyes narrowed slightly as he waited for the man's reaction.

Lili found she had to turn away to hide her own reaction as the doctor responded coldly, "I expect we have different notions about what constitutes *harm* as well, Agent San-doval."

But her smile, suppressed as it was, faded entirely as she took in her new view. People were lined up at admitting; others sat on the floors. People who should have been in bed, hunched over themselves in misery. Young faces, those of every race and both sexes.

Standing among them, Jonathan Doors.

What—?

Oh. The political thing. He was out here rubbing el-bows with the ill, implanting his own brand of propaganda about the Taelons—his no-holds-barred, no-mercy-shown tactics that he'd used within the Resistance as well. He looked the part; his suit jacket hung from one hand, his shirtsleeves were rolled up. The approachable workingman persona.

His son Joshua might be here somewhere as well . . . she didn't particularly want to encounter him right now, not when she was already juggling her Captain Marquette role with her Resistance role, although bumping into Jonathan in her capacity as Sandoval's pilot and general assistant was something that happened now and then since he'd gone public again. Add Joshua to the mix and she'd have to juggle personal feelings as well.

And ah, yes—the ubiquitous bodyguards. Two of them, hands clasped quietly before them, both in expensive suits that had been expertly tailored to hide any signs of their hand weapons.

With a glance at the bodyguards and another back at Sandoval—he'd brought someone else in on the conversation now—she eased over to where Jonathan applied concern while slipping in his rhetoric. "How'd you hear?" she said, low-voiced. "It's not public yet. Not until Thompson breaks it later today."

"Do you really think I spent all that time underground without developing a good system for getting news *first*?" he replied, his voice not matching his expression in the least as he smiled and nodded at someone who waved to him.

"And never one to waste an opportunity, isn't that right?" She was a little surprised at the bitterness in her voice; when she'd started out with Jonathan, she'd thought herself nearly as ruthless as he. And maybe she still was. Maybe it was he who had crossed some other line, from ruthless to unconscionable—or whatever else lay beyond the qualities needed to survive—to thrive—within a resistance movement.

If he'd understood the censure, he gave no indication of it. "More than you know," he said. "I came here to talk to you, as well."

Her gaze darted back to Sandoval. "It's hardly the best time."

"There's never a *best time*, Captain Marquette."

Ah, then, he wasn't exactly happy with her, either. He used names like a weapon when it suited him; Lili was what he'd called her when they'd worked side by side. Now he took her arm and drew her aside, over to a corner that wasn't crowded with people simply because it caught the cold breeze of the nearby doorway. To shake off his arm and pin him under her *watch it buddy* marine glare would only attract attention—possibly Sandoval's—so she allowed him to guide her. Then she took out her irritation on the single bodyguard who'd followed too closely. "Back off, fella. If I want to hurt him I can do it whether you're here or not."

That actually got a chuckle out of Jonathan. "It's true," he told the man, and then to Lili, "that's not why he's here."

"Then why—"

"He's here to meet *you*."

She gave the man a second look, a more thorough inspection; he still came out looking like standard bodyguard fare—a larger than average man in a good suit with a nondescript haircut. Brown hair on the dark side of that spectrum and with a reddish overtone; hazel eyes. Pleasant but not outstanding features—too much meatiness in his broad face. But it was his eyes she went back to. The look in them. That look held secrets.

It knew hers.

Smothering a curse, she turned on Jonathan. "What are you *thinking*?" she demanded in a voice that strained against the low volume she forced on it. "What the *hell* are you thinking?"

"I've got my reasons," he said, and would have gone on if she'd let him.

She didn't. "Not to play with *my* life, you don't. Not without checking with me first. And right under Sandoval's nose!"

"Losing your edge, Lili?" he asked coolly.

"Not even close," she snapped back.

That netted them a moment of silence, into which the bodyguard—still not introduced—wisely said nothing. Then Jonathan, watching her closely, said, "We have to think ahead, Lili."

"We," she said, keeping an eye on the bodyguard.

"The Resistance." Jonathan said it without hesitation; the bodyguard reacted not at all, maintaining what was already an intense interest in their byplay.

She glanced to Sandoval, unable to stop herself; he'd noticed her conversation, but was deeply enough involved in his own that he didn't seem to care. He met her gaze only briefly, then turned back to the chief of staff as if he hadn't noted her at all. *Good*, she thought. *Be preoccupied. Be really preoccupied.*

"I wasn't aware," she told Jonathan, an eye on the bodyguard, "that you were still part of that *we*."

He snorted. "Did you really think I'd just walk away? Just like that? I started this movement, Captain."

"You *focused* it," Lili said. "It started itself. Black Wednesday, remember?" Worldwide, a movement vaguely known as the Liberation—although of late, in the States, they'd adopted the Resistance handle. "Besides, just what sort of *thinking ahead* did you have in mind? And why does it involve him?" She nodded at the bodyguard as though he weren't part of the conversation. As far as she was concerned, he wasn't.

"I'm thinking of its leadership. Just a little detail that no one else seems to be paying enough attention to."

Lili gave a short, incredulous laugh. "Get *over* it, Jonathan. Hayley Simmons was speaking for all the Resistance cells when she came here. That decision has been made."

"That doesn't mean it'll stay made," Jonathan said, as inexorable as ever he could be. Before Lili could respond, he said, "I know Liam's got the flu. The *Taelon* Flu. And I know what the virus does. Now you tell me, Lili—what do you think that's going to do to your *chosen* leader, with his"— and he glanced at the bodyguard just long enough so Lili could see that he hadn't, after all, revealed everything there was to know—"preexisting condition," he finally chose to call it. The hesitation didn't knock any of the edge from his intensity. "What makes you think he'll even survive?"

"He'll survive," Lili said grimly. "In case you hadn't noticed, surviving when everyone else says he can't is pretty much his best thing."

"Have you even seen him lately? Within the last twenty-four hours?"

She was about to shoot back that of course she had, just out of habit; rarely did a day go by that they didn't at least exchange a few words on the Mothership or at Da'an's embassy. But she realized she hadn't, not quite. "Within a day or two," she said. "I'd have heard if there were any significant problem. From Augur if not Liam himself."

The bodyguard finally spoke up. "I saw him last night."

Lili gave him a startled look; she'd stopped expecting to hear him talk. And she stared at him a moment, letting the background noise fill in—the *ding* of an elevator arrival, the smooth working of its doors, someone crying, the momentary rise in volume of the conversation at Sandoval's end of the hall. The bodyguard stared evenly back at her, waiting her out without pushing her. And then, when she frowned and took a breath to ask, he told her before she got there. "Art Wells," he said, though he didn't hold out his hand. She was just as glad; it wouldn't look right to Sandoval. Bodyguards were invisible, not people to be formally introduced. He said, "At the clinic Simmons set up—where Park and Belman are working on an antivirus." He glanced at Jonathan and said, "They could use better equipment, you know."

"I'm not their banker anymore," Jonathan said shortly.

"Do you want the virus stopped, or not?" the man said. Art Wells. Lili thought she might like him if she hadn't met him this way. But that didn't mean she wanted to trust Resistance matters to him.

Crossing her arms before her, she went into a hip-shot stance and said, "What *about* Liam?"

Art Wells gave her a mildly surprised look. "I don't know how much longer he'll be on his feet, let's put it that way. Hayley called him out there last night"—which Lili knew— "but she shouldn't have." He shook his head, frowning. "It's not quite like with the others. Sometimes he seemed to be there, sometimes not. Wouldn't have looked out of place in an outpatient mental clinic, if you want to know."

Wonderful. She'd have to get in touch with Augur, see if she'd been left out of anything important. Not that Liam wasn't perfectly capable of leaving Augur in the cold, too. *Trust me*, he told them now and then when he had a perspective on a situation that he just couldn't explain. At first it had ticked her off; now she'd grown to understand that his often inexplicable behavior was only inexplicable to someone without three-stranded DNA.

But for the moment, she had Jonathan Doors to deal with. "Okay," she said. "You're worried about the Resistance. I'll take it under advisement. And you brought Mr. Wells here to blow my cover why . . . ?"

"I already knew," Wells said, carefully bland. "I'm not new to the Resistance. I've just kept a low profile."

But Lili looked at Jonathan, one eyebrow raised.

"Because I think you should consider Art. And I think you should consider him now, *before* the worst happens to Liam."

Lili stared at him in flat-out astonishment. She would have sputtered if she hadn't stopped herself; a marine didn't sputter. Instead she pulled herself up, an unconsciously military stance—all long legs and chest, the guys in her basic unit used to snicker at her. It never bothered her; those long legs outran theirs, and the chest held pilot's wings long before they began to acquire honors. Now she kept her words crisp and assured. "When the Resistance decided you were no longer right to lead the cells, they asked me; I deferred to Liam. If it becomes necessary to replace him, then they'll ask me again. The thinking ahead is already done, Jonathan. It *has* been."

Jonathan shook his head. "You used to have the edge for it, Lili. You don't; not anymore. Nor does Liam—and he never did."

"Edge?" Lili said. "You mean being willing to sacrifice people like cordwood if it suits your purpose? That's not the only winning philosophy, Jonathan. You played it that way; we're not. And we're doing just fine." She shrugged. "It doesn't mean we won't face that decision in the future— we'll make it if we have to. But unlike you, we don't go in *assuming* losses. Not civilian, not Resistance. Not even Taelon."

Art Wells apparently couldn't help himself. He shook his head, the slightest of gestures.

"Well, *that* figures," Lili said to him, not caring how enigmatic it might seem. "You might as well go back to what you were doing in the clinic, Mr. Wells. I'm afraid you won't get my support. You'll have to do a lot more to earn it than this little introduction."

Jonathan said dryly, "Like be born of—"

"Like *earning* it!" Lili said, cutting him off short and sharp.

Art Wells didn't give her much of a reaction; only a nod,

which she took to be temporary acceptance of her words by a man still unconvinced. Jonathan was more outspoken.

Of course.

"Don't think I still can't make decisions for this Resistance if I want to," he said. "If I decide it's time for a change, it's going to happen."

"Jonathan," Lili said—slowly, carefully—"don't start believing your own campaign speeches."

"I can't spend any more time here," he said abruptly. He was right, too—people would start to wonder, people other than Sandoval. And Sandoval was quite enough on his own. "You think about it, Lili. And call me. We need to talk about how the Resistance is going to use its new armed personnel—courtesy of the Taelons."

He walked away, leaving her with her mouth open—though it snapped shut in anger just as quickly. He might think he could drop a line like that and have it mean something these days, but he'd have to pick up his own global if he wanted to start another conversation with her. Especially *that* conversation.

Use them. Lili hadn't even thought about it, hadn't thought beyond *cure* them.

Of course, now she would. So maybe he'd get what he wanted from that little throwaway after all. Art Wells' expression, the look he threw back at her as he followed Jonathan down the hall, made it clear he thought that was the case.

Both men headed for Sandoval; no doubt Jonathan had some "official comments" to make for the chief of staff and anyone else who might be standing around making note of the presidential candidate's candid moments. Lili didn't even want to know. She certainly didn't want to watch.

What she wanted, right now, was to talk to Liam. She pulled out her global, but couldn't help another glance at Jonathan.

"Forget him," said Augur's voice from around the corner.

"Augur!" she said, her exasperation level long since off the scale. She quickly moved around the corner, pinning Augur up against the wall in the tiny foyer by the doors. "Shall we just have a full-scale Resistance meeting right here? Why not just invite Sandoval while we're at it?"

"Hey, hey!" Augur said, raising both hands in protest. Somewhere along the line she'd taken a good grip on the front of his jacket, and he gave her hand a meaningful look.

Lili made a noise of disgust—at herself as much as anything—and released him. She needed to pace, that's what, but doing so would put her in plain view of the hallway.

Augur tugged his jacket back into place, smoothing the crimson hood as though it were a living thing. "There, there," he told it. "The mean lady won't hurt you."

"Yes she will," Lili said, rounding to face him again. "Unless you tell me what you're doing here, and *fast*. I've had enough of other people putting my cover in jeopardy!"

"Hey, it's not exactly safe here for me, either," Augur said, using his best wounded indignation.

No. It wasn't. Slow down, Lili. Think. Of course he was here for a reason.

"Okay," she said. "You're right. I'm sorry."

"That's better." He shifted the slim pack he carried and added, "But you're not going to like this."

"Of course I'm not going to like it. If it was good, you wouldn't be here at all."

"I first noticed it at the Flat Planet. Kwai Ling did, actually. Sick customers."

"A lot of people are sick."

"Yeah, but how many of them don't have tags?"

She stared at him a moment, taking it in. "You mean . . . this thing is *spreading*? It's not confined to the people who were tagged at the Fair?"

"At first, it was. At least, I'm pretty sure it was," Augur said, admitting to a rare uncertainty. "But not anymore."

She did pace then, a quick step away and back. "And you're *sure*."

He shrugged. "I came here to see if I was right. Figured it'd be easiest to check where the sick people are. Most of 'em are tagged—especially the ones that are really sick. Had it since the start, you know? But there are some who look like they're just starting up. Sick, but still okay to come in on their own power. And they *definitely* don't have tags." He patted his backpack. "I've got people out checking the other locations, but trust me on this one. I'm not wrong."

"It would skew my universe if you were," Lili said, but her heart wasn't in it. It was off with her thoughts, tangled up in the ramifications of Augur's news. No longer was the flu limited to those people the Taelons had targeted at the Fair—the ones they'd felt most likely to survive it. Now the elderly would get it, and children. The death toll would rise . . . and the rest of humanity would never be the same. For all they knew, no one was immune. "This is trouble, Augur. This is big trouble."

"Would you care to try for another understatement of the year?" he asked.

She made a face at him, lifting one side of her mouth in a reaction that was more or less automatic. "Have you told Park and Belman?"

"I only now confirmed it," he said. "They'll be my first call."

Lili looked around the corner for a pensive glance at the doctors who were so obviously wrapping up their conversation with Sandoval. "The rest of the city has to know, too. We've got to get *everyone* working on an antivirus—and keep people at home if they haven't got it."

"That'll hardly make a difference if we *don't* come up with an antivirus."

"True, but we've got to assume we will. That we can stop this thing before it goes too far. That's why we've got to alert every last person who could be a resource." And, glancing darkly down the hallway, she thought she knew the perfect way. Jonathan Doors. He was so willing to use the Resistance . . . now they'd return the favor. Besides, it would earn him popularity points in his campaign if he was the one to break this news.

Assuming that the campaign went on as planned, and wasn't derailed by a worldwide plague retrofitting humanity to Taelon blueprints.

"Every last person?" Augur said, and when she looked at him, he had his eyebrow raised in that *you know what I'm thinking and I'm right* expression.

At which point she did, and he was.

It had been a while since she talked to Da'an, anyway.

"It is time," Da'an said—or *announced*, Sandoval thought, looking up from his workstation with some surprise, for Da'an's arrival on the bridge had not been expected or noted—"to admit that your experiment is a failure."

Zo'or inquired, most politely, "Do I know what you are talking about?"

"I would not insult you by supposing not."

In any case, Sandoval certainly didn't know. Ta'en might, were he here. But Ta'en was deeply involved in following up on the experiment on his own terms, leaving Bellamy to the details of what Zo'or had wrought.

Sandoval was doing the same, in his own way; when Da'an arrived, he'd been setting up a separate datastream of the tracking process, still attending the niggling feeling it

had more to tell him than anyone else seemed willing to recognize.

The original data was gone, of course; no way to overlay
it on a precise map. But he had his CVI-enhanced memories
of it, and he could see the patterns in his mind just as clearly
as if he'd had the information in front of him. Those odd
groupings, as temporary as they'd been. As if there had been
a subpopulation attending the Fairs in numbers, and they
had departed only to gather again in their accustomed place.

Whatever Da'an was talking about, it was bound to interfere even further with Sandoval's efforts to understand
the significance of those tracking patterns. He drew a slow,
deep breath, and left the workstation to attend the conversation between Taelon eagle and dove.

"If you have something to say, Da'an, it would waste less
of both our time if you simply said it." Zo'or reclined in his
bridge chair, looking much more confident than Sandoval
suddenly thought he might, had he paid more attention to
the expression on Da'an's face. The older Taelon knew
something. Not just the details of the experiment, which he
was bound to discover at some point. Something . . . grim-
mer. He was not here to accuse, but to inform.

Da'an inclined his head to Zo'or's request, and obliged.
"I now know you have introduced a retrovirus into the human population, one meant to create shaqarava. And while I
believe you intended this to be an experiment on a limited
population, that is no longer the case."

"What are you talking about?" Zo'or asked again—but
more sharply this time, sitting upright and with a hint of
alarm in his voice.

Sandoval knew just how he felt.

"The virus is now airborne," Da'an said, quite simply. A
diplomat, knowing the impact of just the right words with
none to spare.

"I have heard no such thing. What makes you think you know more of my own projects than I? You are speculating on all counts."

Again Da'an inclined his head. "Am I not correct about the purpose of the experiment?"

"That means nothing."

"Then consider," Da'an said, making a cursive gesture at Earth, so visible through the virtual glass hull, "that you yourself often deride my close contacts with the humans. Is it truly so astonishing that they themselves have gained an understanding of what is happening to them? And that they are capable of discerning the pattern of its spread and that I, therefore, have heard of it?"

"There is no *spread*," Zo'or said angrily, but Sandoval could see the uncertainty in his pale eyes. "You are simply trying to undermine my status with the Synod."

"You will have no status with the Synod if you do not regain control of the situation." Da'an never held the cold, calculating expression Sandoval saw so often on Zo'or, but he had a version of calm conviction that served the same purpose. "If this virus spreads unchecked, then Earth will have the means to resist us successfully. Even should they choose not to, the entire population will have been sullied, and will no longer be suitable for our further efforts to use them in our battle against the Jaridians—whether those efforts follow your philosophies or mine."

"If the virus spreads *successfully*," Zo'or said, most distinctly, "then we will have all the means we need to combat the Jaridians."

"And do you think the newly empowered humans will be led so easily to slaughter?" Da'an inclined his head once more, at that slightly different angle that meant *he* certainly didn't think so. "Whatever resources you have, Zo'or, you had best call on them to create a counteragent for your rapidly spreading virus. Assuming, that is, that you did not have the foresight to have a counteragent in hand before you first infected the planet."

Zo'or did not reply. And Sandoval, who could read that lack of response better than any human alive, closed his eyes.

As if so small a thing could keep him from seeing what was to come.

onathan, I need to talk to you."
Lili didn't hesitate once Jonathan
accepted her global call; there was no telling how long she'd
have this conference room in the Taelon embassy to herself.
She circled the richly appointed table, but couldn't quite
bring herself to sit down. Too edgy. Too worried. She'd
tried Liam first; he hadn't responded—and while she'd prefer to go over and check on him, or have Augur check on
him, Sandoval had called the shuttle up to the Mothership;
she only had a few moments to spare, if that. And Augur . . .
Augur had to get those tagbots replicating or the Resistance
would remain too vulnerable to act.

"Do you?" Jonathan said, just a bit too sardonically for
her tastes. No doubt he was feeling the sting from their earlier conversation; she'd expected that.

"Yes," she told him, ignoring his tone—she didn't have
time for that, either. "Now. Can you?"

She wasn't sure where he was; not in his office. Somewhere that he felt it necessary to glance briefly over his
shoulder. "Be quick."

She gave him a swift accounting of Augur's news, and
said, "We need someone with credibility in the public eye
to get the word out. If we don't stop this thing *now*—"

She supposed she shouldn't have been surprised when

he raised an eyebrow and said, "Then what?" He was fast on his feet, all right—fast enough that he'd already thought this one through. "Then there's no way Earth falls to the Taelons, that's what." He shook his head. "Sorry, Lili. You won't get my help on this one."

"You're willing to let the Taelons change the entire human race? Not just some of us, Jonathan—*all* of us. You, and me, your son Joshua . . . *children*—and there's no telling how many of us will die along the way!"

He didn't look particularly moved. "Maybe that's the way it has to be. The Taelons have finally made a mistake they can't recover from—and it might be the best thing that could have happened to us."

"It happened to the Atavus, and now we're paying the price because *they* couldn't handle it!"

"According to the Jaridian refugee who kidnapped you," he said flatly.

"Yes," she said, suddenly furious. "I was there, Jonathan— you weren't. *I* was the one who spoke to him. And yes, I *did* believe him."

"And did you believe the part about where they'll continue to make war on the Taelons? How about the part where they come here to do it? With shaqarava, we'll be ready for *that*, too."

"For God's sake, Jonathan, people deserve the right to make that choice for themselves. If you help us alert the public, then we'll have all of Earth's resources working on an antivirus that will give them that choice. If they don't want to take the antivirus, they don't have to!"

Jonathan snorted. There was movement behind him; a staffer he waved away. The global view bounced slightly as he moved to a new location. Near a window somewhere; the light altered, became harsher. The lines of his face, never classically handsome and now too well used, echoed that harshness. "People are fools," he said. "Scared fools. They don't know enough to make the right *choices*."

"And you have the right to make decisions for them?" She shook her head. "I don't think so. Not even if you *were* president. I'm giving you an opportunity here, Jonathan. We'll get the word out, with or without you. You could be seen as the man who warned the people."

"History," he said, "is written by the winners. And I intend to be the winner."

For a moment she was speechless; by the time she was ready for words again, he'd filled the gap. "You ought to think about that," he said. "And face some hard facts. Liam Kincaid isn't going to make it."

"We've had this conversation," she said. "Fairly recently, if I recall correctly. You never mind about Liam, Jonathan. With or without your help, we'll find that antivirus, and he'll be the first to get it."

He snorted. "And just what do you think it will do to *him*?"

That stopped her short.

She *hadn't* thought. She hadn't *faced facts*.

He'll be okay, she kept telling herself, because somehow, in the past troubles, his alien heritage had saved him when the unexpected happened.

This time, it would kill him.

What would an antivirus—assuming they found it in time—do to someone with legitimate shaqarava? Change him forever, stripping him of that which was his by nature? Or simply take him apart from the inside out, as the Taelon Flu threatened to do right now?

"Sooner or later," Jonathan said, with a little too much assurance, "this virus will kill him. You'd better be ready for it. And, Lili—if you don't have the nerve for the tough choices—the ones you have to make *for everyone else*—then you'd better start looking for someone who does."

Was he right? Right to let this virus run its course, right to expect that onerous decision of anyone who put themselves at the head of the Resistance?

It's not a decision you have to make until you have *an antivirus.*

"It's not your concern," she said. "I'll handle Resistance matters. And I'll get the word out that the virus has gone airborne. You've apparently already made your choices, Jonathan."

"Lili—" He frowned slightly, as though realizing maybe he'd pushed too far. She didn't feel like giving him the chance to back out of it; she didn't have the time even if she wanted to. She cut the connection, and then stared at the global, biting her lip. Liam hadn't answered her last call. Hadn't been unavailable, hadn't had his global out of service. Just hadn't answered. She glanced at her watch and hit the code to dial him again.

Nothing. No response. And as she waited, shifting uneasily and looking once again to her watch, the global beeped an incoming.

Sandoval.

She started to move. Out the smooth, heavy door of the conference room and down the hall; by the time she picked up the call, he'd see nothing but the evidence of her long-legged strides toward the shuttle. "Agent Sandoval," she said, holding the global up at face level—the stance people interpreted as being the most open, the most nothing-to-hide within the various communication postures that had developed when live-image calls became commonplace.

"Was I not clear enough in my instructions?" he said, definitely testy. "I require you here on the Mothership."

"I'm on my way," she said, not offering any explanation, hoping he wouldn't—

He did, of course.

"You should have been here by now. To what did you give priority over my orders?"

Be prepared, handy motto of Boy Scouts and Resistance activists. "Bad accident at Seventh and N Street," she said, which—of course—there was. "Fire engine response blocked the whole road."

"Never mind," he said, which meant he didn't really care. "Just get here immediately." And he cut off the call before she could make any further assurances.

Just as well by her. She had plenty to think about, and not very much time in which to do it. The less she wasted on Sandoval, the better.

He made it upstairs, falling heavily and face first onto the bed. He wanted a drink. He wanted warmth. He wanted to rip his own arms off. As if any of those would stop the thirst, ever warm him, or begin to halt the agony pulsating outward from the center of his body—the very inward center, where no doctor would ever see. And then he wanted to cover his ears and eyes together, to stop the sensation of taste and touch and smell; he wanted to run screaming down the streets. As if any of *that* could keep the memories away. They bombarded against him, some flashing so fast he couldn't truly comprehend them—Atavus, always Atavus. Atavus struggling with the shaqarava, growing as a species, beginning to comprehend the presence of the Kimera, and how the Kimera themselves had caused this great change in their lives.

Killing Kimera-*within*-Atavus, it seemed, was not so unthinkable as killing one who was truly their own kind.

For they were beginning to see what they had become, and who to blame.

Kimera-within-Kaluuet, oh-so-carefully hidden. Keeping vigil on those of them who had once worked to better their lives with improved weapons, better houses, better fortifications and planting systems. Those few who now sought to truly understand the nature of the shaqarava, ensconced inside a long communal building with deliberately, asymmetrically windowed walls that allowed the celebrations normally held within to escape and proclaim to the world their joy and victories and accomplishments. Now it was merely the only building large enough to hold the vigorous discussions of those who debated and worked and experimented among themselves, all while Kimera-within-Kaluuet and several others of his caste kept vigil.

Eventually the late-night darkness exploded with shouts and harsh cries of fear, and the windows leaked sudden light and energy. Not the same as the shaqarava, but a more muted thing. And the guarding Kaluuet leaped up from the perimeter they'd been assigned and rushed the building, Kimera among them, pressing up against it, peering through the openings.

Inside sat a being of purest energy, very close—the Kimera saw with some shock—to the basic Kimera form itself, Kimera-when-not-within. One of the Kaluuet had somehow . . . reformed itself with its own shaqarava, turning its use of the energies inward. It stood alone in the middle of the room, neither male nor female nor identifiable as any individual at all, other than by default. And there it examined itself, and cried its wonder and pleasure out loud. Cried its freedom, too.

Freedom from the urges of the shaqarava.

But wonder and pleasure turned to a wail of distress. The newly formed being arched back, jerking with the uncontrolled release of the energy comprising its body, spasming in such sudden, snapping violence that those inside rushed for cover and those outside flinched away. All but Kimera.

No, Kimera—astonished and fascinated that so primitive a being could somehow alter itself with such sophistication—was the only one to see the end of that first experiment. How the eerie, wailing creature of energy lost cohesion and shattered into a thousand, a million, an infinite scattering of separate, fading pieces.

And ending, perhaps. But more so a beginning.

The muted beeping of an incoming global call came and went unheeded.

"All right," Augur muttered, multitasking sublime, shifting—no, bouncing—around the three-monitor workstation nexus and definitely on the jazz. "All *right!*" And where was his punching bag when he needed it, the nice sturdy replacement to the one Liam had once—while making quite a good point, too—blown across his old warehouse lair with one punch and a little shaqarava help? That's what he needed, a nice one-two, one-two session to work the Tigger out of his bones.

This little tagbot didn't have a chance. "You're so lonely," he crooned to it. "You want more of you. You know you do."

"Quit sweet-talking it and pull out your weapon," advised Holo-Lili, drawing her sword in example.

He barely gave her a glance. "Darlin', when I pull out my weapon, sweet-talking is *exactly* what I have in mind."

"No wonder your duel with the tag-creature goes so slowly, if that's all you can think of." She gave him a look of disgust. "You need to concentrate on your battle!"

Affronted, Augur lost the greater part of his bounce. "Slowly? *Slowly?* This is delicate work! I've got to find just the right way to trick this thing into duplicating itself."

"You've still got to find a way to seed it into the population, have you thought of that? Your tagbots cannot conquer what they cannot enter."

"If you don't want more puns, don't use the words *seed* and *population* and *enter* together," Augur said, but in fact . . . he hadn't thought of it. Or what thinking he'd done hadn't gotten that far. Dumping starter tagbots into the city water supply would be handy—except the things were engineered to live in blood plasma pH, not the acid-filled stomach. And Park and Belman *might* be convinced to distribute them in their civilian work, but he doubted it. Even if so, it wasn't enough to make a difference.

Still. He had to have tagbots in a raging rut-phase before the Resistance had anything to distribute. "We need the *on* switch," he said. A familiar phrase of late.

"We haven't been able to find the *on* switch," Holo-Lili reminded him, quite unnecessarily. "A wise commander would look to a different battle plan."

"A *wise* commander wouldn't allow insubordination," he said meaningfully. Okay, they hadn't been able to find the *on* switch, and maybe it *was* time to try something else. "Maybe," he said, "we can convince it to find its own *on* switch."

"Go in the back way!" Holo-Lili said with approval.

"It's got to have some means to gauge its population." Augur moved back to the previous monitor, eyeing the muchly magnified tagbot there. "Some kind of sensor to tell it it's reached *full*." He watched the thing a moment. Its function was to produce sound waves . . . ultrasonic markers for the Taelons to monitor. "Maybe it listens to itself," he said. "*Itselves*, I mean. And when it has enough volume—"

"It turns itself off!" She gave a victorious gesture, a high heft of her sword. "That's fighting the good fight!"

"Don't get anachronistic," he told her. "Now, if that

would function as an *off* switch, then the *on* switch would be if it heard nothing at all . . ." He picked a vial off his system's scan plate, swirling the modest amount of liquid within. Just a few isolated tagbots within a friendly vector fluid, something with which he could play. Cocking an eyebrow at Holo-Lili, he said, "You have the specs on the tagbot frequency. Can you produce a null tone?"

"I can null that tone to pieces," she assured him.

"What have I done to you?" he groaned. He eyed her, admiring his choice in costuming; the bronze arm cuffs and strategically revealed skin of the breastplates were among his favorite parts. Princess Leia, eat your heart out . . . Still. This one had to go. "I promise . . . new persona, just as soon as we get through this mess. Right now . . . give me that tone."

He didn't hear it; he hadn't expected to. To judge by Holo-Lili's posturing, however, it had certainly been accomplished. "Keep a scan going," he said. "I want to know the moment the tagbot population increases." And hopefully they'd included the right components in the vector fluid for tagbot use in replication.

He didn't have to wait long. "Tagbot replication in process," Holo-Lili said, somewhat smugly.

He could have kissed her holo-tube right then and there. "Yes!" he said, air-pumping one arm. "We rule!"

Holo-Lili let out what must have been intended as a war cry.

War squeak, thought Augur, but he just grinned at her.

Ta'en paused at the archway to the lab, squelching his irritation at finding it unsecured.

The project was hardly still secret . . . and no one not already involved would do anything to associate—or taint—

themselves with it. None of Zo'or's glib assurances would do Ta'en any good now. He, like many others aboard the ship, had been assigned to creating a countervirus whose very purpose was to destroy his own work. Even if the Synod saw the merits of his experiments—the results *he* had wanted, before Zo'or interfered—once the countervirus had been released, there was very little point to pursuing the original experiment.

He had told Zo'or that Beta-S was not ready for such a widespread use. He had put his objections on the record. He could now only hope that this would be enough to protect him when this crisis was over, and inevitable inquiries started over the dissemination of the unstable virus.

Ta'en was proud of the virus, even so; that it had gone airborne attested to its strength and viability. Had it done so at a time when the Taelons had *chosen* to initiate genetic manipulation of Earth's entire population, he might even have been considered one of the saviors of their race.

He had held great hopes for this retrovirus from the start—but had also been wise enough to let those hopes trickle away when Zo'or stepped in. Now that the worst had actually come to pass, the final vestiges of that hope were easy to transform into bitter disappointment. He carried the disappointment in the corners of his mouth and ignored it.

Bellamy appeared not to have resigned himself to the state of things, however. Barely looking up from his keyboard at Ta'en's arrival, he said, "Did you know that Sandoval has opened the system to his own workstation on the bridge? He ordered the physical connections made last night. It worries me, Ta'en. It doesn't show enough respect for your work. And it makes this area too vulnerable!"

Ta'en felt a sudden flash of affection for this human and his devotion. Although Ta'en used Taelons as well as humans in the area where he carried out his practical experiments, he had quickly found that Bellamy's human perspective—lacking in brilliance as it was—occasionally brought solutions to light that Ta'en had not anticipated. However, until lately, Bellamy's dedication had been impersonal and often distracted. Ta'en often caught him looking at the flat image of his child, though never quite often enough to comment upon the presence of the image as a distraction to Bellamy's work. Now, however, he seldom glanced at it. Since the news that the virus had gone airborne, he had given his attention entirely to Ta'en's needs.

"I suspect you are correct on both counts," he said to Bellamy. Sandoval had little respect for anything other than Zo'or's wishes, although Ta'en felt this was a fault in his CVI imperative, which, as he understood it, should have given priority to the Taelon welfare as a whole. And indeed, this lab was now vulnerable. "However, please do not concern yourself with it. We may indeed be vulnerable, but there is little to gain from breaching our security at this date."

"All the same," Bellamy muttered. "Seewhyay."

"I beg your pardon?" Ta'en said, and in doing so offered Bellamy a courtesy, rather than simply demanding the explanation. Bellamy knew better than to use obscure human colloquialisms in this lab.

The man looked up from his work, startled that Ta'en had paid him any heed. "It's an acronym. C-Y-A. It stands for cover your—" and at that he stopped short. "It means, be forward-looking in protecting yourself from situations that might arise that aren't your fault."

"Such as a breach of security," Ta'en said, not quite making it a question.

"Yes." Bellamy looked at his monitor screen and let out a particularly human sigh. "I'm sorry, Ta'en, but without more information on the retrovirus's current structure, I don't know what else I can do here. I have some ideas sketched out, but—"

Ta'en's gesture stopped him short. "Zo'or has anticipated this problem," he said. "Even now he arranges to provide us with human subjects carrying the virus. I am readying a containment area."

Bellamy turned away from the keyboard completely, his surprise evident even to one not fully schooled in human expressions. "I thought Earth's leaders were too concerned about the origin of the virus to allow—that is, they haven't seemed inclined to allow us access to anyone with the virus."

A faint humor washed through Ta'en; he was sure the human saw it. "In this case," he said, "Zo'or's . . . impulsive . . . methods may serve us well."

Bellamy turned back to his keyboard. "I understand," he said, no doubt hiding some reaction he thought Ta'en would not be pleased to see. In truth, Ta'en didn't care. Bellamy had no CVI; as humans went, he was still reasonably tractable. Even now he typed vigorously at his keyboard, his hands entirely without grace. Without turning around, he said, "I'll be ready."

Ta'en had the feeling he had indeed just missed some sort of undercurrent, and that it actually stood loudly between them. But such things were for the diplomats; Ta'en would never fully understand this race with which the Synod had cast their future. All he cared was that Bellamy did his job.

Another foodbeast herd died, and another. The long-lived Kimera saw it all, through different Kimera-within-Kaluuet positioned across the continent that until now had provided the Kaluuet with sustenance.

Until now, but not for much longer.

The shaqarava gave the Kaluuet access to those things they had never evolved to resist. The pure pleasure of energy feeding wound them to a fever pitch of activity. Living, loving, hunting, feeding . . . they did it with more ferocity, more intensity. They used their world up. And they knew it. So they struggled to find relief from that which they could not control, while the Kimera watched and infiltrated their tribes and wondered about the wisdom of their decision, so many years earlier, to save the Kaluuet from their natural extinction.

Unable to shapeshift like the Kimera, the Kaluuet focused on the finer art of converting energies, but the shift of self-to-energy remained too great a task, and those who tried it perished. And Kimera-within—he who had seen the Kaluuet's first attempt to shift to an energy form—did more than wonder. He saw the guilt of the Kimera written across the palms of each Kaluuet. And each time the Kimera shed their borrowed native forms and gathered to share information as if doing so were their only goal and obligation, he made it clear he felt differently.

But there was no undoing what had been done so long ago. On that they all agreed.

It didn't mean there was nothing to be done. But on that, they could not agree.

So Kimera-within returned to the Kaluuet and watched them struggle, knowing that he could provide the Kaluuet with the means to maintain the new energy form they sought. He knew he could reveal the missing key, the anchor the Kaluuet needed to steady itself in its new form—and to allow others to join it there.

It would, of course, entail revealing himself.

The attempt to make the changeover had become ritualized. Candidates were chosen early and revered until they attempted the change. It cost the tribes lives, but not young ones—and with the shaqarava energies coursing through their bodies, they had lives to spare. With success so tantalizingly close, they even had hope to spare.

They simply didn't have much time to spare.

Yearly, Kimera-within watched it happen.

Until one year, he couldn't simply watch any longer.

There were to be four of them from his tribe that year, four trying together and dying together. Mature Kaluuet, pampered and cared for all their lives, required to do nothing but study their own shaqarava and those gifts it gave them. Of the four, one had demonstrated remarkable control and skill.

It was this one that the Kimera sought out the day before the ceremony.

When the ceremony commenced the next evening, it was no longer the private thing of the first attempt, but now a gathering of many tribes. The Kimera had no difficulty playing his role; he was armed with the memories of his host and the willingness to keep this form for a lifetime. His host, of course, had had no such choice . . . but his host would have perished this evening anyway, despite the unflagging optimism of the Kaluuet as a whole.

They entered the great common house in an orderly line, clothed in their richest materials—blues and purples and shimmering silver highlights, reflective of the energy beings to which they hoped to convert themselves. Long, sweeping robes and skirts styled for each individual, lovingly made by each candidate's closest family members—those who now lined the stone-paved path to the common house.

Kimera-within saw his host's siblings and parents crowding the well-marked line behind which tradition kept them; he nodded to them with much dignity, as was expected. And then he found in his host's mind an odd little wave that this family used among its members, and he offered them that as well. His female parent contorted her face with an expression of both grief and joy, while the younger siblings responded with great excitement, waving back at him.

The ceiling of the common house, on this day only, rolled

back to reveal the stars. Staggered seats, rising from ground level at the front to many seats high at the back, surrounded an open area, upon which was an oval stage, the edges of which were comprised of thick living vines. A rarity on this world, to find vines so thick; it took constant, expert attention to keep them thriving. Kimera-within took his place on the stage in the formal circle with the others, pleased by the spicy scent the vines lent the air. He and the other candidates took up meditative poses perfected over years of practice while the observers took their seats. Honored Kaluuet all, for no others would fit; the rest surrounded the common house and would observe events from there as the candidates lit the sky with their newly acquired energy forms.

Family, of course, had a reserved section down in the front. This time, Kimera-within did not wave or even acknowledge his relations. None of them did. Even before the commotion of movement died down, before the throat noises and excitement faded into respectful silence, the candidates slipped away from their awareness of their harsh, beleaguered world, their shaqarava slowly blooming to life, turning into a complex interplay of energies that connected the circle members. Palm to palm, not touching other than with those energies, and yet suddenly more intimately connected than any two beings—many of them strangers—could ever imagine.

Kimera-within held an awareness of himself aside from the circle, knowing that it would betray him and disrupt the circle beyond mending. Knowing, too, that he must act quickly to initiate the conversion, for he could not keep himself—his true self—hidden forever.

One of the others must have felt his eagerness, for sudden light flared to his left, and the observers gave a collective grunt of reaction. The female directly beside him form-shifted in response, and another, and then the remainder, almost simultaneously—Kimera-within included. For that moment, he lost himself to the moment, caught up in the conversion to a form so similar to his own natural state and yet rather delightfully different. There were more restrictions here, and yet a freedom of sorts from the restraint he had always imposed on himself. From the constant effort of control over the shaqarava . . .

On the other side of the circle, perceptible through senses other than his eyes, one of the candidates flickered, losing stability. As the observers grunted their startled dismay, Kimera-within acted. He reached to his true self and the abilities this Kaluuet form had never known, and he reached *out*. To the female beside him, to the male beyond that, feeling the new changes in those distinct sexualities. To the candidate beyond, and beyond, and beyond . . . around the circle he went, reaching through each candidate to the next, stretching himself, borrowing energy . . .

Until he had done it. The candidates shone with the glow of their stabilized energies, a network of define meridian pathways for each form—and a beguiling hum of awareness of each individual, pooling together to make a singular whole.

Now, of course, they knew of him. Now, as the observers leaped to their feet, their shaqarava pulsing with the depth of their emotions and the common house literally shaking with their foot-stomping approval . . . now, the other candidates fully realized that he was not quite one of their own. In an instant of shared knowing, they learned the depth of the Kimera involvement in their world, and as one they turned to look at him, their shock and accusation shuddering through their common link.

He did not hesitate. *I gave you this, which you have sought so long. I can bring others into this link, as you cannot; all who choose to join us.*

Or—and he did not have to say *if you threaten me,* for they understood his nuances perfectly without such elucidation—*I can take it away, and you will die.*

No. They did not want that.

Lili expected to find Sandoval waiting for her in the shuttle docking area; he was not. Next best bet was the bridge, but she didn't rush off. She took the moment to grab a look at the incoming message stored on her global, the one that had arrived shortly before docking. There'd been no caller ident, not even one of Augur's, and while an occasional piece of junk messaging slipped through her filters, she wasn't about to take the value of the message—or lack thereof—for granted. Not these days.

So with a glance to make sure Sandoval wasn't striding up to the shuttle, she unclipped her global, pulled it open, and said shortly, "Play unheard stored messages."

Text scrolled obediently to fill the screen and waited for her to tap a PAGE DOWN command. She didn't; she stared at it for an uncomprehending moment, taken aback by the unusual presentation. *Someone really doesn't want to be found.* If she wanted to, she'd eventually set Augur on the sender's trail. But first she needed to understand what she had, for it was a jumble of meaningless data—at least to her eyes—with indications of several embedded images that would take a more sophisticated machine than this global to decode. She pulled the global open to its full width, a complete display of both data and call screens, and scrolled through it, hunting for something that would make sense.

She found it at the very bottom of the data, a few discreet lines of text. *You'll know someone who can use this to Earth's advantage*, it said. And then, in a typo-filled addendum minus punctuation, *t acquiring new viruspatients asap for antivrus cant vouch for their sfatey.*

It took a moment to decipher it simply because the warning was such a change of style. The Taelons were about to grab up a few sample patients carrying the airborne virus. For the purposes of developing an antivirus, if she understood correctly.

Lili slowly lowered her global, staring out at the bustle of the docking area and seeing none of it, filled with a swirl of conflict. They needed an antivirus . . . they needed it badly. *Unless Jonathan was right, and it was truly man's salvation against both Taelon and Jaridian.* Although . . . until they had an antivirus, they had no way to protect the weak ones who would succumb to the viral process.

And if the Taelons come up with an antivirus, would you trust it?

Jonathan's voice in her head again, point to her counterpoint. But while Jonathan would have been willing to sacrifice a few civilians to the Taelons if it meant the development of something he wanted, Lili was less so inclined, and less so yet when they could hardly make trusting use of the results of any Taelon-based antivirus.

Especially not when she held in her hand that which the Resistance doctors so badly needed in their efforts. Lili might not be able to decipher it, but Park and Belman would understand it—because she was now almost certain of the contents. She even thought she knew who sent it— someone she had apparently not fooled half as well as she'd thought when he'd caught her in the lab.

And then, in the next moment, she knew what she was doing here . . . why Sandoval had called her.

He was the one who meant to procure these patients. And she would be part of it, at his orders.

She hit a quick code sequence on her global, still expecting Sandoval to come striding up at any moment, still keeping a constant watch on the hallways that spilled from the center of the Mothership to the docking area. As soon as Augur completed the connection, she started talking. "Augur—"

"Whoo hoo!" he said. "Lili, you are beautiful today!"

She did a double take at his handsomely beaming face and got out no more than, "Keep it dow—"

"I can make as much as you can dish out," he said, disregarding the warning she hadn't been able to complete.

"Shh!" she said, one impulse short of slamming the global shut on him; several of the human workers had turned to look at her.

This time, Augur seemed to see the look on her face. "What," he said. "No *good for you, Augur?* No *I knew you could do it, Augur?*"

"I knew you could do it," she said in rushed tones that were anything but congratulatory. It took him back, and she relented, her voice barely above a whisper. "You figured out how to replicate the tagbots? That's great, Augur, it really is, but I've got trouble up here and I don't have any extra time."

"Yes to the tagbots," he said. "Distributing them is up to you. What trouble?"

"*I'll take care of any trouble!*" cried an all-too-familiar voice in the background.

"Shut up!" Augur hissed at it, and Lili would have jumped on him if she'd been any less pressed. "I'm forwarding you a message I just received," she said, suiting action to words. "See that Park and Belman get it. And take a look at the last few lines. I think I'm about to be on my way to kidnap a few unsuspecting virus victims—new ones, with the airborne version—but I have no idea where. I'm going to put my global on standby. Trace it—and get someone there to stop us. You got it?"

"Yeah, but—"

"But nothing—do it! And, Augur—"

"Yes, your highness?"

She ignored it. Let him pout. "Have you been able to get through to Liam?"

The pout vanished instantly into concern. "No. And I've been too busy here to run out there—"

"I know," she said, and then regretfully, "This has got to come first. And see if the doctors have an idea about the distribution while you're at it. I have the feeling my hands will be full for a while."

"Yeah, I can see that," he said. "Maybe we can figure out how the Taelons distributed the virus in the first place. That would work—none of us were any of the wiser about it, that's for sure."

"Good," she said. "I'll try to keep in touch." He made a face indicating the likelihood of *that* possibility, and she closed the global on it.

Sandoval was still not in evidence.

Time to track him down.

Augur kept his vidscreen hopping. Plenty of calls to make, far too many arrangements on far too short a notice. Not that there'd actually *been* notice . . . but Augur knew how to plan ahead. He cut contact with the last of his Flat Planet franchises and considered the next step. He'd already assigned Holo-Lili the task of keeping tabs on the real Lili via her global trace; she'd notify him when Lili headed for a landing. He'd tried to reach Liam again; couldn't. Thought about taking an additional dose of Virex, and did. Weighed the decision to run over to the Flat Planet and Liam's apartment against that of going straight to Belman and Park with his tagbots and information . . . and hovered there for a

while, his personal loyalties weighing against his responsibilities and his very personal fears.

In the end, Augur found himself back at the clinic warehouse. Its dim entry lighting annoyed him, but he supposed
it was good enough in terms of strategy. There'd be no
bursting into any of the various compartments without a lot
of squinting and blinking; it was easy to see they were
brightly lit through the thick plastic that made the walls—
some with so many layers that the plastic might as well have
been opaque plaster. Ah, well, even Resistance members
liked privacy in the bathroom.

The sickroom was one of those; he went to there first,
peering in through the door. They'd enhanced it since he'd
been here last . . . or maybe he hadn't stuck around long
enough to notice how the sickest of the patients were
screened off, and the best off of them in a communal area by
the door. They looked up at him; he lifted a hand in a low,
let's-not-be-friends greeting—the thought of the airborne
virus did that to him—and they went back to what they
were doing.

Practicing, it looked. Practicing control over their
shaqarava.

They all had them.

Augur concealed a shudder. He'd had enough of the
Taelons messing with *his* body parts, thank you very much.

He didn't particularly feel any better when he noticed
that toward the curtained-off area, there were several recovering patients tending those who were still profoundly ill.
Tending them with offerings of *energy*, sweeping their softly
glowing hands down the spines of the recumbent men and
women. It just wasn't . . . right. He'd barely grown used to
seeing it in Liam, and he'd seen Liam grow from babe to
man in less than a day.

Back against the wall—the true cement block wall of the

warehouse—was a discreetly curtained-off area. Not so discreet, though, that he couldn't see the body-shaped outlines lying there. What did they do with them? he wondered suddenly, and then wished he hadn't. He glanced again at the shaqarava-bearing patients and wished he hadn't done that, either, not with the thought of body disposal in his mind.

He shuddered again, simply because he knew there were people in this world who *wouldn't*—and the way things were going, those people would have shaqarava soon enough, to do with as they pleased.

Lili strode through the Mothership corridors at a no-nonsense pace, taking herself to the bridge. She could call Sandoval on her global, of course . . . but if he'd gotten himself preoccupied with something since demanding her precipitous arrival at the Mothership, then she wanted to know what it was.

As much as any of them, Sandoval knew how to mislead someone on the other end of the global. If he wanted you to think he was on Earth in a conventional Earth building, you would think just that—no matter that he was calling from the bridge of the Mothership.

Lili preferred to find him, and to see for herself what had captured his attention.

It didn't prove to be a difficult task. Within moments, she stood quietly on the upper level of the bridge, unnoticed by those below and uncommented upon by the drones above; they moved past her in their quiet, purposeful way.

Zo'or was absorbed in a datastream display; not unusual. A discussion with another Taelon . . . Da'an, she thought, though the image wasn't clear enough at this distance to be sure. For once their conversation stayed in low tones; she'd learn nothing from it. She switched her attention to Sandoval's workstation, off to the side, unheeding of the Taelon flight engineers in their little niches, one of them so close he could reach out to grab her if he chose. She'd never seen any of them involve themselves in real-world byplay, so caught up were they in their connection with the ship itself, the nuances of its health and function. So she moved even closer, using the curve of this one's niche to obscure her presence as she got a good close look at Sandoval. At what occupied him so.

Tagbot maps.

He flashed up one after the other, none of them the file she'd so painstakingly destroyed. They shifted in the data-stream like flash cards, far too quickly for anyone without a CVI to do more than glimpse. And then with sudden, stabbing movements, he stopped the displays, merged them all into one. A jumble, to Lili's eye.

Then again, she didn't have the gift of Sandoval's memory. "Here," he murmured, indicating a spot with movement so precise he might have been piloting a Taelon shuttle. The computer obligingly sprinkled the area with a thick concentration of tag indicators. "Here," he said, doing it again.

Sure enough, he was plotting out the original tag map.

Dammit.

She hoped Augur had planned for this possibility. Her hand crept for her global, even though it knew better. Not now. Not here.

Below her, Sandoval shook his head, wiped out the new additions, and deleted all the maps but the current one.

There, too, the Resistance betrayed itself, if one was inclined to look past the obvious, and to ascertain which of those tag gatherings belonged to which official clinic . . . and which was unidentified.

"Agent Sandoval," Zo'or said, annoyance in his voice,

"why are you not already on your way to acquire specimens for Ta'en?"

"Da'an said—"

"Da'an still intends to make his plea within the County Hospital tomorrow, yes. But *I* do not intend to wait to see if he is successful, which I seriously doubt will be the case. We must provide Ta'en with the means for ending this plague. Unless you *want* to see your people irrevocably changed?"

"I want what I've always wanted," Sandoval said. "What's best for the Taelons." But his glance at the workstation gave him away to Lili; he might want what was best for the Taelons, but he wanted to do it his own way. That pesky little CVI imperative wasn't quite as strict as it used to be. And Sandoval . . . less earnest, and much more calculating.

Lili thought he was probably safer when the CVI had him in a tighter hold.

"I am informed that Captain Marquette has docked. Whatever holds your attention can wait. I have provided you with the necessary documents; all that remains is for you to collect the patients."

"Yes, Zo'or," Sandoval said, and keyed a few last entries into his workstation even as he moved away from it.

Lili knew the right moment when she saw it. She eased back slightly and then strode forward in her normal ground-eating pace, hesitating as she saw Sandoval take the first step up the ramp. "Agent Sandoval," she said. "I thought you'd be in the shuttle bay."

"You should have contacted me when you docked, Captain," Sandoval said, his voice making the reprimand clear. "We've wasted valuable time."

"I'm sorry." Lili ducked her head slightly as he walked right by her, then turned to watch him with narrowed eyes that didn't match her voice in the least. "It won't happen again."

"Don't make me wait for you," was all he said.

Who's been waiting for whom? But of course she didn't say it. She caught up to him, made use of her longer legs to reach the shuttle just before him, and settled quickly into the pilot's seat, waiting for him to enter the shuttle before activating the virtual glass and interface shield. By the time he sat, she was ready to go. Except—

"Destination?" she asked him, her hands poised over the nav interface.

"Georgetown University Hospital," he said. "Roof access."

Pay attention, Augur, she thought, and guided the shuttle into a minimalist takeoff, easing out into open space as she plotted and cleared an entry course with D.C. air traffic control.

Not that there were a lot of conventional flights to avoid, given the growing numbers of ID portals—and Washington had been among the first to get them. In moments they swooped down upon the hospital, a long, shallow descent. Coming out of ID space at some distance from the building was the best she could do to delay for Augur; if whoever was left to lead the local cell—for as far as she knew, their upper-level people were all down with the virus—had any wits, they'd have sent someone to each of the likely locations. Of which this, fortunately, was the most likely of all. Nice and central . . . and the place, of course, where Sandoval had vehemently quarreled with the chief of staff. Come back to make his point, as he was wont to do.

TWELVE

Alarge man came Augur's way down the rigged hallway of the clinic warehouse, wearing a medical scrub pullover shirt and stylistically clashing black cargo pants. The well-dressed Resistance member on nursing duty, Augur thought, taking a second look at the man's no-nonsense expression. *And not friendly.*

"I don't know you," the man said when he reached the door, looking down on Augur. A big one, all right.

"I don't know *you*," Augur said, looking back up at him without backing off, although the big guy had come in close, trying a little body language bullying. "But I do know Hayley. Where is she?"

"I asked you a question first, I think."

"In point of fact, you didn't," Augur said. "You made a statement. You need to get this stuff down a little better before you start trying to intimidate people."

An exasperated groan came from the compartment across from them; a decidedly feminine groan. One of the little break areas, if Augur recalled correctly—microwave, coffee, and snacks. All it lacked was a junk-food machine, but he doubted the suppliers were into dealing with customers who moved around so often and who made themselves so hard to find.

Hayley stuck her head out the door just long enough to say, "Don't be such a pain, Art. We've got guards up, don't we? Let them do their job."

"Just looking out for you," he said, surprisingly mild. And when Augur went to the break room, unwelcome Art followed, ignoring the scowl Augur gave him.

Augur turned his attention on Hayley, lovely Hayley. Not as big a woman as the impression she projected with her authoritative bearing, she had the kind of figure that caught his eye every time. Plenty to fill a man's hands in all the right places. And though her features weren't convention-ally beautiful, even with the remnants of illness upon her they had such life to them that she made herself beautiful on her own. "Why the *Northwest* Resistance cell?" he asked. "The east coast is nice, too. And it's much, much closer."

She gave him an amused if small smile. "It's my home," she said, not bothering to add anything that would erase the somewhat bemused look on Art's face. Now *that* was not a pretty face.

"*This* could be your home," he said, never one to lack persistence when it came to the important things. Speaking of which . . . "Assuming, of course, that the Taelons don't wreck it too thoroughly with their petty little schemes."

"There is that," she said, returning to the white round plastic table that someone had probably picked up at a Wal-Mart store. On sale. Coffee, doughnut, a small white rectan-gle of a napkin, and her gun. Freshly cleaned, by the smell of it. Very homey. Hayley sat, picked up her coffee, and said, "You wouldn't be here without a reason."

"Wooing you isn't reason enough?" He offered her hurt surprise, but she didn't take the bait, so he dropped the wooing altogether, shifting to business. "I'm here to see the doctors, mainly—got some goodies for them—but have a little something for you, too."

She raised her eyebrows; Art moved in closer and Augur felt compelled to make himself some space. "Shoo, shoo," he said, once again leaving the man bemused—enough so that he moved to the other side of the room to stand by Hayley's chair. "Information, mainly. Lili thinks the Taelons are going to make a grab at a few unsuspecting citizens with the new airborne Taelon Flu; she doesn't know where. I've got the local Resistance on it—what's left of them—but I don't know that they'll think to contact you. They're working light on leadership right now."

Hayley put her coffee down. "Going to try to stop it?" she said, her tone making it clear that they'd darn well better.

"Unless you've got a better idea? Like letting the Taelons experiment on more of us against our will?"

"Including throwing an antivirus at anyone and everyone, now that their little retrovirus has bitten them on the ass," Hayley said. She tapped the table a couple of times. "But we need that antivirus. We need to be able to protect the people who can't live through this change."

"But we don't want the Taelons to have that kind of power over us," Art said, and added pointedly, "again."

"No," Hayley said, but it was clear she'd already come to that decision and was speaking absently while her thoughts raced ahead somewhere. "We don't." She looked at Augur and stood up. "I'll take care of it."

"Hey, hey," he responded, suddenly aware of just how willing she was to go her own way. "Don't step on any toes, okay? Don't make me sorry I told you—"

She smiled at him. "Quit worrying. We're on the same side." She reached for her pistol . . . and hesitated, looking at her palms. Normal palms, aside from the faintly darkened areas in the centers. She shoved the automatic in its holster and wrapped its harness around it; clearly, it wasn't going along for the ride. "Have you been able to—"

For some reason, his temper flared. Not worry, no. Nothing to worry about. But he snapped at her anyway. "No, I haven't. Liam isn't answering his calls." *And I should have gone over there instead of coming here. Some friend I am.*

She looked at him, not bothering to conceal her own feelings. He must have thought his too loudly, for she said, "We do what we have to, Augur. That's how it goes these days."

Whatever. He wasn't about to discuss it with Art hovering around like a misplaced oak tree. Or even, after a second look at her, to ask her just how she *did* feel about his boy Liam. And if she felt his unspoken question, she was spared from making any response; Augur's global demurely chimed for his attention.

Holo-Lili. "Go," he said, and she started talking as soon as the connection completed.

"I have a projected location for shuttle landing," she said. "No one tracks 'em better than me!"

"Who's *that*?" Art asked, leaning over to look at the global screen. Augur pointedly turned it to a more private angle.

"You never mind," he said. "Someone who knows what she's doing, because *I* programmed her that way."

"Georgetown University Hospital," Holo-Lili said. "The roof. I can be more precise once they start moving within the building—"

"Good," Augur told her. "Check your records for Hayley Simmons' contact information. You call *her* when you've got that information." He glanced up at Hayley to see that she concurred.

She did. She definitely did. "Thanks, Augur," she said, and grinned at him. Hayley on the jazz.

Art scooped up her gun and followed her as she rushed out of the room. Augur could only shake his head. If that lug thought Hayley's shoulder harness would fit *him*, he had another thing coming. "Good job," he told Holo-Lili, and cut the connection. Enough of the chitchat. Time to find the doctors.

Dr. Park, he knew, had made herself fully available to the Resistance simply by telling her chief of staff she'd caught the virus and was at home; Belman had put aside her current research to join in. Together they were a formidable team—brilliant, determined, and vastly experienced.

So Augur didn't consider it a good sign when he hesitated outside their expanded work lab to hear Julianne Belman saying, "If only we had some of the history on this virus . . . the background of its development. Without it . . . frankly, I don't know where to go from here."

Not good. Definitely not good. However—

"Ladies," he said, stepping through the door, "I come bearing gifts."

They turned to look at him with identical expressions— the *you're interrupting our work* look combined with something of hope. He winced inside to see how tired they already looked—neither of them was in their prime anymore, and Park had already been up to her elbows in this mess. But he knew better than to wince visibly on the outside. Instead he held out the vial of tagbots, within which the population had grown so thickly it was visible as a dark cloud in the vector fluid. Presumably the tagbots had run out of some vital component for reproducing themselves; they had ceased to do so.

But Augur had brought them; he'd brought an enhanced precision oscilloscope, pre-set to the null tone, to prod the little bugs into jump-starting their multiplication tables.

"The tags!" Park said, recognizing the vial. "Were you successful?"

"Were you in doubt?" Augur said. "All we need is more of whatever you put into that vector fluid, and we can make as many of these babies as you please. I've already got Lili hunting us a way to distribute them in appropriately sneaky fashion. Though we're open to suggestions . . ."

Park shook her head. "We can distribute them with an antivirus, if we come up with one—"

"I don't think we've got that long—we've got to obscure our trail before Sandoval comes sniffing it out." But he took another look at their fatigue and decided not to push it; Lili would have to keep at it from her end. Setting the vial on a lab table littered with research tools he couldn't begin to recognize, he pulled out the oscilloscope. "All you have to do is set these things up in new fluid and turn this on, and they'll make like rabbits," he said. "It nullifies the noise they send out, so they think they need more of themselves to reach proper signal strength."

"Nice and simple," Belman murmured. "At least there's that."

"Oh, there's more," Augur said. "Not my doing, but I have the honor of presenting it to you." And he pulled a spare global from his jacket pocket and gave it to Park with a flourish. "Open it," he suggested when she took it and only gave him a puzzled look. "I'm not just handing out freebie globals here."

She did, holding it so Belman could look over her shoulder; at first her puzzled expression merely intensified, but as it changed to surprise, Belman said, "Notes on the creation of the virus! Augur, where did you get these?"

He shrugged elaborately. "Manna from heaven, more or less. I say we take it and run."

"Assuming we can trust it." Park lifted her head from the display, still holding it so Belman could read if she wished.

"Someone went to a lot of trouble to get it to us," Augur said. "And warned us about the little hospital raid Sandoval was about to pull, too. Besides, what have we got to lose?"

"Not a lot," Belman said. "We're pretty much stuck without this information."

Park gave the global another long look and connected it to the lab system, starting a download. "We can at least analyze it," she said. "If it looks good . . . well, then it's a start."

"More than a start," Belman said, evincing much more relief than her colleague; sometimes Augur thought too much of Jonathan Doors had rubbed off on Park while she'd been squirreled away in the Resistance hideout at its heyday—meaning before it had become Augur's, and improved dramatically in appearance. "It's exactly what we need."

"Good," Augur said. "Then maybe you have a moment . . ." he hesitated. "About Liam. Haven't been able to reach him today. I was wondering if one of you ladies would take a moment—" But he broke off as they exchanged looks.

"Augur," Belman said, "I saw Liam last night, when he was here. I took a pretty close look at him, actually."

"Why am I not liking the expression on your face?" he said, eyeing her warily.

She rubbed the bridge of her nose. "For good reason, I'm afraid. He's having a severe reaction to the retrovirus overlay on his existing shaqarava, as I think you know. Augur, right now we can't even do anything to help those whose physiology was *meant* for this virus—nothing but keep them comfortable. At the moment, the only one who can help Liam . . . is Liam."

Anger flushed through him, even though he knew it wasn't fair. Liam had devoted his life to the Resistance literally from the day he was born . . . and now when he needed it, the Resistance couldn't return the favor? *Not fair* was the term for it, all right.

"Augur," Belman repeated, "I'm sorry. I gave him something to take for the pain if he wants it. But don't give up on him, by any means. There's still a lot we don't know about his makeup. And if there's anything the Kimera were good at . . . it was manipulating the nature of their bodies. Ha'gel alone taught us that much."

Nothing much truer than that. "I'll just go check in on him." He reached for his lean leather backpack, now empty.

"Actually . . ." Dr. Park said, looking up from what she was doing, "we could use your help getting this information coded to our system."

Augur stopped in the act of slipping the backpack strap over one arm, conflicted loyalties pulling at him. "No one's even spoken to him today—"

It was Belman who decided it; she gave him a look of such regret that he knew she'd never ask him to stay unless they really needed the help.

"All right, then," he said, slipping back into brash mode by default . . . and because it allowed him not to feel how he felt. "With me at the wheel, it shouldn't take long."

He hoped.

The visions became a refuge. They piled one atop another, and between them Liam Kincaid had just enough awareness to hear the frequent signal of incoming calls. And to realize, with dark finality, that his alien nature—having so many times saved his life—now threatened it. More than threatened it.

And that it did so just when he was beginning to understand the complex and long-standing relationship between the races whose conflict was responsible for his very existence . . .

It really pissed him off.

But the anger did nothing to abate the struggle within his body; it did nothing to keep the visions away, or to allow him to retain his sense of self when they took over. As soon as he came to himself, realizing who he was, where he was, and what was happening, another would rush up upon him.

Kimera-within stayed with the other converted Kaluuet at the tribal spot known as Taelanon, the location of the very first temporary conversion, of the following conversion attempts, and—thanks to his interference—of the first successful conversion. Now it had become a place of pilgrimage, where Kaluuet came and trained for their own conversions, held in batches in the common house and assisted by those who had already made the journey. Those who now existed in what they were coming to call the commonality, and who no longer felt the siren call of the shaqarava's indulgences, gaining much of their sustenance from the energies provided by the sun that had once threatened to kill them.

Only once the new candidates made the transition did they learn the truth, simply by merit of their connection within the commonality. That the original conversion had been successful because of one who was not their own. That further conversions would be successful for only so long as he remained among them; without him they did not have the ability to join new souls to the commonality.

And they inevitably realized that others of his kind were among them, watching them. Realization led to the understanding that his kind were responsible for the changes to their species so many years earlier, for introducing the shaqarava they had been so ill-prepared to deal with.

Inevitably, they responded with anger.

"He should not be allowed to continue among us," the loudest of the most recent additions said, pulsing with his strident words.

Kimera-within said, "Without me, no more of your people may join you." It was not a new conversation to him.

"Then we must reveal the truth to those of us who remain without the commonality," said another. This one was already exploring the ability to layer a shell of flesh over the energy form, but was unable to maintain it throughout the conversation.

This, too, he was used to. As were the others, one of whom said, "Do not waste your thought so. Receive the information available to you through our link. He will not remain among us should we betray his kind, and then we will lose our ability to save the remainder of our own."

No one spoke of what would happen when all were saved. They already knew that their newborn would be part of the commonality from conception onward, because with much effort over many years, one of them had finally conceived.

"Not all of them want to be saved," said the pulsing one. This one had been a female, and was still used to thinking of herself in those terms; it caused her difficulty. Even joined to the commonality, not all of the converted Kaluuet were able to maintain themselves. And those who couldn't, perished. They dispersed in the manner of those who first attempted conversion.

They were not much spoken of.

This one's information was new to those long-established, even to Kimera-within—who had no contact with his own people since the conversion, and knew he would pay the price for his actions once he did—if he indeed survived to that point. The new one continued. "They don't like what they hear of this new state; they claim we have forsaken the passions that made us what we were."

"They say that if conversion is the alternative, they can learn to control the shaqarava," said another.

"They are fools," said a long-established individual. One of the longest, for none of the original had yet perished and Kimera-within did not expect them to do so anytime soon. This new form brought with it other advantages besides control of one's urges.

Although Kimera-within himself missed his natural form and the various urges that came with it, as well as missing the Kimera colleagues with whom he had once communed on a regular basis. He regretted that they had not had the time, so long ago, to save the Kaluuet with a Joining; a Joining would have more fully integrated the shaqarava into their systems, and perhaps made it easier to accept and control.

But it was far too late for such thoughts.

"Then let them be fools," said another of the earliest conversions. "We will continue to do what we know is right. If they do not destroy themselves before we're done, we'll reassess the situation then."

Kimera-within heard the words with alarm, perhaps more so than they merited. Certainly more than he could hide. The rest of the converted beings in conference with him—some clothed in flesh, some not—turned to look at him.

"Yes," one of them said. "We are what you have made us. Now you must live with the consequences."

Sandoval swept into the hospital with Lili at his heels; she knew he expected her to back him up with or without explanation—usually without, of course. And she was used to the role, of putting on her stern military face to remove her personality from whatever distasteful situation in which she found herself.

She didn't feel tainted so much that way.

Now she stood by a hospital-room door in a formal posture while Sandoval said briskly to two uncomprehending and alarmed young men, "Put your clothes on. You're coming with me."

They were sick all right, but not yet to that point where they didn't care about anything but surviving through their misery. "I'm not going anywhere," said one of them, gripping the bed rails as though someone might rip him right out of the bed. A distinct possibility, Lili supposed. The other reached for the call button, thumbing it wildly. The room itself offered them no place to hide—standard-issue hospital room, the curtain between the two beds drawn aside, personal items littering their bedside tables, leftover breakfast still waiting by the foot of each bed for pickup.

She'd left the door cracked; now Lili peered down the hall, hoping to see some sign of Resistance. More likely to encounter them on the way back up to the roof. *She hoped.* If they saved these two, they'd probably only delay the inevitable—the Taelons would acquire their human subjects one way or the other, and sooner rather than later—but Lili was not inclined to give them one more easy victory than she had to. The delay would help give the Resistance the edge in producing the antivirus first.

Sandoval told the young man, "I'm afraid you're mistaken." He reached into his suit's inside pocket and removed several sheets of folded paper, which he briskly shook out. "Since you're obviously too ill to think straight, you've been declared wards of your families. They believe it to be in your best interests if the Taelons take over your treatment from here."

Translation: *They're afraid for you. Someone convinced them that your only chance to survive would be if the Taelons cure you. They have no idea you'll be used as lab rats.*

If only the Taelons would truly be satisfied to limit their use of these men to examining their blood—but then, if that was the case, they could take the samples here and now. Lili took another look out the door, only barely masking her surprise to see two white-clad people striding briskly down the hall. Not hospital personnel. She'd have guessed it from the way they moved even if they hadn't been pulling knit masks down over their faces.

And had she not recognized Hayley Simmons' height and shapely form, or the bulk of Art Wells behind her.

Casually, she moved aside, putting herself in a position to be taken by surprise. Sandoval was entirely embroiled with his protesting patients, one of whom continued to press the call button.

"No one will respond to that call," he said. "They know I'm here. They know why. You'll make it easier on yourselves if you'll just get dressed as I've requested and come quietly. Or," Sandoval said thoughtfully, and his voice grew suddenly hard, "we will simply haul you away with your various assets or lack thereof exposed for the world to see."

At the cracked door, Hayley's blue eyes peered at her from behind the mask. Lili had a moment's confusion—why was Hayley not armed?—and then the door opened so hard it hit the wall stop with a crack, catching Sandoval completely by surprise. Lili took a hard shove—too hard, her head cracked against the wall just as hard as the door—and by the time she could see straight, both Resistance members had taken a stance within the room. The man held a gun on Sandoval, and Hayley . . . just stood there. But she also had her hands slightly raised. *Shaqarava . . . already?*

The two virus-ridden patients were out of bed, uncertainly standing together; Hayley snapped at them, "Go ahead and get dressed. You either come with us or you go with him."

"You're interfering with a legal assumption of care," Sandoval said tightly, eyeing the gun, his hands rising as anyone's might. *Hands in the air* was a tried and true response to looking down the barrel of a gun.

"Do you think we care for your fiction? Taelon influence can get anything on paper." Hayley's tone matched his, and then went sharper. "Keep your hands down where they are. Unless you want to see which is faster—skrill or shaqarava." Then she grinned at him, evident through the mask. "And I'm already aiming at *you*." It was a point she drove home by tilting her hands slightly and bringing the shaqarava to life.

Wisely, Sandoval said nothing. But Lili, rubbing the back of her head and slowly regaining her feet—careful to stay against the wall as Art's gun swung to cover her—knew the look on his face. He wasn't going to take this quietly. Oh, no, not Sandoval.

As if coming to a silent mutual decision, the two young men scrambled for their clothes, pulling on their jeans, stuffing wallets into their pockets, and grabbing up their shirts and jackets. Hayley nodded at the door. "Out you go," she said.

"We'll find them again," Sandoval said. "And we'll find you."

Hayley gave him a short laugh. "You haven't managed it so far."

But there was a new look on Sandoval's face, a thinking look. It had far too much *ah-ha* in it for Lili's tastes, and she followed his gaze to Hayley's shaqarava. "You were at the Fair," he said slowly. "Of course. The Resistance attended the Fairs. And then you got together to talk about it—"

He must have thought he could catch her off guard, that she wouldn't expect him to try anything while thinking out loud. And maybe he would have managed it . . . except that she'd been right the first time. *She* was already aiming at him, and she didn't hesitate—as his arm flicked out to put her in the line of his skrill, she took him down. Neatly. Almost quietly, if you didn't count the thump of his body against the wall and the tearing noise of his suit catching on something as he slid down.

Lili ran to him. "Dammit, you'd better not have killed him!"

"We'd be a lot better off without him," Hayley said, sounding completely unruffled.

He breathed. His heart beat. No, not dead. Lili glared at her. "Kill him, and there *will* be retribution. He's far too important to Zo'or. Keep that in mind when you start throwing bolts of energy around!"

"I *didn't* kill him," Hayley said. "I did just what I meant to do. You're going to have to get used to the fact that some of us have new firepower to back up our words, Lili. And that you don't get to play big sister when it comes to how we use it."

Lili bristled . . . but stopped herself. Not easily, but a deep breath helped. Not to mention that Hayley was right. She'd used just the right amount of power . . . and Sandoval was much safer than if she'd fired a bullet at him. Under Lili's hands, Sandoval stirred. "Okay," she said. "You're right. But you'd better go. And, Hayley"—she lifted her head, meeting Hayley's eyes to give her words emphasis—"you heard him put it together. As soon as he gets to the Mothership, the first thing he's going to do is locate the nice big mess of tag traces from your clinic. Disperse your people *now*."

Hayley hesitated, then gave a short nod. "Immediately,"

she said. "The ones who are going to make it . . . pretty much already have. I've got a standby location for the docs to keep working. I'll be in touch."

And she was gone. Lili waited a decent moment, looking down at Sandoval and beginning to understand just how useful it would be to have shaqarava on their side, and then went to the door to call for help.

Kimera-within, recently assigned to the Taelanon area, waited in her Kaluuet body to greet the one who had been within Kaluuet, and was now converted to something new. The one whom she missed so badly, and had not seen for so long.

They met outside the developing enclave of converted Kaluuet, an area that had grown into an unofficial meeting zone between the converted and their unconverted family members. There was little to it other than its location; it was as rough as any of this land, with rocks sharp-edged, abrasive, and abundant. Within the enclave, things were already different; those in the new form were experimenting with their energies and their ability to manipulate their environment, and young trees of all varieties grew in astonishing numbers. This Kimera-within had even provided some seeds from the lowlands earlier in the season. But she had more on her mind than the native gardening habits.

She sat atop her chosen rock, knees to chest, and waited.

When he finally came, it was not without notice. The numerous small gatherings of mixed Kaluuet—old and new—hushed their conversation, watching his progress. Once it might have been with respect and even awe . . . but now their regard had a darker feel to it.

He gave them no acknowledgment. He came to her, holding up his hand so they might touch palms, a touchstone of their devotion.

She spoke in the low, guttural voice of this species, though her words were in her native language, and her thought processes were not limited to those of the Kaluuet. "You should have thought before you acted." Words aimed at a decision made long ago.

"I thought." His voice sounded a distinct contrast to hers, a voice clear and liquid and yet with a reverberating undertone of the old Kaluuet vocalizations. "I thought long. You know this. You know I felt we should do something to alleviate the problems we ourselves caused."

"We kept them alive. They can overcome the rule of the shaqarava if they so wish; they indulge themselves."

"This was not my belief. Have you been instructed to spend our time together after so long by scolding me over actions taken in the past?"

She grunted, a very Kaluuet-like response. "No. But you should be aware of the new changes, ones taking place other than here, but as a result of what you have done here."

He looked away, not to the enclave but to the distant horizon, as if his vision could extend so far. "I have heard that those who choose not to take conversion now feel compelled to gather in their own enclave, far from here in the Jarideen tribal lands. That they say the converted are no longer of their kind. I believe they feel threatened, as if somehow we could force them to take conversion."

"There has been no physical confrontation," she told him. "But we feel the potential. And you, the only one of us among the converted . . . do you see any truth in the fears of the Jarideens?"

He hesitated, which alarmed her; when he saw it, he offered his hand palm out, a reassuring gesture. "I have no access to the private thoughts of converted individuals, and they strive to keep me as isolated as possible within the commonality. They, too, have fears, which I can say with absolute certainty are unfounded. We can only hope that the fears of the Jarideens are equally unfounded. Perhaps we should—"

She knew him well enough to know where *that* thought was going, stuck on the other side of the commonality or no. "We have already interfered twice. It is enough."

"Perhaps that is the trap of interfering at all," he said. "It never ends."

"It ends now," she said, her voice especially guttural in her emphasis. "We already have many of our resources tied up in this planet. It changes us as much as it changes them, and we do not believe it is for the better."

"We," he repeated.

"Yes," she said. "Those of us still able to withdraw from our hosts and convene off-planet at the assigned times."

"I am able," he said. "I choose not to. I believe it would panic the remaining individuals who desire to convert; they cannot take new candidates without my help."

"Take care you do not remind them overmuch of that fact," she said, looking up at him from small eyes beneath her remarkably rugged brow. "It will breed resentment and fear, and complicate this already complicated situation."

He looked at those around them; they had gone back to their own interactions for the most part, but even she could sense the changed atmosphere, a tinge of lingering hostility. *No*, she told herself. *Hostility is too strong a word.* Maybe so, but he must have felt it too, plus whatever he received through the commonality. "I fear it is too late for that," he said. "In fact, I begin to feel that we must no longer meet like this. We must be more circumspect, lest you be tainted by association."

Regretfully, she agreed. "Let it be soon that you can shed that body, at least for a while. You can always take another and return to them."

"If they let me."

"If they do not, then that is their choice. You need not sacrifice every aspect of your life to them. You need not sacrifice *us*." It was this Kaluuet body, she knew, that increased her longing for him to this level. It was passionate in all its feelings, and not schooled to patience. If it was able, it took what it wanted, when it wanted . . . the very thing that made the species so susceptible to the abuses of the shaqarava.

But it turned out that she was wrong. For after he expressed his regret, after he shared of himself with her for another long, delicious moment, she heard the faint, low growls of displeasure. This preternaturally alert body reacted without thought, jumping up to face those who approached from behind.

She was one of the Kimera and they knew it. Her grip tightened on his hand, hard enough to have broken bones with that astonishing Kaluuet strength had he not been *other*.

She willed him the last of her memories as they killed her.

"I trust Agent Sandoval will fully recover."

Trust wasn't a word Lili liked to use in conjunction with Sandoval. But as startled as she was to see Da'an approach the nurses' station, she still managed a nod. "Yes, he'll be fine." The doctor who'd arrived in response to her call had simply installed Sandoval in a bed belonging to one of the young men he'd been trying to abduct; he'd been heavily stunned, but not injured, and in truth Lili expected to see him come walking out of the room at any moment. Perhaps lurching a little, not willing to wait until he was fully recovered before returning to work.

Which in this case would probably be the process of tracking down Hayley's clinic.

Da'an was not slow to note her surprise at his presence, or her quick assessment of his security. Companion Agent

Lassiter and another, in place of Liam . . . enough protection, if they'd done the necessary homework. "And what of Liam?" Da'an asked. "I have not been able to contact him."

"Neither have I," Lili said, frankly worried. She tucked her hair behind her ear and said, "I have friends trying to reach him. As soon as I'm done here, I'm going over to his place."

"I am concerned," Da'an said, looking away with a subtle blush that sent dread through Lili, "that his nature will make it impossible for him to survive this virus."

Not you, too. "You know, I'm getting a little tired of hearing that," Lili said. "It doesn't look good, I'll give you that. But impossible? That, I won't give you." And still, she wished she could walk away from Sandoval and straight to the Flat Planet.

"Your faith is admirable." Da'an looked as though he might say something else, but settled into a moment of silence instead. When he did speak, it was to say, "I felt it necessary to come as soon as I heard of Agent Sandoval's injury. Although perhaps not for the reason you think."

The response to that was easy. "I've learned not to make assumptions where you're concerned, Da'an," she said with easy sincerity.

He gave her the smallest of smiles, an acknowledgment of what they'd once shared—for even without the shaqarava, the Taelons still retained the ability to exchange of themselves with another being. "I would not have these people think that all the Taelons condone what has happened—what almost happened—here today." Then he gave her another kind of smile, more of a wry acknowledgment. Da'an's was a face of subtle expressions, and following them all meant paying strict attention. "Although perhaps," he said, "not in so many words."

"You don't think the Taelons should help find an antivirus?" Lili said. It was baiting him, but so be it; sometimes you had to play those games.

"I do not think," Da'an said, giving her a look from those pale blue eyes that made it clear he knew exactly what she was doing, "that we should further alarm your citizens in the process of finding an antivirus. At the moment, your global leaders have asked that we keep a distance from these efforts. Much as I regret this stance, I believe we should respect it."

"And would you respect a request for help from humans who were trying to help their own kind?"

Da'an came to a sudden, complete stillness, in that moment looking as androgynously alien as he . . . she . . . it . . . ever did. He said quietly, "Perhaps not. It would depend on the nature of the request."

She was careful. Oh, so careful. He knew she was Resistance; he'd seen her in the hideout before it became Augur's place. "If an antivirus was developed, we would need a quick, efficient way to distribute it." *And the tagbots before it.* "I have reason to believe the Taelons could supply a device for that purpose."

Saying things without saying them; that was the way to work with Da'an. She *knew* they had a device that would serve the purpose; the Volunteers had used something of that very nature to distribute the retrovirus in the first place.

Da'an gave her a canny look. "You might simply request this of Zo'or. Although I respect and even understand humanity's desire to resolve this problem on its own, I do not think it practical or viable. It is for this reason I will appear at County Hospital tomorrow in a more official role, pleading with your world leaders to accept our help."

And a good move, too. Offering help from a hospital, no doubt with strategically placed and desperately ill patients in the background? Definitely a good one. Lili gave him a twisted half smile. "Zo'or would help in a way of his own choosing, not ours. I think that *you* would honor the actual nature of our request."

"Flattery?"

"Truth." She eyed Sandoval's room uneasily. This conversation was over as soon as he emerged. "What do you say?"

"I say," Da'an replied slowly, "that it may be possible to acquire that which you need. But to whom would it be delivered?"

He knew, then. The devices would be used within the Resistance, and she could hardly waltz into the embassy and pick them up herself. But she grinned at him, not at all worried. When conventional means suited the purpose, the Resistance was quite willing to use them. "That," she said, "is what messenger services are for."

Cowley kept his hands in his pockets and lingered by the appliance store display window along with a gaggle of other people on the street. Astonishingly few people, actually— most everybody was at home today. Home sick, or home trying not to get sick.

Cowley found he didn't much care about them one way or the other.

What he cared about was that Da'an was in the news. Making noises about the newshound rumors of an aborted abduction at County Hospital today, although their vid footage showed no more than an extremely rumpled Agent Sandoval emerging from a hospital room—brief vid footage at that, for he'd put his hand up and someone to the side— that woman pilot, he'd bet, the one with all the legs and chest, she always seemed to be lurking in the background when Sandoval was in the news—had pulled the cameras down so they showed an instant of blurred legs and feet and went dark.

The newsies could have edited the blurry jumble out. They'd left it to show how crassly they'd been treated. Cowley didn't care about them, either—what did they expect, sticking their cameras in everyone's faces?

The others around him had heard enough, and moved on to whatever business they'd been about, but Cowley hung around and listened to the recap. "Again, Da'an announced his intentions to appear publicly at County Hospital tomorrow to bring his offer of Taelon help to the people. World leaders have repeatedly refused such help, citing issues of trust in their belief that the Taelons delayed revealing their knowledge of the virus origins . . ."

Whatever. Cowley knew the origins of the virus; he'd never had any doubt. Neither would anyone else around here, if they'd just open their eyes instead of being led around like the Taelon version of sheep.

Just maybe, he'd help open some of those eyes tomorrow when he killed Da'an on the steps of the hospital.

Or maybe not.

He really didn't care.

THIRTEEN

Stunned by the shaqarava of a Resistance member.

For some reason, this particularly annoyed Sandoval. He'd been shot at, he'd been flung into sharp and damaging objects, he'd been stuffed in a Kimera cocoon, he'd had his skrill ripped off, he'd nearly lost himself to a failing CVI.

But Resistance with shaqarava?

He was definitely in a bad mood.

And he'd evidently left the hospital too soon, just as Captain Marquette had suggested upon helping secure his seat restraints in the shuttle. The mildly variegated blue walls around the workstation seemed to pulse at him; the sweeping support ribs of the bridge made him feel slightly dizzy. Marquette, rather than going off on her own, pursued her work in the background on a secondary station; he felt her gaze upon him. That, too, irritated him. The day he needed coddling was the day he'd . . . he'd . . .

He'd probably make a fatal error. There were, after all, so many of them available for him to make.

Sandoval tried again to focus on the datastream before him; damned things could be hazy at the best of times, and he'd long suspected the Taelons perceived them differently than humans. Giving up, he switched to a flat screen display in the workstation, which was little better. All those dots . . .

Marquette had also suggested that the only reason he was on his feet at all was because of the recuperative powers his CVI gave him, and that he shouldn't push it. He'd snapped at her, of course. It didn't mean she wasn't right. He rubbed his eyes and reapplied himself. In the background, Marquette snatched her global on the first beep and apart from her greeting responded only with a short affirmation, sounding inordinately pleased; he heard the global slide shut with a satisfied snap. One of several incoming calls since they'd returned . . . it crossed his mind to remind her that personal calling privileges were not to be abused. All too vaguely, he wondered what she was up to.

But he had his own problems. Problems that now coalesced before him, represented by the single being who approached. Zo'or.

Sandoval drew himself up. He was lucky he'd had this much time at his own pursuits. On the other hand, it probably meant Zo'or had been occupied with the Synod, an activity which—given the circumstances—was not likely to have put him in a pleasant mood.

Zo'or walked up with a formal posture that only emphasized his androgynous nature, his hands held stiffly in a neutral carriage at hip level. "Agent Sandoval," he said, to which Sandoval stood straighter and clasped his hands behind his back, the only response for which Zo'or allowed him time. "I am given to understand that you have failed me."

"We had an unexpected setback—"

"Did you or did you not fail to acquire the subjects I provided for you?"

Sandoval hesitated. "The Resistance anticipated our move. I have reports that they were at every hospital and clinic. Had Captain Marquette been watching the door more carefully—"

"Against one armed with shaqarava? *You* are the one

gifted with a CVI. You are the one who can be expected to overcome such an opponent."

"None of us expected the Resistance would have working shaqarava at their disposal," Sandoval said. "Not at this stage. You gave me no warning of this possibility, Zo'or."

Zo'or's eyes narrowed; for a moment Sandoval thought he'd overstepped that fine line. One of the things Zo'or liked about Sandoval was his refusal to accept defeat, but one could only take that so far when dealing with a being who considered himself superior. Zo'or's next words surprised him.

"This woman truly had full control over the shaqarava?" He didn't wait for an answer. "If this is so, we have less time than expected to produce an antivirus. Once the retrovirus completes its process, we cannot simply 'cure' those who have it. We will become enmeshed in tracking down those newly endowed humans and disposing of them. It will be a disaster." He gave Sandoval a sharp look. "Ta'en will simply have to continue his work without airborne-contaminated subjects. Meanwhile, I will make the necessary arrangements with new families; you will acquire those subjects as soon as possible."

From behind him, Marquette said, "But I thought Da'an was making a public appeal tomorrow. Wouldn't it look better if we gave the president a chance to officially accept—"

"I have no intention of waiting for Da'an *or* your president," Zo'or said. "If President Thompson had not taken the lead in refusing our help, none of this would be necessary in the first place."

"Yes, Zo'or," Sandoval said. "And if the Resistance is waiting again . . ."

"Then take care of it," Zo'or snapped. "If they choose to use shaqarava against us, then they will pay the consequences."

Of course, Sandoval thought, but it was a muzzy thought, and Zo'or and the workstation both seemed to lose stability. He grabbed for it, steadying it. Or maybe steadying himself. In the background, Marquette's global beeped; she instantly slapped the mute.

Zo'or looked at him with alarm. "Have you brought the virus here? We cannot afford to have our human support crew infected—"

"Maybe someone should have thought of that before the virus was released on Earth," Sandoval muttered, clutching the indistinct workstation.

Zo'or's response came in a dangerous purr. "I do not believe I heard you correctly, Agent Sandoval."

Marquette rushed up behind him, her slender fingers firm on his upper arms. "He took a pretty hard stun," she said, her voice hurried. "In his rush to serve you, he left the hospital before the doctors wanted him to. Let me take him to rest."

"Do that," Zo'or said, words fraught with warning. "I trust he'll be recovered in time to collect our new subjects."

"I'm sure he will be," Marquette said. She waited until Zo'or's unfocused form moved away, and then applied a guiding pressure to his shoulders. "Let's get you somewhere horizontal," she muttered.

Perhaps a good idea. Except his gaze, in a moment of clarity, caught the display on his workstation. The tag distribution map . . . except it had changed. Was *changing*. He frowned at it. "Wait," he said. "That's not right—"

Her hands didn't disappear. "Whatever it is," she said, "you'll figure it out later. If you don't rest *now*, you won't be able to act when Zo'or demands it."

In one thing, she was right—failing Zo'or could not be allowed to happen. But he could swear . . . the tag traces were growing denser within the affected cities, beginning to obscure the intense gatherings at the clinics, and at the unidentified area he now so strongly believed to be a Resistance gathering. Resistance with developing shaqarava . . .

"Let's go," Marquette said, and her voice didn't have the proper amount of respect in the least. More like an exasperated adult to a child . . .

Sandoval pulled out of her grip, turning to berate her . . . and found himself sliding gently down the workstation to the floor.

She looked down at him, hands on hips, and sighed with much exasperation. With more strength than he would have given her credit for, she grabbed his arm, fitted it over her shoulder, and pulled him upright, muttering, "You should have just listened to me and stayed down in the hospital in the first place."

He was beginning to agree.

"Move, move, move!" Hayley's bellow sounded out across the warehouse, which little resembled the organized conclave it had been even moments earlier. Augur stood in the doorway of the medical lab area and caught her arm as she jogged by, deeply intent on some goal.

"What's going on?" he demanded. "We're just starting to make some headway here—I think they're on to something!"

"Yeah, well so is Sandoval," she said, giving her arm a pointed look; he released her. Behind her, two men in hospital gowns and jeans pushed a third patient on a gurney. "It's finally occurred to him that not all of the tagbot gatherings are clinic locations. We've got to get out of here before he tracks us down here. I'm dispersing what's left of us to the street clinics."

"Oh, yeah," he said. "We're going to blend right in."

GENE RODDENBERRY'S EARTH: FINAL CONFLICT

"You got a better idea?"

"As a matter of fact, I do," he said. "Which should come as no surprise. You have a fallback location?"

"Of course." She didn't like to be questioned, that much was clear. She had that in common with Liam; so often he had the insight to provide solutions, and just as often he found it impossible to explain why. As if his daddy's extra DNA wasn't explanation enough. She nodded her head to the east, an unconscious giveaway of the new hideout. "I've just come from there. All the equipment will be trucked to the new location, since none of it's tagged."

"Then I think you should send your sickest people there, too," Augur said. "Keep it in the family, and out of the public clinics where the Taelons can round them up."

"Aren't you listening? Sandoval will know it's not a new bona fide clinic showing on his map. He'll just come after us there."

Augur held up a finger, a *wait here* gesture, and caught a glimpse of her impatient reaction as he ducked back inside the lab. He returned with his hands full: tagbot vial and quick-shot. "We've been busy while you were gone," he said, justifiably pleased with himself. "These arrived, courtesy of Da'an and several relay couriers. Handy little things, aren't they? You don't even feel the shot go in. Which explains how they infected so many people without anyone knowing about it."

"You've started tag distribution?" Hayley said—more of a demand, really, but what did she say that wasn't?

"Bingo." Augur hefted the little treasures in his hand. "By the time you get settled in the new place, this whole city will be one big blot of tagbots on Sandoval's scope."

She hesitated; he wasn't sure over what. Then she said abruptly, "Good. I've got something to do. You know how to handle touchy equipment—make sure the doctors get moved with the least amount of disruption."

He frowned. "Yeah, but I don't exactly take orders from you."

"Then consider it a favor." She was relentless, he had to give her that.

Not that he still didn't find himself resistant. "And you'll be doing what, while I baby-sit the docs?"

She looked down at her hands and their quiet shaqarava. "I'm not sure," she said. "But . . . helping, I hope." And she turned on her heel and left.

"Oh, fine," Augur said. "Be specific, why don't you." But she was gone, and after a moment he sighed, grabbed a few sturdy-looking men and women, and began issuing his own orders.

Peter Bellamy rubbed the back of his neck, turning it into a stretch; for a moment he just sat on the low padded lab stool, not caring if Ta'en did turn around and see him taking this much-needed break.

Taelons often forgot that the human body had needs different from their own. That the human soul had needs different from their own—though they understood those needs well enough when it suited them, and then they twisted their human employees in the grip of those needs, wringing out loyalty that Bellamy would have given freely, had he been allowed the opportunity.

Not loyalty beyond that to his own species, however, or beyond that to his own *family*. That's where the Taelons erred, in thinking they could control that loyalty with threats and coercion.

The moment they had introduced their oblique threats

to his little Eileen—their references to their hopes for her continued well-being, that her cured blindness would remain so—they had lost any loyalty he'd once had. And they'd apparently thought him too lacking in imagination and initiative to do anything about it.

Wrong again.

He rose from the stool, stretching again.

"Have you completed your task?" Ta'en asked, swiveling to look at him in the way the Taelons had of moving their entire upper bodies when a twist of the shoulders would do.

Bellamy glanced down at his display screen, where he'd been cataloging other known viral mutations from contact-borne to airborne, with the hope of finding a pattern they could assign to the shaqarava retrovirus that Ta'en had piggybacked on what he considered a benign and stable flu template. "I'm almost done," he said. "But I have bodily needs to attend to."

That did it, as he knew it would. Bellamy wasn't sure how the energy-based beings dealt with intake and elimination, and he didn't care. All that mattered was that they were elitist about mammalian needs, and it was one subject on which he wouldn't be queried.

Because along with availing himself of the special human facilities, he also found a quiet nook and pulled out his global, hitting the autocode for his home.

The nanny answered, justifiably surprised to hear from him. He never called during work hours, which of late had been almost around the clock. "Mr. Bellamy!"

"Just listen," he said. "I want you to pack up a small suitcase for Eileen. And make up a travel pack." The indispensable backpack containing snacks, activity books, and a favorite stuffed animal . . . Eileen wouldn't go on a trip without it. "Make sure there are plenty of healthy snacks in it. Keep these in the closet by the front door."

The woman hesitated, and then asked, "Should I prepare her . . . ?"

"Yes. As we talked about last year. And . . . you might want to think about joining us." He'd told her that before, too. She was too closely associated with their household not to come under scrutiny if he walked off this ship and didn't return. Her own extended family lived in France and she was accustomed to long absences from them; in time she might even return to them.

She merely nodded. The less said, the better, and she knew that, too. Along with the fact that it might be days before anything actually happened . . . or it might be minutes.

Bellamy was betting on something in between.

Until then, he'd go back to work. Maybe Ta'en would come up with an antivirus for this contagion before Earth's population had changed irrevocably, and maybe he wouldn't; maybe the researchers on Earth would provide their own solution.

And maybe not.

Either way, Bellamy was done here. It had become less safe to stay than it was to leave, a moment he had feared.

But one he'd hoped for, too.

FOURTEEN

Liam woke and stared, uncomprehending and dazed, at the high
ceiling of the loft. He was himself—for now—and not stuck
in the world of Kimera and Kaluuet. That self—for now—
was Liam Kincaid. That self was sick, and becoming lost in
the sickness.

Face it. Eventually, that self wasn't going to come back
from one of these memories. And *eventually* wasn't all that
far away.

It angered more than frightened him. Kimera. The last of
his kind, and it was killing him. *It didn't have to be this way.*
"Dammit, Ha'gel," he muttered, "you should have left an in-
struction book." And then laughed at himself, short and sharp.

It was enough to get him, if not to his feet, at least sitting
up, fumbling to toe off his shoes and divest himself of his
jacket, scarf and gloves, and the blankets he'd pulled over
them. That still left him hot, and though he knew it was false
warmth, that the fever would chill him again without warning,
he pulled off his shirt, too. Then he defied gravity to stand;
the room rolled around but didn't quite collapse on him.

Shaqarava. They had protected him; they had defended
him. They forged a path for Da'an to rejoin the Commonality; they recaptured Augur's life essence as it slipped away
and held it long enough for Augur to snatch up a new
breath. They were his *strength*, not his weakness.

Or they were supposed to be.

Weren't they?

He stumbled more than walked to the sink, knocked his toothbrush to the floor and left it rather than risk bending over, and filled a glass with water. The moment the liquid touched his lips he became ravenous for it, and drank it fast and carelessly, spilling the water down his chest. Another glass and a half and he was just as suddenly slaked; he left the half-empty glass sitting precariously on the edge of the stainless-steel sink.

Shaqarava. He had seen what they did for and to the Atavus; he had seen them use it in love and hunger and fear; he'd seen them comfort one another with its touch. But what had the *Kimera* been able to do with it? What secrets was he still hiding from himself?

And how stupid if he had the means to save himself and didn't, like a man dying for lack of air with his hand on the knob of an oxygen tank.

He glanced at the bed and its rumpled mess of blankets and clothes; he didn't want to go back there. He'd had enough of it. And yet the memories murmured at him, demanding his attention. Clawing at his ability to think. He made his slow way to the rail that edged the loft, looking out over the spare furnishings below. There was little of a truly personal nature there; the thoroughly modern shelves and wall hangings reflected Augur's tastes as much as his own, simply because for the first part of his life, Augur's decor and Taelon architecture had made up the bulk of his experience. Most of the furnishings were rejects from the bar—a long wavy-edged stand-alone bar running just below the railing of the second floor, with two different levels that he used for a work surface, old overhead coffee bean dispensers now filled with M&M's, the similar wet bar counter next to the kitchenette. Eclectic, yes . . . but there was nothing to indicate who he was, even in the short time he'd been alive.

Maybe because I don't know *who I am.*

As ever, that's what it seemed to come down to. He longed for Siobhan Beckett's assured confidence with her place in the world. In *her* world. No matter that she'd made mistakes along the way; she'd always known who she was. *Sowelo.* She'd worn the rune around her neck; she'd truly lived it. *The force within that guides you on your path.* She would grieve, he thought, that he so often felt lost from that force. "Don't worry about it," he told her. "You gave me *othila.* You gave me everything you had." And so had Ha'gel; he had simply neglected to let Liam know how to access it. "A sense of being connected to heritage and kin," he said out loud, and then laughed, a little over the edge even to his own ears. To have so much of it, and yet so little . . .

Fire washed through his chest, sparking along his arms; the laugh turned to a gasp as his knees gave out on him. A muted glimmer of energy flickered along the lines of his arm, blue lightning flashing briefly under his skin. He stared in a fascinated kind of horror, and was staring still as the agony surged through his body again, collapsing him the rest of the way to curl around himself on the cold iron floor with no strength left to fight the memories.

Death.

They'd sought only to give the Kaluuet life, and in the end, death had found the species anyway. Or the death of its nature, as it split into factions that evolved away from each other, leaving little of the actual Atavus itself.

And then death had turned on the Kimera.

This Kimera-within, a female newly assigned, was trapped in the lowlands when it started.

Here the Taelanon tribe had moved, refocusing their efforts to change the environment to their liking . . . encouraging foliage, altering the water cycles to retain more on the land. Here had come the original members of the commonality, many centuries earlier, bringing with them that infamous Kimera-within who had made their commonality possible in the first place—and making their knowledge of other Kimera-within such as herself clear. Making their intolerance of Kimera study just as clear; duty on this planet had now become danger-fraught, and was left to only the most expert of the Kimera anthropologists.

By now the Kaluuet had completed its species polarization . . . those who chose to convert to energy forms had done so, and those being born into the commonality were already a part of it from the moment of conception. The others . . . the Jarideens now crowded the opposite end of the continent, immersed in their fiercely joyful way of life . . . slowly learning control over their urges, but not abandoning them. They bred freely and swiftly, and despite themselves were spreading toward Taelanon territory.

There were few Kaluuet left in this area. This Kimera-within was one, unwilling to join the commonality in her study of this emerging race, knowing as such that her time on the planet was limited. She stayed in the crude, unaligned tribe who clung to the Taelanons, living in the thatched huts—for the climate had turned too wet for the sun-baked clay roofing—and working under the magenta-tinted sky.

She was excruciatingly careful in her studies. She did nothing to draw attention to herself. She had taken the form of an older being, and her responsibilities were few. There were no young ones to care for; those who wanted to breed in the tradition of the Kaluuet had taken themselves to Jarideen territory. Their arts had been absorbed by the Taelanon community; all that remained was to feed themselves, and the converted ones controlled even this, meting out hunts like misers, governing the resources around them.

The remaining Kaluuet meant little to them besides a lesser species to be tolerated and in many ways patronized. Kimera-within, as an aging Kaluuet, was among the population to which they paid very little attention.

So she was astonished when she saw one of the converted heading for her—astonished and not a little bit alarmed, for rarely did they leave their own complex compound singly, and even more rarely did they approach the Kaluuet as individuals. Crouched by a fire, mixing an herbal paste to treat one of the other Kaluuet whose recent injury had become infected, she was in no position to rise quickly, not with these old bones.

But the Taelanon saw her distress and made a quick and soothing gesture. "Be at ease," he said, his movement causing a shimmering ripple in the thin, sheer layers of his robes, currently much in vogue among the converted.

Or *she* said. There was no telling what this one had once been, although it never seemed to bother the Taelanons themselves.

Slowly, Kimera-within relaxed, but she put the crude bowl of paste aside. Within the converted compound they were experimenting with more advanced materials than this woven, clay-lined bowl, but they saw no need to share their advances with the dwindling Kaluuet.

The dying Kaluuet, neither Jarideen or Taelanon.

"How," she asked, lowering her head slightly, "may I serve you?"

"By not serving me at all." The converted's mouth twitched in a more individualistic expression than many of them made. "I have been watching you. I am of your own kind at heart."

"Within?" she whispered.

He inclined his head; it was too slow to call a nod. "I come with warning."

Deep inside, fear stirred in response to his words. "They have changed so much," she whispered.

He shook his head. "Perhaps not. Perhaps this was there to see from the beginning, had we so chosen. Their refusal to deliberately cause harm to one of their own speaks not of compassion or loyalty, but of an intensely high drive for species survival. Under the influence of such a drive, they do not hesitate to kill that which is not their own."

"And they have redefined what they consider their own," she said, half guessing—but guessing with many lifetimes full of memories within her.

Again he inclined his head, but this time he did not return his gaze to her; he looked off over the compound. "For these," he said, "anything outside of the commonality does not count as their own, despite common origins."

"Still," she said, "none of these others—the Jarideens, those Kaluuet who remain here—are of any threat to them. Nor are we, for all that they harbor ill will against us. Do they not require even a justification for their behavior?"

He bestowed upon her another quirky smile, a deeply wry expression. "Ah, but they have one. They fear for their commonality."

"That we—our *true* community—would dissolve what we once created?"

"That very thing."

She shook her head. "We are certainly capable of such. And I cannot say that I disagree with the notion. But it would take an act such as yours, an individual act. We will come to no consensus over such an extreme step."

"It was rare enough that we did so in time to bestow the shaqarava on this species in the first place," he admitted.

She stared at him a long moment, her neck grown uncomfortable with the angle of looking up at him. "What of you?" she whispered, as much of a whisper as this harsh voice could manage. "Do you think of it?"

He took an even longer moment before responding. "I fear to answer you," he said. "There is much I can hide from the commonality, but . . . I think, not enough."

She hid her leathery, coarse features in her taloned hands, unable to absorb the implications of his statement without intense grief for what her own people had come to. This was not the Kimera, they who traveled the galaxies in search of life to catalog and share. Not even of late, when they had been forced to concentrate so tightly on this one species; never was it their intent to mire themselves in the development of a species so closely that they could not quietly retreat, leaving no mark.

They had left their mark on the Kaluuet. Perhaps they deserved to pay the price.

"You must return to the others," he said to her, finally intruding on her pain. "I have not been able to reach others within; I am under close supervision at all times, and cannot delay any longer here, lest I put you in danger." *As I have others before.* But he didn't have to say that; they both had the memories of it, intense memories of death-within-Kaluuet that he had contributed to the Kimera racial memory. "But you must not delay. Leave this place now." And so saying, he did the same, walking serenely away—not toward the compound, which would have assigned this conversation the significance it deserved and perhaps betrayed her, but toward the developing lake where many of the converted lost themselves in meditation.

Do not delay. There would be no worry about that. All Kimera-within wanted now was to escape this planet.

Someone had to warn the Kimera of what was to come.

She left the paste by the fire and gathered what she would need for the tiring journey to the place of contact, still carefully hidden from the Taelanons after all this time. And as she left her hut for the last time, choosing to maintain this form for her own safety until she was extracted from this planet, she turned once to look back at the Taelanon compound, with its living vine structures and the constant wink of energies in play. "Good-bye, Ha'gel," she said. "May you fare better than I think you might . . . and perhaps better than you deserve."

·   ·   ·

Hayley strolled into the Flat Planet, amused to find it so similar to the one she'd once visited in Denver. Big curving red bar, a modest gathering of tables, the dance floor, the currently unoccupied bandstand . . . all with the same stamp. Augur clearly bought in bulk.

But she was only briefly amused, for she had other things on her mind.

She knew Liam's apartment was here somewhere. With a glance at the late-afternoon patrons, she went to the un-populated bar, resting upon it the thermos she carried. An Asian woman in an excessively tight silver outfit stood at the opposite end of it, issuing orders to a young blond woman who absently wiped the same glass clean over and over. Naive, Hayley pegged it right off. She had a soft look to her pretty features, and what Hayley thought of as a Bambi eye. Either she had no idea the Resistance hung out here, or she was much, much better than Hayley gave her credit for.

When the Asian woman was through with her, the blonde noticed Hayley and came over with a smile, al-though the thermos clearly had her baffled. "What can I get for you?"

Hayley said, "Directions. There's an apartment in here somewhere; I need to get to it. Which door do I take?" If this *was* anything like the Denver Flat Planet, there were a plethora of little back rooms she could waste time exploring.

The blonde's eyes narrowed slightly. "Liam's apart-ment, you mean?"

"That would do it," Hayley said.

"He's sick," the blonde said, as if that was an answer.

"No kidding." Hayley leaned her elbows on the bar with an expression that any one of her Resistance cell members would have known to avoid. "The question is, where's his apartment? Because I can go around kicking doors in, but I don't think your boss would like that very much."

The blonde blinked, an uncertain look, her gaze flickering out to the floor; Hayley interpreted it as a cry for help. She was right, to judge by the speed with which the Asian woman appeared. On second glance, the silver thing actually worked. Somehow.

"Problem?" the woman said, her accented voice mild— although Hayley heard the steel beneath it. Good. Someone she could deal with.

"I'm trying to find Liam's apartment."

"Ah," said the woman. "Here's the thing—when he wants someone to visit, he tells them just where he is."

"Okay." Hayley shrugged, picking up the thermos and counting three obvious doors right off the bat. "Kicking doors it is. You just tell Augur to put it on my tab. Because Liam's sick, and while *you* can't help him"— she nodded at the blonde—"and *you* can't help him"— a nod to the Asian woman— "*I* can. And I'm probably the *only* one who can."

The woman gave her a startlingly dismissive wave, along with a little hissing sound. "Oh, one of *you*. That door there." And she pointed to one Hayley hadn't yet noticed, quietly set in a nook to the left of the bar.

"Kwai Ling—" the blonde said, as if this hadn't been what she expected when she so discreetly signaled for backup.

"Piffle," Kwai Ling said, and nothing more; she headed back for the floor, where she'd apparently been in discussion with a band rep next to the dance floor.

Obviously, Taelon Flu or not, life went on at the Flat Planet.

Hayley gave the blonde a little shrug and picked up her thermos. The blonde abruptly said, "Wait!" and went to work behind the bar, filling a large mug with a carefully measured mix of coffee and thick hot chocolate. "He likes these," she said, pushing it across the bar to Hayley. "Tell him Suzanne sent it in."

Hayley raised her eyebrows, took the coffee, and headed for Liam's apartment without comment. Someone had a crush on someone, she'd bet on it.

Too bad someone was totally without a clue.

Or maybe not.

She tucked the thermos in her elbow and knocked on Liam's door; once, twice . . . no answer. He had to be here. As luck would have it, the door was unlocked when she tried it; with a glance at Suzanne—yes, she was watching—Hayley let herself in.

"Liam?" she said, closing the door behind her and taking the liberty of locking it as it should have been. Still no answer; she took a moment to orient herself. Whatever she'd been expecting, this wasn't it. She found the recliner she'd seen him in, and the wall screen he'd used for those calls, the giant bank of windows looming in the background. Wet bar/kitchenette—she deposited thermos and coffee cup along with a bakery bag that upon inspection held handmade chocolates—a barely noticeable sleek black leather couch along one wall that looked like it didn't get much use, and then this multilevel work table curving sinuously across the room.

Add the gleam of glass and metal, the plethora of thick candles, and the odd silver interior walls—soundproofing?—and visually, it was hard to hold together as a whole.

She wandered over to the work table; his slim portable computer sat unopened on top of it. From there she saw the stairs—they hadn't registered as stairs at first, so tightly spiraled, all open metal structure—and followed them to the open catwalk flooring of the loft.

Something shadowed the light trickling down through

the flooring. Almost above her, a dark form curled in upon itself, not moving.

"Liam!" she breathed, and ran for the stairs. So still, so still—*be breathing*—

Yes. Still breathing.

She knelt by him, afraid to touch him at first—the energy play beneath his skin was eerie and unlike anything she'd seen at the clinic, his breathing shallow and erratic and strangely matched to that flickering light. He lay shirtless and dressed in the worn jeans she'd seen the night before, curled around his hands, obviously crumpled on the spot with the hard iron catwalk floor offering nothing to pad the fall. "God, Liam, you should have called," she muttered. "You should have *called* before it got this bad!"

Maybe he hadn't had the chance.

"Dammit," she muttered, her hand hovering to touch his shoulder and then not daring. She covered her face to think, then abruptly lifted her head to look around. There, there was the bed, a simple thing with no head or footboards, shoved up against the wall with the covers thoroughly trashed and mixed in with what looked like the rest of his clothes. Nothing else up here but the sink and a shower stall, a chair . . . stark. And the bed was farther away than she cared to drag him when she wasn't even sure how to touch him.

Touch him, then. Find out.

Her hand was shaking. It remembered what had happened before. She clenched it, willed it to stop, and then reached for him.

Nothing met her but the cold, clammy skin of his back. Too cold, way too cold. Her natural assurance took over, along with the hours of practice she'd had in the clinic, hours of careful shaqarava energy offerings to those who needed it most.

Inching closer, she carefully pulled him up over her

knees, running her hands across the width of his shoulders, down his spine. Taking in the feel of him as he was, for when she activated her shaqarava, she would experience only the pull of the energies. Solid weight and size across her thighs, smooth skin, bone and muscle beneath, all trembling with the uncertain nature of his breathing.

Don't waste any more time. She closed her eyes and tapped into the warmth that now lived within the center of her being. A small spot, still growing by the day, but consistent and welcoming; she asked only for the quietest it could offer. The warmth spread to her arms and hands; when she opened her eyes it glowed serenely within her palms.

A regular Florence Nightingale. She rested her hand at the base of his neck, there where the hair grew long and curled in a little cowlick that matched the boyish grin he offered far too seldom, and swept it down the length of his spine.

Be enough, she told the energy. *Be enough.*

If only for a reprieve.

Something of the real world touched him. Bringing him back partway, enough to realize he wasn't quite on the floor anymore. Soothing warmth spread across his shoulders and down his back, easing the muscles, trickling in energy. Enough that his body, in the process of rallying, regained the strength to respond to the surges of internal lightning— it caught him unaware, streaking from center to arms like a razor racing across his nerves; he grunted in surprise, clenched in its grip with muscles corded, gripping his own ribs as though he could squeeze the torment out.

But the warmth flooded through him with insistence, and when the pain released him, leaving him panting and half sobbing with relief, he finally began to recognize the real-world elements around him. A hand, gently stroking down his bare back, offering the healing energy his body so readily absorbed. An arm crossing under his upper chest, awkwardly holding him in place over folded legs.

Someone had found him on the floor, pulled him into his . . . no, *her* . . . lap, and was . . . what? How? He pushed himself up to figure the puzzle out, but the hand on his back stayed him.

"No," she said. "Just a few more moments."

It was a voice much more troubled than he was used to, enough so that it took him a moment to recognize it, and even then he wasn't sure. He mumbled, "Hayley?"

"Yes. Be still. This isn't a cure, but we've had plenty of experience to know how much it helps."

That sounded more like her. And in truth, he wasn't in any great hurry to move. He relaxed into her grip and let her wash him with the controlled energy of her shaqarava. Something to remember, this. If he had the chance. *This isn't a cure.* Of course not. That would be too easy. *What of the others?* What of the tagbots and an antivirus?

They were things he should ask . . . and he would. In a moment. His mind cleared rapidly, but the rest of him was too relieved by the surcease of struggle to climb to his feet and start shooting questions at her.

And then her touch changed. Something subtle, something that warmed him more than soothed him and made him want to . . . to—

He shoved himself off her lap and to his knees, and found her looking down at her hands with a sheepish expression.

"Oops," she said, and her voice again was different, lower than normal. "I'm not sure how that happened."

"I'm not sure I care," he said, taking in the strain in her face—she'd given much to him, and it showed—and the flush that settled over her features as she again glanced at her hands, opening and closing them as if testing what she'd felt through them, her eyes gone dark as she looked up once more. She raised an eyebrow at him. Cocky Hayley.

He didn't even think about it. He felt his own expression change—acceptance of the challenge, just the same as he'd given her when they'd made the run for the wall at Second Chances. And he kissed her. He took her in with the gentleness of a man's first kiss . . . and the hunger of a man with the memories of a thousand kisses. He captured her head in his hands and kissed her again, and this time when her hands ran down his sides there was no question at all what kind of energy she shared with him. This time when he trembled, it had nothing whatsoever to do with pain.

The Atavus had felt this. So had the Jaridians.

But never the Taelons.

She didn't give him time for second thoughts. No, not Hayley. And response hummed through him, growing into raw hunger, his hands working into her short hair as the energy within him surged, suddenly zinging through his arms—

Hayley's eyes opened wide; he felt the lashes move against his own skin. Not wide with any kind of pleasure, but *alarm* as she stiffened against him and the shaqarava power tingled into internal lightning—

He threw himself aside, landing outstretched on the hard iron-latticed floor as his wayward shaqarava discharged unbidden. Then he rolled onto his back and just lay there, breathing like he'd just crossed a finish line, tumbled up with so many different sensations he couldn't even begin to untangle them.

Hayley eased over to his side, eyeing the floor just beyond him, her expression a mingling of leftover alarm and dry amusement. "Nice hole in your floor," she said, wrinkling her nose at the smell of hot metal. "That was a little *premature*, wasn't it?"

He stared at her a moment, not quite understanding the humor behind that comment and in no condition to go searching memories for clues.

Hayley laughed out loud, brief as it was. "Never mind. If we're lucky, I'll have the chance to explain it to you later."

Fine by him. "Augur's going to kill me," he said, and realized the irony of it. "If he gets the chance."

She leaned over and gave him a quick, hard kiss. "Well, I'm not sorry," she said. "You get what you take out of life, whatever else is going on." She rested a hand on his chest, watching it rise and fall with his breathing. Then, with regret and one last caress, she stood, holding out a hand to help him up. "You were shivering when I got here," she said. "Much as I hate to say it, put a shirt on before you chill again. And you should eat something, if you feel up to it—I brought some soup from the clinic. Get it down while you still feel like it."

He reached for her hand, letting her do the brunt of the work as he struggled to rise from the floor; she set her feet solidly and didn't seem to find it too much of an effort. "Soup?"

She shrugged. "We had to move on short notice—better than throwing it out. It's been the easiest for our people during the worst of it, and I spiced it with electrolytes and neutricals. It's downstairs by the microwave. Big kitchen you've got in this place, by the way."

He found his turtleneck on the bed and pulled it on. "Who needs a kitchen with the Flat Planet next door? I'm not here often enough to use one, anyway."

"Yeah, well, the Flat Planet is pretty much closed," Hayley told him, pulling out her global. "Since the virus went airborne, there aren't enough people out to—"

He almost missed it, thinking of what had passed between them, from the gift of energy—however long it might last—to the more humanly intense exchange. Definitely thinking of the feel of— "Since the virus did *what*?"

She finger-combed her hair back into place—more or less—with one hand. "You really *have* been out of touch," she said. "Things have happened. Things *are* happening—"

Da'an on the steps of a building, people screaming, an energy blast—

"Liam?"

He shook off the foresight. "I'm okay," he said. Or not, but for now as close as he'd get, and not about to lose the moments. "Bring me up-to-date."

She gave him what could only be described as a regretful look, and then seemed to shake it off, turning into Hayley the Resistance cell leader. "Back to business, then. The short version—the virus has gone airborne, the Taelons are in a panic that their little experiment is out of hand but still not admitting they had anything to do with it, the public is in a panic, Doors thinks it's the best thing to happen since the Taelons landed and is setting up a guy named Art Wells to challenge Lili for Resistance leadership—"

Now *that* didn't slip by him. "Counts me gone already, does he?"

The anger on her face was meant for Doors. "That, or he's just taking an opportunity to bypass you. He's never been happy about how that decision went down."

"And he's been so careful to hide it," Liam said dryly; that wrung a grin out of her. "Is that it?"

"Not by a long shot. Sandoval's on our trail, thanks to the tagbots, but Augur made more of them and we should be okay now that we've moved." She gave him a rundown on the mechanics of that operation, the confrontation with Sandoval in the hospital, explained the download Lili had received and passed on, and finally added, "And tomorrow

Da'an is appearing at County Hospital to urge humanity to accept Taelon help."

Da'an on the steps of a building, people screaming—

He shrugged it off as if he were shaking snow from his shoulders; Hayley looked at him, but didn't immediately say anything. Then, carefully enough so he knew she'd *wanted* to say something and had used unusual restraint, she told him, "The big thing is this—thanks to our mysterious informant, it looks like the doctors will come up with an antivirus soon. If they do, we have to decide what to do with it."

He paused at the head of the spiral stairs, his hand on the railing, the metal of the top step cold against his toes. "Meaning?"

"Meaning I'm beginning to wonder if Doors isn't right. Things would have gone much differently in that hospital room with Sandoval if I hadn't had my shaqarava. Things would have gone much differently for *you* in these past few moments if I hadn't had them—you should lock your door, by the way."

"Must have slipped my mind," he muttered, his mind focused on her words as he descended the stairs. "You can't seriously be thinking—"

"Wait for Lili and Augur," she said, cutting him off without apology. "Right now, you eat. And don't waste what I gave you; you'll need to be as full of yourself as ever when they get here, if you want to discuss this with them."

He held up his hands in acquiescence in the middle of the first floor, putting himself where she could see him from upstairs. He knew better than to argue when he could already feel the gabble of Kimera memories at the edge of his thoughts and the faint burn of errant shaqarava energies down his arms to his palms.

She'd given him time . . .

But not much of it.

FIFTEEN

Brian Cowley walked the sidewalk in front of County Hospital. Easing back and forth, back and forth, taking notice of when the extra security guard arrived, and that his sidearm was the particle beam gun that the ranking Companion Agents carried.

Yes, Da'an would be here tomorrow, all right.

He knew the front of the hospital by heart, now. Three tiers of five steps each, with a broad landing between each. A long, curving wheelchair ramp off to the right. Immaculate evergreen shrubs lining each set of stairs, a slice of currently bare flower beds alongside the ramp. The lowest landing spread into a welcoming delta of sidewalk, lined with bare-branched plantings that would flower riotously in another month or so.

His wife would have known what kind of bushes they were. Cowley had no idea.

But Cowley knew every crack in the sidewalk, every little weathered crevice that might cause him to stumble or draw attention. He knew which bushes offered the perfect cover for a man on his stomach, sighting from the palm of his own hand. He'd scoped out vantage points for each potential position Da'an might take up—although Cowley was figuring on the spot at the top of the upper tier of steps.

The most dramatic visual for the cameras. Behind him the hospital would tower, a prize of modern architecture with its white stone and gleaming steel lines, made welcoming by pleasantly asymmetrical sections. The parking garage, a low square off to the left. The main doors, with a covered entry area and brick planters, and the hospital itself rising behind it in two different levels—one for the outpatient and labs, another for the inpatient beds. He knew them well, of course. He'd spent plenty of time here before the Taelons had enticed his wife into their ill-fated plans.

Cowley figured he'd let the Taelon complete his speech . . . an ironic act of mercy. Not to mention that his security people would be drawing a deep breath of relief, figuring the time of exposure was ending safely, and the rest of the crowd would be fixated on the Taelon's words, as sheeplike as ever.

Cowley had other things on which to fixate. And finally, after years of obsession, he would be at peace.

He didn't particularly expect to live out the moment. But that, too, would be a kind of mercy.

He was ready for it.

Augur gave Doctors Belman and Park a quick look over his shoulder and walked away from them as he thumbed his global open, the *snick* of it lost in the bustle. The new warehouse was literally in construction around them, just as it took form around the virus victims who were still too sick to help, already ensconced in beds in very much the same general location as they'd been within the old building. Outside this research section, people shouted to one another, conveying directions and *no, don't put that end down yet* and *grab it, grab it!* But those involved in putting up walls around the doctors and their equipment kept their comments muted, trying to be as unobtrusive as possible—thanks to a few pointed words from Augur.

He'd already accompanied the equipment from the old location, stashing the doctors in a hotel for a few much needed hours of sleep while the worst of the chaos worked itself out. They'd needed it; they both looked the better for it. And Julianne Belman had that expression she sometimes got, the one that appeared right before she wrapped her brain around an errant solution.

His work here was pretty well done. Fine by him; he preferred to stay a little more low profile than this. Let Hayley take over from here, whatever she was up to.

Calling him, apparently. His global beeped with an unidentified caller before he coded in his own call; after a moment, the ident flickered through its automatic subroutine and displayed Hayley's ID number. He told it, "Go, incoming," and her face appeared on the small screen. Whatever she'd been doing between then and now, it had wiped the renewed signs of energy from her face and replaced it with fatigue. Although there was a certain bright look in her eyes and a smudginess around her lips . . .

Augur was not slow to pick up on such things, but this once he forbore to say anything. "I was just about to call you," he told her. "Your lab equipment has been moved with tender loving care, and the docs are rested and raring to go. I think they're getting close—"

"Even if they are, we still have to find a way to manufacture and distribute the antivirus," Hayley said, not as moved by his news as he had hoped.

"You really think that's going to be a problem? Hell, even the government can handle that one."

"Which government?" Hayley asked. "The one that until now has taken every chance to cringe submissively at Zo'or's feet? Joshua Doors is the only one who ever took them on straight, and Thompson pushed him out as soon as he could."

Augur shifted uncomfortably. "The U.N., maybe?"

"Right. Remember Russia, Augur? They're putting people to *death* for crimes against the Taelons."

"Hey," he said sharply. "That little incident was wiped from the records—just how did you get your hands on the information?"

She shook her head. "You underestimate the other Resistance cells—just because we're not right there in D.C. But it doesn't matter. What matters is that I'm right about Russia—and who knows how many other countries. If the big tough United States allows itself to be pushed around, you can bet it's a lot harder on the countries who were struggling before the Taelons got here."

He fought a flash of irritation; he didn't like being wrong, and he didn't like that Hayley knew about his arrest in Russia. "Then *you* come up with an answer."

The look she shot him was plain enough—*grow up, little boy!*—but she didn't say anything other than, "I've got people on it. Right now, we've got bigger worries."

"We do?" Augur said, surprised out of his pique. "I thought that one pretty much topped the list." And then he recognized the brick walls behind her, the spare modern lines of the sink in the upper level of the Flat Planet's apartment. "You're with Liam." Someone came up behind Augur, then, moving in close and staying there in an unapologetic eavesdropping position. Hayley saw him, too, to judge by the faint exasperation that appeared on her face. A glance told him all he needed to know—the walking wall, Art Wells. There were others of his size in the Resistance, but no one who'd recently been such a consistent pain in the neck. "Hello, Art," he said, not turning to look at the man.

"Anything you'd care to say to Hayley during *my* conversation with her?"

"Not yet," Art responded.

"This doesn't concern you, Art," Hayley told him, but didn't dwell on his presence. "Augur, I need you here."

"You do?" Augur said, not quite following.

She lowered her voice, brought the global in closer after glancing in what he knew to be the direction of the railing and the first level below it. "Let me put it this way. If you want to talk to Liam again, *you* need you here. You get that?"

He felt like he'd been kicked in the gut. Yes, Liam was sick. *Yes*, everyone was doom-and-gloom about it. But Augur had simply been through too much doom-and-gloom with Liam to take it seriously. Hell, they'd been *dead* together; they'd seen each other's afterlife as sustained by the psycho-kinetic near-death machine the Taelons created. And though Park had even declared Liam dead, Augur could still remember the very *alive* feel of his friend as he hoisted the taller man off his feet with the joy of discovering Park was wrong, wrong, *wrong.*

Well . . . Liam had created his version of the afterlife *without* the machine. But that was just the point—he was always doing the unexpected, from the very moment he'd grown up before Augur's eyes. Augur had somehow . . . come to *expect* it of him. And blinking, suddenly realizing that Hayley was waiting for his response, her expression more understanding than he'd anticipated, he said roughly, "Are you sure?"

Again she glanced over the rail; Liam was there, whatever he was doing. "I found him down," she said. "If I hadn't revived him with the technique we've been using in the clinic, I think you'd already be too late. But it wasn't a cure. It was . . . a temporary reprieve. I think you want to be here before it fades." An odd expression flickered across her face, as if she'd remembered something. "I'm going to call Lili, too—is there anyone else you can think of? We've got some things to talk about . . . I think we need Liam's"—and she looked at Art, obviously reshaping her words—"unique perspective on them while we still have it."

Augur recovered from the initial shock of her announcement. "That's a little cold, don't you think?" he said, his voice just as cold as her intention. But she shook her head, startling him with the glint in her eyes. Were those *tears*? From hard Hayley Simmons?

"Don't make assumptions," she said, and there was a little anger there, too. "Didn't you just get into trouble doing that with what I know? Don't think you can make assumptions about how I feel, either."

Art cleared his throat. *Good timing, buddy*, Augur thought at him, but apparently the man couldn't—or wouldn't—read his annoyed glance. Instead he spoke up. "If there's some kind of discussion going on, I'd like to—"

Hayley didn't let him finish. "That's not necessary," she said. "I've got other calls to make, Augur. Will you be here?"

"Yes," he said, once more distracted by the implications of needing to join her at all. "Of course." He pushed the global against his stomach to close it, and turned around to glare at an unapologetic wall. The wall met his gaze evenly. A wall who'd shown up so recently, and now seemed to feel obliged to stick his nose in everything Resistance, as though he had a perfect right to be involved in leadership decisions.

A wall he'd seen with Jonathan Doors at the hospital.

He said flatly, "Doors is paying you."

To give him credit, Art didn't look surprised or guilty or even regretful. He hesitated only a moment before saying, "Yes."

Okay, now would be a good time to blow the whistle. They didn't need this; they didn't need Doors, and they didn't need his attempts to manipulate the Resistance from the outside. Doors had *made* his choice. Now would be a good time to blow the whistle, but . . . "For what, exactly?" Augur asked. "To get things done his way? Or are you just snooping?"

"A little of that," Art said, shrugging linebacker shoulders. "A little of the other. He wants me in a position to affect major decisions. If he thinks I'm going to be a figurehead for him, he's wrong about that."

"Of *course* he thinks you'll be a figurehead," Augur said, lacing his voice with scorn. "Of *course* he wants you to puppet for him." He eyed Art a moment longer, frowning. There was always an advantage to knowing things that other people didn't . . . sometimes it came in the form of monetary remuneration, sometimes not. But as soon as Augur said something to someone else about the unknown, it became the known; the advantage was gone. "We'll talk about this later," he told Art.

This time, the man showed his surprise; he hadn't missed the significance of those words. After a moment, he nodded. "All right," he said, appraising Augur openly. "We'll talk."

Right now, Augur had somewhere else to be.

Lili left Sandoval still sleeping off the effects of Hayley's shaqarava. "You might want to dial down the next time you nail a Companion Protector," she told Hayley in their brief global conversation, tacking it on after Hayley's suggestion that Lili come see Liam, and come see him *now*. Tackling the subject now, bringing the irritation to her voice, was one way to keep her anxiety hidden from those around her. Those whose questions she didn't want to answer—for if they couldn't hear her words, they could still see her face and catch her tone. "If he hadn't had a CVI, you'd probably have done some serious damage."

"I didn't mean to leave him comfortable," Hayley had said. "He's not dead—what else do you want?"

And while Lili might have wished for more responsiveness from the Resistance cell leader, she couldn't argue that particular point. She simply said, "I'm on my way," and headed for the shuttle dock, glad that the route to the embassy shuttle pads was so ingrained in her mind as to become automatic—for there was plenty else to keep her mind occupied.

Such as the news report that had flashed across her workstation monitor only moments before Hayley's call, citing an increasing number of new virus victims. The airborne version seemed especially virulent, sneaking up as a few days of malaise and then suddenly ripping through body systems, stressing the victims to such a degree that only the strongest would survive.

And, too, she had another anonymous global message to think about. Text again; not even voice with video blackout. *I helped you*, it said. *Now it's time to return the favor. But I need to know I can trust you.*

That was something, demanding a favor and implying mistrust in the next breath. But she understood it; whoever had sent her the virus background information had done it on a gut feeling, and didn't know for sure she was involved or even sympathetic to the Resistance. He—or she, because while Lili had her own gut feelings, she wasn't *certain* of the sender's identity—had left the reply code for an anonymous message storage service; now it was up to her to figure out a way to reassure him without completely giving herself away.

It could be a trap, of course. It might not be the person who sent the virus background at all, but someone who'd found out about it and was trying to snare her. She didn't think so.

But caution ruled, all the same.

When she exited the embassy, she walked a swift half block in the chilly air to the nearest public global booth and left a text message of her own, cold fingers typing awkwardly on the reduced keyboard; the single small lightbulb in the booth did little to offset the looming dusk. *Come to Judiciary Square, your choice of time. Don't expect to leave until you've been verified.*

If it was their informant, he'd be safe enough, and well met. If it was someone with backup around the corner or who didn't check out . . .

Then things wouldn't go so well for him.

She returned to the embassy's private parking area, grabbed her sporty little Mercedes Kompressor, and headed for the southmost part of Georgetown, where the looming brick edifice of the Flat Planet nestled among the other nightlife options of the area. The former warehouse had two panels of towering multipane windows high on each outside third of the front edifice—red brick with two rows of giant, bulging light stone along the bottom. More of that stone, this time in a more refined crenellated pattern, lined the old black double delivery doors in the center of the building, to which there weren't and never had been steps. Neon art-deco lettering over those doors proclaimed the establishment's name; Lili headed to the left corner, where sat a smaller black door labeled ENTRANCE in that same neon-blue.

From the outside, you'd never guess the interior held a sprawling entertainment complex complete with a band stage, secluded nooks for those who wanted to quietly imbibe of their chosen mind-altering chemical, private and public dining areas, a dance floor—and of course, the long swoop of a bar. Not to mention the back rooms that no one knew about, those where Resistance members often passed along information and where Lili herself had had plenty of arguments with Jonathan Doors and William Boone.

Will Boone. It had been bad enough when they'd lost him—when *she'd* lost him. Now, if Hayley was right—she winced at the thought—Liam.

But Hayley wasn't always right. She just always *thought* she was right. Lili took comfort in the fact as she parked the car, set its alarm, and approached the offset door to the Planet, her breath pluming in her wake. One of these days spring would arrive for good—hard to believe they'd had such a nice day for the Fair.

And too bad, too. There'd have been fewer people exposed to the introduction of the virus if everyone had been huddled out of a more typical dreary and drippy day.

Kwai Ling met her in the entry area, backed by an unobtrusive bouncer who, as far as Lili knew, remained naively unaware of the Planet's Resistance connections. Augur's bouncers, of anything in this place, were just what they appeared to be. Questioned, they could reveal nothing. Which was why Kwai Ling, standing there with modified global in hand, greeted her cheerfully and then followed her to the actual bar entrance before saying, "You're not tagged yet, Lili. I don't usually give our customers a choice, but . . ." and opened her palm to display a quick-shot.

Lili gave her head a quick shake. "I'd better not." If she

showed up on the Mothership with a tag, she might be questioned about it, and while she could plead ignorance . . . best if she not draw that sort of attention to herself in the first place.

"That's what I thought," Kwai Ling said wisely. And then, eyeing the unobtrusive door to the left of the bar that led to Liam's apartment, she said, "Give him a smooch for me, then," hesitated, got a wicked look in her eye, and added, "Give him *two* from Suzanne!" and returned to her post by the entrance.

Lili shook her head, glad for even a moment's humor, and slipped through the door.

The others were here, as she expected. She *hadn't* expected to find them gathered in the sparsely furnished lower level of the apartment—Hayley, Augur, and Liam—each with a mug of what looked like tea in hand, and a half-empty bowl of soup on the floor by Liam's bare foot along with a Flat Planet mug. Augur was on his feet—too restless to sit, as often—but Hayley and Liam were parked on the black leather couch along the wall opposite the loft, looking surprisingly casual.

Or maybe not. A second look revealed the hollows under Hayley's eyes; she held the mug wrapped in both hands as if its warmth offered significant succor, and her tightly fitting slacks and combat sweater looked pulled from a laundry bin. Liam, long legs encased in jeans, a rumpled, close-fitting black turtleneck on top, rubbed absently at one arm and then the other, strain setting his face into sharper lines than she'd seen before. She'd expected worse . . . but then, Hayley had said something about reviving him.

But Augur was reassuringly Augur, even if unhappily so; his black and red shirt blasted jagged-edged Batman POW!, BLAM!, and SOCKO! balloons at anyone who could bear to focus on it, and even though he scowled, he looked every bit himself in the process.

An acrid odor hit Lili's nose, disrupting her thoughts. "What's that *smell*?"

Augur rolled his eyes. "Just a little home remodeling," he said, nodded toward the second level; Lili moved closer to him and found light shining through a small hole in the floor of the upper level. "Don't bother to ask. They're not talking, other than to say it was an accident."

The memory of a Texas farmhouse with its side blown out flashed through Lili's mind, and she said, "Could be a lot worse, Augur."

"Easy for *you* to say. It's definitely not up to code anymore." He gestured with his mug. "Hey, you want some tea? It's my own recipe—"

"Will I be able to think clearly once I've had it?" She walked to the spot under the hole, tilting her head to regard it for a long moment. Slaggy metal edges looked down at her. No carpet; the flooring upstairs was strictly functional, no luxury to it at all. Just as well. The fumes from *that* would probably kill them.

"It's *interesting*, Lili, not incapacitating," Augur said. "Would I do anything to mess with my precious gray matter?"

Like hooking yourself into the Taelon Commonality without checking it out first? But out loud Lili said, "Love some, thanks. It'll shake the cold."

"You're not—" Liam started, turning to look at her.

She shook her head quickly. "No. Just plain old fickle spring in D.C., that's all." She came back to the end of the couch by Liam and held out her hand. After a moment, he provided her with his. An ordinary human hand, big to go with his height but built like the rest of him, lean and with the play of muscle and bone evident beneath the skin. Ordinary hands, even with the faint dark areas marking the shaqarava.

Well. They were ordinary if you didn't count the errant surge and ebb of energies at that shaqarava, and the involuntary twitching of his fingers that came with the pain of it. Or—and she closed her grip more firmly around his wrist and pushed up the soft sleeve of his shirt, ignoring his faintly bemused expression at the handling—if you didn't notice the shadowy glimmerings of Taelon-blue energy tracing random pathways under the thinner skin of his forearm. She opened her mouth . . . and closed it again. There wasn't much point. If there was anything anyone could have done about it, it would have already been done. What she did say, finally, catching his eye for a good strong moment, was, "Don't quit."

He hesitated, and for an instant she was afraid he already *had*. That he'd had enough, had *already* quit before Hayley came along and pulled him back with her own . . .

Shaqarava.

But now he looked at her and gave her a slight shake of his head. "No," he said, "I won't."

She wished she didn't have the feeling that he'd made up his mind about that right then and there. But there wasn't anything she could do about it, except hold his gaze a moment longer and give his wrist a squeeze before she released it. He gave her the faintest of smiles in return.

"See now," Augur said. "Art would have been totally out of place." But the faint gathering of his brow between his deep brown eyes belied his cockiness and bespoke his worry, his fear for his friend. And it was not a state he handled with ease—so Lili left him his cockiness and took the mug he handed her. He'd brought it up from the bar, she saw, not surprised that Liam was hardly equipped for entertaining.

"Art?" she said, taking a sip and then hardly noticing the

spicy way the taste crept all the way up her sinuses. "Art *Wells*?"

Augur nodded. "The same." He might have said something else just then, but the moment of hesitation disappeared into more sarcasm. "Hayley's walking wall."

"He's not *my* wall," Hayley said. "I'm not sure, but I have the feeling Doors sicced him on me. That man has some real control issues, you know?"

"I think that's a pretty valid suspicion," Lili said. The apartment wasn't strong on seating; she joined Augur near the wet bar.

"Good, eh?" he said, nodding at the tea.

"What *did* you put in it?" she said, and then quickly shook her head. "Never mind. I don't want to know."

"I'm not telling, anyway," Augur said with a flippant shrug.

Hayley ignored their byplay. "I want you to know I'm not fooled by him," she said. "I don't appreciate anyone who thinks he can shove his way into an organization that relies so heavily on trust."

Liam gave her a wry grin. "Like I did?"

"It seemed that way at first," she admitted. "But you proved yourself."

Augur snorted. "You didn't shove your way anywhere. You were born in the middle of it. You name me anyone else who can say that—Doors included."

Hayley gave an irritable frown, lifting her chin slightly and looking straight at Lili. "And anyway, it's not the issue here. I just want you to know that none of us is susceptible to that sort of power play."

Lili hesitated, glancing at Liam. He didn't rise, which was unlike him; he tended to pace his way through thinking, focused and already heading for action. He shook his head with some impatience and said, "Don't bother talking around it. There's a real possibility that someone else is going to have to coordinate for the Resistance. There's no question in my mind that it should be you. It almost *was*, not so long ago."

But there was some question in *her* mind. *Thanks to Jonathan and his hardline position on ruthless decisions.* "Jonathan said some things to me . . ." she started.

"Oh, let me guess." Liam was never reticent when it came to Jonathan; the trouble between them had started as soon as Liam was born of alien seed within Jonathan's stronghold, culminated in Jonathan's attempt on Liam's life, and finally settled into an uneasy alliance. "As usual, he's as bad as the Taelons when it comes to using people . . . and he doesn't like it that you won't work that way. Am I right?"

"He thinks humanity should be allowed to develop shaqarava . . ." Lili said slowly. "That we shouldn't even try to stop it. And I hate to say it, but I'm beginning to see his point." She gestured at Hayley. "They could be of tremendous benefit to the Resistance."

"On more than one level," Hayley said, glancing quickly at Liam and away, a mere flicker of her eyes. "We pulled a number of Resistance members through this illness who wouldn't have otherwise made it, I'm certain of it."

Lili nodded. "And while Sandoval may be sleeping off your stun, he's not *dead*. If he'd been killed, the Taelons would be all over us."

"Do you know how many people *will* die if they catch this virus?" Liam said, looking askance at them both. "Too many have *already* died!"

Hayley shrugged. "So make it a choice. Those who want the antivirus can have it."

Augur made a dismissive noise, a quick *pfft* of sound. "What makes you think you'll *have* a choice?"

"What do you mean?" Lili didn't like the implications of that, not when he sounded so certain. Augur was full of himself, but . . . he usually had reason to be. He was usually *right*.

"You're all concerned over distributing an antivirus, if the docs ever get one put together. Well, yeah, it's a concern—for those who are already sick, like Liam. *They* need help ASAP. Direct introduction, just like the retrovirus. But I've spent the last little while hanging around the lab, translating that file for them, watching them work. Now that they have the background materials, they're doing just what the Taelons did—they're piggybacking the important package on top of a mild existing virus. And no one's told *them* that we might not want it to be communicable. *They're* thinking in terms of keeping the human race *human*."

"In other words," Liam said, "once it's released, it's out of our hands. Anyone who wants it can make sure they get it . . . but anyone who *doesn't*, won't have that choice."

Augur spread his arms in a *don't shoot the messenger* gesture. "That's how it looks to me. I suppose you could ask them to start over, but don't count on *me* to be anywhere in the neighborhood if *that* happens." He crossed those arms solidly over his chest, taking his stance. "*You* tell Belman she's done it all wrong," he said meaningfully, just in case they hadn't gotten the picture.

But Lili had. She'd gotten it good and clear. "Then it's one or the other," she said. "We all have it . . . or none of us has it."

"Why is this even under discussion?" Hayley cried, jumping up from the couch so suddenly that she spilled tea over her hands. She put the mug on the glass-topped end table beside the couch with a clink, too impatient to care about the fragile nature of both mug and table. "With shaqarava, we can defend ourselves against the Taelons! We can even defend ourselves against the *Jaridians*! Humanity would control its *own* destiny."

"No," Liam said, so darkly full of certainty that they all looked at him, that even Hayley stopped in midtemper to stare at him. "If we go down that path, humanity will *lose* control of its destiny."

In the silence that followed, Lili was the one who finally spoke. "Liam, I hate to admit it, but it looks to me like Hayley's right on the mark. It might not be right, it might take away the choice from individuals and we might lose a lot of vulnerable people in the process, but in the end, we'd be stronger for it. We wouldn't be at the mercy of Taelon *or* Jaridian."

Liam took a deep breath. She could see it in him, that urge to get up and move around, to think on his feet; she could see it just as plainly when he decided against it. "We'd be at the mercy of *ourselves*. I *know*—I just watched it happen to the Taelons."

"You could make more sense," Augur suggested, in the guise of someone being extremely reasonable with someone who isn't actually making any sense at all.

"I told you," Liam said, giving Augur a sharp look. "This flu—I've been seeing things . . . living my racial memories. Learning about what it's like to be the Kimera-within . . ." He glanced at Lili, gave a short shake of his head as if he'd decided not to go there, and started again. "I don't think it's coincidence that these past few days I watched the Taelons go from their natural Atavus state to something that turned on that being. They nearly destroyed their world then, and they went on to destroy it later!"

The others responded with silence, but it was of anticipation. Liam seemed not to notice, looking off at some mind's eye view, lost perhaps in the very images to which he referred—but it was a normal distraction, and not the dis-

traction of a man gripped by visions. Lili said quietly but
with insistence, "I think we need to know more about that,
Liam."

He did get up, then, moving away from the couch with
none of his normal vigor, trailing an inconspicuous and
steadying hand off the recliner on the way by. He said dis-
tantly, "The Kimera gave the Atavus shaqarava because the
Atavus were dying, and it was the only way to save them. It
was a selfish decision . . . the only way to continue studying
a life form that intrigued the Kimera." He looked directly at
Lili, a movement that chilled her; he spoke to her as the one
on whose shoulders the decision might rest. "Da'an once
told me that the Kimera *joined* with the Atavus; I've heard
other Taelons say the same. They also say the Kimera are
genetic predecessors to the Taelons. But that's revisionist
history; it's true only in the loosest fashion."

Lili started. "I'd almost forgotten . . ." she said, and
looked up to see she had not only Liam's intent interest, but
Hayley's and Augur's as well. "Something Boone said," she
told them. "It was right before he died, and the semantics of
it didn't seem that important. That at one point, the Kimera
used chameleonlike abilities to conquer the Taelon home-
world, and infected them with a genetic virus."

"Conquer," Liam mused. "Not the word I would use.
But the rest of it is closer to the truth than what I generally
hear."

"There aren't exactly any Kimera left to refute whatever
the Taelons want to say, are there?" Augur said. "Except for
you, and you're—polluted."

Liam looked startled, but then his face cleared. "With
my human side, you mean? Doesn't matter. I'm not exactly
stepping up to a microphone."

"Every time I think the Taelons have finally come clean
about their true purpose here, I get a nice big slap upside

the head to remind me they're the absolute masters of spin," Lili said, more disgusted at herself than anything else.

Liam said dryly, "Oh, the Kimera gave the Atavus something of itself, all right—the shaqarava and some of the abilities that came with it. But it was a unilateral decision; the Atavus had less to say about it than we do right now. They couldn't handle the power the shaqarava gave them; they misused it and they threatened the existence of everything else on their world. They sacrificed themselves trying to create the Commonality, because they discovered that within that state, the darker side of the shaqarava didn't call to them."

"That pesky Dark Side of the Force," Augur said, but his tone wasn't as light as it might have been. They all knew that Liam had been through his own struggles to deal with the temptations and the power of the shaqarava. *Thurisaz*, he'd once told Lili. Beckett's runes, this one representing the dark things within. The things to be overcome.

"When Da'an reverted to the Atavus state, Zo'or told us the Taelons couldn't bring him back to the Commonality." Lili lifted an eyebrow at Liam. "It took *you* to do that."

"Because Zo'or was telling the truth. The Atavus failed in its attempt to create the Commonality until the Kimera stepped in. A single individual who'd taken the Atavus form; it was his interference that allowed the Taelons to create their Commonality. Once they had the Commonality, once they had a true understanding of the Kimera's abilities . . . they were afraid of them—afraid the Kimera wouldn't like what their one individual had wrought and would somehow take away the Commonality. And so they started a war, and they wiped Ha'gel's people out. *My* people." He hesitated by the recliner, as if just realizing the true personal import of that fact. After a moment, he shook it off and looked back to Lili. "After that they started on their own kind. Or what had once been their own kind."

"The Jaridians?" Hayley said.

He nodded. "They were just too different from each other . . . but they were inextricably bound together. They still are."

"Gahh," Augur said. "Like the universe's worst marriage."

Liam gave him a brief grin. "More like conjoined twins who were separated, and each of them resents the parts that the other ended up with. Worse than that, they eventually discovered they *need* those parts to survive."

"That doesn't have to happen to us," Hayley said, hanging on to her original contention with typical tenacity. "We *know* what's happening to us. We can handle it. I'm handling it."

"You think so?" Liam shot back at her, garnering resentment. "You haven't *begun* to experiment with what you can do!"

Augur cleared his throat, tentatively if only figuratively stepping between them. "According to the docs, even the first affected aren't all the way through the transition yet. That's why it's so important they get this antivirus circulating. It's not going to be effective on anyone who's truly completed transition."

Lili gave Hayley a pointed look. "So you *don't* know what it's like. Not yet."

"That didn't keep me from using them effectively against Sandoval," Hayley said, unswayed, and looked just as pointedly at Liam. "Or from helping you enough so you even have the chance to tell me I don't know what I'm doing!"

There was silence after that in which even Liam looked

taken off-stride, and then Augur growled, "Low blow, Hayley."

Hayley sighed and threw herself back down on the couch. "Yeah, maybe," she admitted. "It's still true."

"*I've seen it,*" Liam said, repeating everything he'd said with just those three words. "And for all the Atavus are—as primitive as Da'an seemed to us when he reverted—they had something that humans have never had. They refused to kill their own kind. It's why the Kimera were so entranced with them, and broke their own rules to save them. They had an unrelenting moral code, and they still ended up where they are."

Augur snorted. "That didn't stop Da'an from killing two people—or from going after *me.*"

"You aren't Atavus," Liam said. "But the Atavus, the Taelons, the Jaridians—none of them kill within their species, and they've still managed to bring themselves to the brink of destruction—and maybe us along with them—because of the shaqarava. We *already* kill each other. Maybe *you* can handle your shaqarava, Hayley . . . maybe you can't. But not everyone will—and they're the ones we'll have to worry about."

"We'll handle *them,* too," Hayley said. "I'm not saying it'll be easy. I'm saying it'll be worth it." She shot Lili a look, a challenge. "You got quiet, Lili."

Lili gave her an even stare. "I'm thinking. It's a big decision . . . and we don't have a lot of time to make it. The last thing we want is to be too late, so we guarantee that some of us have shaqarava and some of us don't. We can barely handle different races within our species . . . we aren't likely to do well with different subspecies."

"Oh, I think it's guaranteed that we'll end up with two different versions of humanity unless we stop it in time," Liam said. He returned to the couch, hesitated there, and lowered himself into it. "Not everyone who's infected and survives will have the shaqarava. Some of them are bound to throw it off."

Reluctantly, Hayley said, "That's true. Two of my people did."

Great. Just great. Lili threw her hands in the air and turned to face the bar, taking a moment for herself. Or she meant to. Her global beeped just as her hands found her cooling mug of tea. She checked the ident and held up a hand to halt the murmur between Hayley and Liam. "Sandoval," she said, exasperated. The last thing she needed; he was probably ready to go on his second little patient raid, and she wanted nothing of it. She wanted to stay *here*, dealing with the retrovirus problem, and not go contribute to it.

On impulse, she scrubbed her fingers through her hair, gave her cheeks a brisk rub, and knuckled her eyes hard enough to at least briefly redden them. Then she activated the global. "Go, Sandoval."

"Captain . . . I've been informed you returned to Earth. I require you here at the ship immediately—"

"I don't think that's such a good idea," Lili said.

"No one asked you for your opinion," he said, but it was an automatic response, and he hesitated almost immediately, looking at her more closely. "Are you well, Captain Marquette?"

"No, I don't think I am." She made herself pause, as if thinking thickly. She'd seen it often enough in recent days to imitate it well. "I don't think I can provide you adequate backup."

"You should report to a clinic immediately."

Yeah, right, where a Taelon flunky can walk in and appropriate me. "If I don't feel better in the morning, I will," she told him.

It didn't satisfy him; it never satisfied him when anyone

did anything other than immediately complying with what they were told, and sometimes not even then. But he gave a short nod. "Report to me first thing," he said, and cut the connection.

Lili snapped the global shut to find Augur staring at her with admiration. He said, "Did I ever tell you how much I love you?"

"All the time," she said. "And you're so sincere."

"No, I mean it. We could really do good things together—"

"Hayley," Lili said, "time to play with those shaqarava again, if you're lucky enough to hit the right target."

"He's going after more guinea pigs?"

"That's my bet."

Hayley stood, glancing at Liam with a reluctance of a different nature than that she'd shown during their heated discussion. "I'll handle it," she said.

"You won't have my global to trace," Lili said. "Get manpower at all the clinics and hospitals. He'll probably be coming in from the roof, but you should cover all the—"

"I'll *handle* it," Hayley repeated.

Lili stopped herself in midword, hesitated, and nodded. "Okay," she said. "It's all yours, then."

Hayley crossed in front of Liam, pausing just beyond him; he propped an elbow on the arm of the couch and put his hand up. She gave him the smallest of smiles and took it—no, she didn't. She held her hand up to it as though she *would*, but stopped with an inch of clear space between them, standing that way long enough that Lili exchanged a puzzled glance with Augur, even opened her mouth—

And then closed it again as Hayley glanced at her—a shuttered, warning sort of glance that claimed privacy—and headed for the door.

Lili, thinking about that look, returned to her tea.

SIXTEEN

Augur pretty much watched it happen.

Not a big surprise to anyone, of course, though as he saw Liam's eyes losing focus more and more frequently he cornered Lili by the wet bar under the guise of warming up some buffalo chicken wings he'd brought up from the bar. The scent of them was enough to make his eyes water, but his mouth wasn't particularly interested. "Isn't this just surreal," he said. "Mom and Dad baby-sitting the kid."

Lili gave him a wry smile, one that faded quickly. "Too close to being true," she told him. "We were there when he was born . . . we both saw him grow up. The only thing we missed was his conception."

As if Augur could let a line like that just pass him by. "Darn," he said. "Would have liked to try that alien sex."

"Augur!" she hissed, her gaze flicking to Liam and back most meaningfully . . . just before she hit him.

"*What?*" Augur gave her a wounded look, but she didn't relent. "Must be a guy thing . . ."

"No doubt," she muttered.

But the fun was over, and he, too, glanced over his shoulder to see how closely Liam was paying attention to them. Not much; caught up in his own thing. "Look, someone's got to say this," Augur said, keeping his voice low—

although he'd taken the precaution of firing up the big wall-screen monitor and bringing up the surveillance view of the Flat Planet; the action was slow as slow, but the girl band was doing their best to keep things loud nonetheless.

"Somebody's got to say what?" she said, arching a brow high over one of those exquisite eyes.

Augur didn't let it deter him, though he was more than susceptible where Lili was concerned. "What do you think? The thing that everyone's been *not* saying. Maybe the Taelons can do something for him, Lili. *We* sure can't."

"Maybe they can," she agreed, readily enough that he frowned. It couldn't be that easy—

It wasn't. She added, "And maybe they'll tell us he died and put him in a box like they did with the Jaridian, keeping him to experiment on for year after year—"

"Da'an would never allow that."

"Not if they told him." Lili reached behind him and flicked the door bar on the microwave, snagging herself a piece of chicken that she then seemed to forget about except as a gesturing tool. "Even if Da'an managed to keep Liam safe for the moment, what do you think his life would be worth once the Taelons know the truth about him?"

Augur scowled at her, unable to find any argument to that, until the frustration built into a harshly inarticulate growl. "Nothing!" he said. "But it's not going to be worth anything if he's *dead*, either!" And then he winced and looked over his shoulder, checking to see if the subject of the discussion had caught on.

The subject of the discussion was missing.

"He's in the bathroom," Lili said; she, obviously, had been paying attention—although of course she was facing the right direction to manage that without bodily contortions. She set the chicken wing on a napkin on the counter, untasted, rubbing her fingers on the corner of the napkin.

And then—lowering her voice in a way that made Augur think Liam had reappeared, she caught and held Augur's gaze for quick and final words. "Look, Augur . . . Liam's no fool. If he wants to go to the Taelons, he can make that decision on his own. I'm not going to make it for him."

"It's not a decision he can make if he's *unconscious*," Augur muttered, but it was more to get the last word than to extend further argument.

"Chicken wing?" Lili said, which was as much warning as he'd get that Liam had barefooted up behind him. He moved away from her, making room for someone else to join the conversation in this small space, but found Liam leaning on the bar counter from the other side, and making an amused grimace.

"I don't think so," Liam said. "I think I'll stand pat with Hayley's soup."

There was a moment of awkwardness, which Augur hadn't expected, and then Liam said, "Lili . . . if you end up making the call about the antivirus . . . do what you think is right. Don't let Doors intimidate you."

"Or you?" she said, as archly as ever.

He shrugged, elbows still on the counter. "I happen to think I'm right. But you'll have to do what you think is best. You're the one who'll have to live with it."

She made a wry face. "That makes me feel so much better all around."

Liam eyed her a moment and then his attention abruptly seemed elsewhere; for an instant Augur thought he'd gone off to a memory, and then at the sudden tension on Liam's face, the brief frown that settled on his forehead and lifted again, he was sure of it. Gone, and fighting to come back. Liam refocused on Lili and said, "I'm sorry," and though he didn't explain himself, Lili seemed to understand.

"It's a position I wanted at one time," she said. "I can't blame anyone but myself."

"I'm still sorry."

She said softly, "I know."

"Gah," Augur said. "This is hard enough without everybody being all sincere and everything. Look, Liam, I don't know what's gonna happen with you, but I'm staying. Lili's staying. And you—you go sit down or something." He waved his hands at the couch in a shooing motion. "Go on. If you keep wobbling around on your feet I might feel obliged to spoon-feed you more soup, and I don't know if I can stand the overwhelming *niceness* that would involve."

Liam grinned. "You always know just what to say, Augur."

"I'm gifted like that," Augur admitted.

A global beeped; they played an interesting game of looking at belts and slapping pockets before Liam found Lili's global on the counter and shoved it toward her. "Again?" she said, exasperated, and thumbed it open—only to roll her eyes at what she saw. "Text Guy is back," she muttered.

"Who?" Liam said, baffled.

"The source of the retrovirus development file," Augur said, and tilted Lili's global so he and Liam could see, too, although Liam had to lean way over the counter to do it.

"He's been trying to set up a meet," Lili said. "I think he wants extraction."

"A new ID courtesy of yours truly?" Augur murmured, reading the message twice to make sure he hadn't missed any sneaky spylike references. Nope; nothing but a time, and a single comment: *There will be three of us, nonhostile . . . we entrust ourselves to you.* "Three new IDs," he said, disapprovingly.

"If the file he gave me leads to an antivirus, he's earned as many new IDs as he wants," Lili said. "I've got to make a call about this."

"Don't send Hayley," Augur said, noting that the middle of the night timing would make her available. "She's a little too eager to play with those shaqarava."

"No need to send Hayley." Lili gave him that eyebrow again. "We still have a few people of our own in play, you know." And she took control of her global and turned her back on them, not so much to hide the conversation to follow, but—from the look she shot over her shoulder at Augur—to avoid peanut gallery remarks.

Fine. He knew when he wasn't wanted. "I say we go make up some life stories," he told Liam. Turn down the Flat Planet surveillance sound, watch the bar patrons chat to one another, and make up stories based on their attire and body language. If the other Flat Planets weren't in the process of moving lock, stock, and barrel to new locations, he could split the monitor into a screen for each of them. And maybe this one should have moved, too . . . but they'd acted quickly to protect it, he thought, especially with Sandoval's current fixation on Hayley's ex-clinic. "I've had my eye on this fellow who thinks he can dress like me, only he's got this pale, pale skin and—" He cut himself off when Liam didn't follow along, recognizing the change in Liam's posture, the fact that the counter was actually the only thing keeping him on his feet. With what he hoped was airy panache, Augur said, "Here, then. Have a shoulder."

"Don't mind if I do," Liam murmured, reaching. "The guy who keeps hitting on Suzanne, you mean?"

"Ah, you noticed. What was it, the fact that he was hitting on Suzanne, or his sad effort to emulate *moi*?" Augur hid his wince at the heightened warmth radiating from Liam's body and deposited his friend safely on the couch, tossing him the woven cotton blanket that hung sloppily over the recliner.

Liam smiled faintly. "I'm not telling," he said. And was gone, so suddenly motionless that Augur sprang back to him, checking the rise and fall of his chest—yes, still happening—before falling heavily onto the couch next to Liam.

To wait.

The memories reached for him, their now-familiar collage of images pushing at the edges of his thoughts. But this time when he lost the struggle to stay in the real world, he didn't tamely let those memories take control, dragging him where they would. He didn't have the time to give them . . . and he'd already learned what he needed to know. *For now.* For now, he had other needs.

Like how to survive.

When the memories enveloped him, this time he plunged into them—into and beyond, to a more nebulous place—where, for a panicked moment, he floundered, disoriented and lost.

"Ha'gel!" he shouted, a cry muffled by darkness and formless not-being, muffled right into soundlessness.

He'd spoken to his Kimera parent once before, as near to death as he was now. And though while living the memories he could not feel his body, in this place he could feel it with preternatural awareness—the struggle of organs dealing with constant and rising fever, the labor of his heart pumping blood through each artery and vein and the smallest capillaries . . . the fire of the inflamed nerves ripping from the center of his being and out toward the shaqarava, where secondary pathways tried to form and fought rejection. A body never more alive as it struggled not to die, calling out for the help of its parent.

But there was no one else here. There was no *here* for someone else to be.

All right. Then change that. Make *a here.*

Last time it had been a featureless atmosphere of brilliant, rushing clouds. This time . . .

Siobhan Beckett's Ireland. Strandhill, where the Taelons had kept so many secrets for so long. Sheep-cropped green hills, light woods edging in from the sides. A gray sky, mottled from nickel to bright steel, threatening mist.

"As once I said," came a voice within his ear, "what the Taelons create, my son, *you* can transcend."

"Ha'gel," Liam breathed.

"Or the spirit thereof," Ha'gel said, a smile in his voice; this time the sound came from without, and when Liam turned he found the smile on Ha'gel's face as well.

His father's face.

Or one form of his father. For the Kimera, in native form, were all energy and light. But this was not, as far as Liam knew, any of the forms that Ha'gel had ever assumed— ever *borrowed*—while alive. This man's form came as a reflection of Ha'gel himself—a mature man nearly as tall as Liam, with silvered hair and a weathered face that smiled much more easily than Liam expected.

Maybe it was that he himself simply didn't smile enough.

Not that it had been easy to see Ha'gel's features that first time, with silvery nimbus-lights slipping off the surface of his skin and nondescript clothing. Here he faced Liam with much the same effect, a distinctly green cast to the light that came from nowhere and everywhere to define his form, never holding position long enough to quite sort out the chiaroscuro lights and shadows.

It was the best Liam's unconscious could do at filling in the details of a being he'd never even known.

"To be called thus is a pleasure for me," Ha'gel said. "But I sense not the same for you."

"No," Liam said. "If I had a better understanding of my heritage, that might be possible. But finding this place without . . . extraordinary . . . circumstances doesn't seem to be one of the skills you've given me."

"Things change."

"Things won't have the opportunity to *change* unless you can help me get through this illness."

Ha'gel considered that, the unearthly light playing across his face here in the most earthly of surroundings, and his features became distracted, then more solemn—as if he'd taken some internal inventory of this son in whose consciousness he existed. And then he inclined his head, spreading his arms slightly to indicate Liam himself.

"I can only tell you that you must help yourself."

"Spare me!" Liam snapped. "You sound like a movie of the week."

Ta'en walked freely into the lab, hesitating a moment to get used to the bustle of human drones in the background; they were installing equipment suitable for humans—as opposed to the existing Jaridian-based monitoring systems—so Ta'en could complete his work right on the premises upon the impending arrival of the human subjects.

The arrival of which had once more been delayed. "Mr. Bellamy," Ta'en said, not taking any particular note of the fact he had interrupted the human's work, "I wish your insight on a human matter."

Bellamy swiveled his chair away from his monitor, which was now clear of any sentimental images of his daughter. "How can I help?"

"I fail to understand why the human Resistance continues to counter our attempts to procure samples from those who have acquired the airborne version of the virus."

Bellamy gave Ta'en a stare that indicated total lack of understanding, making Ta'en set his hands at waist-level impatience. But the man's face cleared suddenly, and he said, "They did it again?"

"Yes. They have done it again. We wish only to use these subjects to develop a cure for that which ails all of Earth. Why would they act against us in this matter?"

Bellamy hesitated. It wasn't the hesitation of one without an answer, but of one who wasn't sure of offering the answer.

"Speak freely," Ta'en said.

Bellamy crossed his arms over his chest, a curious muffling of his hands. "When the Taelons choose to act, it's because acting is in their best interest."

That was an explanation? "Of course," Ta'en said. "How would it be otherwise?"

Bellamy made an aborted movement of his eyes that Ta'en suspected wasn't respectful, or the man would have allowed himself to complete it. Still, in some odd way, he seemed freer with his reactions than he had been during all the time Ta'en worked with him. "If it's in the Taelons' best interests, then that doesn't necessarily mean it's in humanity's best interests."

"May these conditions not overlap?"

Bellamy shrugged. "Sure," he said. "They could. But they usually don't. What if it were in the Taelons' interests to provide an antivirus that tags individuals with the kind of tracking system you wanted to use for the retrovirus experiment in the first place?"

Ta'en looked at Bellamy with renewed respect. "That is an excellent suggestion, and one I will pass along to Phe'la."

Bellamy made an unintelligible noise with his mouth, freeing his hands to flap briefly in the air. "That's exactly what I'm talking about. Humans know that Taelons won't think twice about piggybacking something that may be against humanity's interests onto what otherwise seems like something we badly need. So they don't dare *not* look a gift horse in the mouth."

"The idiom escapes me, as usual," Ta'en said. "But I gather the point of it. All humans feel this way?"

"No, I don't think they do," Bellamy said. "But the Resistance certainly does, or they wouldn't even exist."

"And *you*?" Ta'en moved closer to his assistant, watching his reaction closely. "How do you feel about those things Taelons do for humanity?"

For a moment, Bellamy merely toed his chair in a slight arc, back and forth, back and forth. Then he said, "How I feel depends on what I've seen. It changes. I think some things are worth the risk. If I didn't believe that what benefits the Taelons can also benefit mankind, I wouldn't be here."

"And that is why you stay, and apply yourself with such diligent effort. Because you believe you are benefiting your own kind."

"Of course," Bellamy said, his voice flatter than usual. Da'an would have known what that meant . . . Ta'en did not. "What other reason could there be?"

Ta'en thought to the way Zo'or often worked . . . that instead of focusing on goals and the benefits of obtaining them, he chivvied his subordinates along with threats and implications. Ta'en had felt that particular lash; Zo'or would hardly think to spare the Mothership humans the same, including Bellamy. But he said, "I am gratified that you maintain your belief that the same developments may benefit both our species. I only wish you could convince those who keep us from obtaining the human subjects we need."

Bellamy said nothing; this, too, was a human cue that Da'an would have been able to interpret, and Ta'en reconsidered Bellamy's most recent words, looking for clues. But Bellamy sidetracked him by standing. "I've completed the compilation of virus strains you asked for, Ta'en, and sorted them according to characteristic. There's nothing more I can do until we have some samples to work with . . . I'd like to request a short Earthside break; I have personal business to take care of."

"This is an unusual request."

"I've never made it before. That's why I'm hoping you'll grant it now."

Ta'en hesitated. "We may acquire samples at any time. I would prefer for you to be available the moment that happens."

Bellamy looked away from him. "I didn't want to say anything . . ."

"I have indicated you may speak freely."

"The truth is, I've heard from a friend who's sick. It sounds like the airborne version, and . . . I may be able to talk him into coming up here. I just didn't want to say anything in case I can't convince him."

"Then we will have a Companion Agent accompany you—"

"No, that's just the point." Bellamy was indeed speaking freely, to interrupt in such a manner. "That would scare him off for sure. He's old, and he's not likely to survive without help . . . I can convince him, I'm sure of it. If you send someone official, there'll just be a big stink, and that won't look good for the Taelons, I assure you."

"I think I understand," Ta'en said, although there was

something here that he was sure he did not, some unusual stress in Bellamy's voice that first impulse attributed to the human need for significant break periods when working on a project of the magnitude of that which Bellamy had just completed . . . and second impulse said was something new, something different altogether. "See if you can convince your friend to join us here."

Bellamy said nothing more, merely nodded as if it had been Ta'en's idea in the first place. He stood, draped his lab coat over the back of the chair, and walked briskly out of the lab area.

Ta'en looked at the coat, and looked at the area of Bellamy's workstation where the image of his daughter had always rested but now did not.

He was suddenly certain that his second impulse was the more accurate.

Augur had persistence. He knew how to ignore *no* and *it can't be done* and *that's impossible.* He had the tenacity to lurk in the dark areas of cyberspace until the right person peeked out, showing him how to get in. He knew how to bypass every authority but his own.

He was absolutely no good at *this* sort of waiting.

Waiting for a friend to die?

"This sucks," he muttered, sitting at one end of the couch with his arms crossed defiantly over his chest. "God, this sucks."

"Don't think I could put it better myself," Lili muttered back from across the room. "But let's keep the out-loud thoughts positive ones, shall we?"

"What, like *best wishes in the next life*?" Augur snapped. "Got a Hallmark card for that?"

She didn't respond, and after a moment he looked at her

from under his brows. Wished he hadn't. She was tired, she was sorrowful, and she had a look on her face that he'd helped to put there. He took a deep breath, and went back to muttering. "I didn't mean that," he said.

"You did," she told him. "It's okay. It's . . . you."

"And that's a good thing, right?" He sounded more hopeful than he'd prefer, and that made him frown, too. *Just keep your mouth shut. Sit here and hold Liam's hand.* Which he wasn't doing, except in a figurative sense.

Liam, at least, seemed more or less at peace. Fine beads of sweat gathered on his forehead and upper lip, but he was no longer twitching or jerking or making little sounds of distress. Propped up in the corner of the couch in a quiet way, breathing not quite right but not raggedly enough to send Augur into paroxysms of worry. And while at first glance his face was slack, a second glance showed the faint frown of concentration.

Augur hadn't said anything to Lili. Didn't intend to. Let her get her hopes up when they didn't have so much chance of getting dashed.

Liam, he knew, hadn't given up. Maybe once, to judge by the way he'd responded to Lili not long ago, but not now.

He glanced at Lili to make sure she wasn't looking, and straightened the blanket so it covered Liam's exposed jeans at one knee. He had an image to maintain, after all.

A fact that completely escaped his mind when his global beeped. Distraction! Anything for distraction. He grabbed it from its clip at the shirt pocket in the center of his chest, right over a POW!, and found Hayley's ident in the window. She thought she was running anonymously, of course.

For most people, she was.

Let her go right on thinking it. "Incoming, go."

"Augur," she said, diving in without hesitation. "Just

wanted to let you know we were successful. You can tell Lili that the shaqarava came in damned handy again. And no one's dead."

"Since when am I your messenger boy?"

"Since she's standing there in the room somewhere with you," Hayley said, unaffected by his sarcasm. "And since I thought you'd like to be the one to get *this* message, considering the way you've been working with Belman and Park."

He did perk up, at that, and gave Lili a quick glance. "They've done it?"

"Yes," she said. "They've done it. It's been given to those of us who aren't going to make it otherwise. Things look good so far. It'll just sit dormant in the system of anyone who doesn't have the Taelon Flu, so you're welcome to have a dose anytime you want. Belman told me to relay that, specially."

"Yeah, but she had a twinkle in her eye when she said it," Augur said, hiding his immense relief with bluster. Or trying to. Lili eased closer, eavesdropping. "What about giving it to Liam?"

She gave a short, sharp shake of her head. "Nothing's changed on that front. How is he?"

"Hanging in," Augur said, deliberately light. "How about distribution? Any solutions?"

Another shake of her head, more resigned now. Until she took a deep breath and slanted a wise look at him. "It's not like we've decided to distribute the thing at all, other than to these few test cases. And we'll keep them isolated from now on if we have to, to keep the cure from spreading."

Augur shook his head as if dislodging foreign matter from his ears. "You know, there's something about that that just doesn't sound right."

"There is, isn't there?" Lili murmured from behind and

GENE RODDENBERRY'S EARTH: FINAL CONFLICT

off to the side, savvy enough to stay out of the range of the global and close enough to have heard every word of the call.

And Augur had a thought. The kind of thought that made it almost impossible to keep a smile to himself, a things-coming-together smile. "Listen, is your pal Art around?"

She snorted lightly. "When is he not, lately?"

"Good. Have him call me from somewhere private."

Hayley eyed him a good long moment, and finally asked the brewing question. "What for?"

"If I wanted you to know, I'd tell him to call me from somewhere private with you attached to his elbow." No apologies there; Augur's business was Augur's business. Lili knew enough to sit quietly in the background, not drawing so much attention to herself that he'd feel obliged to shoo her off.

"I'll find out," Hayley said, shaking her head. "A lot sooner than you think I will."

"Yeahyeah. Now hang up and give him the message, okay?"

Hang up *on* him was more like it; she cut the connection without any social niceties.

Lili said nothing. Quite loudly, she said nothing. Good girl.

When his global beeped again, Augur activated it so swiftly that Art Wells looked startled. He recovered quickly enough. "Your timing sucks."

"I said we'd *talk*," Augur told him.

"It takes two for that," Art said, and Augur knew, *knew* that the man was about to cut him off.

"I wouldn't." His most deadly voice, quiet and oh-so-confident. Knowing more than anyone, because he made sure that he always did.

Art Wells didn't. He didn't know what Augur knew; he'd never know. But he feared it all the same.

As he should.

"Got a job for you," Augur said, all cheer now that he had Art's attention.

"Do you, now?" Art's broad features—though surely his nose hadn't *come* like that—settled into a sullen expression.

"Ah-ah," Augur said. "Attitude adjustment, my friend. Do this right, and you get to walk away with beaucoup karma; everybody loves you."

"What're you talking about?"

"We need a patron," Augur said. "Someone with lots of money. Lots of resources. A trusted public face. We need someone to stand at the door and hand out the Halloween candy."

The sullenness disappeared completely, replaced by honest bafflement. "You *what?*"

Not enough imagination, apparently. Nor from Lili, who whispered in the faintest possible voice, "Augur, *what?*"

Augur waved her off below the level of his global. "The cure, Art. The retro-retrovirus. The keep-us-human magic the doctors have provided to treat the world."

Immediately, he grew wary. "That decision hasn't been made yet."

"No one said it has. But if and when it is, we've got to be ready for it. And we're not. You can change that. You've got the right connections."

"You think—" Art cut himself off just short of naming Doors, and then laughed out loud. Not a pretty sight. How many fillings did the man have, anyway? "Not from that source," he said finally. "I think you know his philosophy on keeping the gifts the Taelons have been spreading around."

Lili swung around to face Augur, silently—and somewhat incredulously—mouthing, "Doors?"

The hand that had once hushed her from beneath the
global now nodded in lieu of his head, a sock puppet without the sock. To Art, Augur said, "The thing is, it doesn't
really matter how he feels about it personally. This is an opportunity for him to get some high-profile poll points to
kick off his bid for the presidency. It's an opportunity for
you to make good . . . to do your own thing. That way, if it
were later revealed that you have a certain paid association
with this potential patron, you'd already have a spin on
damage control. You can follow that, can't you?"

Art's response was disgruntled and not entirely convinced.

"On the other hand, if you weren't interested in even
trying, I would imagine that that certain paid association
would become common knowledge much sooner than you
were prepared to deal with it. Those Resistance are a touchy
bunch, wouldn't you say? They don't like it when they find
out someone's been keeping secrets."

Lili's eyes widened; her hands went to her hips at the
juncture of the tightly tailored vest and the equally tailored
pants. Augur really liked that vest. He waved her down anyway, and repeated with a knowing smile, "No, they *really*
don't like it if you keep secrets from them."

"You've made your point. You don't seem to get that I
can't control the man."

"Then *don't* control him. *Manage* him. If he doesn't
help, we'll use other channels. We'll get help from Thompson's people, or maybe the Taelons. But we'll make it really
clear who turned us down first. And if that happens, no
karma for you, walking wall or no."

Art seemed to have caught on to the rhythm of ignoring

the extraneous in Augur's conversation. "We do it this way, I get him to agree . . . then it's *my* idea."

"Absolutely," Augur said. "Credit's all yours. He owes you, we owe you, the world loves you."

Lili made a terrible face, scrunching her nose up and trapping her eyes between the wrinkles it made and her quirked-down brows.

"I'll . . . let you know," Art said. But it was clear enough . . . his mind was already racing. Already spinning scenarios of conversation between himself and Doors.

"Do that," Augur said, and cut the connection to meet Lili's gaze with his own look of extreme satisfaction.

She shook her head, helpless in her search for a response. "You—" she said. "You're . . . you're—"

Augur smiled. "Yeah."

Liam whirled away from Ha'gel—from his *father*—closing his eyes on the deep green of the hills before him in an effort to quell the cry of disbelief burning in his throat. Words that swelled and beat against him from the inside . . . words like *how can you do this?* And more painful yet, *how can you do this to* me? *I'm your* son!

Ha'gel, an ancient being with an intimate knowledge of his own nature. The *only* being with any intimate knowledge of the still-hidden secrets of Liam's nature . . . and not willing to share it. Not out of compassion, not out of respect, not even to save a life.

Worse than all that. Not even father to son.

Finally, fists clenched at his sides and eyes still closed to the beauty of the Irish countryside, he managed to push words past his throat. Even to his own ears, his voice came harsh and strained. "Why do you make it so damn *hard?*

You could have trusted Boone at St. Michael's—you could have worked with him instead of causing both your deaths. You could have *been here* for me!"

Ha'gel moved up beside him; even through his closed lids, Liam saw the glimmer of that shifting light. And, ever so gently, Ha'gel said, "I *am* here for you."

Liam turned on him, hard and fast, so full of the anger that words fled him completely and after a moment of silent vehemence he retreated again, looking away over hills that had grown abruptly, significantly darker, the clouds thickened and dropping.

Ha'gel cleared his throat, his presence at Liam's side full of unexpected warmth and solidity. *More real than most,* he'd once said of his own existence on the spiritual plane. "I *did* choose to trust Boone," he said quietly, his voice a rumble. "I simply didn't do so fast enough." He cleared his throat again, another rumble. "I am old, son, but not perfect. The Taelons have chased me across the universe, painting themselves as martyrs even as they destroyed the Kimera."

With pointed bitterness, Liam said, "The Taelons are anything but martyrs. That doesn't make what the Kimera did to them *right*. That doesn't make your choices *right*."

"It does not. And now I have paid for those mistakes. I spent untold lifetimes interred in stasis captivity, from which they occasionally removed me to point and murmur before returning me to their latest technological prison. When I finally escaped, I had but two imperatives. You are the result of one. The other was to survive. They were both entirely self-serving motivations. Trust was part of another lifetime, one I knew before the Taelons came into it. And so I did not do that which would have saved Boone and me."

"No," Liam said, taking a deep breath. "You didn't."

But this isn't about you. It's about me. He opened his eyes again, looked across the landscape—or what there was left of it. The clouds obscured the opposite hillsides completely, an oppressive mist that had only now made its way to Liam to bead on his shoulders, face, and hair. Ha'gel's light reflected, flickering, in the condensation on his lashes; Liam wiped his fingers over his eyes and looked at his father, finally under enough control to do so. "You never answered my question. Why leave me to fight for every little bit of self-understanding I have? Especially when so often it means the difference between life and death." *Like now.*

"If you didn't have to fight for the knowledge, it would mean little to you. You would perhaps disregard it even in those times when you need it most." Ha'gel hesitated, considering Liam with eyes that were suddenly easier to meet in the altered light. "I *am* here for you, Liam. In ways you have seen, and in ways you're not yet ready to accept."

Liam snorted. Loudly. "Don't give me that. You know more about me than anyone else dead *or* alive. Give me a nudge, or a clue, or hide a note in a Cracker Jack box. Anything! Or is it really your intent that I die, all because you wanted me to solve some internal puzzle?"

Ha'gel seemed genuinely taken aback. The deepening mist obscured everything but Ha'gel's form, graying both light and shadow toward neutral and making him as easy to see as he'd ever been. A strong man in his sixties, hair combed back without style, the lines on his face emphasized with emotion, one hand half lifted as though he wanted to clasp Liam's arm and had thought better of it. "Can you really think I want you to die?"

"You're not doing a very good job of convincing me otherwise." Liam felt the mist's dampness, now, seeping through his shirt to his shoulders. He realized with sudden, brief amusement that he was not wearing the black turtle-neck and jeans, but linen. Natural linen button-front shirt darkened with water over his shoulders, pleated linen pants darkened at the knees and across the back of his calves. Summer in Ireland. Right.

Ha'gel shook his head in a very human gesture. "It is true, should you fail to find your answers, I would not mourn—for rather than not see you again, I would see you always. But, Liam . . . I would not take from you that which waits you on Earth—those joys and passions and struggles to which you once before made the decision to return. It is a brief interval, in the larger scheme of things, but it is yours." He stared at Liam as if he was searching for something. "The answers you need are within yourself, if they're there at all. You are the result of a joining between human and Kimera . . . there *are* no others of your kind. *I* am not of your kind, even if you are the last of mine. You have thought to bring yourself here . . . to bring me here. Now it's time to look further. Look within yourself."

Liam's anger surged anew. No wonder the Taelons were so damn good at evading direct questions. They'd learned from a master.

But Ha'gel's face did not hold the expression of one in evasion. The age-carved features were open, even a little concerned. As if he needed Liam to understand . . .

Something.

And his hand, once in retreat, now waited for Liam's. Open, waiting . . . steady. Around them, the rest of the world had disappeared; Liam glanced down to find even the sheep-cropped turf turned to featureless gray. They were alone, he was dying, and his father was reaching out to him.

For an instant, he didn't dare respond. They were not real in this place . . . could two not-real beings touch each other? And how much worse would it be to try and fail than not to try at all?

Worse. It would be worse.

Slowly, he met Ha'gel's grip.

It was as solid as any he'd ever felt, a hand as big as his own, dry and warm against his mist-clammy palm.

I am more real than most.

Maybe he was.

Look within yourself.

Maybe that, too, was real.

Maybe it was more real than Liam had been able to imagine.

He'd made this place, after all. Strandhill, as obscured as it now was. The very mist that soaked and chilled him. It was all more or less within him.

Ha'gel released Liam's hand; he, too, was graying with the mist, less distinct with each passing moment. Liam looked at his hands—looked at both his hands, at the faint birthmarks of the shaqarava. For the first time since coming here, he felt his own body again—gripped by a sudden shiver, startled by the shock of pain that came with the faint, transitory bloom of the shaqarava.

And when he looked up again, Ha'gel was gone.

Look within . . .

He didn't know how. The thought invoked a short laugh—since when did he know how to do half of what he did? He just kept taking chances. Diving in, making his own way . . .

He closed his eyes to the shaqarava, still seeing them in his mind's eye.

He went within.

He found himself in another inner landscape, the very real landscape of the energies that made up his existence—

energies expressed in a painter's palette of hues and shades. White-blue shaqarava energy forked against a backdrop of violet blues in the subtle variations of a watercolor wash. The red of passionate emotion, woven strong in some places, made way for the weaker, washed ocher of hesitation in others. There were handfuls of dancing yellows and oranges and ceruleans, there were colors he couldn't even name, nor guess their function, all tracing pathways across the backdrop haze, all an expression of the energies moving within his own body.

Except the black. No, not *black*—absence of light. It globbed around the other colors, choking them, leaving withered strands in its wake; it crawled in slow jelly-movements, plastering itself to parts of his being. Taking over, remaking him.

Killing him.

As he watched, a patch of the solid darkness heaved; it bubbled and glimmered and then exploded in shaqarava light, a rogue shaft of energy that left the corruption shredded in its wake even as the sharp pain of it rocked him, graying the inner vision, threatening to evict him back to the gray mist of his outer landscape.

Not. Yet.

With the tenacious persistence of all three parents—the mother who had seen her Ireland united, a human father who still fought his own private battles, and a man—a *being*—who had finally escaped the Taelons after untold ages of captivity—he clung to that inner landscape, battling to maintain the vision even when the emergent shaqarava light went rogue, scattering a section of quiescent normality and shrieking a response through the body he now felt all too keenly.

The corruption spread inexorably through his system, killing him in its very efforts to remake him . . . while the existing energy, blocked by viral changes, destroyed him simply by bursting free of its normal boundaries.

Then guide it.

Use the shaqarava energy that had been within himself all this time, ripping through his system to raze everything from a militia farmhouse to his very self—except this time . . . guide it.

Destroy only the destroyer.

He found a new gathering of white-blue energy, building from the center of the backdrop, following established pathways; he diverted it to the darkness—and gasped at the clash of the two, an internal sizzle that faded as soon as his concentration waned.

No relief, then. Only the white-hot pain of the cure. No wavering.

And very little time.

Liam took up the battle.

SEVENTEEN

Hell, Lili decided, would be like this.

Like this endless night during which sleep never quite claimed her, but nevertheless hung heavily enough to create distorted nightmares. Nightmares in which she watched people die from the virus, knowing she could have prevented it . . . dreamy slow sequences of pacing hospital halls, ducking away from Sandoval's astute and far-reaching gaze, peering into overcrowded rooms, looking at face after desperate face.

The worst was looking for Liam and waiting for someone to tell her he'd died, knowing that somehow she could have prevented that, too.

Retrovirus. Anti-retrovirus. Taelon Flu. The cure.

The decision, it seemed, would be hers.

Freedom from the Taelons forever through shaqarava?

The beginning of the end for a humanity unable to handle the darker side of those shaqarava?

Or back to what they'd always been, and still facing the Taelons and their agenda . . . maybe the beginning of the end for a humanity unable to resist that agenda—not to mention the Jaridians.

Damn.

It should be more than her. It should be the U.N. and

the Resistance and the elderly lady who lived down the hall from her. *They* should decide.

Hospital halls. Liam dead. Augur dead. Hayley dead. Stacks of child-sized corpses overflowing rooms, aged great-grandmothers smiling sweetly at her and slumping to the floor, outlined in shaqarava light.

Not me. I didn't do this. Tell me I didn't do this!

Jonathan, her dreams seemed to tell her, was right. She wasn't cut out to make the hard decisions.

Finally, something twitched against her, breaking Lili free of a maelstrom of guilt for something she hadn't even done yet. She rubbed fingers over sleep-filled eyes, trying to focus on her watch; her eyes widened, then closed again. *Almost nine in the morning.* Da'an would be speaking at the hospital soon. Sandoval would want her there, or her doctor's report in his hand explaining why she wasn't. And before she got there, before she got caught up in the Taelon side of things again . . .

Before then, she'd have to make that decision.

Another twitch against her, less gently. She realized suddenly where she was, that she'd ended up on the other end of the low black couch from Liam, that somewhere during the night she'd been unable to leave him as he was, slumped into the corner diagonally, his neck crooked and legs falling off the edge of the couch; now his legs stretched across her lap and it was her own neck that ached from falling back against the low edge of the upper cushion. And the legs . . . they twitched, after a night of being nothing more than dead weight on her thighs.

He's alive. At least he's alive.

She rested a hand on his shin, jostled it slightly, watching his face for reaction. "Liam?"

The answering twitch of his leg came as randomly as the one before. Lili sighed, running her hand down the shin in a sad gesture. Alive, yes . . . but how much more he could take, she didn't want to say. Hell, she didn't even want to *think*. Again, she fought the impulse to rush him to help . . . to the warehouse clinic doctors, to a hospital, to the Taelons. But the first had already admitted there was nothing they could do, and the alternatives meant revealing his secrets to the Taelons.

She'd told Augur he might as well be dead before that happened. She still believed it.

She sighed, feeling very much alone . . . except she hadn't been alone, falling asleep here last night. Augur had been in the recliner, watching the monitor. A quick glance showed him gone; no doubt he'd taken himself to the second floor and the empty bed. Typical Augur thinking . . . *some*one might as well use it.

A grumbling noise from the floor made her think twice about that assumption. She craned her neck, found Augur's feet, and twisted even farther to find him stretched out on the floor, hugging her coat.

He cracked open his eyes, discovered the eyebrow she had raised at him. "You got the couch," he said, and yawned hugely. "Don't begrudge me a pillow."

"Wouldn't dream of it." But she kept her eye on him as he sat up and scrubbed a hand over his depilated head, yawning again, noticed her continued scrutiny as he reached over his shoulder to scratch low behind his neck. "You're staring."

"You don't look very good." His rich color had a definite tinge of gray around the edges.

"Hey, this is my morning face. Love it or leave it. How's Liam? I checked about an hour ago . . . same old same old."

Lili glanced back at Liam, frowning anew. "I really don't know. And I hate to leave, but . . ."

"But Sneezy, Sleepy, and Grumpy are waiting for you. Grumpy—that would be Sandoval."

"Thanks," she said, absently patting Liam's leg again. "I got that. You caught the virus, didn't you?"

He looked at his hands; the fingers trembled slightly. Annoyance and resignation flashed across his face; then he gave up and buffed his upper arms through the thin material of his Zowie shirt. "You'll be next, you know."

No kidding.

Unless she did something about it.

And that was the moment she realized that she could, nightmares notwithstanding. That *someone* had to, and if it was to be on the shoulders of any *one* person, hers were sturdy enough. She understood as well as anyone the ramifications of each decision. Better her than a man like Jonathan Doors, who saw only one side to everything. His side.

The decision wasn't made yet . . . but she could and would make it and live with it and still look Augur in the eye. Still look herself in the eye, even if her reflection was that of a woman with shaqarava.

Or not.

Liam kicked her. "Whoa," she said, grabbing his leg. "Maybe I'd better move."

"What's up?" Augur said, climbing stiffly to his feet to join her by the foot of the couch.

"I don't know," she murmured, giving Liam a more critical glance. How strange to spend the night in what amounted to a deathwatch, offering nothing more than an extra blanket along the way. Even if Liam had made it perfectly clear that having them there was all he wanted.

Now Augur pointed wordlessly, a sharp and accusing motion—but by then Lili had seen it too: the new play of shaqarava energy beneath Liam's skin, following his brow and cheekbones like rolling sparks, making his face ghastly beneath its pallor. "Ugh," Augur said, ever eloquent. "Do you think—"

But he glanced at Lili, unable to bring himself to finish the thought. Not that she blamed him; neither could she. *This is it.*

They stood together in one silent, breath-held moment—and then Liam exploded into motion, energy-lit spasms that would have thrown him off the couch if Lili hadn't dived to grab his shoulders, snapping, "Get his legs!" as if Augur wasn't already on his way. Lili winced against the bright luminescence that played under Liam's face and neck, turning away from the glare of it as he arched against her hold—

No, not against her. Not against her grip, not against Augur's losing battle with those long legs, but against something within himself, an agonizing battle from the inside out that left tears of effort leaking from the corners of his tightly closed eyes and left Lili breathless and buffeted as she tried to stop him from battering himself here on the outside.

Augur staggered away with the solid thud of ribs taking a kick, and an instant later Lili lost her grip, crashing back against the glass-topped coffee table even as Augur dived back to try to break her fall and Liam came off the couch to sprawl atop them both.

Limp and still, but breathing—all of them—gasping, trying to reorient . . . just taking in air. Until Augur said, "I've been looking forward to this, but it's not quite what I had in mind," and Lili realized just how high his grip on her waist had slipped, but that his arm was trapped beneath Liam as well.

So she shifted Liam aside as much as she was able, as gently as she could; fortunately, the thick table glass had popped off its metal frame but hadn't broken—no danger of lacerations to either of them while she was at it. She and Augur disentangled themselves with much grunting and effort, and as she climbed to her feet, tugging her shirt back down, she found herself meeting one puzzled pair of blue-gray eyes.

She sucked in a startled, hope-filled breath, clutching Augur's arm; in turn, Augur stiffened. "*Liam!*"

Liam reached out to her, and she met his grip. A trembling but warm and otherwise normal grip, devoid of rogue shaqarava light or the tension of pain he'd been carrying for days.

"Liam," she said, and a smile caught her mouth as she pulled him up from the floor and then let him drop back to the couch, not quite able to let go of his hand. He returned the squeeze she gave it and she allowed the full relief of his recovery to flood through her. *He's back. We got him back. We got him back.* "Welcome back," she said softly, blinking suddenly watery eyes. Human joy.

That wasn't demonstrative enough for Augur, who pulled Liam right back up again and caught him up in a suddenly ebullient grip, whooping without restraint as he hefted Liam off his feet; even Liam laughed, still looking bemused and pale and entirely disheveled. When Augur released him they dropped down to the couch together, and Augur turned on him in a sudden about-face and said seriously, "If *you* gave me this thing, you and I are going to talk."

"Later," Lili said, ignoring Augur's grumble that he

might not *have* a later. "Talk, Liam. What's going on? What just happened? Are you . . . are you okay?"

He looked at his hands. They appeared to be behaving perfectly; he closed his eyes and then pulled his fingers in to cover his palms, sighing with relief. "I think so," he said. "I think . . . I got rid of it from the inside out."

"Don't tell me," Augur said. "Another of Papa Ha'gel's tricks? Another one of those things he didn't think to mention to any of us?"

"He didn't exactly have time to write his memoirs," Lili said, shooting a quelling look at Augur.

But unexpectedly, Liam grinned at them, the boyish grin. "No," he said. "Just something of my own."

"And you're okay?" Lili prodded. "You're really okay?"

He didn't answer immediately; he hesitated, his gaze gone inward. And then he nodded slowly. "I'm okay. Just don't ask me to move."

She wanted to grab his shoulders—upright again, as they should be—and shake him and yell that he was *never to do that to her again.* Instead she nodded, and answered his still-dazed grin, and said, "I think we can manage that. For now." She straightened her clothes again—they'd been slept in and looked it, but that couldn't be helped, and her coat would cover the worst of it. Of course, *it* had been slept *with*, and hardly looked any better; she clipped her global to her belt and snatched the coat from the floor. "I've got to make Da'an's appearance at County. You two stay out of trouble and I'll be back when it's over. We've got some thinking to do." This time, at least, they'd make the decisions together.

Liam frowned, the look of a man trying to remember something.

"What?" she said, buttoning her coat, a thigh-length, dark-green lined oilcloth with a close-fitting cut, perfect for a professional fade-into-the-background look. At the last minute she remembered her hair, and moved to check her reflection in the black-faced microwave glass. Okay, the mussed look was in; she'd have to give herself that. When Liam still hadn't answered, she turned back to find the frown remaining in place—but Liam shook his head.

"Nothing," he said. "I thought . . ."

"You're lucky to be thinking at all." She discovered her trouser cuff caught in the heel of her shoe, freed it, and headed for the door, where she paused to give Liam a stern look. "No more surprises. Stay here, be quiet, and be glad you're still with us." But she softened; she couldn't help it. She said, "*I* am," and closed the door on the welcome sight of his wry grin.

Back to reality.

Or at least, the reality that most people were used to.

Liam sat on the couch, feeling far too drained to do anything but. Augur slumped at the other end of it, eyeing him with a distinctly cranky air, one cheek propped on his fist. Liam raised an eyebrow at him.

"You had to wait," Augur said.

Liam added the other eyebrow.

"To figure it out!" Augur scowled at him. "Right till the last minute, when we were sure you were a goner. I even spent the night on the floor!"

There was a bed upstairs, but Liam decided not to point it out. "Then I guess it's a toss-up which of us looks worse right now."

"Oh, no it's not," Augur said. "I may have the Taelon Flu, I may have spent the night on your floor, but I'll *always* be prettier than you."

Da'an, danger, the explosion of his defensive shaqarava—

The past? The now? The almost? Or just leftover moments from another reality?

"Don't go getting that look on your face," Augur said, prodding Liam's bare ankle with his sneakered toe. "I've had enough of that."

"Goes with the territory," Liam said absently, eyeing the dismantled coffee table, deciding to leave it as it was for a while and then trying to decide if *he* could make it upstairs to the bed—a little dreamless sleep would go down smoothly right now—or if it was better to tank up on caffeine, shower off, and wait for Lili to return; no doubt they'd take Augur to Hayley's relocated clinic. He glanced again at Augur; aside from the slept-in look Liam himself wore, he didn't look too bad yet.

He would.

Interpreting Liam's scrutiny, Augur said, "I don't care what you and Lili and Hayley and the rest of the Resistance decide. This body's perfect just as it is—I don't want to accessorize with shaqarava. What I *want* is that shot."

"And if they decide to withhold the antivirus?" *They*, because he wasn't sure the rest of the Resistance would tamely follow his lead on this one. Not without Lili's backing. "You'd spend quite a while in confinement."

"I spend all my time under St. Michael's anyway."

"You're *here* now," Liam said, quietly but making the point. "I'm serious. For the short term, you wouldn't be going *any*where. Not until the Taelon Flu spreads throughout humanity, and everyone's past the point of no return. Even Hayley hasn't reached that point yet, from what I heard last night."

Augur scowled, opened his mouth to say something, hesitated, and then crossed his arms over his chest with defiance. "And you're just going to let them get away with that? Forcing shaqarava on the entire human race?"

"You must have me confused with someone else," Liam said. "Someone with unlimited power, maybe?"

Or maybe just with his father—Ha'gel, the Kimera-within who'd made the decision the rest of the Kimera couldn't face, and who'd done something to help the Atavus save themselves from the shaqarava.

Except . . . instead of repeating Ha'gel's mistake, Liam's looming burden was to take the shaqarava *away* before it was too late . . .

Kimera-within, of a sort. Making decisions for an entire race. Again.

"You've got that look on your face . . ." Augur warned him.

"No . . ." Liam said. "No, I don't. That was a different look entirely. I think . . . I think we'd better get over to the clinic and get our hands on some of that antivirus. *Now.*" Now, while he still had the chance. Not to act with . . . not immediately. But to have.

Just in case he had to.

For an instant, Augur looked like he might hesitate, might complain about moving. The defiance of his arm-crossed posture had turned into a self-hug for warmth, and his expression had drifted to a kind of distraction that Liam knew well . . . attentiveness to the inner world, the world that wasn't working just right. But Augur shook off the hesitation in a catlike gesture, his eyes widening slightly as he understood the implications of just what he was about to become part of. "Well, then," he said. "Hi-ho Silver, away."

Liam had to search for that one, hunting down the familiar sound of the phrase until he found Sandoval's limited exposure to *The Lone Ranger.*

Augur just shook his head. "We have *got* to get you a better-rounded education."

"Getting an education in the first place would be a start,

don't you think?" Liam said, shoving himself to his feet and checking out the feel of it, hunting up his shoes.

He felt almost too heavy to move . . . but not quite. He held out a hand, hauled Augur to his feet, staggering as he did so. "Come on," he said. "You're the one who knows where they are."

Augur groaned volubly on the way up, but once in motion he scooped up his coat from the floor near the door and preceded Liam out the door. "Car," he said. "We're going to want a car."

Liam shook his head; he had no inclination whatsoever to get behind the wheel of the classic Datsun 280Z Augur had snared for him—a side effect of one of his deals, apparently—not even with the unusually deserted state of the streets. "Taxi. Assuming we can find one."

"Hey, those drivers don't exactly get sick days. If anyone's on the streets, it's them."

The Flat Planet itself was still closed, with chairs on tables, the floor cleaned, and one lone bottle sitting on the bar. Champagne. Augur snagged the note sticking out from under the bottle, read it, and tucked it away in his wallet. "You wait here, baby," he said to the champagne. "I'll be back."

Not much point in asking . . . whoever it was from, the next would be from someone else. Liam headed for the exit—*Da'an. Danger*—and brought himself up short—*shaqarava light. Screaming. Cameras*—as Augur bumped into him and backed off to give him a wary look—*the hospital. County Hospital.*

"Okay, *that* was one of those looks," Augur said accusingly.

"Yeah. It was." Liam threw on the black leather jacket he'd grabbed on the way out and headed for the door, leading them out into a sunny spring morning—almost as warm as the day of the Fair. "Change of plans. We've got to get to the hospital—"

"I thought you were *fixed*," Augur said, bumping into him once more as Liam stopped at the curb, gesturing to the taxi at the end of the block. "No, let me rephrase that—"

"Not me. *Da'an.* There's going to be trouble—" Liam turned on him as the taxi slid in at the curb, giving him a sharp look. "You don't have to come. Wait here, I'll be back—we'll still go for the antivirus."

"Oh, please," Augur said, sliding into the backseat before Liam could dive in. "Why start doing the sensible thing now? Besides, it'll be faster to go straight to the clinic from there, and believe me, getting to that clinic is a top priority for me right now."

Their taxi driver turned on them; he wore a neatly wrapped turban and a carefully applied surgical mask, and his black eyes narrowed at them. "You're not being sick, are you?"

"No, no," Augur hastily assured him, if falsely so. "We're on business. Besides, we're not getting out now, so you might as well go. County Hospital, and don't spare the gas."

The man just stared at him, frowning. "You're sure you're not—"

"We're going to see Da'an speak," Liam interrupted. "We're not going *in.*"

"And we're in a *hurry*," Augur pointed out. "We'll even *pay* to be in a hurry."

They pulled away from the curb.

"Remember that," Augur said, leaning in toward Liam. "Money talks, my friend."

But Liam was more concerned about their progress than Augur's rules of acquisition, and by the murmur of the foresight against his thoughts . . . murmurs, just like the memories, only this time he still had a chance to change them.

Or so he hoped.

The taxi driver, however, pulled to the curb while they were still a good block and a half from the hospital. "No closer," he said. "Not with the Taelon speaking, you see?"

Liam did see. The street was blocked off; no doubt the other approaches were just as inaccessible. He dug in his pocket for his ID. "I'm a Companion Protector," he said. "They'll let me through."

"Very good for you. But *I* am driving, and I am not a Companion Protector. You walk from here."

Run, was more like it. Liam flipped a generous cash card into the front seat and hit the sidewalk at full speed—or as close to it as he could get in the aftermath of the Taelon Flu, his coat flapping open to catch the full chill of his own breeze, Augur trailing behind him. The first block was easy; adrenaline fueled his speed, his ID warded off the three cops who closed in to check on the man charging toward their Taelon guest, and the otherwise empty sidewalks left him plenty of room to move. After that he ran into a fourth cop who wanted to check the ID up close and personal, and by the time the crowd grew thick enough to impede his progress, Augur was at his heels again, his more compact build giving him the advantage on the dodge.

"Do you see Lili?" Liam said, getting pushy enough to draw annoyed glances from those lining the sidewalk in front of the hospital, hesitating as he reached the wide area below the steps. There was security everywhere—hospital security, uniformed officers, even a few familiar Companion Agent faces. Evergreen shrubs lined the slope beside the several tiers of steps, blocking much of his view from this angle. Tall enough to see over almost everyone there, he still couldn't spot Lili, Da'an, or Sandoval . . . no familiar faces from the usual entourage that discreetly surrounded Da'an's appearances. But as his gaze swept over the landing above the top tier of stairs, the murmur of foresight broke through the hold he'd put on it, jarring him with the force of the intrusion. *Da'an, screaming, shaqarava light—*

"Don't go all woo-woo on me," Augur said, shoved up close beside him. "We'll find them. We're early, not late."

Someone behind them muttered, "And you're in the *way*," and jostled them both.

Augur turned; Liam put out a hand to caution him, but Augur ignored it. He said, his voice full of surprise, "Is that *your* cash card on the ground?" and suddenly they had plenty of room as the crowd tightened around the jostling man, hunting the phantom card. Augur, somehow managing to look miserably flu-ish and triumphant at the same time, gave him an oh-so-casual shrug.

"My mother would have raised me to watch out for people like you," Liam murmured, still scanning the grounds, "if she had raised me at all."

"And she would have been right," Augur said, not a trace of apologia in his voice.

At the top of the steps, a portable podium and microphone went unattended; a small crowd of reporters waited off to the right, standing on the spring-soft turf and gently jostling for position. Behind the podium stood two stern-faced hospital security guards and several representatives for the hospital—two mature women and an older man, all looking distracted; they had better things to do during this crisis, and they didn't bother to hide it.

Finally, Liam found what he sought—movement behind the reflecting glass doors of the hospital entry . . . a vague form, with its alien and yet still utterly familiar posture and shape. On its way out to the podium.

He lost any pretense of moving politely through the

crowd. He left Augur behind with a look, knowing Augur's carefully honed preference for anonymity would keep him out of the spotlight. A shove here, a nudge there, weaving between shoulders, avoiding feet; he kept his gaze on Da'an's glass-muted form.

Lili emerged from the entrance overhang first, just as Liam broke through the crowd in the front. He dodged a determined and reaching police officer, giving a practiced flash of his ID and the automatic shout of "Companion Protector!" that went with it, bounding for the stairs.

For a moment, just at the base of them, he couldn't see beyond the top landing, couldn't see or assess the danger to Da'an. But if nothing else, he'd gotten Lili's attention with the fuss; he took the steps two and three at a time and reached the top to find that she'd stepped in front of Da'an, holding one hand behind herself to stop him, the other reaching for her laser-sighted pistol—easy access through her carefully unbuttoned coat. Behind Da'an, Lassiter did the same, and a third agent stepped in front of Da'an to serve as a body block. Lili hurried out to meet Liam, angling her body so she could search half the area before them while he turned and hunted the other. Parking garage boundary, more shrubs, the hospital administration, the two security guards, the top step—

"What?" she asked shortly, not even looking at him, sweeping her search across the area bounded by the main hospital building and the reporters.

"Don't know," he said. "I keep . . . *seeing* . . . someone attack Da'an—here. Near the podium, I think. He can't give this speech, Lili."

"You think *you* can talk him out of it?" Lili said; her gaze swept the area before them again—people were reacting to Liam's presence, the crowd below had gone noisy, the reporters swinging their cameras around to focus on Liam and Lili. Nothing out of the ordinary. She relaxed, letting out a deep breath, and brought her weapon to rest at her shoulder, pointing to the sky. "Liam, a *vision*? You've been too damn full of them to pay any particular attention to this one, don't you think?"

He shook his head, short and hard. "I saw this before I was sick, too. I just didn't understand its significance—not until I realized Da'an was speaking *here*. Someone here is after him, Lili."

"The crowd's been swept for weapons," Lili said, not with any considerable amount of patience.

Again, he shook his head. "I know what I saw."

From behind them, Da'an called, "Liam, is there a problem?"

Liam held up a hand to forestall any answer, still watching the area before the hospital, frowning with frustration. "I *know what I saw*, Lili."

Exasperated, she said sharply, "And just what *did* you see, Liam? Because I don't see anything but a publicity incident in the making."

Da'an. Screaming. People running. People diving aside. The shaqarava light of Liam's response—

Or so he'd thought, the first time he'd seen it. The day of the Fair, when the Taelon Flu hadn't yet struck. When only he himself had shaqarava to wield. He turned to catch Lili's gaze directly for the first time. *"Hayley's not the only one with new shaqarava,"* he said, driving the words home, keeping her gaze until he saw her eyes widen.

And then, behind them, from much too close, Da'an said, "As much as it delights me to see you recovering from your illness, Liam, I am not pleased at this delay. My message will not be heard by a people intent on the disturbance you are causing."

"Da'an, you have to go back inside," Lili said, her voice

gone slightly breathless with new understanding. "Liam has seen—"

Reality.

A man burst from the low shrubs, shedding plastic and cardboard and a ratty blanket on the way. He propelled himself up the short hill, aiming a close-contact blast to take out the officers who whirled to confront him. *Screaming.* Lili threw herself in front of Da'an as the first energy blast came their way, badly aimed from the distance but enough to take out a support pillar of the entrance overhang. *Da'an, astonished, hitting the hard concrete with Lili over him.*

Habit had Liam reaching for his particle beam gun, and found him grasping at air. Not there—left at the apartment. Idiot! But even as he threw himself before Lili and Da'an, he realized that he wasn't crippled in the use of his natural defenses. Not this time. Even as the hospital administrators scattered, as the reporters crouched and covered their heads and their camera operators contorted to keep recording while doing the same, as one brave security guard tried to intercept the attacking man and found himself blown back down the hill in reward, Liam glanced at his hands, almost unable to overcome the habits that concealed his true nature from the world.

But when the next blast of energy came their way, even lifesaving habit didn't stop him from deflecting it—not at the attacker with innocent people behind him, but into the turf, which exploded upward in a sizzle of steam and popping rocks and a few blackened worms that pelted into Liam's face and thumped off Lili's back.

Even as Liam shook his head to clear his face and hair of debris, Lili was up again and at his side; behind them, Lassiter had Da'an, who ran for the hospital entrance in the typical Taelon combination of grace and awkward speed, picking his way through the debris of the overhang destruction. "There," she said, pointing decisively. "The parking garage." She activated her earpiece. "This is Marquette—Team One, block off interior exits from the parking garage—every stairwell, every elevator. Team Two, cover the exterior exits. Kincaid and I are going in. I don't want anyone else in there unless I request it." And she looked at him to assess his readiness. "You okay?"

She didn't mean did he have dirt in his eye or dead worms in his hair. She meant, *you almost died last night—do you want out?*

"Let's go," he told her—and though she hesitated an instant, she finally gave him a short nod and together they sprinted for the garage, pounding through the entrance just as several Companion Agents moved into place.

There they stopped.

Listening. Assessing.

"What did you see?" Lili asked him, a whisper.

"About thirty. White man, black watch cap . . . dressed for cold—I'd say he spent the night there. Dirty off-white down jacket, torn. Dark pants, probably jeans. Maybe five-eleven. He could pull off his cap and jacket and look like just about anyone else we might find in here."

"Figures," Lili muttered. And there were bound to be others trapped in here, they both knew it.

They started the search. The ceilings loomed close above them, a maze of colored pipes and beams and flickering fluorescents that did little to dispel the gloom of the place even with the daylight from the drive-in entrances behind them. They trotted from one row of cars to another, looking behind them, under them, and then trotting along to look between each one, methodical and silent teamwork with nothing more than gestures and the tilt of a head for communication.

At the second level, Liam paused for breath, suddenly very much aware of the way he'd spent the night. The night and the last how many days?

Lili came up beside him. *"Okay?"* she mouthed at him.

Not anywhere near it. And while he struggled with himself for the right answer, she made up her own mind. She moved in closer, close enough to be able to murmur almost soundlessly and still be heard. "This was a mistake. You weren't ready. Take a break, Liam."

He started to protest; the thought of her moving on alone gave him a foreboding that was perhaps as dependent on human intuition as anything else.

"Stay here," she said, lifting both eyebrows as an *I mean it* warning. "I'll just do this level and come back for you."

"Just this level," he said, and slumped back against a square cement support pillar in acquiescence. Or partial acquiescence, because *this* had been no mistake. Saving Da'an had been no mistake. Making sure someone armed with shaqarava and already willing to use them didn't escape was no mistake, either. Not when Liam more than any of them knew how to handle shaqarava energy.

Trying to do it so quickly . . . that, maybe, had been a mistake. He leaned his head back against the pillar and sucked in air.

"You don't look so good." From behind him, behind the pillar. The man hadn't panicked, hadn't rabbited wildly through the parking garage to hole up where they could flush him out. He'd used his head, found a cranny, and doubled back after Lili moved on. And his voice . . .

Calm. Not the voice of a man who'd just tried to assassinate a Taelon Companion.

The voice of a man with nothing to lose.

As Liam turned to face where he stood between two parked cars, the man added, "Maybe you and I have something in common, then."

Liam shook his head, a slow gesture. "I don't think so."

The man had removed his coat, all right, but hadn't discarded it; it dangled from his hand with the look of something precious and irreplaceable. His hunter-green chamois shirt was of an expensive make, but worn to threads across the shoulders and elbows; his jeans suffered likewise. Beneath the black watch cap, a rubber band fastened his slack brown hair at the nape of his neck; the hairstyle of a man who couldn't afford to *get* his hair styled, and likewise his untrimmed beard. But it was his eyes that caught Liam's attention. Clear and calm and, like his voice, the eyes of someone who'd known he wouldn't walk away from his actions a free man if he even walked away from them at all. Now he gestured at Liam's hands, the coat flopping against his leg, and said, "I saw what you did out there."

"What I did, I did in defense. What you did, you did to kill the very people I was defending. That doesn't leave us much in common."

"People!" The man sneered and kicked the tire of the car beside him. "You're human. *I'm* human. What're you doing defending them? Don't you know what they'll do to us? What they've *already* done to us?"

"More than you'd believe," Liam murmured, not caring if the man either heard or understood, though in the next moment he took back the man's gaze. "It's still wrong to kill them."

"Was it wrong when they killed my wife?" For the first time, the man lost his detached calmness. His expression twisted with grief and defiance. Defiance, Liam thought, not to the authorities or to any argument Liam himself might make, but to what his wife would have said had she known of his actions this day.

Reel him in, then, before he got more upset. End this. "Of course that was wrong," Liam said quietly.

"Then why did you stop me?" the man cried. He gestured again at Liam's hands. "Look what they've done to *you*! You could have *joined* me—we could have *done* something about them—"

Liam looked at his hands, flexed the fingers. "I *am* doing something about them. Every day, I do something about them. I do it in my own way." But he didn't like the wild look in the man's red-rimmed eyes, growing behind the grief. He reached inside himself, just enough to touch the heart of the energy waiting there. Just enough to be ready.

Except that warm spot in the center of his being had gone cold. Out of reach in an overused body, giving him nothing but a susurrous of familiar pain along the pathways within himself. He winced, clenching his hands closed reflexively, as startled by the failure as the discomfort.

Nor was the man slow to notice, although he misinterpreted it entirely. "You see?" he said. "You see what they do to us? Let me go, and I'll be the beginning of the end for them. I'll pay them back for everything!"

Gently, Liam said, "You knew you wouldn't leave here when you came. Not once you made that first move against Da'an. Come with me now; I'll make sure you're safe. You'll be in human hands, not Taelon."

The man snorted; though his eyes remained red, he'd regained his self-composure, and his purpose. "I don't think so. You have no weapon; you'd have pulled it on me by now, or been running around waving it like your lady friend. She went on to the third level, I think, no matter what she told you." He held out his hands. Glowing palms, gently swirling shaqarava energy. A display more than a threat. "That leaves you with these. Can you use them to stop me? Can you take advantage of what the Taelons have made you, even as you defend them?"

Well spoken. A man of the street who'd had a wife he'd loved, and probably an entirely different life. Somewhere along the way, the Taelons had done something to change that. To change *him*. They'd driven him to act in ways he'd probably never dreamed of until the Taelons had given him both cause and means.

Liam reached for the energy again. The cold spot remained within him, the reaction to his internal request the same. But he kept the difficulty of it off his face and tried once more, invoking a sluggish response that drew as much from his fleshly body as from his connection to the energies around him. "I am what my father made me," he said, not expecting to be understood and not caring; he said it for himself. For the man in front of him, he added, "And I do what I must."

They held each other's eyes for a long, measuring moment, and then a new kind of sadness came into the man's eyes.

"Ah, well," he said. "I was ready for this." His shaqarava brightened; his eyes closed. Liam knew, he *knew*, even as the man's hands raised, that *he* was not the one in danger.

"*Don't*—" he started, even as Lili came pelting down the center of the parking ramp, blocked from his sight if not sound by the pillar beside him, unable to see that he was far from helpless or taken by surprise.

"Liam, look out!" she shouted, and fired a warning shot that pinged off the ceiling over the man's head, spraying him with debris, startling him into turning on her even as the shaqarava blossomed with a surge of energy—

Liam made it around the pillar fast enough to see Lili's *oh shit* reaction, to see her dive for another of the square pillars—to see the look on her face that meant she knew she wouldn't make it.

Liam made it first. He drew mercilessly on his body when the energy source within him stayed torpid and reluctant, and he met the blinding shaqarava bolt with his own, throwing up a second, stationary glow to protect Lili from the backwash. The man hadn't thought to do as much; he slammed into the car beside him an instant before the car blew in a gaseous fireball that took out the car behind it as well, and would have taken the next had the spot not been empty—and the one before it, had Liam not drawn relentlessly on himself to push against the roiling energies, and to keep pushing until he realized there was nothing left—

By then it was too late.

Lili tucked her ID so it hung out of her jacket's breast pocket for the sake of the personnel that swarmed the parking garage, gathering evidence and body parts. Down feathers settled around her through the air; a good hunk of the man's coat hung in the pipes overhead, intermittently releasing its insulation into the garage. She crouched by Liam, who sat against one of the pillars, legs crossed and looking dazed enough that some of his youth showed through on the face that was so deceivingly thirty-something. He'd gone down, but only for a moment, and not apparently as a result of the blast; something had happened, she thought, that she didn't yet understand.

Something that maybe *he* didn't understand.

"You okay?" she said.

When he glanced at her, something in his expression

shuttered out, leaving the competent thirty-something behind. Resistance leader. Companion Protector. Not so vulnerable . . . and not quite as reachable. "I will be," he said. "Once we're through here."

"We *are* through here," Lili said. "The rest is for the locals. They'll figure out who he was . . . maybe even what drove him to this."

His brows drew together; his mouth tightened. He looked at the destruction before them and said, "I think we pretty much know what drove him to this. Maybe not the details . . . but we know enough." And then he looked at her, making sure to catch her eye, holding her gaze even when she grew uncomfortable and might have looked away. "We know that he's not the only one with that kind of story. If we don't release that antivirus, this is only the beginning. The first shot in an ugly, uncontrollable war, and those with the weapons won't care who is hurt in their crusade for personal justice."

She took a deep breath. "You don't have any doubt, do you?"

"No." He shook his head with finality. "I've seen too much. And so have you. Don't let Doors do your thinking for you; his eyes have been closed for a long time."

"No one does my thinking for me," she said firmly. She stood, and held out her hand. "Come on. Let's do something about this before it's too late."

And he smiled at her as he took her hand and climbed wearily to his feet, but the relief in his eyes wasn't as deep as she'd expected . . . he kept something hidden there.

Something he'd seen, she thought, something from these past days of looking within that had also given him the strength to make his own decisions and act on them with or without her.

She told herself it didn't matter, brushed a down feather from just above his ear, and put a companionable hand on his arm before leading the way out of the parking garage, two tired Resistance leaders balancing the need to stay human against the need to save humanity, and making a choice for them all.

EIGHTEEN

Augur sat at his main workstation, contemplating the thing of beauty he'd just finished programming—but when he heard the computer's warning about an impending visitor, he murmured, "Later, darlin'. I'm not ready to share you just yet."

Besides, he was expecting Lili, and he *really* wasn't ready to share with *her*. So he flipped the screen view to the file he did plan to share with her, and stretched in his chair, shifting his Tootsie Pop from one side of his mouth to the other.

"Look, ma," he said, turning his hands to display his palms to her as she strode out of the elevator and down the several steps to the main floor, "no shaqarava!"

"No kidding," she responded, coming right up beside him to look at the file structure he'd displayed. "It's been a week, Augur. No one's got them anymore. And you never *did* have them."

"A fact which continues to delight me, so excuse me if I share."

"What'd you find?" she said, nodding at the monitor, and then at the candy. "And do you have any more of those?"

Augur used the sucker stick to point vaguely off behind and to the side. "On the table. A bag of them. On special this week. But hurry back, because you're gonna like this."

She was back beside him in a moment, taking a chair

from down the workstation and rolling it over to sit next to him. She'd shed her light jacket and settled in to cross her legs and arms and stare at the monitor, idly rolling the sucker in her mouth. He began to regret offering her one.

"Grape," he said longingly, not thinking of the Tootsie Pop. "My favorite flavor."

"This week," she told him smartly.

He muttered, "Aren't you just no fun," and opened the waiting video file, putting it on pause to display a cavernously empty room, big enough to be a small convention center and utterly devoid of identifying characteristics. There were only a few capped plumbing fixtures sticking out of the cement block walls, and a high, forlorn bank of windows lining the side above the entrance. From the illumination, it looked like there were probably also skylights. And not much else.

"What's this?" she said, leaning forward to look more closely, then—when no clues were forthcoming in the image—giving up to relax back again.

"When I learned Sandoval was on the track of the tagbot gatherings—the first tagbot gatherings, the ones the Resistance members made—I knew sooner or later he'd find the exact locations. We could erase that file, but not his CVI memories."

"Right," she said, in a *that's not news* voice.

"Our Flat Planet here in D.C. was safe enough—what with Liam living there and Hayley's clinic tagbots drawing the heat from it so nicely—it never did peak as high as the others. The rest of them . . . well, it's not like I don't plan ahead for these things."

She made a loud, distracting sucking noise on the Tootsie Pop, her expression all innocence, prodding him to get to the point. Augur gave her an excessively annoyed glance. "It's so nice to be appreciated," he said. *"This"*—and he gestured at the screen—"is where the Denver Flat Planet lived before the Taelon Flu." He thumbed a key, releasing the pause.

It was a short file, but the scene that played out before them nevertheless struck deep notes of satisfaction within him. The door, bursting open. The Volunteers, pouring into the empty former barroom. Sandoval, on their heels, entering with skrill in firing position. Hesitating, disbelieving, slowly standing down.

An expression of utter fury on his face.

Augur glanced at Lili from the corner of his eye; she wore a small smile around the sucker stick.

"He tried them all," Augur said. "Same results—I have those on file, too."

"And there's no evidence to tie the locations to the franchises?"

He smiled broadly. "Nope. Nada. None. Those buildings are currently listed as having been empty for years. And the Flat Planets continue to do a booming business a block or so away in their respective cities. Doors' franchise buyer wasn't as lucky; the Orbital Spin is history. But Doors got cleanup teams there in time for the fellow; Sandoval won't track him down."

"Lucky? I don't think so," Lili said. "You *make* your luck, Augur."

"Yeah," he said with satisfaction. "I do. And plenty of it." And by now the tags were distributed so thoroughly— worldwide, not just the States—that he'd be surprised if the Taelons were bothering to track them at all. Let them, if they wanted . . . the Resistance was no longer in any danger from it, and neither were Augur's interests.

In fact, things were altogether quieter than the norm. The antivirus was in the air for good, the doctors had probably slept this whole week, Liam had gone surprisingly withdrawn and needed a kick in the pants, and even Lili's virus informant had made his way to safety. Three new identities, courtesy of Augur the Magnificent. He'd taken special care with the one for the little girl. No one would ever know her father had once worked for the Taelons . . . and had once shared their secrets.

"So that's it," he said, concluding his thoughts out loud. "The good guys win."

"Did we?" Lili said, removing the sucker from her mouth to give him the kind of soul-searching look he wished he could evoke from her under entirely different circumstances.

"Don't tell me you're still worried about whether you made the right choice," he said in disbelief. "Believe me, *I* don't have any doubt."

Still thoughtful, she tapped the sucker against her lower lip. "No," she said, looking more inward than out, "I think it was the right choice. I just don't think we *won*. I think maybe we lived to fight another day."

"Hey," Augur said as she crunched down on the sucker to reach the chewy center, "I happen to think that as long as we're still human, we've won. We won yesterday, we won today, and I plan to win tomorrow."

She shrugged. "That's one way to look at it, I suppose."

"Yeah, a *cheerful* way to look at it. Tell that to Liam next time you see him, why don't you?"

Lili stood, hunting a wastebasket. "He's keeping to himself these days."

"Yeah, well, maybe someone should do something about that." He swiveled his chair to give her a pointed look.

She reached for her jacket. "Give him space, you told me once. I'm doing it."

Not much to say to that. Not without contradicting his own wisdom.

"By the way," she said, "I've been meaning to talk to

you . . . about that latest version of wish-fulfillment you've programmed into your computer—"

"Say no more," he interrupted with some haste. "I've moved on."

She looked at him long enough to make sure he was telling the truth, and slid her crop-cut jacket on with the whisper of smooth lining over her tightly cut vest and brilliantly red, clinging shirt. He berated himself for not turning to look directly at her sooner, but didn't let himself get so distracted he didn't add, "Honest. She's history. I'm . . . still working on an alternative."

"Uh-huh," she said, and walked by *Guernica* and the conference table to grab another Tootsie Pop on her way out. "See you later, Augur. Don't forget to mention it if you move *this* Flat Planet, will you?"

As last words went, they weren't much; Augur let her have them. And then he turned to the holo-tube and said, "Computer, time to rise and shine."

A new image of Lili appeared within the tube. Lili with a tight spangled black top and black leather pants, a three-legged stool behind her, a coil of chain next to that. In one hand and puddled around her feet was a long, stout leather whip.

Lion-tamer Lili.

Augur smiled.

Da'an briefly contemplated the delicate tree shrubs in his embassy receiving area. Its frond shapes, once so common in the flora on his beloved planet, were also distinctly reminiscent of many species of Earth trees. Generally he found it soothing to consider this an indication that humans and Taelons did not have such a vast gulf between them after all, and that this kinship would, if nurtured, help save the Taelons from their Jaridian enemies.

It was not soothing enough, however, to offset a data-stream interface with Zo'or. Taelons were not given to an excess of external expression, but Zo'or's current expression could only be termed what the humans called pugnacious. Another of his aggressive programs in failure . . . Da'an understood this child of his well enough to know that Zo'or hoped to avoid direct assumption of responsibility with this assertive strategy.

Zo'or was nothing if not assertive in everything he did. Perhaps being the last of one's kind did that.

Da'an, interrupted from a satisfying contemplation of the recent successful development of a golden rice that would not breed outside itself and thus sully native rice gene pools, was not inclined to play the game. Best, therefore, to preempt it. So when Zo'or said, "I am preparing to give my final report to the Synod regarding the shaqarava retrovirus," Da'an didn't wait for the actual question, the request to know how Da'an intended to slant his report on the incident.

"I consider the experiment a success," he said.

Zo'or gave him an intent look, as much of a challenge as ever. "I find this difficult to believe."

Da'an gestured his understanding of that fact, and explained, "It proves once again that the humans are more than you yet comprehend. It is they who directed the outcome of this incident, and they who prevailed despite the dangerous flaw in your methodology." No small thanks to the Resistance—and the newly revitalized Doors International. No doubt Jonathan Doors would enjoy an improved standing in the presidential polls.

"The experiment," Zo'or said, speaking most precisely, "was Ta'en's."

"The original experiment may have been Ta'en's, but the premature directive to take it to Earth was yours."

Zo'or did not acknowledge the point, which was how he

ever dealt with facts he could not refute. His posture remained confident, and his face relaxed and serene; he said, "Although the final results were not anticipated, I, too, consider this experiment a success. We not only deflected blame from ourselves with our cover story about the probe, but we learned just how susceptible the humans will be to our bio-engineering techniques, and that is a valuable insight indeed."

"The probe story deflected only official blame. Rest assured there are many who know exactly where the retrovirus came from. However, as to your second point . . . I cannot argue it," Da'an conceded. He was always willing to concede truths, although he knew Zo'or felt this was a particular weakness. Zo'or was inclined to concede nothing.

Which meant Zo'or would not cease in his efforts to place the blame for the runaway virus on Ta'en's methods, a matter the disappearance of Ta'en's assistant and the apparent leak of Beta-S research information only complicated. And while Da'an felt Ta'en was indeed inclined to be difficult to work with, it was because he clung to excessively conservative ways—and not, as Zo'or would claim, because he was careless.

However, these were days during which special care need be taken. Days in which a scientist of Ta'en's inclinations could be valuable, were they not overridden by others. Da'an said, "Given the results of the retrovirus experiment, I expect you have lost confidence in Ta'en."

"That would be an overstatement. However, it would be accurate to say that I can no longer allow myself to be associated with his work."

"Then allow me to offer a solution. I believe I have some genetics work that would suit him. It is restricted to crop manipulation, and would not involve human experimentation."

Zo'or's eyes widened slightly at the unexpected opportunity to put distance between himself and the scientist he intended to blame for his own poor decisions. But he didn't jump at the opportunity; doing so would put him in Da'an's debt. Instead, he considered it, and said, "If you need additional assistance, then you may transfer Ta'en to your staff."

"Thank you," Da'an said, "for your generosity."

He did not expect Zo'or to recognize the human sarcasm. He was not disappointed. Zo'or merely nodded and cut their communication, leaving Da'an to contemplate the tree shrubs and recent days, and to glance at Liam, engrossed at his workstation, relentless in his insistence upon certain securities for an upcoming appearance. He bore no signs of his recent affliction, nothing other than a few pounds lost, evident in the fit of his sleek gray shirt, the faint hollows under his cheekbones—and a certain tendency to look inside himself when he thought no one was paying attention.

Now *there* was something to contemplate. Da'an didn't know how his Companion Protector had survived his illness. He knew his own advice had been woefully inadequate; he knew he wished he'd been of more help.

But he was beginning to understand that Liam—as much as he struggled, as little as he understood himself— did not need Da'an in order to find his answers. And that, in turn, gave Da'an a sharp pang of what he could only call regret . . .

And loss.

NINETEEN

Liam parked the 280Z behind the Flat Planet, sliding it into a spot against the back of the building, tight between the neat brick walls that held the Dumpster and the Flat Planet itself. Few cars fit there; no one else ever tried. His spot, by default.

He glanced at the back door—he had a key, but coming in that way tended to startle the kitchen staff—and walked the sidewalk around to the corner and official entrance. Augur no longer had anyone lurking there, neither checking tags nor surreptitiously distributing them. He eased past the handful of couples crowding the entry area to wait for an open table, and nodded as Kwai Ling bustled toward them, a pencil behind one ear and a chopstick behind the other, shuffling a stack of menu cards back into order. Her silver and black eye makeup matched the enameled chopstick to perfection.

He'd meant to head straight for his apartment, but Suzanne caught his eye, lifting her head in a slight nod to make sure she'd also caught his attention. At that he could tell it was business, or at least not purely personal, for her fair complexion tended to pink right up if she actually tried to make conversation. He changed course and headed for

346   GENE RODDENBERRY'S EARTH: FINAL CONFLICT

the bar, leaning on it next to the lone empty seat in its center, waiting for her to serve up the drinks she had in progress.

"Looks like business is back to normal," he said when she finally set a champagne punch in front of him.

"More than," she said, tucking blond hair behind her ear. "It's like they're making up for lost time."

There were still plenty of people filling the hospitals. Those who had only just caught the retrovirus before receiving the antivirus, like Augur, experienced fleeting illness, but those who had caught it first were just now recovering from the reversal process.

Hayley was one of the latter. She'd left town that morning, taking her people with her—but not without meeting him in the bustling anonymity of the ID portal terminal. The past weeks had taken their toll on her; her clothes, once just-snug-enough, hung loosely on her frame. He'd never thought of her as delicate, not until he'd spotted her waiting and didn't quite recognize her at first glance.

It must have shown in his expression, because she made a wry face at him. "Give me a month," she said, then upped her own ante. "Less than that. I'll be ready to raid anything that needs to be raided."

He supposed he was meant to play along, to say *no doubt* and smile. But he wasn't inclined to take lightly those things they'd been through, both alone *and* together.

She gave him that. She came straight to the point. "I still think you were wrong," she said. "You took something from me that I didn't want to give up . . . something I believe would have saved us all. So just because I wanted to say good-bye . . . don't think it won't take me a while to forgive you for that."

"I know," he said.

"It's just—" she started, but stopped, looking away, juggling unspoken words—without, apparently, finding any.

"I know," he said again, and this time lifted his hand, palm out, fingers slightly spread.

She stopped her attempt to find words, and briefly bit her lip. After that instant's hesitation, she raised her smaller hand to mirror his, not quite touching. What passed between them was only an echo of the connection they'd shared once before, but it was enough. It said enough.

She added out loud, "I'll be back. Sometime." Then she kissed him . . . and she left.

He'd stood in the terminal for a while, just feeling the wistful reverberation of the sharing. And then he, too, had left. Back to the business of being a Companion Protector/ Resistance leader. To the embassy and work, and now home to the Flat Planet, where he'd hoped to find solitude but had instead apparently found more business.

"Hey, you okay?" Suzanne asked him, leaning over the bar to look at him more closely.

"Yeah," he said. "Just thinking about someone."

She backed off immediately. How women could tell when you were thinking of another woman was an utter mystery to Liam, but it at least was one of those things that mystified all men.

"There's a fellow waiting for you," she said, nodding vaguely at the dining tables; Liam twisted to look. In the far back, the latest girl band trickled onto the stage and began checking amps and jacks and microphones. Only one of the tables held a single diner; a big man with a square face, little in the way of neck, and shoulders only a custom-tailored suit could hold. Not a man Liam knew . . . but one he thought he knew *of.* "He say what he wanted?"

"Nope." She lifted a finger to let a customer at the end

of the bar know she'd seen him. "Just came in and grunted something about waiting when I said you weren't here."

"Thanks." He picked up the tall glass with his drink and made his way to the table, standing opposite the man and his heaping plate of appetizers. From sushi to fried cheese sticks . . . he hadn't wasted his time here. Nor did he dive right into conversation, instead regarding Liam for a good long moment.

Liam gave him the moment only; he knew when he was being assessed, and just now it wasn't how he cared to spend his time. "If that's all you wanted," he said, "I'll be going."

"It isn't," the man said. He stood, extending a meaty hand. Liam glanced at it, glanced at the man, raised an eyebrow. "Art Wells," the man said, keeping his hand where it was.

The man who Doors had set up to undermine Lili, already counting Liam out of the picture. "Liam Kincaid," Liam said, setting his drink on the table. "But you knew that."

Art dropped his hand with a shrug. "Don't be hard about it, Kincaid. There was never anything personal. You pulled it out of the fire; gotta respect that."

"That I'm still here has nothing to do with how things worked out for you. Lili's heart is with this organization. You can't replace that with hired help."

Art grinned, a predatory expression. "Don't be so certain," he said. "I'll do the job I'm hired for with the best of *my* ability—I'm no one's puppet. I left because I won't work the way Doors expected, not because I couldn't have gotten what I set out to get."

"I guess we'll have to disagree about that," Liam said, meeting the predatory look head-on, but not taking it any further. Then he backed off a step, because when all was said and done, Art Wells had been useful in his own way. "Is that why you're here? One last shot at Lili before you ride into the sunset?"

Art Wells laughed, genuinely amused. "Not really. I just wanted to make my position clear . . . about why I'm leaving. It's a small thing, I suppose. It might not mean much to you. But it means a lot to me. And making sure people know such things also makes a difference who I can count on when we meet again."

Couldn't argue with that. Liam nodded acknowledgment, picked up his drink. "Let's stay on the same side, then."

"That's the point," Art said, picking up the check next to his plate and pulling out a cash card, dismissing Liam as much as Liam chose that moment to walk away, turning Art into a thing remembered but no longer making an impact on his life—or on the Resistance.

This time he made it through the door to his apartment; the soundproofing closed off the noise of the bar behind him. He didn't bother to take off his coat; he climbed the spiral stairs to the second floor, and the cramped ladder steps to the roof door in the corner beyond that.

The warmth of the spring air took him by surprise even though he'd just been in it; after a long fall and winter that comprised a great deal of his life . . . of *this* life . . . he'd grown to expect the cold, and not the sporadic fits of pleasurable weather that preceded true spring.

Weeks had passed since he'd last been on this roof, alone with his thoughts and simply trying to figure out how to live—how to be who he was. In that time, he'd learned more than he'd thought possible . . . but as much about Taelon heritage as his own.

In that time, he'd changed. He sat in the waiting chair, set his drink beside it, the glass bottom grating against the gritty roof coating, facing the fact that he wasn't even sure how *much* he'd changed. He'd blundered around inside his own body, wielding cleansing energies of which he had nothing but instinctive knowledge, scouring his body of the destructive retrovirus with little finesse. He hadn't felt quite the same since then.

Then again, he often didn't feel quite the same from week to week. So who knew? Not Liam, that was certain. And apparently, not even Ha'gel.

So changed, but back where he started. Still struggling through the world alone, one of a kind, Kimera-within hunting answers and heritage.

Except he thought of Lili's hand, closed around his wrist, squeezing encouragement; her command of him not to quit. And he thought of Augur, asleep on the floor, unable to bring himself to go as far away as the bed upstairs.

Maybe not so alone after all.

ABOUT THE AUTHOR

DORANNA DURGIN is the author of a number of fantasy novels, including *Dun Lady's Jess, Changespell, Barrenlands, Touched by Magic, Wolf Justice, Wolverine's Daughter, Seer's Blood, A Feral Darkness,* and *Star Trek: The Next Generation—Tooth and Claw.*

After obtaining a degree in wildlife illustration and environmental education, she spent a number of years deep in the Appalachian Mountains, where she would have avoided the Taelons if they'd actually arrived on Earth. When she emerged, it was as a writer who found herself irrevocably tied to the natural world and its creatures.

Ms. Durgin, who isn't sure whether she lives in New York or Arizona, hangs around with three Cardigan Welsh Corgis—Belle, Carbon Unit (Kacey), and Jean-Luc Picardigan—and drags her saddle wherever she goes.

She answers mail between writing books, and you can contact her at:

EFCH@ doranna.net

or

PMB 207
2532 N. 4th Street
Flagstaff, AZ 86004

or visit

http://www.doranna.net/